Maxime de La Rocheterie, Cora Hamilton Bell

The Life of Marie Antoinette

Vol. 2

Maxime de La Rocheterie, Cora Hamilton Bell

The Life of Marie Antoinette
Vol. 2

ISBN/EAN: 9783337414603

Printed in Europe, USA, Canada, Australia, Japan

Cover: Foto ©Raphael Reischuk / pixelio.de

More available books at **www.hansebooks.com**

Crowned by the Académie Française

THE LIFE

OF

MARIE ANTOINETTE

BY

MAXIME DE LA ROCHETERIE

Translated from the French

BY

CORA HAMILTON BELL

IN TWO VOLUMES

Vol. II.

LONDON
JAMES R. OSGOOD, McILVAINE & CO.
45, Albemarle Street
1893

CONTENTS.

VOLUME II.

CHAPTER I.

CHAPTER II.

CHAPTER III.

CHAPTER IV.

CHAPTER V.

CHAPTER X.

CHAPTER XI.

CHAPTER XII.

CHAPTER XIII.

CHAPTER XIV.

CHAPTER XV.

CHAPTER XVI.

CHAPTER XVII.

CHAPTER XVIII.

CHAPTER XXVI.

CHAPTER XXVII.

LIST OF ILLUSTRATIONS.

VOLUME II.

LIFE OF MARIE ANTOINETTE.

CHAPTER I.

WE now enter upon the militant period of Marie Antoinette's
life. We shall present it, as we have the rest of this
history, with perfect impartiality, but with a feeling of melancholy which we have not experienced to the same degree in the
earlier part of this work. Until now we have seen the queen
comparatively happy, despite the fleeting clouds which darkened
the blue sky, despite gloomy forebodings and moments of
repressed sadness, still retaining the radiance of youth and the
dignity of the crown. Although she is marching toward an
abyss, yet she advances slowly; and the splendour of the throne
and the bright joys of maternity half conceal the yawning gulf.
But now the veil is torn asunder; the danger appears urgent and
inexorable. On the very brow of the mother a new light is
about to go out. The queen of Trianon has vanished; the
queen of Versailles is about to vanish. Behold! the queen of
the Tuileries advances, while awaiting the queen of the Temple
and of the Conciergerie. The sovereign is despoiled; the woman
is exalted. Her character acquires new strength, and adversity
transfigures her. All the latent vigorous traits in her nature,
which prosperity had, as it were, hidden under the more seductive gloss of agreeable qualities, — proud dignity, intrepid courage,
contempt of danger, buoyancy, indomitable firmness of spirit, —
are developed, and stand out in bold relief. The elegant woman
gives place to the strong woman; the pastel of Boucher becomes

a painting by Rembrandt; and to borrow Mirabeau's words, after 1789 there is but one man near the king, and that is the queen. If her political understanding did not rise to the height of her character; if Marie Antoinette, despite her masculine courage, exhausted herself in vain and often ill-conceived efforts, — it was because her mind was not great enough to dominate such a difficult situation as hers; she should have been prepared for the struggle by an education and an experience which she lacked. It is also true that God, in his inscrutable designs, sometimes chooses pure and striking victims, that their fall may command respect.

And yet in the spring of 1789 who could have foreseen the bloody catastrophe? Everything was tinged with hopefulness; the world was dreaming of the Golden Age. It is difficult to-day to form an idea of the panic that seized France at the approach of the reunion of the States-General. Despite the previous disorders, and seeds of discord contained in certain *cahiers*, the prevailing sentiment was confidence. The nation, which a century of revolutions had not yet rendered sceptical, had faith in the monarchy which had founded it, — in that dynasty sprung from its entrails, which had brought it peace with Henri IV., glory with Louis XIV. It had faith in that sovereign, still young, who had never had other thought than for the happiness of his people, and who was willing to surrender to them his absolute power; "the best of kings," said one pamphlet, whose "paternal bounty" was extolled by every one. It had faith, also, in the "immortal Necker," a minister "precious to France," — an able financier, whom public opinion, no less than the monarch's favour, had raised to power; in that Third Estate which, although not convened for the first time, as was falsely asserted, seemed destined, by reason of its double representation, to play an important part in public affairs, and that with the consent of the crown. It had faith even in the privileged orders, who seemed ready at least to sacrifice their pecuniary privileges. The people everywhere hailed with enthusiasm the new era which was dawning. With a firm king, with a statesman who knew what he wished, and was determined to accomplish it, this confidence would have been an incomparable force. With a feeble prince like Louis XVI., with an irresolute minister like Necker, it was an appalling danger. The public, inflamed by the anarchy that had preceded the convocation of the States, disposed, through its inexperience, to accept all Utopias, and impelled by its peculiar character to desire their immediate realization, naturally grew more exacting in proportion as they were promised more, and more impatient and irritable as their hopes became livelier and appeared better founded.

In the midst of this general satisfaction there was but one dark spot, — the queen. The cheers which greeted the king were silent before his wife. Calumny had done its work; and all the nobles from the provinces, the country curates, the citizens of the small towns, came from the confines of France imbued with the most contemptible prejudices against this unfortunate princess. Pamphlets, poured out against her by malicious enemies; vague and mysterious rumours, circulated everywhere, repeated in whispers, without giving any clew to their source, — the more dangerous because indefinite, and the more readily believed because infamous and absurd, — had so often reiterated that the queen was author of all the evil, that the world had come to regard her as the cause of the deficit, and the only serious obstacle to certain efficacious reforms. "The queen pillages on all sides; she even sends money, it is said, to her brother, the emperor," wrote a priest of Maine, in his parochial register, in 1781; and he attributed the motive of the reunion of the Notables to these supposed depredations. If, in 1781, such reports had penetrated to the remotest parts of the country, and found credence with such enlightened men as the Curé Boucher, one can judge what it must have been two years later, when the convocation of the States-General had inflamed the minds of the people. If the States should encounter any inevitable obstacle in their path; if certain imprudent promises should be unfulfilled; if promised reforms should fail, — public resentment and ill-will, always on the alert, would be sure to blame Marie Antoinette; they would impute to her all the evil done, and all the good left undone.

The symptoms of this distrust were manifest at the outset.

"The deputies of the Third Estate," Madame Campan observes, "arrived at Versailles with the strongest prejudice against the court. The evil sayings in Paris never failed to be spread through the provinces: they believed that the king indulged in the pleasures of the table to a most shameful excess ; they were persuaded that the queen exhausted the State treasury to gratify her inordinate love of luxury; almost all wished to visit Little Trianon. As the extreme simplicity of this pleasure-house did not correspond with their ideas, they insisted on being shown even the smallest closets, saying that richly furnished apartments were being concealed from them. Finally they designated one, which according to their account was ornamented with diamonds, and twisted columns studded with sapphires and rubies. The queen was amused at these mad fancies, and told the king of them. He judged from the description of the room that the deputies had given to the guards of Trianon that they must have been seeking the decoration of paste diamonds which had been made during the reign of Louis XV. for the theatre at Fontainebleau."

On the 4th of May the solemn procession which was to precede the assembling of the States-General took place at Versailles. People did not then believe that it was unnecessary to invoke the blessing of God upon the transactions of a great assembly; the religious ceremony preluded the political. The weather, rainy on the day before, had cleared. A vast crowd of people filled the streets. The windows, rented at exorbitant prices, were adorned with curious spectators gathered from all parts of the kingdom. At ten o'clock the king left the palace, accompanied by the queen, the royal family, and the principal officers of the crown, and proceeded in state coaches to the church of Notre Dame. "The horses, gorgeously harnessed, had their heads covered with high plumes. The entire household of the king — equerries, mounted pages, falconers with birds on their wrists — marched before the superb train." The deputies waited in the church; the commons were dressed in black, with a short silk mantle, white muslin cravat, flowing hair. and a hat turned up on three sides without cord or button, called at that time a *chapeau claband;* the nobles in mantles with gold trimmings, and hats turned up after the fashion of Henri IV., with white plumes; the clergy in cassocks and long cloaks; the cardinals in scarlet capes; the bishops in *rochets* and *camails*, violet *soutanes* and square caps. The procession began, the Third Estate at the head, in two parallel lines; then the *noblesse*, after which the lower clergy; the bishops surrounded the Holy Sacrament, borne by the archbishop of Paris, under a sumptuous canopy, the *cordons* of which were held by Monsieur, the Comte d'Artois, the Duc d'Angoulême, and the Duc de Berry. Behind the canopy walked the king, bearing a wax taper, and wearing a robe of cloth-of-gold covered with precious stones. Near him the queen, gorgeously dressed, with crown imperials intertwined in her hair. "Her sad expression," remarks an eye-witness, "added yet more to her noble and dignified bearing."

The procession advanced through the streets, hung with rich tapestries, between two lines of troops formed by the French and Swiss Guards, and in the midst of an enormous throng of spectators. Choirs stationed at intervals made the air ring with their harmonies. "Military marches, the roll of drums, the sound of trumpets, the noble chanting of the priests, heard in turn, without discord and without confusion, enlivened the triumphal march of the Eternal."

Frantic cheers greeted the deputation from Dauphiné as it passed; they burst forth with greater energy at the sight of the Duc d'Orléans, who, scorning to take his place among the princes of the blood, had chosen to walk among the deputies of his bailliage, — a threatening demonstration which at bottom expressed more hate than sympathy. It was not the prince whom the crowd applauded; it was the queen whom they wished to humiliate, and the very tone of the cries emphasized their purport. Madame Campan relates that "the women of the people on seeing the queen shouted 'Vive le Duc d'Orléans!' in such hostile tones that the unhappy woman, overwhelmed by these insulting plaudits, almost fainted." Some one supported her, and those who surrounded her feared for a moment that the procession would have to be stopped. She recovered herself, and, it is said, bitterly regretted that she had been unable to hide the effects of this shock. She was, however, deeply wounded by this manifestation, the significance of which she fully realized, and the unseemliness of which offended the chivalric sentiment of a republican. If we are to believe Gouverneur Morris, Madame Adélaïde had the lamentable courage to add the sting of her sarcasm to this popular outburst.

The *cortége* proceeded from Notre Dame to the church of St. Louis; the deputies seated themselves on benches; the king and queen took their places under a canopy of purple velvet covered with golden *fleurs-de-lis*. The Holy Sacrament was carried to the altar amid the sound of "most impressive music." The archbishop of Paris celebrated the mass. The bishop of Nancy, Monseigneur de la Fare, delivered the address. When the orator, in the midst of flights of eloquence, began to draw a picture of the evils caused by the salt tax, a clapping of hands burst forth on all sides. This unprecedented act of applauding in a church, and in the presence of the Holy Sacrament, made a deep impression upon the spectators, who drew gloomy prognostications from it: they asked anxiously if those who had so little respect for God in his temple would have more for royalty in the palace.

On the following day, the session of the States-General was solemnly opened in the Salle des Menus-Plaisirs, which had already been used for the Assembly of Notables. The hall, magnificently decorated after designs by Paris, who had designed the king's cabinet, presented an imposing spectacle; at the end, the throne; to the left of the throne, a large armchair for the queen, and stools for the princesses; to the right, folding-chairs for the princes; along the right of the hall, benches for the clergy; along the left for the nobility, and at the end opposite the throne those for the Third Estate. The steps and galleries around the hall were filled with more than two thousand spectators. Between nine and ten o'clock the deputies began to arrive, then the secretaries of State and the ministers, the governors of the provinces, and the lieutenant-generals, all in full uniform. Monsieur Necker alone, with intentional singularity, which was remarked, wore citizen's dress; he was applauded at his entrance. The Duc d'Orléans and the deputation from Dauphiné, who had been cheered on the preceding day, were likewise again greeted with acclamations. "Some were disposed," so Grimm relates, "to render the same homage to the deputation from Provence; but they were arrested by a murmur of disapprobation, the personal application of which could not escape the shrewd comprehension of the Comte de Mirabeau."

When the king entered, the entire company arose, and cries of "Vive le roi!" burst forth "with reverential tenderness, a most touching overflow of affection." The queen accompanied him, "exquisitely attired," declares a witness of the scene, "wearing a single fillet of diamonds, with the beautiful plume of the heron, a violet mantle, and a white petticoat spangled with silver." But the same ominous coldness which had greeted her during the procession met her again in the Salle des Menus. "Not one voice is heard to wish her well," Gouverneur Morris records. " I would certainly have raised my voice if I had been a Frenchman; but I had no right to express a sentiment, and in vain solicited those who were near me to do it."

Louis XVI. read his address in a firm voice and with impressive dignity. As he was about to begin, he invited the queen to be seated; she declined with a low bow, and listened standing, like all the Assembly. After this address, which was only an appeal to the wisdom and moderation of the people, in which virtues he set them an example, the keeper of the seals, Monsieur de Barentin, recalled the sacrifices which the king had made, and those which he was still disposed to make, "to establish universal happiness upon the sacred foundation of public liberty." He pointed out in a few words the reforms to be effected and the questions to be solved, but without indicating the solution or allowing it to be surmised that the ministry had any plan except for the assessment of taxes and the renunciation of pecuniary privileges. Then Necker, in a report which lasted nearly three hours, exposed the financial situation, and declared a deficit of fifty-five millions. "His long enumeration of figures," writes an eminent historian of Louis XVI., "dampened the enthusiasm which had been aroused by the words of the king." Nevertheless cheers still followed the monarch as he retired; even some shouts of "Vive la reine!" were mingled with those of "Vive le roi!" She acknowledged them by a bow, at which the cheering redoubled; but it was easy to see, an eye-witness remarks, "that the applause was more than anything else an act of homage to the king."

On that very day, and at the adjournment of the meeting, difficulties began. Through improvidence or ignorance of the human heart, the government had excited the passions and ruffled the vanity of the public, without seeking, however, to direct the conflict. In granting to the Tiers-État a double representation, it had, it would seem intentionally, inflamed their pride. While abandoning what appeared to be one of the fundamental principles of the early Constitution of the States, it had preserved the most superannuated forms. At the very moment that it had doubled the importance of the Tiers-État, it wounded their self-esteem to the last degree by distinctions in costume and etiquette, and by a puerile series of regulations. They were not slow in expressing their dissatisfaction, and making known their pretensions. Instead of retiring like the other orders into the place reserved for them, the Tiers-État remained in the Salle des Menus after the royal session, taking possession of it, as it were, and in consequence seeming to assume and represent the whole States-General. Then the grave question of voting by order or by person was presented at once, which threw a brand of discord among the three orders, inflaming the passions, embittering all minds, and calling forth recriminations which were sustained by animosities from outside; and the government, which had not known how to prevent these contentions, did not interfere in any way to effect their cessation. Thus the gulf in which the monarchy was to founder began to deepen between a royalty which seemed impotent and an Assembly which tended manifestly toward the seizure of power.

This situation grieved Marie Antoinette deeply. She exerted herself in vain to win the good feeling of the deputies. She gave orders, but to no purpose, that the palace and the gardens of Versailles and of Trianon should be opened to them at all hours. She had a card giving them free entrance to the theatres of the town and of the court distributed to each of them, but without avail. The few deputies who dared respond to these advances were marked out for popular vengeance as partisans of the queen and enemies of the nation. The unhappy sovereign was cut to the heart, and I know not what gloomy forebodings agitated her thoughts. An anecdote related by Madame Campan gives an idea of the painful state of her mind: —

" The queen," she writes, " retired very late, — or more truly, this unfortunate princess was no longer able to enjoy any rest. Toward the end of May, as she was seated one evening in the middle of the room, she recounted several remarkable things which had taken place during the day. Four candles were placed upon her dressing-table ; the first one went out of itself ; I soon relighted it ; the second, then the third also, went out. At this, the queen, pressing my hand with a movement of alarm, said to me, ' Misfortune makes one superstitious ; if that fourth candle goes out, nothing can keep me from regarding it as an evil omen ; ' the fourth candle went out.

" Some one remarked to the queen that the four candles had probably been made in the same mould, and that a defect in the wick was naturally to be found at the same place, since they had gone out in the order in which they had been lighted.

" The queen would listen to nothing ; and with that indefinable emotion which the bravest hearts cannot always overcome in momentous hours, gave herself up to gloomy apprehensions."

Events, alas ! appeared to justify her superstitious fears. A very few days after, the first of those lights which seemed destined to illumine the horizon of France was extinguished. The dauphin died at Meudon.

A delicate infancy, a frail constitution, and still more, perhaps, mental precocity and a development of the affections, by which Providence, it would seem, wished to compensate for the shortness of his life, had long foretold this sad event. Despite the devoted care of the Duchesse de Polignac, despite a free existence in the open air, exempt from comforts which enervate and formality which restrains, the young prince had never been able to acquire that vigour of constitution which seemed the heritage of his family, and which his younger brother, the Duc de Normandie, possessed in so eminent a degree. Was his death the consequence of his feeble health, as his mother thought, or was it, as the secretary of his tutor, the Duc d'Harcourt, wrote, the result of an unsuccessful inoculation, the eruption of which had been suddenly arrested by emotion? However that may be, when he passed from the hands of women to those of men, the dauphin, then six years of age, was submitted, in accordance with the regulations, to an examination by the faculty; the witnesses were obliged with regret to note an impediment in his walk, a tendency to deformity, and a weakness of the entire system which allowed of but little hope. After this examination, the child felt depressed on rising; and though he seemed brighter after he was dressed, he never again exhibited the vigour of a strong child.

"My oldest boy causes me much anxiety," the queen wrote on the 22d of February, 1788. "His figure is misshapen; one hip is higher than the other; and the vertebræ of the back are displaced, and project. For some time he has had continual fever, and is very thin and feeble." But with that power of illusion which love gives to mothers, she fancied that it was only a temporary derangement, due to teething and growth, and that the fresh air would triumph over these evil humours as it had triumphed over the weakness of Louis XVI., who had been delicate, like his son, in his early years. The child was, in fact, established at Meudon in the beginning of April. Under the influence of the change, the spring, the air, the open country, he seemed for the moment to improve; his gayety and appetite returned, his strength increased, and the unhappy mother felt a new confidence born within her. It was but a fleeting hope, however; for three months later, she was driven to write, "My son has alternations from better to worse which, without destroying hope, do not let us rely upon it." The disease made rapid progress; the back became hunched; the figure lost its shapeliness; the legs were so weak that the young patient could no longer walk without being supported, nor go for an airing without being mounted on a donkey. Medicines ceased to have effect; gangrene reached the spinal column; the face grew long, and acquired that expression of pain and anguish which, when seen in a child, makes the heart ache. The intelligence still remained clear, and the taste for reading strong; the mind seemed to live at the expense of the body. But under the sting of suffering, his nature became embittered; and if Madame Campan is to be believed, the prince manifested a veritable antipathy for his former governess, Madame de Polignac. A touching tenderness for his mother at least survived. One might have said that before leaving her, he wished to lavish upon her all the affection pent up within his heart. He begged her to stay near him; and to give him pleasure, she occasionally remained to dine with him in his room. Alas! the poor mother swallowed more tears than bread.

On the 4th of May, 1789, lying on a pile of cushions on a balcony of a small stable, the heir of the throne could witness the procession of the States-General. A month later, he was no more. His father having come to Versailles to see him the day before his death, the Duc d'Harcourt sent his secretary to entreat him not to enter. An eye-witness relates, —

"The king stopped short, exclaiming with sobs, 'Ah, my son is dead!' 'No, Sire,' I replied; 'he is not dead, but he is in the last extremity.' His Majesty sank down upon an armchair near the door. The queen entered almost immediately, and threw herself on her knees between those of the king, who cried, 'Ah, my wife! our dear child must be dead, since they will not let me see him.' I repeated that he was not dead. The queen, shedding a torrent of tears, and with both arms still resting on the knees of the king, said to him, 'Have courage, my friend! Providence can do all things, so let us hope that he will yet preserve to us our well-beloved son.' Both arose and returned to Versailles."

And the author of this touching story adds simply and briefly, " This scene called forth my admiration, although cruelly painful for me, and will never fade from my memory."

A few hours later, on the night of the 3d and 4th of June, the cause of so much joy, who had now become the cause of so many tears, was no more, and the afflicted monarch wrote in his journal: " Thursday, the 4th, death of my son at one o'clock in the morning. Special mass at a quarter to nine. I saw only my household and the princes on duty." On the 8th, the last honours were rendered the dauphin at Meudon; twelve archbishops and bishops, accompanied by twelve curates, twelve gentlemen of the court, and twenty-eight members of the Tiers-État, represented their respective orders at this sad ceremony. On the 4th, Bailly, the oldest member of the Tiers, presented himself at the palace in the name of his order, to " express to the king the sympathy of the Communes on the death of the dauphin," and to ask at the same time that a deputation from the Tiers be received to deliver to him in person an address upon the state of affairs, " the deputies of the Communes being unwilling to recognize any intermediary between the king and the people."

He urged it in so imperious a tone, says Weber, and in such pressing language, that the king, absorbed as he was in his grief, yielded to his demands, and received the deputies of the Tiers on Saturday, the 6th of June, even before the funeral of the dauphin; but few encroachments on his authority affected him so much as this violation of the inner sanctuary of his mourning. " Are there no fathers in the Assembly of the Tiers-État?" he asked with bitter anguish of heart.

Seven days later, on the 13th of June, the body of the dauphin was carried without pomp to St. Denys. It was not long to rest there.

CHAPTER II.

THE grief of the father could not obtrude upon the duties of the king. Complications born at the outset became every day graver, and dissensions grew more marked. The Tiers-État on the one side, the *noblesse* and clergy on the other, were in open conflict ; and the king's efforts to bring about an understanding failed. The contest was embittered by the pretensions of the one party and the opposition of the other. Men were rare who, like Malouet, wished to effect the reunion of the orders by common consent, without force. On the 17th of June the Tiers-État, on a motion by Sieyès, declared themselves by a majority of 491 voices against 90 a National Assembly. After this encroachment, which, in the words of Malouet, signified a "disastrous division," the government could not observe silence. It announced a royal council for the 22d of June, and in consequence closed until that day the Salle des Menus. When, on June 20, the Tiers-État presented themselves at the door of the hall, soldiers barred their entrance. Upon the proposition of Dr. Guillotin, the deputies from the Communes assembled in the hall of the Jeu de Paume, or Tennis-Court. Incensed by the rebuff which they had experienced, exasperated by the alarming rumours which ill-will constantly circulated concerning the intentions of the court, carried away by one of those contagious enthusiasms which a large gathering can with difficulty resist, the deputies took oath not to separate until they had, either with or without the king, and indifferent to his consent, given France a Constitution, — an audacious pretension, which neither the instructions of their constituents, nor the traditions of the country, nor the constitutional principles of the States-General, authorized; a "fatal oath," — the expression is Mounier's, — which its very originators soon regretted and disclaimed. The current was so irresistible that when a single deputy, Martin d'Auch, dared to oppose it, the populace, which was already beginning to assert the power so soon to become supreme, very nearly made him pay dearly for his brave and conscientious resistance.

If we are to believe Malouet, there was still time, with resolution and a fixed plan, to put an end to these encroachments, the audacity of which was injuring the success of the wise and pacific reforms demanded by the *cahiers*. Necker was only capable of half-measures, the foolish weakness of which was an encouragement to the leaders, in guaranteeing to them an impunity, which they attributed, as has been justly said, to a lack of power to punish. The royal council was postponed a day; it took place on the 23d of June with pomp rather more irritating than imposing. Soldiers and body-guards surrounded the hall of the States, and the imperative form used several times by the king offended the representatives of the Tiers-État, over-sensitive through their exaltation, and rendered stronger by the adhesion of one hundred and forty-nine members of the clergy, who had joined them on the preceding day.

The text of the discourse prepared by Necker had been modified at the last moment in a council, at which Monsieur and the Comte d'Artois, who were suspected by the popular party, had assisted. Dissatisfied with these alterations, of which he disapproved, the minister took occasion to absent himself from the royal session, thus sacrificing his duty to his popularity, and crippling the government, of which he was still a member. Despite unfortunate omissions, the declaration of the king marked a genuine progress; it realized a considerable portion of the reforms demanded by the *cahiers*, and it exposed the principles which, if they had been developed with wisdom and precision, would have led France, slowly, perhaps, but surely, to the possession of that constitutional form of government the establishment of which she had vainly been endeavouring to obtain for a century. The consent of the States to loans and taxation, the publication of a list of receipts and disbursements, the renunciation of pecuniary privileges by the *noblesse*, the guarantee of personal liberty, the freedom of the Press, the suppression of internal customs, the reform of the administration of justice and of the government, the abolition of the *taille* and *corvée*, a change in the duty upon salt, the establishment of provincial States, in which the Tiers should have double representation, and where deliberations should take place in common, — all these were accorded or promised. "Let any one study the declaration of Louis XVI. in the council of the 23d of June," a distinguished writer has said, "and he will find therein the beginning and even the development of all the political reforms which have since been set down in the oft-renewed editions of our Constitution and our charters." But the king preserved the distinction between the three orders, and was satisfied at a moment when the struggle between them, and the animosity against the two higher orders, was the strongest sentiment of the public, merely to invite the *noblesse* and clergy to deliberate in common with the Tiers-État "upon matters concerning the general welfare." He touched only vaguely upon the much-debated question of the Constitution and the periodic meetings of the States-General; he maintained the feudal rights, and observed silence as to the admissibility of all to public offices. Finally he gave them to understand that if by immoderate demands or impertinent objections harmony between the States and royalty was rendered impossible, he should carry out these reforms alone.

"Any distrust on your part," he said, "would be a gross injustice. Until now I have done all for the happiness of my people; and it is rare, perhaps, that the sole ambition of a sovereign is to persuade his subjects to agree at last to accept his benefactions."

This personal and somewhat threatening tone, despite all the paternal feeling which there was at bottom in the declaration, strongly irritated these men, still elated by their newly acquired power, and made suspicious, moreover, by the absence of the popular minister. The king was heard in gloomy silence. When he went out, after having commanded that the Assembly should break up at once, the clergy and *noblesse* alone followed him; the members of the Tiers remained in the hall. "Messieurs," exclaimed Mirabeau, thus rendering involuntary homage to the generous and patriotic intentions of the sovereign, — "Messieurs, I admit that what you have just heard might be the salvation of our country if the gifts of despotism were not always dangerous." Distrust was thus revived, discontent reawakened; and when the master of ceremonies, the Marquis de Brézé, came to remind them of the king's orders, Mirabeau again replied, "We are here by the wish of the nation; physical force alone can compel us to leave." And the Assembly, siding with the tribune, who, despite the repugnance which he had heretofore inspired, was beginning to acquire a predominant influence in the body, refused to disband, and declared itself inviolate.

Thus this day, from which the era of Liberty might have dated without social upheaval, had failed of its purpose. In the evening Necker tendered his resignation. The queen sent for the minister, and implored him to retain his office. It was she who had secured his appointment to the ministry; it was she who begged him to remain in it. The king added the weight of his authority to his wife's entreaties; and Necker yielded a consent which accorded perhaps with his secret wishes, and was tantamount to a popular triumph for him.

But Necker's return was only momentary. Louis XVI. could not, after his attitude on June 23, regain absolute confidence in him. Besides, the king's natural irresolution prevented even himself from following any fixed course. Contradictory advice crowded upon him from all sides; the unhappy prince vacillated in the midst of these contradictions, now inclining toward concessions, now toward resistance, and often overturning on the morrow what he had done on the preceding day. After having maintained, on June 23, the right of the orders to deliberate in separate bodies, he induced the *noblesse* to join with the Tiers-État. This reunion took place in fact on June 28, amid great rejoicing. Versailles assumed an air of festivity; cries of " Vive le roi! " were shouted under the windows of the palace, and even the queen on that day received her share of cheers. The enthusiasm was universal; and a few ingenuous citizens were heard to declare that the Revolution was at an end.

The illusion did not last long; and this tardy reunion brought peace neither to the Assembly nor to France. Soon the fever which inflamed the minds of the people, the turmoil which threatened to descend into the streets, even acts of violence, of which several members of the clergy and nobility, having resisted certain popular injunctions, narrowly escaped being victims, and the recent insurrection of the French Guards, made the necessity of holding a sufficient military force at the disposition of the government obvious. The king assembled the troops round Versailles, under the command of one of the heroes of the Seven Years' War, the Maréchal de Broglie; but the disorganization which had invaded every class of society had not spared the army. " The soldiers cannot be relied upon," wrote the Count of Fersen on the 26th of June. Be that as it may, this concentration of the military forces irritated the people instead of calming them. The Assembly pretended to be alarmed, and to see in this an attempt against its independence. It demanded, through the medium of the ever-ardent Mirabeau, the withdrawal of the troops. The king, while protesting against the project of a *coup d'état*, which was urged upon him, proposed to transfer the States-General to Soissons or Noyon. Perhaps this would be a solution of the difficulty. The Assembly, removed from the exciting influence of Paris, might show less vehemence; and the prince, who was anxious to be in harmony with it, might then secure this accord. " But," Gouverneur Morris observes, " in recording this news, and expressing this hypothesis, the evil lies deeper than the king's counsellors are aware of, and the business now broached must have its complete course."

What part had the queen taken in all these proceedings? In the absence of any positive documents from her or her confidants, it is difficult to ascertain clearly. In general, one must regard with singular distrust the authors of the memoirs and chronicles of this disturbed period; for they frequently draw inferences without proofs, and make assertions without authority. They usually choose to confound the queen and the Comte d'Artois in the same party, as the leaders of the people had confounded them in the same sentiment of hate. It must not be forgotten, however, that on the occasion of the convocation of the States-General, a serious controversy had sprung up between Marie Antoinette and her brother-in-law. Monsieur de Ségur even relates that during the first interview which he had with the queen after his return from Russia, this princess — at the end of a long conversation, in which she had expressed herself with a sadness full of dignity, yet without bitterness against those of her friends who were then at the head of the popular party — had remarked, " I see, from what you have said, that you think me averse to your ideas. But to-morrow you will hear from me, and you will find that I am not so unreasonable as many suppose." And in fact, on the next day she sent him, through Madame Campan, a sealed package, which contained a pamphlet by Mounier, the undisputed leader of the moderate constitutional party. Nevertheless, taking into account the queen's proud character, and her exalted opinion of royal power, it is justifiable to believe that she was in favour of resistance rather than of concessions; but it is also probable that, absorbed as she was at this time in the grief caused by the recent loss of her son, she thought more of tears than of politics, and that the sorrow of the mother trammelled, if it did not altogether impede, the activity of the sovereign.

On the 11th of July Necker received an order, couched in most courteous terms, to hand in his resignation, or rather, an authorization to retire; and he departed in silence, with unquestionable dignity. A new ministry was formed under the presidency of the Baron de Breteuil, with the Maréchal de Broglie as minister of war, and Monsieur Foulon as comptroller-general. This news, which spread quickly, threw Paris into great agitation. A crowd gathered at the Palais Royal, which was the usual centre of all disturbances. Camille Desmoulins, jumping upon a table, pistol in hand, snatched a leaf from a tree, made a cockade of it, and inveighed against the enemies of the nation. The people bore aloft in triumph the busts of Necker and the Duc d'Orléans. They showered imprecations upon the names of the Comte d'Artois and the queen, to whom they attributed the dismissal of the popular minister. They assaulted the troops drawn up on the Place Louis XV. with stones. The Prince de Lambesc, incensed on seeing his men stoned without defending themselves, and threatened by the mob in the Tuileries, pushed his way with a detachment into the garden, in order to clear it. The crowd took flight, doubling the disorder by their haste, and adding to the tumult by their cries. The rumour spread that innocent citizens were being slaughtered; in default of a corpse, which one invariably finds in revolutions, a wounded man was shown, and the soldiers, to whom the most pacific orders had been issued, passed in the popular imagination as the murderers of the people. The multitude surged toward the Hôtel de Ville, demanding arms and the tocsin; the French Guards sided with the rioters, and marched against the royal troops, whom their commander, the Baron de Besenval, irresolute and without instructions and orders, ordered to fall back toward Versailles.

On the next day the agitation grew more violent. While the

electors, assembled at the Hôtel de Ville, decreed the formation of a Parisian militia, which was soon after famous under the name of the National Guards, the rioters sacked the house of the Lazarists, whom they accused of monopoly, freed the prisoners of St. Pelagie, plundered the Garde-Meuble, and erected barricades in the streets. In the face of this constant and growing disorder, the government remained in incredible inactivity.

The mob, emboldened by immunity from punishment, and tacitly encouraged by the Assembly, who, in the midst of the fermentation at the capital, continued to demand the discharge of the troops, no longer contented itself with the easy feats of burning barriers and pillaging convents. On the morning of July 14 it proceeded to the Hôtel des Invalides to search for the arms of which it stood in need. The governor, Sombreuil, wished to close the doors; the *invalides* themselves opened them and surrendered the guns. The spirit of revolt breathed everywhere. Bands, now armed, rushed toward the Bastille. After a siege, which was only a wretched farce; after strange negotiations, an account of which would be too long to give here, — this old fortress, so terrible in appearance, so feeble in reality (for it was without other guard than thirty-two Swiss and eighty-two *invalides* who refused to fight, without ammunition, almost without cannon), was taken; or to speak more exactly, it surrendered without having been defended. The governor, or rather the garrison, seeing itself without orders and without succour, capitulated. The crowd, which had fled before the one cannon-ball fired from the Bastille, dashed into the enclosure of the fortress as soon as there was no longer even an appearance of danger to fear. They butchered the principal officers, the *invalides*, the governor himself, De Launay, whose head, set up on the end of a pike, served as a trophy to the victors of the day, along with that of the provost of the merchants, Flesselles, to kill whom the mob had gone to the Hôtel de Ville.

The Reign of Terror had begun; so an eye-witness, one of the most moderate and far-seeing men of the time, declares. The murder of De Launay and Flesselles was the prelude. The wild beast, the populace, had been loosed; intoxicated by the smell of blood, it was preparing to shed still more. "If the court had been at Paris instead of at Versailles," Malouet writes, "they would have massacred the ministers and princes instead of Foulon, Berthier, and De Launay." The Palais Royal had drawn up the list of victims; the murderers were ready. The Comte d'Artois, the Condés, the Polignacs, the Baron de Breteuil, the Maréchal de Broglie, Foulon, Berthier, and many others also were inscribed upon that fatal list. "Prince," the Duc de Liancourt, who had just returned from Paris, had said to the Comte d'Artois, "your head is doomed; I have read the announcement of the terrible proscription." Even at Versailles the prince had been several times insulted; and Madame Campan had overheard a disguised man say to a veiled woman, "The duchess is still at Versailles; she is like the moles, — she works under ground; but we shall know how to dig in order to unearth her."

The king bestirred himself in the face of these threats, which might soon become bloody realities. He persuaded his brother to seek out of France the safety which he felt himself powerless to promise him. The queen did likewise for her friend. At eight o'clock on the evening of the 16th of July, she sent for the Duc and Duchesse de Polignac, and entreated them to leave at once, that very night. For a long time they refused to do so. At last the queen, not knowing by what means to prevail upon them, and trembling for every instant that delayed their departure, said to her friend amid a torrent of tears, "The king goes to Paris to-morrow; if one were to ask him — I fear the worst; for the sake of our friendship leave. There is yet time to rescue you from the fury of my enemies; if they attack you, it will be much more because of hatred for me than for you. Do not be a victim to your affection and to my friendship." At that moment the king entered, and the queen appealed to him: "Come, Monsieur, and help me persuade these good people, these loyal subjects, that they ought to leave us." The king, going up to the duke and duchess, assured them that the queen's advice was the only one to follow, and added, "My cruel destiny forces me to send from me all those whom I esteem and love. I have just commanded the Comte d'Artois to take his departure; I give you the same order. Pity me, but do not lose a single instant; take your family with you. Count upon me at all times. I will keep your posts open for you."

At midnight, the duchess received this short note from the queen, "Adieu, tenderest of friends. How frightful is this word! But it must be spoken. Adieu. I have only just strength enough to embrace you."

· Despite the estrangement of these last years, Marie Antoinette could not, without anguish of heart, part from this friend, to whom fifteen years of affection and all the memories of a happy life bound her. It was the first tie broken; it was friendship forced to flee before criminations and murder, — a sad and clear augury of the fate reserved for the queen herself! Had not a woman, veiled in black, said to Madame Campan on the day before, "Tell your queen not to meddle further in our government, but allow the king and our good States-General to care for the happiness of the people"? "Yes," a man apparently disguised as a market-man continued; "say to her that it will not be with these States-General as with the others, who have accomplished no good for the people. Be sure to tell her that. Do you understand?" Thus popular ill-will persisted in regarding the queen as the sole obstacle to reform; and if the people did not secure that happiness which had been so loudly promised to them with more boldness than wisdom, it was she who must bear the blame.

The Duchesse de Polignac, on arriving at Basel, met Necker, and communicated to him the first news of his recall, which was soon after confirmed by the arrival of a royal courier. Louis XVI., frightened by the revolt in Paris, which, according to the word of the Duc de Liancourt, had risen to the height of a revolution, determined to shed no more blood for his cause, and yielded. On the 15th he went to the Assembly on foot, without guards, accompanied by his two brothers, to announce in person the withdrawal of the troops. On his return the crowd acclaimed him; flags floated in the air; drums beat; the troops drawn up on the Place d'Armes shared in the universal intoxication. The queen appeared upon the grand balcony, accompanied by her family, holding the dauphin in her arms, and Madame by the hand. Soon after, the children of the Comte d'Artois were led out by their tutor. They kissed the hand of the queen, who bent toward them, her son in her arms. The two young princes embraced their cousin; the little Madame, affected by the scene, joined her caresses to those of the Duc d'Angoulême and the Duc de Berry; and for a moment all of these young blond heads were blended in one common embrace, overtopped by the graver yet smiling face of the queen. It was a touching picture, and there was a moment of indescribable enthusiasm; but among the people who thronged below the balcony this enthusiasm was mingled with imprecations against the Comte d'Artois and suppressed murmurs against the queen.   Louis XVI. observed this; and not wishing to have his brother share the dangers which confronted himself, he gave him, as we have said, orders to depart.   During the night of the 16th and 17th, the Comte d'Artois and his children, the Prince de Condé, the Duc de Bourbon, and the Duc d'Enghien set out on the road to Belgium, where the last three arrived only after having with difficulty escaped a furious mob, who wished to throw them into the Oise.   The ministers who were compromised in the cabinet of the 11th of July, Messieurs de Barentin, de Villedeuil, de la Vauguyon, de Breteuil, the Abbé de Vermond, the Prince de Lambesc, who was guilty of having commanded the charge of the Royal Germans in the garden of the Tuileries on July 12, followed their example.   The Maréchal de Broglie retired to his government of the Trois-Évêchés, whence the excited clamours of the populace against him soon forced him to fly to Luxembourg.

Some days later, the horrible assassination of one of the ministers of July 11, Foulon, and of his son-in-law, Berthier, justified only too well the sombre forebodings of the king and queen, and proved the necessity of the first emigration.

For a moment, however, Louis XVI. entertained the thought of resisting the insurrection.   He wished to abandon Versailles and retire to Metz, under the protection of the troops, to whom he had just given orders to withdraw.   The queen urged it strongly; she herself had already made preparations for the departure, had burned her papers, collected her diamonds in a casket easy to carry, and delivered to Madame Campan an order to accompany her in the capacity of governess to Madame. A council was held, in which the king proposed the question frankly; the discussion was long and animated; but the majority decided against the departure.   Monsieur besought the king to remain; and the Maréchal de Broglie, when interrogated in his turn, replied, " Yes, we can go to Metz; but what shall we do when we are there? "   Louis XVI., overcome by the prayers of his brother, the hesitation of the commander-in-chief of his troops, and the prospect of the civil war which might follow, renounced his plan; and the queen, taking back the paper which she had given to Madame Campan, tore it in pieces, saying with tears in her eyes, " When I wrote it, I hoped sincerely that it might be of use, but Fate has decided otherwise.   I am very much afraid that this will prove a misfortune for us all." She was not deceived; and the king regretted later the course which he had chosen on that day. "I missed the right moment," he remarked with sadness to Fersen three years later; "and since then I have never found another."

It was decided that the prince, instead of taking the route to Metz, should go to Paris to try to calm the people. Gloomy apprehensions troubled his heart; and before starting, he insisted on ordering his conscience as Christian and as king. The Christian heard mass and received the sacrament; the king gave over secretly to Monsieur an act which appointed him lieutenant-general of the kingdom in case an attempt should be made on the life and liberty of the sovereign. Then, at nine o'clock on the morning of the 17th, Louis XVI. set out; if he had not the courage of aggression, he had that of resignation. Only twelve body-guards followed him, with the Duc de Villeroy, the Duc de Villequier, the Maréchal de Beauvau, and the Comte d'Estaing; there were no princes of the blood or ministers. The remainder of the escort was furnished by the National Guards of Versailles, who accompanied him as far as Paris. There they met the Parisian National Guards, still in citizen's dress, and commanded by Lafayette on his horse. A double file of armed men — one hundred and fifty thousand, it is said — extended from the Pont du Jour to the Hôtel de Ville. In the streets, at the windows, on the roof-tops even, there was an immense, rough, impatient crowd of young men bearing pikes and fowling-pieces, monks in arms, half intoxicated, market-women carrying immense bouquets, jumping and frisking; musicians playing the tune, "Où peut-on être mieux qu'au Sein de sa Famille?" cannons wreathed with flowers, bearing this inscription, "Your presence has disarmed us." Everywhere — on the hats, on the caps, on the uniforms, even on the statue of Louis XVI. — was to be seen the cockade in the colors of the capital, red and blue.

At the barrier, the mayor of Paris, Bailly, presented the king with the keys of the city upon a crimson cushion. "Sire," he said, "I bring to your Majesty the keys of your good city of Paris; they are the same which were presented to Henri IV. He had reconquered his people; here it is the people who have reconquered their king."

Bailly was right. It was, in truth, a vanquished man, "an illustrious captive," the Marquis de Ferrières observes, who " with a

sad and anxious look " slowly advanced in the midst of two or three hundred members of the Assembly, marching through the streets of the city without guards, with a retinue in disorder, and yet with a pomp "which in the eyes of all had something funereal in it." The cries of " Vive la nation ! " which re-echoed on every side almost to the exclusion of the old French cheer, " Vive le roi ! " indicated clearly the situation. The humiliation was completed at the Hôtel de Ville, where the king, after having passed under a threatening arch of swords crossed, confirmed the power conferred upon the rioters. Bailly presented the monarch with the new cockade, which was taking the place among the Parisians of the old royal cockade. The king took it, put it in his hat, and appeared on the balcony. Wild cheers burst forth, greeting the disarmed and vanquished sovereign, and then only the cry " Vive le roi ! " was heard again. This was, however, no longer the madness of loyal devotion ; it was the madness of triumph.

The king felt it. Tears, which were not tears of joy, dropped from his eyes ; and it was with a downcast mien and a heavy heart that he returned to Versailles.

The alarm at the palace was intense. The queen, although she " had shown great courage and an extraordinary firmness of mind," had been unable to contemplate this journey to Paris without anxiety ; she had done all she could to keep her husband from it ; she had implored him on her knees, and in tears, to abandon a project which offered great insecurity and danger. Would not the citizens try to hold him prisoner ? Would they not do still more ? And, in fact, these fears were not groundless. A few days later did not Lafayette boast to Gouverneur Morris that he had been sole master on July 17 ; that if he had wished, he might have detained the king prisoner ; that he had marched him through the streets as he pleased, and that he himself had prescribed the degree of applause which it was proper to accord to him ? Had not the crowd on the Champs-Élysées seen a woman struck by a bullet aimed in the direction of the king's carriage ; and did not this act, although it was probably the result of chance, appear " extraordinary " even to Bailly ?

The day had, in consequence, seemed very long to the poor queen. She had passed it in apprehension and in tears, shut up in her apartments. She had given an order that a carriage should be held in readiness ; and while repeating unceasingly in broken tones the words, " They will not let him come back," she had even attempted to sketch out the address which she would deliver to the Assembly if the malcontents, from whom one might expect anything, should oppose his return.

He returned, however. At six o'clock in the evening, the first page, Monsieur de Latour, hastened at full speed to bring the good news. At nine o'clock the king himself arrived, prostrated with fatigue, but congratulating himself that no disaster had marked this journey, which had been undertaken with so many misgivings. " Luckily," he said, " no blood has been shed; I swear that there shall never be a drop of French blood spilled by my order." The queen with the dauphin rushed halfway down the stairs to meet her husband. In an instant the prince was in the arms of his family. His wife, his sister, his children, surrounded him, weeping for joy. The alarm had been so terrible that his return filled every one with happiness. They forgot the anxieties of the day; could they forget those of the morrow?

" Your Majesty," Bailly had said to the king, " is come to enjoy the peace which you have established in your capital." Five days later the murder of Foulon and Berthier showed upon what basis this peace was founded, and how well the Parisian people understood respect for the laws. These two unfortunate victims, arrested far from the capital, led back to Paris by a furious populace, who heaped upon them insults and ill-treatment, abandoned by those who should have defended them, were butchered with all the horrible refinements of barbarism. Their heads, placed on the ends of pikes, were paraded through the streets amid cannibal-like songs and dances; and the bloody heart of Berthier was brought in before the very eyes of the electors assembled in the great hall of the Hôtel de Ville. In the provinces the excitement was no less intense, nor were acts of violence less frequent. Vague rumours, too much in accord with one another, however, not to be the outcome of one word of command, diffused alarm through the country districts : bands of brigands, it was said, were coming to plunder the crops and burn the wheat. " A panic of terror," observes a reliable witness, "spread throughout all parts of the kingdom on the same day." The women fled; the men took up arms; they fell upon the imaginary brigands; and not finding them, they threw themselves upon those who were accused of hiring them. They demolished the châteaux, pillaged the convents, burned the registers and deeds, massacred the nobles and all whom they suspected, with or without reason, of being hostile to the Revolution. Law was powerless; anarchy reigned supreme. "Property, of whatever nature it may be," said the deputy Salomon on the 3d, in the name of the Committee of Reports, "is a prey to the most reprehensible brigandage. On all sides châteaux are burned, convents destroyed, farms given over to plunder; taxes, seigniorial fines, all are suppressed; the laws are without force, the magistrates without authority; and justice is a phantom, which one seeks vainly in the courts."

It seemed as if the decrees of August 4, in abolishing the feudal rights, ought to put an end to the disorders which then had no further pretext. This was not the case: new conflagrations, new outrages, new massacres, were the only response to the generous outburst of the privileged orders. Against such excesses it was necessary to act; the Assembly was content to talk. But its proclamations, which were without colour or vigour, remained without result. All-powerful to destroy, it found itself without strength to preserve. And how could it have any? Did not the most violent agitations start from its tribune? Had not the man who exercised undisputed sway over it been heard to exclaim one day, "The nations must have victims; every one should harden himself to public misfortunes, for one is not a citizen except at that price"?

And at the moment of the assassination of Foulon and Berthier, had not Barnave spoken those words, which he was to regret so bitterly, "Is the blood which flows so pure, after all?"

"My health continues good," the unhappy queen wrote to the Duchesse de Polignac; "but my soul is overwhelmed with troubles, sorrows, and anxieties. Every day I dread fresh misfortunes; one of the greatest for me is separation from all my friends. I no longer encounter hearts which understand me. . . . Be undisturbed; adversity has not diminished my strength or my courage, and it has taught me prudence."

While waiting for better days, she had, remarked her brother, "taken the only expedient for her, that was, to live in seclusion, wholly absorbed in her children."

Necker had returned on July 28 amid general enthusiasm. But his return had neither restored order nor the finances; patriotic gifts, the announcement of important reforms in the households

of the king and the queen, even the sending of the royal plate
to the mint, had not replenished the empty treasury. Taxes were
not paid. After August 4 the peasants believed themselves exempt from all State taxation as well as from all feudal fines. Nor
was Necker more successful in politics. In the month of July,
as in the month of May, he had no plan of action, and the fear of
injuring his popularity led him into compromises which even a
hostile statesman like Mirabeau would not have been willing to
accept. Thus it was that in the grave and vital discussion upon the
veto the tribune was seen sustaining the royal prerogative which
the minister abandoned; but even this submission was not enough.
The word " veto," misunderstood, became the injurious and deadly
epithet by which the people designated the king and the queen.
The danger grew from hour to hour. Anonymous letters denounced not only friendly deputies, but all those who did not
blindly obey the decrees of the Palais Royal.

"All bonds are broken," wrote the Count of Fersen, on the 3d of
September; "the authority of the king is null; the National Assembly itself
trembles before Paris; and Paris trembles before forty or fifty bandits or
vagrants established at Montmartre, or in the Palais Royal, whom no one
can drive away, and who persist in fomenting disturbances."

The situation was intolerable; the Assembly was not free.
The clamours of the galleries, the cries of the street, anonymous
letters, threatened its wisest and most eminent members. The
police reports made known a plan of invasion of Versailles by the
ringleaders of Paris. It was necessary to leave there. The court
gave serious thought to the subject, and the Royalists of the Assembly considered it no less earnestly. Was there at that time a
project to carry off the king by way of Champagne and Verdun,
and transport him to Metz under the protection of Bouillé's
army? The Comte d'Estaing asserts it in a letter to the queen,
the rough draft of which was found in his house. It was openly
spoken of at Paris; and Madame de Tourzel confirms it in her
memoirs, but the scheme seems always to have remained vague.
The place of retreat even was not decided upon, and it was soon
given up. At about the same period three deputies, Malouet,
Redon, and the bishop of Langres, believing themselves sure of
carrying the majority of the Assembly, who were frightened by
the boldness of the factious members, proposed to the ministry, in
the name of a certain number of their colleagues, to transfer the

Assembly twenty leagues from Paris to Soissons or Compiègne. Several of the ministers, Necker and Montmorin among them, had advocated the project; **but when it** was submitted to the king, he objected.

What was the reason of this objection? Had not the prince confidence in the success of the scheme? Did he recall that on July 14 he had wished to adopt a similar resolution, and that he had been obliged, by arguments of the very men upon whom he believed that he could most surely count, to relinquish it? Did he think it necessary to remain near Paris, in order the better to hold it in check? Did he not believe in the reality of the danger? Was he ashamed to appear to flee from the uprising? All that history can say is that on that day, as later, Louis XVI. manifested an unconquerable reluctance to abandon Versailles. The deputies withdrew in consternation.

It was on September 29 that this measure was proposed and defeated. A few days later, the king and the Assembly left Versailles to enter Paris as prisoners.

CHAPTER III.

MEANWHILE the plans to invade Versailles were no longer secret; alarming reports multiplied. On the 30th of August, one of the most censured, and for that very reason one of the most influential, among the Parisian demagogues, the Marquis de Saint-Huruge, had tried to lead fifteen hundred rioters against Versailles. The attempt had failed; but the project had not been abandoned. A little later, in September, Camille Desmoulins had declared at the Palais Royal that fifteen hundred men must be sent to Versailles to bring back the king and imprison the queen. Rumours of insurrection and invasion of the palace were in the air. Mounier says, "Horrible designs against the queen were proclaimed." At Paris, and in the provinces as far as Toulouse, people discussed them openly. They talked of carrying off the Assembly and the king, and "of treating according to their deserts those deputies who had shown themselves ill disposed toward the people." Mirabeau said one day to the bookseller, Blaisot, that he foresaw there would be some unfortunate occurrence at Versailles, but that good citizens had nothing to fear; and finally the French Guards, who had formed the paid companies of the National Parisian Guards since their disbandment after the capture of the Bastille, boasted loudly that they would go out and resume the posts which they had formerly occupied at the palace, and if necessary get possession of the king. Their commander, General Lafayette, watched intently the disposition of the troops; and while believing himself able to neutralize them by his authority, he considered it his duty, toward the middle of September, to warn the minister of the king's household, Monsieur de Saint-Priest, of their evil designs.

The court became alarmed; the defence of the palace was no longer undertaken except by the Swiss and body guards, who, although faithful, were few in number. The defence of the town was given up to the National Guards, the majority of whom were untrustworthy, and who were, moreover, worn out by continual expeditions to secure provisions. In August they had been forced to send to the Trois-Évêchés for two hundred *chasseurs*, and to Lorraine for two hundred dragoons to aid them. This would not suffice against a possible and foreseen invasion. Monsieur de Saint-Priest expressed himself on the subject to the commander-general of the National Guards, the Comte d'Estaing, whose attachment to the new ideas' was unquestionable, and he undertook to obtain the consent of the municipal authorities, whose requisition was necessary for the entrance of troops into Versailles. On his motion, and in view of the statement of the staff captains of the National Guards that their forces were insufficient, and "of the diverse rumours of more and more alarming import which were constantly arriving," it was decided on September 18 that it was indispensable for the safety of the town, of the National Assembly, and of the king, to procure as soon as possible a relief of one thousand men from the regular troops, who should be under the orders of the commander-general of the National Guards of Versailles. The regiment of Flanders was chosen because its good-will and discipline seemed to guarantee fidelity, while the name of its colonel, the Marquis de Lusignan, who sat on the left of the Assembly, would reassure the patriots against the project of a counter-revolution. The Flanders regiment arrived on September 23, and was "very well received;" Comte d'Estaing, with a staff and a detachment of National Guards, and the president of the municipality, with the members of the municipal corps, met it at the barrier. The regiment was conducted to the Place d'Armes, where, in presence of the mayor, it took the oath of allegiance to the nation, the law, and the king. It consisted of eleven hundred men and two cannon.

The king was so well satisfied with the militia of Versailles on the occasion that he wrote a letter with his own hand to the commander-general, the Comte d'Estaing, expressing his thanks to them; and the queen resolved to offer a proof of her gratitude to the National Guards. On the 29th she herself announced to the staff that she wished to present a flag to each division; and on the 30th these two flags were solemnly blessed in the church of Notre Dame by the archbishop of Paris, in the presence of the governor of Versailles, of the municipality, of a large number of the members of the Assembly, of the notable citizens of the town, and of the officers of the entire military corps. After the ceremony, a banquet brought the invited guests together; the greatest cordiality prevailed throughout, and toasts were drunk to the king and to the prosperity of the nation ("insep- arable factors"), to the queen, the dauphin, and all the royal family.

On the next day another banquet was to take place. It was the account of this one which, shamefully perverted, served later as pretext for frightful massacres. It was then, as it is still to-day, the custom in the French army to offer a mess banquet to the regiment that arrived at a new garrison. At the time of the journey of Louis XVI. to Cherbourg, the body-guards had received similar attentions from a great number of regiments of infantry; they determined to repay them to the Flanders regi- ment, and thus tighten the bonds which united all the troops of Versailles. It was decided that they should tender them a ban- quet, and the date of it was fixed for Thursday, October 1.

As the Salle du Manège and the auditorium of the town the- atre were not suitable for the purpose, the originators of the entertainment asked the king — who granted it willingly — for the use of the opera-house in the château, in which, some years before, the body-guards had given a ball to the royal family. The hall was tastefully decorated; a table of two hundred covers, arranged in the shape of a horseshoe, was set on the stage, where about eighty of the Life Guards, all the officers of the regiment of Flanders, the *chasseurs* and dragoons of Lorraine, who were then in garrison at Meudon, several officers of the Swiss Guards and of the Prévôté, and some twenty National Guards were to sit down. At three o'clock on the afternoon of the appointed day, the historian of Versailles, Monsieur Le Roi, recounts, —

"Every one assembled at the gate of the palace, which was the meet- ing-place named. The company then proceeded through the corridor of the palace to the Salle de l'Opéra. On entering they were charmed with the appearance of the hall; the guests took their places, and the repast began. The trumpeters of the guards, and the band of the regiment of Flanders, were in the orchestra; a parterre was reserved for the grena- diers of the regiment, and the *chasseurs* and the dragoons of Lorraine."

No unusual incident marked the first course. At the second the Duc de Villeroy, captain of the Light Guards, invited the grenadiers from Flanders, the Swiss grenadiers, and the *chasseurs* from the Trois-Évêchés to enter the hollow of the horse-shoe. These good people, pleased with this distinction, begged to propose the health of the royal family. Their glasses were filled, and they drank to the health of the queen, the king, and the dauphin. The spectators whom this feast had attracted, and who had packed themselves in the boxes, responded with cheers, which were at that time still familiar to the people of France. Whatever may have been said by writers who were interested in perverting the facts, the health of the nation was not proposed, and consequently not refused. At the moment of dessert the royal family appeared in a grated box. The queen, disturbed by the rumours which came from Paris, and greatly saddened by the hostility which was shown to her, had retired early to her apartments. Several times her ladies-in-waiting had praised the magnificence of the feast, and begged her to witness it; she had refused. They represented to her that the sight would amuse the dauphin; through maternal love she consented to go. The king was just returning from the hunt; she carried him with her.

On perceiving them both in a box, shouts of "Vive le roi!" burst forth on all sides. The company besought them to come down into the hall; they descended, overcome by their importunities. The Vicomte d'Agoût, as a sign of rejoicing, fastened a handkerchief to the end of his commander's baton. The queen, taking her son by the hand, made the tour of the hall. The guests rose, drew their swords as if to defend this noble and unfortunate family, swore fidelity to them, and promised them love and devotion. One of the bystanders asked that the tune, "Où peut-on être mieux qu'au Sein de sa Famille?" be played. As the musicians did not have it, they substituted the well-known and captivating melody of a composer dear to the queen, "O Richard, O mon Roi!" The shouting redoubled; the enthusiasm was at its height. Marie Antoinette, touched by these cheers, which were raised for her husband, herself, and her children, felt herself happy as queen, wife, and mother; gentler thoughts filled her mind, and she experienced unmixed delight at this return of popularity. Poor woman! it was her last day of happiness.

The royal family soon retired; a large number of soldiers climbed to the boxes and jumped over the railings to accompany them through the chapel corridor, through which they returned to their apartments; then every one — musicians, guests, spectators —repaired to the marble court below the king's windows. A crowd of the inhabitants of Versailles had assembled here, in the courts, and on the Place d'Armes to assist at the festivities. The guests, heated by the wine, and exalted by the visit which they had just received, indulged in noisy demonstrations; they sang; they danced; and a soldier who five years later became one of the most dangerous insurgents, succeeded, by climbing up a column, in scaling the balcony of the king, who, despite the shouts, remained in his apartment, and did not appear.

That was all. It has been alleged that there were counter-revolutionary manifestations, that the tri-coloured cockade was trampled under foot; but these allegations were false. The officers of the Life Guards who had organized the banquet always denied it with haughty vehemence, and the queen herself took care to refute the calumny. "It is incredible," she replied to the revolutionary tribunal, "that such devoted subjects should trample under foot or wish to change the badge which their king himself was wearing." That white cockades were seen at the banquet is true, and with reason. The army at that epoch still wore the white cockade; only the king and the National Guards wore the tri-coloured; and if, as is told, some ladies of the court made white cockades out of paper and gave them to the officers whom they met, they only gave to these officers the legitimate customary badge, the one which Mounier still called "the French cockade."

On the 3d of October the queen received a deputation from the National Guards, come to thank her for the flags which had been presented on the 30th of September. Still affected by the sympathetic demonstration of two days before, she replied to them, "I am most happy to have given the flags to the National Guards of Versailles. I was overjoyed by the events of Thursday; the nation and the army should be as devoted to the king as we are to them."

On the same day another banquet took place in the quarters of the Life Guards; eighty soldiers of the regiment of Flanders and of Lorraine, and a man from each company of the National Guards at Versailles, were invited. The repast was gay; the health of the king, of the nation, of the Assembly, and of the National Guards was proposed; then toward the end, as the banqueters grew excited, they sang, shouted, broke the bottles and glasses.

In what banquet of two hundred persons, of two hundred young men, do not scenes of this sort occur?

On Sunday, the 4th, the municipal authorities of Versailles in their turn entertained the Flanders regiment; the National Guards were present at the banquet, and drank to the health of the king and the queen ; but everything passed quietly.

Such was the series of festivities and banquets which was transformed into a series of attempts against the national supremacy. Nothing (the simple recital above is sufficient to prove it) could have served as pretext for such an accusation. There were undoubtedly enthusiastic demonstrations in honour of the royal family, but these demonstrations were then echoed in the hearts of the great majority of the French people; as for attacks on the reforms of the Assembly, there were none. The Life Guards, the army, the National Guards, had been in perfect accord. Moreover, it must not be forgotten that these Life Guards, although devoted to the king, were in no way hostile to the new ideas. They had recently given proof of this; they lived on very friendly terms with the deputies, and passed in the Assembly for excellent patriots. This evidence was given in the trial by a thoroughly unprejudiced deputy.

But an excuse was necessary; and this was chosen as one. The signal was given by Laurent Lecointre, lieutenant-colonel of the National Guards of the district of Notre Dame, — a man who later played a melancholy part in the convention, and who was at that time one of the bitterest enemies of royalty, although he called himself one of the king's most loyal subjects. He was offended because he had not been invited to the banquet on October 1, and in consequence, personal rancour added flame to his political enthusiasm. One of his friends, Gorsas, editor of a revolutionary newspaper, the "Courier de Versailles," at his instigation began in his journal a whole series of articles directed against the banquet of the body-guards ; this repast, of which we have given an account taken from the most authentic documents, was represented as a "genuine orgy." The "staggering guests" had offered a "disgusting and horrible sight." Some one having proposed the health of the nation, the body-guards had rejected it, and it was with such a scandal that the queen had declared herself overjoyed. What better proof could there be of the counter-revolutionary designs of the court, and of the Austrian's schemes of vengeance against the people?

It is easy to conceive what effects such furious denunciations would produce, falling like seeds of hatred upon the well-prepared soil of the Parisian populace. Gorsas's account was read with avidity, and odiously commented on. Marat, Camille Desmoulins, Loustalot, in their journals, thundered against the court and the queen, and denounced the great counter-revolutionary conspiracy. They revived an old rumour which had been formerly circulated concerning the abduction of the king, and his transportation to Metz. They did not stop to consider that Louis XVI., in order to execute such a plan, had it been thought of, had at his disposal only six hundred Life Guards, the majority of whom were warm partisans of the Tiers-État, two hundred dragoons, two hundred *chasseurs*, eleven hundred soldiers of the Flanders regiment, commanded by a patriotic colonel; and that with this feeble corps of two thousand men, he could not have rushed into so hazardous an enterprise in the face of the National Guards, who would surely not have lent their co-operation. But popular masses, when excited, are blind; and the leaders in this case did not allow the mob time to reason.

The opportunity, moreover, was a good one. A scarcity of food, for which one need not go far to seek the causes, but which at the moment certainly had something factitious in it, — a "docile famine," as Lally-Tollendal calls it, — prevailed in Paris. There was some real suffering, and, as always, it was upon the government, the king, the court, the most unpopular members of the royal family, — upon the queen, consequently, — that people laid the responsibility of this suffering. Gorsas's calumnies threw oil upon the fire, which was smouldering under hot ashes. The populace collected at the Palais Royal; troops were formed; orators declaimed. The people swore vengeance against the Life Guards, who, it is said, began to display the black cockade. They indulged in the most frightful denunciations against the queen; they stimulated the populace against the populace. A woman, whose dress indicated a woman above the middle class, cried out that she had no bread, and the people must go to Versailles to ask the king for some. Then when one of the bystanders laughed, she dealt him a blow in the face, and other women present applauded.

"To-morrow," they said, "things will go better; we shall place ourselves at the head of affairs." Some of the National Guards who were sitting round the tables of the Café de Foy joined in

with the women.   The police remained inert, and made no attempt to scatter the groups or re-establish order.

Nothing had been neglected to organize the attack and weaken
the resistance.   " The Machiavellis of the public squares and
low haunts," Monsieur Taine has said, " recruited men from the
gutter and women from the pavement."   Gold was distributed in
abundance among the people and in the army ; seven millions, it
is stated, came from Holland.   Since the arrival of the Flanders
regiment every means of corruption, even the most shameful, —
wine, money, women, — had been employed to bribe the soldiers ;
and in the beginning of October this regiment, which had been
called to protect order and the monarchy, was only a new danger.
It was with these feeble resources, with these half-corrupted
soldiers and a few faithful guards, against the National Guards
as a hostile party, that Louis XVI. was to combat a conspiracy
which his enemies had been weaving for a long time, with
most infernal cleverness.

CHAPTER IV.

THE women gave the signal. Those who directed the insurrection, Mounier observes, had judged it expedient to have it begun by the women; they felt that their presence would inspire less uneasiness; that the soldiery would less easily be brought to drive them back by force of arms; that they would spread confusion; and that then the men who followed them would run less danger.

Nor was this calculation a mistaken one. On the morning of the 5th of October, a riot broke out at Paris. A girl from the district of the *halles* pushed her way into a body of guards, seized a drum, and ran through the streets beating to arms, and crying out against the high price of bread. The tocsin was rung; the women assembled; a certain number of men in disguise joined them, and the crowd moved toward the Hôtel de Ville, which it invaded about nine o'clock. It forced open the magazines of arms, sacked them, and took possession of seven or eight thousand guns, insulted the members of the municipal council and their employees; and women armed with torches entered the halls, and prepared to set fire to them. A significant fact, upon which too great stress cannot be laid, is that most of these women were dressed in white, with their hair curled and powdered, as if they were going to a *fête*. Very few seemed to belong to the populace. Some laughed, sang, and danced in the court; while others sounded the tocsin and freed the prisoners. Almost all had their pockets full of gold.

At half-past eleven, a band of men, armed with axes and hammers, forced the door of the Arcade St. Jean, invaded the Hôtel de Ville in their turn, scattered in every direction, broke open the closets, pillaged and destroyed everything.

Here appears one of the most sinister figures of the Revolution, — the bailiff Maillard, the future instigator of the massacres of the Abbaye. An official errand had brought him to the Hôtel de Ville. Recognized by several women who hailed him as one of the conquerors of the Bastille, he was proclaimed, or proclaimed himself, their leader. He seized a drum, placed himself at their head, and set out toward the Louvre. The ranks were swollen by a crowd of women who were forced to march with the band. When these ladies, as Maillard called them, arrived at the garden of the Tuileries, and wished to cross it, a Swiss guard opposed them; they threw him to the ground, beat him, and passed on. The Place Louis XV. had been assigned as headquarters. They went a little farther on to the Champs-Élysées; here they met detachments of women, provided with pikes, sticks, and guns. Maillard ordered them to lay down their arms; he harangued his troops, drew them up in line, and started off at their head. A certain number of armed men who had joined the band were consigned to the rear; the women, following the word of command, marched first.

Everywhere along their route shops were closed, houses were vacated, doors were barricaded. They broke down the doors, carried off the signs, stopped the couriers, and forced all whom they met to go with them. At Sèvres they made a halt; they were hungry, and besides this, they feared lest the bridge across the Seine might be guarded. Through a fatal piece of negligence the passage was free. After having indulged in the popular amusement of smashing the doors and sign-boards of the wine merchants, who could give them nothing to eat, the horde rushed off in the direction of Versailles, dragging two cannon with them.

During this time a new disturbance had broken out at the Hôtel de Ville. The disbanded French Guards, who formed, under the name of the paid companies, a notable part of the Parisian Guards, thought this an excellent opportunity to resume their former posts at Versailles, now filled by the body-guards. They assembled on the Place de Grève, and raged and shouted.

Toward noon, five or six grenadiers went up to police headquarters, where Lafayette was to be found. One of them, who, besides a most beautiful face, possessed a flow of language which astonished all those who listened to him, and a coolness which astonished them still more, acted as spokesman. "General," he said, "we have been sent by the six companies of grenadiers. We do not believe you a traitor; we believe that the government betrays you; it is time that all this should come to an end. We cannot turn our arms against women who ask for bread. The Committee of Subsistence are deceiving you; you must dismiss them. We wish to go to Versailles to exterminate the Life Guards and Flanders regiment, who have trampled the national cockade under foot. If the king is too weak to wear the crown, let him lay it down; we will crown his son; a council of regency will be named, and all will go better." The delegates were proud of their orator. "Let him speak," they said; "he can talk well." Lafayette tried in vain to recall them to their duty; their decision was manifestly made beforehand; the word of command had been given. "It is useless to convince us," they all cried together, "for all our comrades are of this opinion; and if you convinced us, you could not change them."

Lafayette went out upon the square, harangued his soldiers, reminded them of their oath, appealed to their feeling of affection and confidence for him, protested his devotion to liberty; but words and supplications were unavailing. Tumultuous cries arose: "To Versailles, to Versailles! If the general does not wish to come, we must choose an old grenadier to place at our head. It is astonishing that Monsieur de Lafayette should wish to command the people, when it is the people's right to command him!" This was the sole response given by the troops, among whom the malcontents had not loosened all the reins of discipline in vain. Lafayette re-entered the Hôtel de Ville. He hesitated, waited for orders from municipal authorities. The municipal authorities, honest like Lafayette, and like him weak, were no less a prey to anxious fears. The turbulent, surging mass upon the Place de Grève grew denser; the troops, worked upon by mysterious agents, became impatient. Threats of death were uttered against Bailly and Lafayette. The municipal authorities gave way; and in view of the entreaties of the people, of the representations of the commander-general that it was impossible to refuse them, they gave orders to the general to set out for Versailles. The power of law was once again conquered; the rebellion had triumphed. Loud cheers greeted the victory of the populace and the downfall of authority.

It was six o'clock in the evening. Lafayette mounted his horse with bowed head, downcast spirits, and his mind full of gloomy forebodings, — of remorse, perhaps. In the front he detached three companies of grenadiers, a battalion of fusileers, and three cannon. Seven or eight hundred men in rags, bearing pikes and cudgels, with hideous faces, bare arms, and voices thickened with wine, — brigands which the gutters vomit up in times of riots, — marched behind the vanguard, interspersed in the ranks. Lafayette followed with the companies; led by his soldiers rather than leading them, like a living trophy of the rebellion, he set out for Versailles.

There a secret agitation reigned. The disclosures of Lecointre and his friends, the calumnies of Gorsas, had produced their effect; and the National Guards, who had been so warmly in sympathy with the Life Guards on October 1 and 3, had become hostile to them. Every one was expecting the Parisians, a trustworthy witness reports. From the 4th the people knew of the invasion contemplated by the French Guards; the malcontents fomented disturbances in the cafés, and prepared cartridges, saying, " These are to assassinate the Life Guards to-morrow."

At the Assembly, the leaders of the Left were likewise aware of the plan about to be executed against the corps. On Monday, the 6th of October, it was easy to see at the opening of the session, by the tone which some members of the Assembly assumed, that something extraordinary was pending. The galleries also appeared more animated; and the crowd which surrounded the chamber was consumed by that fever which portends popular storms. The president, Mounier, announced that he had received the king's reply to the Declaration of the Rights of Man, and to the last article submitted for his sanction. The king accepted them, but with certain reservations, and with observations of unquestioned wisdom upon them. The discussion opened with extreme violence. Robespierre and Lapoule denounced the king's very natural comments as a censure of the Constitution; Adrien Duport saw in them a whole scheme of counter-revolution, and seized the opportunity to inveigh against the " indecent orgy" which Versailles had witnessed on October 1. Virieu protested in vain; and the Marquis de Monspey demanded that the accusation be put in precise terms. Mirabeau arose and said, " Let the Assembly decide that the person of the king alone is inviolable, and I am ready to furnish the details and sign them." In giving definite form to his odious and transparent insinuations, he remarked in a low voice to those who stood around him, " I shall denounce the queen and the Duc de Guiche." These accusations stirred up a violent tumult in the Assembly; the Left exhibited wild excitement; the Right protested with spirit. The excitement in the galleries redoubled.

Meanwhile the rumour of the approach of the Parisians began to spread. Between eleven o'clock and noon, Mirabeau walked up to the desk and addressed Mounier, saying, "Mr. President, forty thousand men are coming from Paris; hurry the session; adjourn the meeting; say that you are going to the king." "I do not hurry deliberations," Mounier replied; "I find that they are too often hurried." "But, Mr. President," Mirabeau continued, astonished at this calmness, — "but, Mr. President, these forty thousand men — " "Well," Mounier answered, "so much the better. They have only to kill us all; but *all*, you understand clearly. The affairs of the republic will run more smoothly." "Mr. President, your remark is charming," Mirabeau could not resist saying, as he returned to his seat.

Of the inhabitants of Versailles, the royal family, alone perhaps, remained calm; and the ministers, although so often apprised of the designs of the Parisians, through a strange blindness shared their serenity. The king had set out early for the chase; Madame Elisabeth was at Montreuil; Mesdames at Bellevue; the queen at Trianon, through whose beloved groves she was wandering for the last time. She was seated in the grotto, trying to shut herself off from the noise of the world, when a courier, sent by Monsieur de Saint-Priest, came hastily to find her. At the same time Monsieur de Cubières, equerry of the prince's household, had started out on a gallop to notify the king. He overtook him about three o'clock in the preserves of Meudon, and gave him a note from the minister. The king took the note, read it, and involuntarily exclaimed aloud, "The women ask for bread. Alas! if I had any, I would not wait for them to come to ask for it." He ordered that his horse be brought; and just as he was setting foot in the stirrup, a chevalier of St. Louis, whom no one had remarked until then, threw himself on his knees, and cried out, "Sire, they are deceiving you. I have just come from the École Militaire; there I saw a gathering of women, who said they were coming to Versailles to demand bread. I beg your Majesty to have no fear." "Fear, Monsieur!" the king replied sharply; "I have never experienced a feeling of fear in my life." Then descending one of the steepest slopes of the woods of Meudon, he set out at full speed along the road to Versailles, and returned to the palace, where he rejoined the queen.

On his arrival, the council assembled. At this critical moment the ministers were weak, hesitating, irresolute. Necker, as ever, concerned for his popularity, which was already, however, much weakened, advocated yielding. Monsieur de Saint-Priest alone seemed to have a full realization of the danger, and an understanding of the means to avert it. He, together with an energetic officer, Monsieur de Narbonne Fritzlar, begged that the bridge at Sèvres be put in a state of defence, and that the king go at the head of the faithful troops to drive back the Parisians at the passage of the Seine. During this time the royal family should withdraw to Rambouillet. Several ministers — among whom was Monsieur de la Luzerne — supported the plan; others, with Necker, opposed it. Was the king convinced by the arguments of the latter? Did he mistrust the troops, or did he fear that he would not find a sufficiently firm devotion among them? Was he influenced by the queen's repugnance to separation from him? Whatever the cause, Monsieur de Saint-Priest's suggestion did not prevail; and this last chance of safety was abandoned.

The government confined itself to insufficient means of defence; the municipality of Versailles had requested the Comte d'Estaing, commander of the national militia, to take every precaution, and to employ all the forces at his disposal to shield the king, the royal family, the Assembly, and the town from insult. The body-guards and the infantry were placed under his orders. About half-past three the Flemish regiment was drawn up in line on the Place du Château; but despite the urgent appeals of the mayor, Monsieur de Montmorin, it had been unable to obtain cartridges. The Life Guards, three hundred in number, had been placed before the gates of the ministers. A few *chasseurs* from the Trois-Évêchés, and some of the guards belonging to Monsieur and to the Comte d'Artois, were among them. A detachment of dragoons had been stationed on the Avenue de Paris opposite the door of the Assembly hall. The Comte d'Estaing, aware of the hostile disposition of the National Guards, who for ten days had been constantly stimulated by the malcontents against the king's defenders, had not dared order them out; but Lecointre had commanded a general call to arms to be beaten, and had assembled a certain number of companies from the district of Notre Dame at the old barracks of the French Guards, to the right of the quarters of the Life Guards.

At the palace the deliberations continued. Louis XVI., held back in part by kindness of heart, which, as has been justly said, appeared to be in him only another form of weakness, was, as always, irresolute, and could not bring himself to resist or withdraw. When Monsieur de Luxembourg, captain of the Life Guards, asked for orders, he replied, "Come, come! against women? You must be jesting." A little later, Monsieur de Saint-Priest proposed a retreat into some loyal province, — Normandy, for example. The king regarded the proposition with repugnance. It seemed to him that to flee from the rebellion was to abdicate. "A fugitive king, a fugitive king!" he repeated sadly. Meanwhile the danger was pressing. "Sire," Monsieur de Saint-Priest exclaimed earnestly, "if you are taken to Paris to-morrow, your crown is lost!" They decided to set out for Rambouillet. The municipality of Versailles placed no obstacle in the way. It even commanded the Comte d'Estaing to cover their departure. The carriages were ordered; and the queen had sent a note to her ladies-in-waiting, "Pack your effects; we are to leave in half an hour; make haste." But it seemed as if the resolution were only made to be abandoned. A little later the queen sent word to these same ladies, "All is changed; we are to remain here."

The order for the carriages was countermanded. When in the evening, the cabinet, owing to a sudden turn of events, wished to return to the plan of retreat to Rambouillet, it was too late. As the carriages appeared at the gate of the orangery, the populace, the National Guards, even the servants of the royal stables, forced them to turn back, and the queen could not then have left, perhaps, without imperilling her life.

During all this vacillation, the Parisian populace had arrived; all the actors were on the stage; the great drama was about to begin. The band, led by Maillard, had left Sèvres after a short rest there; a collarless individual, who, so he pretended, had narrowly escaped hanging that morning for having wished to sound the tocsin, had assumed command of the men, as Maillard had that of the women. On the way the mob continued to arrest the king's couriers, allowing only those of the Duc d'Orléans to pass; they laid hands on all travellers, and ill-treated those who wore the black cockade, forcing them to march in the middle of the troops, with an insulting inscription on their backs.

The weather was frightful; rain fell in torrents; the roads, soaked through, had become a quagmire. This disorderly train of women, drenched with the rain, soiled by the mud, yelling and shouting, was horrible. "See how we are tricked out," they said; "we are like devils, but the b—— shall pay dearly for it." Others sang and danced, giving expression to gross insults, and swearing that they would tear the queen to pieces, carry off the fragments, and make cockades of them. "We shall bring back the queen, dead or alive!" they cried; "the men shall take charge of the king."

When they arrived at the barriers, Maillard harangued his troops, placed the women in three ranks, sent the cannon to the rear, and ordered the tune of Henri IV. to be sung; and thus this terrible band made its entrance into Versailles to the sound of the royalist couplet, shouted in cruel irony by these shrews, who were going to force the grandson of the good king from his palace.

Their first visit was to the Salle des Menus, where the Assembly was in session. Maillard penetrated into the hall, followed by a part of his company, and addressed the meeting, saying, "Paris wants bread; the people are desperate; their arm is raised. Let every one be on his guard, or they will be driven to excesses. It is for the Assembly to prevent bloodshed. The aristocrats wish to make us perish from hunger." "Yes; we want bread," the women continued; and some of them, drawing from their pockets a piece of mouldy bread, cried, "We shall make the Austrian swallow this; then we shall cut her throat!"

The tumult increased; deliberation became impossible. Upon a proposition of one of the members, it was decided that a deputation should go at once to the king, to inform him of the condition of the town and of Paris, and to solicit at the same time an unqualified acceptance of the constitutional decrees.

The president, Mounier, repaired to the palace, escorted by some of the women, whom he had perforce promised to introduce into the presence of the king. Among these women there were two who did not seem to belong to the people, although they affected their language. Louis XVI. promised to have all the bread collected which could be found; and after some hesitation he signed the decrees. The women withdrew; they seemed content; and not concealing the fact when they returned, they aroused the anger of their companions, who had waited outside.

Some, believing everything at an end, since they were to have bread, returned to Paris in the court carriages; others, who were in the secret, refused to leave, — they had, so they said, express orders to remain.

In the mean while, great confusion prevailed in the palace. The ministers had assembled, but did not know what course to choose; the most contradictory counsels were proposed, adopted, then abandoned. Louis XVI., with passive resignation, continued silent and irresolute. The queen alone, in the midst of this inactivity and pusillanimity, preserved her proud attitude. " Her bearing was noble and dignified, her face calm; and although she could not delude herself as to her perilous position, no one could perceive the slightest trace of uneasiness. She reassured every one, thought of everything, and concerned herself much more about those who were dear to her than about her own person." " Every one except herself seemed terrified," the president, De Frondeville, testified, who had passed the night of the 5th at the palace. " I know that the people have come from Paris to demand my head," the heroic woman said, " but I learned from my mother not to fear death; I shall await it with resolution." Some one offered to convey her and her children to a place of safety. " No," she replied; " my place is here, near the king; I shall remain." The sole precaution which she consented to take was not for herself, but for her children. It was agreed that at the slightest disturbance they should be brought to her. When informed of the danger which threatened her, she gave a counter-order, and sent word at eleven o'clock at night to Madame de Tourzel to conduct her son and daughter, in case of alarm, not to her, but to the king's apartments, where they would be in less danger. And when her attendants urged her also to go there to pass the night rather than in her own apartments, which were exposed to the blows of the assassin, she replied, " No; if there be any peril, I prefer to encounter it alone, and avert it from the person of the king and of his children."

Alarming reports followed one another in rapid succession. The body-guards had been attacked on the Place d'Armes; the other soldiers had given way. The queen alone " showed a calm and serene brow, reassured those who trembled for her, and forced even those men who had condemned her principles to admire her courage." These words are taken from the " Moniteur," and the "Moniteur" is to be trusted. A certain number of gentlemen, assembled to defend the royal family, asked for instructions and horses. The president, De Frondeville, acting as their mouthpiece before the queen, requested permission to take the horses from the palace stable. "Very well," she replied simply ; " I consent to give you the order, but on one condition : if the king's life is in danger, that you put it into immediate execution; if I alone am in peril, that you make no use of it whatever."

" In the midst of so much duplicity of every kind," writes Rivarol, " but one strong nature was to be found on this scene, where fear and cowardice were dragging weakness to its ruin, and this was shown by a woman, — by the queen." She stood out from among these bewildered and terrified men by reason of her noble and resolute bearing; and when all around her was error and madness, she was conspicuous for extraordinary presence of mind. She was visible during the evening of October 5, received a numerous company in her large cabinet, talked with energy and dignity to all who approached her, and imparted her assurance to those who were unable to conceal their alarm. She was soon to display the magnanimity of her mother, when perilous circumstances required it; and if, though possessed of the same courage, she was not equally successful, it was because Maria Theresa had to do with the nobility of Hungary, while Marie Antoinette appealed to the *bourgeoisie* of Paris.

Meanwhile Mounier returned to the Assembly; he cleared the hall, which was crowded by the populace, and convoked the deputies for a night session. In this moment of peril he judged it expedient to retain the Assembly until daylight. But a little later, about three o'clock in the morning, he adjourned the meeting, having been reassured by Lafayette, who had just made the round of the different guard-houses, and was ready to answer for the public order.

Lafayette, having arrived at midnight at the head of his army, had proceeded immediately to the palace; he entered alone with the deputies of the municipality of Paris. The apartments were full of people. When he appeared, a voice murmured, "Behold Cromwell!" "Monsieur," Lafayette replied, "Cromwell would not have entered alone." His democratic ardour had not made him lose his sense of propriety, nor the tone of the society in which he had been born. " I come, Sire," he said, "to bring you my head, to save that of your Majesty. If my blood must be spilled, let it be in the service of my king, rather than by the ignoble light of the torches on the Grève." He added that he also guaranteed the loyal disposition of his army.

The king, naturally inclined to trustfulness, felt reassured, and, to make use of the piquant saying of Rivarol, "placed his entire confidence in a general who himself was sure of nothing." At two o'clock in the morning, the queen, who was also reassured, in appearance at least, retired to her apartments to rest. Lafayette insisted that the defence of the château be given to his army, and that the French Guards should resume their former posts; Louis XVI. consented. The bodyguards, who had been exposed to the rage of the populace, and assaulted with stones and guns by the mob, as well as by the militia of Versailles, received an order at eight o'clock to evacuate the Place d'Armes, and to withdraw to their hôtel, whence they could regain Trianon or Rambouillet across the fields. Those who were on duty at the palace quitted the Cour de Marbre, and retreated to the terrace opposite the queen's apartments. They retained the inner posts only; the outer posts were occupied by the French Guards.

Lafayette, after having attended to the execution of his orders, visited the Place d'Armes, went to the Assembly, where he communicated the "contagion of his confidence" to the president, again crossed through the court, conversed an instant with Monsieur de Montmorin, then, reassured by the measures he had taken, relying, moreover, on his power over the populace, and full of illusions as to the integrity of the rabble, repaired to the Hôtel de Noailles, and being very tired, went to bed. It was then four o'clock in the morning; the awakening was to be terrible.

Every one in Versailles slept. The royal family, exhausted by the emotions of this trying day, and quieted, moreover, by Lafayette's assurances, were resting for the last time in the palace of Louis XIV., whose majesty had not been violated. The National Guards, drenched by the rain, fatigued by a march to which they were not accustomed, had sought quarters everywhere,— in the churches, in the barracks of the Life Guards, in private houses. Pikemen and women, to the number of eight or nine hundred, were stretched out on the benches of the

Assembly hall; others, who had found no place of shelter, had lighted great fires on the squares, and after having cut up and roasted a wounded horse, had lain down round this improvised bivouac.

Crime alone, as some one eloquently asserts, did not sleep. The rabble had not done its work; these women, these disguised brigands who asked for bread when their pockets were full of gold, had not yet earned their hire. On the preceding evening, they had indeed given themselves the pleasure of throwing stones at the defenders of the crown, and of seriously wounding one of the body-guards. But they demanded more illustrious victims; and it was not for nothing that they had sworn to wring the neck of the queen and make district badges of her skin.

At the Assembly, a woman with haggard eyes, reeking of wine and repulsively dirty, had gone up to the President de Frondeville, and showing him a poniard, had asked if the queen's apartments were well guarded. At the château a deputy, the Marquis de Digoine, had noticed that the entrance to the Cour de l'Opéra, through which a troop of ragged men had just gone out, had remained open; he had spoken of it to the porter, who had replied that at the moment he had not the keys, but that he would close it. The Marquis de Digoine had passed by again at midnight, then at three o'clock in the morning; the gate was still open, and was guarded by a soldier of the Versailles militia. Also, an officer of the National Parisian Guards, in which Lafayette had such blind confidence, had carefully inquired "the shortest way to the queen's apartments, and the hidden passages by which one could go there unseen."

At daybreak the rabble awoke. At half-past five groups of men and women, armed with pikes, lances, sabres, and sticks, formed on the Place d'Armes and rushed toward the château. "Drums summoned them; banners bearing red and blue flames rallied them." One band penetrated into the Cour des Ministres, the entrance to which had been left open, and finding the Porte Royale closed, turned back, went through the Grille des Princes, which was guarded by two members of the militia, who allowed them to pass, and gathered in the park under the queen's windows. The queen, awakened by the noise, rang for her first lady-in-waiting, Madame Thibaut, and asked her what was the meaning of the tumult. Madame Thibaut replied that it was without doubt the women from Paris, who had not been able to find a place to sleep; and the queen, reassured, remained in bed.

The crowd continued to swell; fresh masses arrived at every moment. The major of the body-guards, the Marquis d'Aguesseau, stationed several guards to defend the Passage des Colonnades, which gave access from the Cour des Princes to the Cour Royale. But what could a few soldiers do against this human tide which was steadily rising? The passage was forced; the populace with shouts rushed into the Cour Royale. Bands were formed, each one directed by chiefs who appeared thoroughly to know the place; one of the bands, led by two men disguised as women, ran to the entrance of the Cour Royale, seized one of the Life Guards, Monsieur de Varicourt, who had just been posted there as sentinel, dragged him to the Place d'Armes, and massacred him. A miserable ragpicker, dressed in a short frock coat with large white buttons, and wearing a long black beard, with bare arms and head covered with a high-crowned round hat, broke through the crowd, and setting his foot on Monsieur de Varicourt's breast, cut off his head with one blow of his axe.

Almost at the same moment, Monsieur Deshuttes, another guard on duty in the vault of the chapel, was torn from his post by the bandits, dragged through the gate of the Cour Royale, where the sentinels made no effort to protect him, and was struck down from blows from the butt-ends of the guns. The man with the long beard cut off his head, and went with his hands covered with blood to beg a pinch of tobacco from the Vicomtesse de Talaru's Swiss guard, saying with a triumphant air, "One is done for, and he 'll not be the last."

Nor indeed did this suffice: the mob wanted other and more illustrious victims. "It is not enough," the shrews yelled; "we must have the heart of the queen. Let us take her entrails and make cockades of them for ourselves."

The leaders sounded again the horrible battle-cry; and the rabble, breathless, intoxicated by the taste of murder, rushed to the assault with still hotter fury. "Kill, kill! no quarter! To the queen's apartments!" they cried on all sides. A huge red-haired woman brandished a sickle; another sharpened her knife. One of the Versailles militia, a small dark man, who seemed to be well acquainted with the entrances to the château, placed himself at the head of a band which dashed up the marble stairway, shouting cries of death and everywhere asking for the queen's chamber. "It is this way; it is this way!" several voices cried. Two body-guards, Monsieur de Miomandre and Monsieur des Repaire, sought in vain to check the furious mob. They were thrown to the ground, struck down by blows dealt with pikes or with the butt-ends of guns; but Miomandre, before falling, bathed in his blood, had time to open the door of the queen's antechamber and call out to one of the women there, "Madame, save the queen! These people have designs on her life."

The heroic resistance of these two brave young men saved Marie Antoinette. One of her women, Madame Anguil, who had heard the body-guard's cry of distress, bolted the door of the second antechamber, then ran to the queen, with whom she found Madame Thibaut. Together they hurriedly put on her skirt and stockings, threw a little cloak over her shoulders, and drew her along the small passage which led to the Œil de Bœuf. The door was closed. They waited five minutes, — five minutes, an age! What throes of agony in that brief moment of delay! They knocked, made themselves known. The king's valet opened; the queen was saved! When the brigands, after ransacking the large drawing-room, succeeded in forcing the doors and penetrating into the royal apartments, they no longer found the victim there, and could only spend their rage upon an empty bed. "The attempt has failed!" one of the disappointed assassins was said to have murmured.

By a touching coincidence the king was hurrying to the queen by a secret stairway at the very moment she took refuge in his apartments; not finding her, and learning that she had gone to him, he hastened back to his apartments, where he at last found her, "with a sad but calm mien." Almost at the same instant Madame de Tourzel brought the dauphin; and the queen ran to get her daughter, whom she soon led back, "with a pride and dignity remarkable at such a moment."

The danger, however, was not averted. The mob filled the palace in mad pursuit of the body-guards. Luckily Lafayette, finally notified, galloped up at the head of his grenadiers, took the unfortunate guards under his protection, and drove away the bandits, who were occupied in destroying and plundering. He went into the château, the apartments of which were full of people. The king and his ministers were in the council-hall; the Duc d'Orléans was also there, talking with an air of unconcern to Duport; Monsieur, Madame, their aunts, and the rest of the family were in the king's chamber. The queen, standing erect at the side of a window, gazed out sadly; near her were her daughter and Madame Elisabeth; before her the dauphin, standing on a chair, toyed with his sister's hair. "Mamma, I am hungry," the poor little boy murmured; and the queen could only reply, with tears in her eyes, "Have patience, my child, this disturbance must first be brought to an end."

The mob grumbled under the windows of the château and in the Cour de Marbre. "The king! The king! We wish to see him." The king appeared; cries of "Vive le roi!" and "Vive la nation!" burst forth on every side. Soon, however, with these shouts was mingled another, "The queen! Let the queen appear on the balcony!" Some one went to notify her; for an instant she hesitated. "Madame," Lafayette said to her, "this measure is necessary to calm the people." "In that case," she replied, "were I going to my death, I should no longer hesitate. I will go." She took her children by the hand and appeared at the window. "No children!" yelled the crowd. "The queen on the balcony alone, alone!" The queen, with a sublime gesture, pushed her children back into the room, and alone, erect, her hands crossed on her breast, a thousand times more beautiful in her modest coat of yellow striped cloth than in the gorgeous attire of fête-days, stood upon the balcony, pale, her hair dishevelled, her lips pressed together, her head high, commanding involuntary respect and defying bullets. A man dressed in the costume of a National Guard took aim at her, but did not dare to fire.

There was a movement in the crowd; the heroism of the queen and her sublime imprudence had worked a reaction in her favour, and these shrews who an instant before had wished to tear her to pieces now applauded her; "Vive la reine," they shouted. "Her spirit," writes Rivarol, "suddenly restored the intelligence of this demented multitude; and if her enemies had need of crimes, conspiracies, and long proceedings to accomplish her assassination, she needed only one action to excite admiration."

Strange fact! This woman, so unpopular and so unjustly slandered among the people, had regained her power the moment that she found herself face to face with this people, and by the sole force of her dignity and truth, forced the hostile mob to bow before her and applaud her. However, some women, more stubborn in their hatred, continued to pour out infamous insults against her.

But popular enthusiasm passes quickly; and there are animosities more deadly and surer than bullets. Marie Antoinette knew this, and on leaving the balcony, went to Madame Necker and said to her with stifled sobs, "They will force the king and me to go to Paris with the heads of our body-guards carried on the ends of their pikes." And folding her son in her arms, she covered him with kisses and tears.

Alas! the queen was not mistaken; fresh cries were heard: "Le roi à Paris!" ("The king to Paris!") The king hesitated, consulted his ministers, conferred with Lafayette. But how could he resist? It was decided that he should go; and to calm the crowd, strips of paper were thrown down announcing the determination, or rather the capitulation, of the monarch. Deafening cheers burst forth in the court; as a sign of rejoicing the soldiers discharged their muskets, the gunners their cannon. Lafayette questioned the queen, saying, "Madame, what is your personal intention?" "I know the fate which awaits me," she replied; "but my duty is to die at the feet of the king and in the arms of my children."

At twenty-five minutes past one o'clock the royal family descended the marble staircase, still stained with the blood of their defenders, and got into carriages. The populace was growing impatient; scarcely victorious, it had all the arrogance of sovereignty. This new master of France had almost been kept waiting; it was even unwilling to allow the old royalty time to make its preparations for departure. The way was so blocked that the carriages were not able to set out until two o'clock.

The Avenue de Paris was thronged with armed people. Two men marched at the head of the procession bearing on the ends of their pikes the livid heads of the unfortunate Deshuttes and De Varicourt; several of the king's guards on foot, escorted by half-drunken brigands, walked behind these hideous trophies. After them came two other guards without arms; one of them wore boots; he had a wound in his neck, and his shirt and clothes were covered with blood, and two men in National uniform, carrying drawn swords, held him by the collar. Farther on rode a group of the king's guards mounted, — some in the croup, some in the saddle, almost all having a companion in the National uniform on the horses with them; a portion of the populace and women who surrounded them obliged the king's guards to cry, "Vive la nation!" and to drink and eat with them. A carriage containing the king, the queen, the dauphin, Madame Royale, Monsieur, Madame Elisabeth, and Madame de Tourzel, followed this strange vanguard; round the carriage marched a lamentable escort of disarmed guards, men in rags, and intoxicated women, shouting, "We are bringing back the baker, the bakeress, and the little baker boy." As if to give meaning to these ignoble cries, some sixty flour-wagons trimmed with green boughs and drawn by market-men were seen in the procession; an occasional cry of "Vive le roi!" was heard, but more frequently, "Down with the *calotte!* Every bishop to the lantern!" Some women, termagants, with Théroigne de Méricourt at their head, all of them decked out with the spoils plundered from the Life Guards, and from time to time shouting invectives against the queen, were mounted on the cannon or crowded into *fiacres* in the rear; to close the procession, and in a way to consecrate the defeat of royalty and announce its own servitude came a deputation of the Assembly, drawn in the court carriages, at the doors of which men with pikes demanded if there were no priests to hang to the lanterns. . . . What a retinue for the grandson of Louis XIV.!

The day was glorious; by one of those bitter ironies of which the 10th of August was to be another example, Nature seemed in holiday attire; all was calmness and gayety. In the woods of Viroflay the birds sang; the leaves were of those beautiful shades of yellow and red with which they reclothe themselves before they fall. "The breeze scarcely stirred the trees; the sky was cloudless; a radiant sunshine, the mellow sunshine of autumn, illumined this funeral train of the monarchy."

Throughout this sad journey the queen preserved her calmness and majestic bearing. She talked with the men and women who surrounded the carriage, saying to them, "The king has never desired anything but the happiness of his people. Many evil things have been told to you about us; they were said by those who wish you harm. We love all Frenchmen." And some of the people, touched by so much kindness, astonished by so much self-possession, murmured naïvely, "We did not know you; we have been greatly deceived."

An eye-witness writes, "I beheld this sinister train. In the midst of the tumult, clamour, and the frequent discharge of musketry, which the hand of a monster or of some clumsy fellow might render fatal, I saw the queen maintain the most courageous and tranquil spirit, and air of nobleness and inexpressible dignity, and my eyes were filled with admiration and grief." Burke was right when he declared in a burst of enthusiasm, "The world loves to know that those who are destined to suffer know how to suffer."

And later, at the public inquiry concerning this criminal attempt of October, when a deputation from the Châtelet came to demand her testimony, she would only give this noble answer, "I saw everything, knew everything, and have forgotten everything."

The journey was long; it lasted seven hours. At the gate of Chaillot, Bailly came to harangue the king and hand over to him the keys of the city. With a lack of tact inconceivable in an intelligent man, he said, "What a happy day is this, Sire, when the Parisians are about to hold your Majesty and your family in their city!" At this remark the king could not repress a sigh, as he replied, "Monsieur, I hope that my sojourn here will restore peace, harmony, and submission to law."

It was necessary to go to the Hôtel de Ville. The king shrank from the thought, and Marie Antoinette would have been glad to escape this last humiliation; but Moreau de Saint-Merry, when asked if she could not be spared this, answered, "I hope that the queen will be able to return from the Hôtel de Ville; but I doubt if she could go to the Tuileries alone." Cries of "À la lanterne!" were heard; thus did Paris welcome the royal family, whom, according to Bailly's words, it had reconquered.

The king entered the Assembly of the representatives of the Commune with a firm step; the queen followed, holding her children by the hand. "It is always with pleasure and confidence," said the prince, on entering, "that I find myself among the inhabitants of my good city of Paris." Bailly repeated these words to the people and forgot the word "confidence." The queen reminded him of it. "Messieurs," Bailly replied gallantly, "you are more fortunate than if I had not made the mistake."

The king and the queen had mounted on a throne, which had been hastily erected; but the people wished to see their conquest; the royal pair were forced to appear at the window of the Hôtel de Ville between two torches, that the faces, more brightly illuminated, might be the more recognizable. Under this new sort of canopy the king and queen saluted the crowd. The mob, as always, variable, applauded with irresistible enthusiasm those whom they had so lately insulted. On the Place de Grève, they shouted, "Vive le roi! Vive la reine! Vive le dauphin et nous tous!" They exchanged congratulations; they embraced one another, weeping with joy and emotion. It seemed as if the presence of the king at Paris had saved everything.

At ten o'clock the mournful procession entered the Tuileries. The royal family were prisoners; the Assembly also. Joseph II. was right when he wrote to his brother Leopold, "The riff-raff of Paris is to become the despot of all France."

CHAPTER V.

THE palace of the Tuileries had remained unoccupied almost without interruption since 1665; nothing had been prepared to receive the august guests whom the will of the new sovereign had housed there. Workmen, notified at the last hour, had been forced hastily to make some indispensable repairs; ladders stood about everywhere. The furniture was old, the hangings faded, the apartments badly lighted; there was a lack of beds; the doors would not close; the dauphin was obliged to pass the night in a room open on all sides, and in which his governess shut herself as best she could. "Everything is very ugly here, mamma," the child remarked on entering. "My son," replied the queen, "Louis XIV. lodged here, and liked it; we should not be more fastidious than he;" and turning to the ladies who accompanied her, she said with a sad smile, as if to excuse the destitution of the palace, "You know that I did not expect to come here."

At daybreak on the following morning an immense throng gathered in the garden; yielding to the pride of triumph, or rather impelled by an old royalist instinct, it was eager to see this royal family, of whose presence it had been so long deprived. The court, the terrace, and the park were full of people;

they cried out loudly for the king and queen; Madame Elisabeth went to get them. "The queen," says this princess, "spoke with all the graciousness with which you are already acquainted." That morning was a favourable one for her. All day the royal family were forced to show themselves at the windows; the court and the garden remained crowded.. When Marie Antoinette appeared, the cheers were so loud and so universal that the sovereign, according to the account of an ardent patriot, could not speak for some time.

Some of the women who had come imbued with revolutionary prejudices went away Royalists. One of them accused the queen of having wished to bombard Paris on July 14, and to flee to the frontier on October 6. The queen replied gently that her enemies only had circulated that rumour, and that these calumnies had been her despair as well as that of the best of kings. The crowd applauded. Another spoke to her in German. Marie Antoinette answered that she did not understand her; that she had become a French woman; that she had even forgotten her mother tongue. Cheers greeted this declaration. Some women begged the queen to make a compact with them. "And how can I," she replied, "make a compact with you, when you do not believe in that which my duty prompts, and which I should respect for the sake of my own happiness?" These women then asked her for the flowers on her hat; she herself detached them; and the whole group divided them among themselves, shouting, "Vive Marie Antoinette! Vive notre bonne reine!" This enthusiasm was general, and at that time it was sincere.

"The same crowd and the same eagerness to see the royal family," Madame de Tourzel relates, "continued for several days with the same inconsiderateness; and it was carried to such excess that several market-women jumped up into Madame Elisabeth's apartment, and she implored the king to lodge her elsewhere." The queen, however, was touched by this ardour; and in her trusting confidence, she almost excused the fury of this people, who, when seen closely and left to themselves, appeared so good. One day she went to visit the glass factory in the Faubourg St. Antoine; she was greeted with enthusiasm. "How good the people are," she remarked, "when one comes to seek them out!" "They are not so good," replied a courtier, "when they seek you out." "Oh!" she answered with animation, "then they are moved by foreign impulses." She still had faith in the good-will of the Parisians on the morrow of those October days. Meanwhile, in the midst of this anguish her beautiful blond hair suddenly turned white; and with her own hand she wrote below the portrait of herself, painted by Madame de Lamballe, "Her misfortunes have whitened her hair."

Official presentations followed the visits of the populace. The conquered royalty still retained its authority, and the king continued to occupy the throne. The Parliament was received first, on Friday, October 9; the deputation counted thirty members, with the first president at their head. "His Majesty received the deputation in his cabinet, having at his right the dauphin standing, with a chair behind him, and at his left Madame, the king's daughter, also standing, with a folding-chair behind her. The queen, after her reply, was pleased to add that since Monsieur the Dauphin and Madame could not receive in their apartment, she had had them brought to her, that the Parliament might not be deprived of the happiness of seeing them."

At noon of the same day the Commune of Paris came, led by Bailly and Lafayette. "Madame," Bailly said to the queen, "I come to convey to your Majesty the homage of the city of Paris with a testimony of the respect and love of its inhabitants. The city glories in seeing you in the palace of our kings; it desires that the king and your Majesty grant it the favour of making this your habitual residence, and when the king has accorded this favour and deigned to give us the assurance of it, the city will be happy to think that your Majesty has contributed toward its attainment." The queen returned Bailly this short response, "I receive with pleasure the homage of the city of Paris; I will follow the king gladly wherever he goes, especially here."

The entire month was given up to ceremonies of this kind. The Cour des Aides was received on the 11th; the university on the same day; the grand council on Wednesday, the 14th; the Chambre des Comptes, the Cour des Monnaies, and the private council on Monday, the 19th. On that day the queen was indisposed, and could see no one. Finally on the 20th, at half-past six in the evening, the National Assembly, which had returned to Paris despite the gloomy presentiments of its wisest members, of Malouet in particular, and had held its first session on the preceding day at the archbishop's palace, unexpectedly presented itself at the Tuileries.

For the first time the deputies had not put on court dress; even the bishops and curates were in short coats. The king received them seated and with head covered, taking off his hat only at the entrance and during the obeisance of the president. From the apartment of the king the Assembly passed into that of the queen by way of the cabinet and the gallery.

"The queen," says the official report, "not having been informed of the Assembly's desire to pay their homage to her Majesty, was at her toilet, preparing to hold her play in public. In her desire not to keep the Assembly waiting, the queen determined to give them audience at once without being in full dress. Therefore her Majesty having placed herself in an armchair in the grand cabinet, the officers of ceremonies introduced the Assembly as they had done in the king's apartment. The room was filled with deputies, a goodly number of whom could not enter. The queen rose to receive the Assembly; and when Monsieur Fréteau in his address made known the desire of the representatives of the nation to see the dauphin in the arms of her Majesty, the queen ordered the master of ceremonies to bring him to her; and when he came, the queen took him in her arms and showed him to all the deputies, who made the hall re-echo with applause and repeated cheers of 'Vive le roi! Vive la reine! Vive le dauphin!' Her Majesty was pleased in this wise to make the tour of the room, that all the deputies might see the dauphin; and at the same time she addressed words full of kindness to all those who were near her. The queen then re-entered her apartment, and the Assembly withdrew, accompanied to the foot of the stairs by the officers of ceremonies. The master of ceremonies considered it his duty on this occasion to call attention to the fact that the queen, 'receiving all bodies in the same manner as the king, need not have risen on the entrance of the National Assembly, and that it was a special mark of consideration which her Majesty had wished to show them in rising and making an excuse for not being in full dress.'"

The master of ceremonies was careful to add a little farther on that these "irregularities," as he called them, arose only from circumstances, and would not form a precedent for the future. Strange preoccupation for such a moment! The monarchy was toppling, and Monsieur de Nantouillet thought only of the subversion of etiquette.

The Assembly was followed by the municipality of Paris,

the Châtelet, the Bureau of the Treasurers of France, the Admiralty, and last in line, on November 16, the French Academy, who delivered a discourse to the queen by the mouth of their director, the Chevalier de Boufflers.

"In all these receptions, whether official or popular, Marie Antoinette bore herself with simple dignity and that seductive charm which her recent misfortunes had but increased." "It is impossible," Madame Elisabeth wrote on October 13, "to show more graciousness and courage than the queen has shown during this last week." This courage was at times nervous, and this graciousness veiled with melancholy. All was quiet in appearance. Bread had returned in abundance; a certain respite seemed to have come. The Duc d'Orléans, intimidated by Lafayette, had gone to England under a pretext of a mission which ill disguised his exile. But how many passions fomented under this calm surface! The little dauphin, with the naïve heedlessness of his age, could write to Madame de Polignac, "Oh, Madame, how unhappy you would have been on the 5th and 6th of October; but at present we are all happy." The queen could not feel either this infantile gayety or this confidence; her enemies were not disarmed.

Indeed, two days after her return to Paris, a riot had broken out at the Mont de Piété. A report had been spread abroad, — one can easily divine with what purpose, — and it even had been announced in the public papers that the queen would redeem all objects in pawn, and a rough and anxious crowd had hurried to the doors of the offices. Deceived in their expectations, they had proceeded to the Tuileries, crying loudly for the queen and demanding the execution of her pretended promise. Some persons urged Marie Antoinette to yield to this tumultuous desire. Madame de Tourzel and Madame de Chimay dissuaded her, and haranguing the crowd themselves, begged them to trust to the well-known bounty of the sovereign, and finally induced them to withdraw quietly. Some days after, the queen, always ready to mark her passage by benefactions, obtained permission from the king to redeem at the Mont de Piété all objects not exceeding one louis in value. They amounted to the sum of three hundred thousand livres. A little later, through her intervention, four hundred fathers of families held for debts to nurses were set at liberty.

Even this generosity, however, did not arrest calumny. A

hired mob often gathered under the windows of the palace to heap contumely upon the unfortunate sovereigns. Their enemies went still further; individuals sprung from the dregs of the populace would, under the title of delegates or under pretext of haranguing the king, gain entrance to the palace and give utterance in the presence of the royal family to gross insults inspired and paid for by others. The abuse was such that the ministers proposed to refuse such people admission to the palace. "No," the king and queen replied, "let them come; we have the courage to hear them."

One day a man of this stamp, in addressing Louis XVI., dared in the most offensive terms to denounce the queen, who was present at the interview. "You are mistaken," the king answered with kindness: "the queen and I have not the intentions which are imputed to us; we act together for your common good." "When the deputation had left," adds Hue, from whom we have borrowed this incident, "the queen burst into tears."

Under such conditions, confidence could not revive, and on the 10th of October, 1789, the queen sent to her jeweller, Daguerre, the larger part of that valuable collection of objects of art which she had gathered together: Japanese lacquers, Chinese porcelain, petrified woods, caskets of jasper, cups of Oriental agate, vases of brown sardonyx, inlaid caskets, ewers of rock crystal, — charming objects, the exquisite style of which still delights the visitor of to-day in the Museum of the Louvre, and the "beautiful and rich workmanship" of which the commissioners of the convention were themselves forced to admire. "It was done," said the inventory proceedings, "in order to have them mounted, or to have some repaired and to have cases and boxes made for them that they might be transported with safety." They were, in fact, to be transported to St. Cloud; but events did not permit it, and it was to the successor of Daguerre, Lignereux, that the delegated commissioners, the citizens Nitot and Besson, came on the 30th Brumaire, in the year II., to make the examination of them and to demand their transference to the National Museum.

The royal family, almost immediately after their arrival in Paris, had been forced to submit to a painful sacrifice. As an act of prudence, Louis XVI. had judged it expedient to send his body-guards away from him. He was forced to part with these loyal servants, whose devotion alone had snatched the queen from the assassin's dagger, and who would have been a sure defence against future attempts if their very devotion did not mark them for the fury of the populace. "This has been a keen sorrow to the king and queen," Madame Elisabeth wrote to the Duchesse de Polignac.

At about the same epoch the disconsolate queen wrote to her friend: "I wept with emotion on reading your letters. You speak of my courage; it needs much less to undergo the terrible moments through which I have lived than to endure our present position, my own sufferings, those of my friends, and of those round us. It is a weight too heavy to bear; and if my heart were not held by such strong bonds to my husband, my children, my friends, I would wish to die; but you sustain me; I also owe this feeling to your friendship. But," she added sadly, "I bring misfortune upon all of you, and your suffering is for me and through me."

The National Guards filled the posts at the Tuileries, as they had, on October 6, occupied those at Versailles. Offspring of a riot, born of a spirit of defiance toward the monarchy, formed of rebellious soldiers and of naïve and fault-finding *bourgeois*, pulled hither and thither by the different parties, condemned by their very origin to share the prejudices of the mob and the illusions of their leaders, they could not, although they had discharged their duties faithfully at the outset, show in the defence of the crown either the devotion of the civil servants or the strength of disciplined troops. The agitation, for a moment lulled, soon broke out afresh. "We are living in the midst of constant alarm," wrote an attaché of the Saxon legation; "the people do not yet appear satisfied, despite all that they have obtained." The *portes-cochères* of those houses which were at all conspicuous had been chalked with red or white, and people feared a riot. On October 21 — in fact, two days after the Assembly had held its first meeting in Paris — the populace assaulted the shop of a baker named François, plundered it, hanged the baker on the Place de Grève, cut off his head, and carried it through the streets on the end of a pike. The queen could do no less than give a small pension out of her privy purse to the widow of the unfortunate man; she sent her six thousand francs.

On the 4th of November the "Charles IX.," of Chénier, which

had been at first interdicted, then authorized through Bailly's weakness, set the spectators of the Théâtre Français on fire. Despite the author's protestations and his enthusiastic dedication to the "magnanimous prince," whom he was, three years later, to condemn to death, the attack on the throne was obvious, and the moment singularly well chosen, as Beaumarchais observed, just when the king and his family had come to reside in Paris. Every evening the allusions were eagerly seized upon by an ardent public, who issued thence, says Ferrières, "drunk with vengeance and consumed by a thirst for blood." The leaders of the Revolution were fully alive as to the value of this play. "This piece," wrote Camille Desmoulins, "furthers our cause more than the events of October." And on the very day of the first representation Danton remarked in the pit, "If 'Figaro' killed the nobility, 'Charles IX.' will kill royalty."

One can imagine that the queen manifested little eagerness to show herself at the theatres where such pieces were being played; she had replied, when solicited by a deputation of the municipality and of the National Guards to appear at the representations, "that it would give her infinite pleasure to accept the invitation of the city of Paris, but that she needed a little time to efface the remembrance of the painful days through which she had just passed and from which her heart had so keenly suffered." Agitated by the trials which had overtaken her, by the dangers which she had gone through and which yet awaited her, though she pretended to feel no uneasiness, alarmed by the indications which she daily discovered, and feeling no security against the threats of the mob from the protection of Lafayette and the Parisian militia, she shut herself in the palace and became absorbed in her family.

After several unsuccessful attempts, inevitable in the disorder of the first moment, the household at the Tuileries had at last been organized. Furniture had been brought from Versailles, and the king and queen had chosen their own quarters and those of their attendants. The king shared his apartments with the dauphin in order to have his son near him; he occupied three rooms on the ground floor facing the garden, and reached by the left gallery. His geographical cabinet was in the *entresol;* his bedroom on the first floor; near it, the council-chamber.

The queen's apartments were near those of the king; her dressing-room, bedroom, and drawing-room below; in the *entresol* was her library, which had been brought from Versailles by her order, — a serious, pious collection of books, "which," says a writer, "betokened an earnest, cultivated mind," and in which were to be found, among the works of Christian theology, of philosophy and history, a few romances, some dramas, and the classic poets. Above the library was Madame's apartment, separated from the king's bedchamber by that of the dauphin. Madame de Tourzel lodged on the ground floor. A small dark staircase connected the young prince's apartment with that of his governess. Only the queen and Madame de Tourzel had keys to it. Other stairways allowed the king and queen to communicate freely with each other and with the children. Madame de Lamballe occupied the ground floor of the *pavillon de Flore;* Madame Elisabeth, the first floor; Madame de Mackau, Madame de Gramont, Madame d'Ossun, the floor above; Mesdames, the *pavillon de Marsan.* Monsieur and Madame resided at the Luxembourg.

At the end of a few days the court had resumed its usual habits. The principal officers, the first gentlemen of the chamber, the Duc de Villequier and the Duc de Duras, the grand provost, the Marquis de Tourzel, the grand quartermaster, the Marquis de Brézé, had returned to their posts. On Sunday and Thursday there was play, and occasionally on Sunday a state dinner. The Princesse de Lamballe, to divert her royal friend, tried to organize some entertainments in her lodgings; but Marie Antoinette no longer had a heart for amusement. There were still, as a remnant of etiquette, some presentations; but most of the time the queen remained in her apartment with her husband and children. She breakfasted alone every day; afterward she saw her son and daughter; during this time the king came to pay her a visit. Then she attended mass; for a while, until there had been time to construct a sort of gallery with planks, she crossed the grand terrace of the palace in the open air, on her way to the chapel, exposed to the curious or hostile gaze of the bystanders. After mass she returned and shut herself up in her rooms. She dined at one o'clock with the king, Madame Royale, and Madame Elisabeth. After dinner she repaired to the gallery of Diana to play a game of billiards with Louis XVI., who, having given up riding or driving since the departure of the body-guards, had need of some exercise. She worked at her embroidery, and again returned to her own rooms to remain until eight o'clock, at which hour Madame and Monsieur arrived for supper. At eleven o'clock the family separated for the night.

In her apartments Marie Antoinette's life was divided between needle-work and her children's education. Her mind, full of anxiety about public affairs, had need of an occupation which busied the fingers without absorbing the attention. Needle-work served this purpose; she had always been fond of it, and she became still more devoted to it now. She undertook elaborate pieces of tapestry-work, — an easy task, which left her thoughts free; and Madame Campan declares that a merchant of Paris, a Madame Dubuquois, for a long time preserved in her shop a rug made by the queen and Madame Elisabeth for the large hall on the ground floor of the Tuileries.

But the best and most precious part of the day was reserved for her children. On August 12 she had written to the Duchesse de Polignac, "My children are my sole resource; I have them with me as much as possible." At the Tuileries, this was still more the case. The morning was devoted to the education of Madame Royale, who had all her lessons under her mother's eyes. When the weather was fine, the queen took a walk with her children in the garden of the Tuileries, which was not open to the public until noon. It was a consolation for her and a genuine delight to the dauphin, who was passionately fond of the open air and exercise. He would have liked to go about Paris, but at the outset his parents did not dare to risk it; and at the end of November or the beginning of December the young prince wrote to his former governess, "We have not yet gone outside the Tuileries; we often walk with mamma in the garden." On Sunday the curé of St. Eustache came to teach the Catechism to Madame Royale, who was preparing for her first communion; the dauphin was present at these instructions.

The dauphin was at this time a charming child, with large blue eyes, long curling hair, fresh rosy cheeks, of a frank, communicative, and gay disposition, full of light-headed impulsiveness, which misfortune was soon to turn into precocious gravity. No one knew him better than his mother; no one had studied with more minute attention, or more severe insight, the defects as well as the good traits of his character.   Some days after July 14, the queen, on appointing the Marquise de Tourzel to the position of governess to the Children of France, left vacant by the emigration of the Duchesse de Polignac, intrusting, as she herself said, to virtue that which she had confided to friendship, wrote the following letter:—

"July 24, 1789.

"My son is four years and four months less two days old.   I say nothing of his figure or of his appearance: you have only to see him. His health has always been good; but even in the cradle we perceived that his nerves were delicate, and the slightest unusual noise affected him.   He was backward in cutting his first teeth, but they came without illness or accident.   It was not until with the last—I think it was with the sixth—that he had a convulsion at Fontainebleau.   Since then he has had two,—one in the winter of 1787 and 1788, and the other at the time of his inoculation; but this last was very slight.   As a result of his sensitive nerves, any noise to which he is not accustomed frightens him; for example, he is afraid of dogs, because he has heard them bark near him.   I have never forced him to see them, because I believe that as his reason develops, his fears will subside.   He is, like all strong and healthy children, very quick and violent in his anger; but he is a good child, tender, and caressing even, when his impulsiveness does not carry him away.   He possesses inordinate vanity, which, if well directed, may some day turn to his advantage.   Until he is quite at ease with any one he will control himself, and even stifle his impatience and anger, that he may appear gentle and amiable.   He is most trustworthy when he has promised anything, but he is very indiscreet; he repeats readily anything he has heard, and often, without meaning to lie, he adds what his imagination has made him see.   This is his greatest fault, and one which it is most necessary to correct.   Nevertheless, I say it again, he is a good child; and with kindness, and at the same time with firmness, but not too great severity, any one can make of him what one will.   Severity, however, drives him to rebellion, because for his age he has a great deal of character: to give an example, from his babyhood the word 'pardon' has always been offensive to him.   He will do and say all that one may wish when he is in the wrong; but he will not pronounce the word 'pardon' without tears and great reluctance.

"My children have always been accustomed to feel great confidence in me, and when they have done wrong, to tell me of it themselves; consequently in scolding them I have appeared more troubled and grieved than angry at what they have done.   I have trained them all to believe that a 'yes' or 'no' pronounced by me is irrevocable; but I always give them a reason within the reach of their comprehension, that they may not think it caprice on my part.

"My son cannot read, and learns with great difficulty, for he is too heedless to apply himself. He has not the slightest idea of haughtiness in his head, and I am most desirous that this should continue. Our children always learn soon enough what they are. He loves his sister well and heartily. Whenever anything gives him pleasure, — whether it be to go somewhere or to be given something, — his first act is always to ask the same for his sister. He was born light-hearted. He has need for the sake of his health to be much in the open air; and I believe it is better for his health to let him play and dig in the ground on the terrace than to take him a greater distance. The exercise which children get in running and playing out of doors is more wholesome than when they are forced to walk, which often tires their backs.

"I will now speak of those who surround him. Three under-governesses, — two Mesdames de Soucy (mother-in-law and daughter-in-law) and Madame de Villefort. Madame de Soucy, the mother, is an excellent woman, very lenient and exact, but vulgar. The daughter-in-law has the same air, — there is no hope for her. For several years she has not been with my daughter, but with the little boy there is no risk. In other respects, she is faithful and even a little severe with the child.

"Madame de Villefort is just the opposite, and spoils him. She is also quite as vulgar, and even more so in appearance. They all get along well together.

"The first two women are both strongly attached to the child. Madame Lemoine, however, is an insufferable gossip and chatterbox, telling everything she knows in the room, whether before the child or not, — it makes no difference. Madame Neuville has an agreeable exterior, intelligence, and polite manners; but she is said to be ruled by her mother, who is very intriguing.

"Brunier, the physician, has my entire confidence whenever the children are ill; but beyond that he must be kept in his place. He is familiar, ill-tempered, and boastful.

"The Abbé d'Avaux may be very good to teach my son his letters; but in other respects he has neither the tone nor any of the qualifications necessary for the charge of my children. It is for this reason that I have at present decided to withdraw my daughter from under him. You must take great care that he does not settle himself in my son's apartments outside of lesson-hours. The intercourse with the under-governess was one of the things which gave Madame de Polignac the greatest trouble, and with all her efforts she could not always control it. Ten days ago I heard of some ungrateful remarks by this abbé, which displeased me greatly.

"My son has eight waiting-maids. They serve him with zeal, but I cannot count much upon them. Lately there has been much evil-speaking in the prince's chamber, but I cannot say exactly by whom. There is, however, one — a Madame Belliard — who does not hide her sentiments. Without suspecting any one, you can be on your guard. All of the men-servants are faithful, devoted, and quiet.

"My daughter has two first women, and seven waiting-maids. Madame Brunier, wife of the physician, has been with her since her birth, and serves her with zeal. Though I have no objections to her personally, I would never intrust to her more than attendance on the princess; she has the same disposition as her husband. In addition, she is avaricious and greedy of the small gains which are to be made in the small chamber.

"Her daughter [Madame Freminville] is a person of real merit. Although only twenty-seven years of age, she possesses all the qualities of mature years. She has attended my daughter since her birth, and has never lost sight of her. I married her; and the time which she does not spend with my daughter she gives up entirely to the education of her three little girls. She has a gentle, pliable disposition, is highly cultivated, and it is she whom I choose to continue the lessons in place of the Abbé d'Avaux. She is well fitted for the task; and since I have the good fortune to be sure of it, I find her preferable to all the others. Besides, my daughter loves her, and has confidence in her.

"Seven other women are excellent persons, and this chamber is much more tranquil than the other. There are also two very young girls, but they are supervised by their mother, — one belonging to my daughter, and the other to Madame Lemoine.

"The men have served her since her birth. They are absolutely insignificant creatures; but as they have nothing to do but wait upon her, and do not remain in her room except for that, this is of no importance to me."

We omit the judgments on people whom subsequent events could and did modify. Who does not admire the watchfulness of this mother, beset as she was by so many and varied anxieties, her clear-sightedness and untiring care for the health and moral education of her children?

A month later she wrote again to Madame de Tourzel concerning a mild fit of anger on the part of the dauphin: —

"My dear heart, our tenderness for this child should be stern. We must not forget that we are educating him not for ourselves, but for the nation. The first impressions of childhood are so strong that I am, in truth, frightened when I think that we are bringing up the king."

Under such guidance the dauphin was growing up, learning much from his lessons with the Abbé d'Avaux, and even more from those with his mother; under her devoted influence, he developed both his mind and his heart. He adored her, was happy in her smile, suffered in her sorrows, and constantly taxed his ingenuity to give her pleasure. He had — the letter which we have just cited asserts it — a rather strong distaste for study; he overcame it from filial affection. One day Marie Antoinette reproached him for not knowing how to read at the age of four years and a half. "Very well!" he replied; "I will learn for your New Year's present." At the end of November, Madame de Tourzel relates, "he said to his tutor, 'I must know how much time I have before the New Year, since I have promised mamma to be able to read on that day.'" In learning that he only had one month, he looked at the Abbé d'Avaux, and said with remarkable calmness, "I beg of you, my good abbé, give me two lessons a day, and I will apply myself earnestly." He kept his word, and on the day fixed, entered the queen's apartments in triumph, holding a book in his hands; the amiable child threw himself on her neck and said to her, "Here is your New Year's gift. I have kept my promise; now I know how to read."

Another time, hearing a woman say of one of her friends, "She is as happy as a queen!" he replied, "Happy as a queen! It is not of mamma you mean to speak, for she is always crying."

The official walks in the garden of the Tuileries under the escort of the National Guards were a constraint. Madame de Tourzel succeeded in having a small private garden arranged for the dauphin on the edge of the water, at the extremity of the terrace. The young prince played here in perfect freedom. He raised rabbits, took care of the birds in the aviary, and of the ducks on the pond. He cultivated the flowers, and the loveliest were always reserved for his mother. At other times he was taken to the house of a relative of Madame de Tourzel, the Marquise de Lède, who owned a beautiful hôtel and large park in the Faubourg St. Germain. More often he accompanied his mother in her round of charity. When the queen visited the hospitals or the poor, she took her son with her, and was careful that he himself distributed the alms which she left in the garrets. Sometimes they went to the Gobelins; and the president of the district coming on one occasion to compliment her, she said, "Monsieur, you have many destitute; but the moments which we spend in relieving them are very precious to us." Sometimes she went to the free Maternity Society which she had founded, where she had authorized the Sisters to distribute sixteen hundred livres for food and fuel every month, and twelve hundred for blankets and clothing, without counting the baby outfits which were given to three hundred mothers. At other times she went to the School of Design, also founded by her, to which she sent one day twelve hundred livres saved with great effort, that the rewards might not be diminished nor the dear scholars suffer through her own distress. Again, she placed in the house of Mademoiselle O'Kennedy four daughters of disabled soldiers, — orphans, for whom, she said, "I made the endowment."

But that which most strongly attracted the dauphin, as if by a mysterious presentiment, was the Foundling Hospital. Marie Antoinette took him there often; and the gratitude of these poor children expressed itself in acclamations, which was most agreeable to him; they shouted often, "Vive le roi!" and not unfrequently, "Vive la reine!' The young prince always left the hospital with reluctance, and all his little savings were devoted to the relief of these little unfortunates. One day his father came upon him as he was putting some écus into a pretty little box which had been given him by his aunt, Madame Elisabeth. "What, Charles," he exclaimed with a look of displeasure, "you hoard your money like a miser?" The child blushed, but recovering immediately, replied, "Yes, father, I am miserly; but it is for the foundlings. Ah, if you could see them! They are truly pitiable!" The king bent over his son, and embracing him with an effusion of joy which he seldom experienced now, said to him, "In that case, my child, I will help you fill your little box."

Madame Royale, older and graver than her brother, felt more deeply the anxiety of the situation. The queen, to bring a little gayety into her life, had organized in Madame de Tourzel's apartments small informal gatherings, to which she went occasionally to drink tea, and where her daughter met young people of her own age. They played little games, ran through the rooms which were thrown open, even played hide-and-seek, which the dauphin later remembered with pleasure. More serious pursuits, however, occupied the time and engrossed the heart of the young princess. Since her arrival at Paris, the curé of St. Eustache came every Sunday to teach her the Catechism, and to prepare her for her first communion. She performed the solemn act at St. Germain l'Auxerrois on the Wednesday of Passion Week, March 31. In the early morning the queen led her daughter to the king's chamber, saying to her, "My daughter, throw yourself at your father's feet and ask his blessing." Madame knelt; the king blessed her, raised her up and addressed to her these grave and pious words: —

"It is from the bottom of my heart that I bless you, my child, while praying Heaven to grant you a full realization of the great act which you are about to accomplish. Your heart is innocent in the eyes of God; your vows should be acceptable to him; offer them to him for your mother and for me. Ask him to accord me the grace necessary to bring about the happiness of those over whom he has given me empire, and whom I should consider as my children. Beg of him that he deign to preserve religious purity in the kingdom; and remember, my daughter, that our holy religion is the source of all happiness, and our support in the adversities of life. Do not believe yourself secure from them. You are very young, but you have already more than once seen your father in affliction.

"You do not know, my daughter, to what Providence destines you: whether you are to remain in the kingdom, or whether you are to go to live in another. To whatever place the hand of God may lead you, remember that you must teach others by your example, and do good whenever you find the opportunity; but, above all, my child, relieve the unfortunate as much as is in your power. God has placed us in this rank of life only that we may work for their happiness, and console them in their sorrows."

Such were the instructions which the "tyrant" gave to his children, and his actions followed closely upon his words. It was customary for the Children of France to receive a set of diamonds on the day of their first communion. Madame Royale did not receive this splendid gift. The ceremony was performed with extreme simplicity. The young princess arrived at the church, accompanied by her governess and her under-

governess, Madame de Mackau; she showed the greatest composure, and approached the Holy Table with marks of sincerest
devotion.   The queen, who had received the Easter sacrament
two days before, assisted at the ceremony incognito and without
attendance, "as simply dressed as a *bourgeoise*," relates an eye-
witness, but with extreme piety, and with her eyes constantly
fixed on the young communicant.   On the same day generous
alms were distributed to the poor of the various parishes of
Paris; they were the price of the diamond necklace, which
Madame Royale had not received.

CHAPTER VI.

THE Assembly, reinstated in Paris in the Salle du Manège, or Riding-School, resumed its discussion. To cover the deficit, it despoiled the clergy. On November 2, it declared, on the motion of the too famous bishop of Autun, that the property of the Church was at the disposition of the nation. This was the first step in the path of spoliation. On the next day the Assembly, at the instigation of Adrien Duport, adjourned the reopening of the Parliaments until a time when it might suppress them. Thus that great body which had suggested the reunion of the States-General became their first victim. Soon after, departments were substituted for the provinces. The ministers accepted these changes with a readiness which made their assent appear suspicious. "The executive only feigns death," exclaimed Charles de Lameth; and the leaders of the Revolution already mistrusted this passive attitude, when the affair of the Marquis de Favras transpired and furnished grounds for their suspicions.

What was at bottom the plan of the Marquis de Favras? Did he really wish to abduct the king and queen and carry them away from Paris? Was he devising a scheme of counter-revolution? Under whose inspiration? With what support? A deep mystery surrounded these points, and probably always will surround them, thanks to the heroic silence of the accused.   It was said that the queen feared an avowal on his part.   Monsieur, frightened by the denunciations of the journals which had connected his name with the affair, thought it his duty to vindicate himself publicly, and repaired to the Hôtel de Ville on the day after the arrest of Favras to protest his attachment to the Revolution,—a strange proceeding and one which was considered little worthy of a son of France.

The trial was conducted with expedition.   Favras, arrested on Dec. 25, 1789, and led before the Châtelet, replied with admirable composure to the allegations of his accusers,— two individuals of low condition, and of little reputation.   The sentence, however, was decided in advance.   "It was necessary," wrote Madame Elisabeth to Madame de Bombelles, "to terrify those who wished to serve the king.   The people demanded blood, and the blood of a man to whom the name of aristocrat could be given."   On the day on which judgment was pronounced, the mob howled round the court of justice, crying out vehemently for the death of the accused, and seeking to intimidate the judges.   The judges yielded; the demonstra· tion of the populace served in place of proofs, which did not exist, and Favras was condemned to be hanged.   "Your life," Quatremère, reporter of the trial, said to him, "is a sacrifice which you owe to the public peace."   Favras replied only by a look of scorn to this singular theory, by which the timid have always since the origin of Christianity attempted to justify their cowardice.

On the next day, Friday, February 19, Favras was hanged by torchlight on the Place de Grève amid shouts of ferocious joy, and with unusual ceremony.   To the end he exhibited the same composure, replying to the insults by a disdainful smile only, and nobly refusing to reveal the secret.   "Fellow-citizens," he said, "I die innocent; pray to God for me.   I die with the calmness which a peaceful conscience gives, and I commend my memory to the esteem of all virtuous citizens, as also my wife and children, to whom I was so necessary.   I beg that mercy be shown to those who witnessed falsely against me, if they were recognized as such, and let no one dread the consequences of the imaginary plot."   Then turning to the hangman, he said, "Come, my friend, fulfil your task."   The mob, incapable of understanding this heroism, insulted the dying man with shouts of laughter, dancing, and derisive applause.   A few wretches even had the courage to cry, "Bis!" and the body was only saved from final outrages by a hurried burial. The king and queen were deeply moved by this condemnation and death. "I witnessed their grief," Madame de Tourzel relates; "and I cannot yet recall without pain the state in which I saw the queen when she learned that Monsieur de Favras was dead."

A more serious project, or at least one better known than that of Favras, — for it has been described in detail by its author, — had been conceived by Augeard, secretary of the queen's commands. Alarmed at the dangers which menaced the royal family, and especially Marie Antoinette, he had proposed to the queen to abduct her and her children some evening in a post-wagon drawn by two horses; she was to assume the costume of governess, and the dauphin was to be dressed as a girl. On the following morning they were to make a halt at St. Thierry, the country house of the archbishop of Rheims, then setting out again after a hasty repast, and taking care to avoid the cities, they were to arrive at the château of Buzancy, belonging to Augeard, from which place a relay, posted in advance, should carry the fugitives to the frontier. The plan was guarded with the greatest secrecy even from the king. The queen at first consented; but when it became necessary to make a positive decision, she could not bring herself to do it, and met Augeard's urgent entreaties with a refusal: "After due consideration, I have determined not to go; my duty is to die at the king's feet." Despite all the precautions taken by Augeard, his project was revealed; he was arrested and imprisoned; but, more fortunate than Favras, he was released after four months and a half of confinement.

These various plots, that of Favras especially, had given rise to so many accusations against the court that the ministers, and Necker in particular, counselled Louis XVI. to take public measures to prove his devotion to the new form of government. The king, favourably disposed toward all suggestions from his ministers, consented. On Thursday, February 4, he notified the president by note that he would visit the Assembly at noon, and that he wished to be received without ceremony. The session was adjourned at once; a covering of red velvet stamped with *fleurs-de-lis* was thrown over the president's armchair, and "every one, while awaiting the august visitor," an eye-witness relates in the sentimental style in vogue at that time,

NECKER.

"rejoiced with his neighbour over the delicious pleasure in store for him in seeing his father and friend. With such an overflow of affection did they speak of the good Louis XVI."

At one o'clock the king appeared, attired simply and without ostentation, and delivered an address, which had been in part composed by Necker. He declared his adhesion to the Constitution, praised the reforms effected by the Assembly, and repudiated every enterprise which might shake its foundation. "I also," he said, in alluding to the sacrifices which the new *régime* had forced upon so many people, — "I too could count many losses if amid matters of greater importance I should stoop to personal calculation; but I have found full and complete compensation in the increased welfare of the nation. It is from the bottom of my heart that I give expression to this sentiment. Therefore I shall defend and uphold constitutional liberty, the establishment of which has been sanctioned by the general wish of the people, as well as by my own; I will do more: I will, in concert with the queen, who shares all my opinions, early prepare the mind and heart of my son for the new order of things which circumstances have brought about; I will accustom him to be happy in the happiness of the French people, and always to remember, despite the assurances of flatterers, that a wise Constitution will preserve him from the dangers of inexperience, and that a just liberty will add a new worth to the sentiments of love and fidelity, such touching proofs of which the French nation has for centuries given its kings."

Enthusiastic applause greeted this declaration; and the Assembly, electrified, took an oath to forget all its dissensions, and to be loyal to the Constitution, which, in reality, had not yet been drawn up. A deputation escorted the king back to the Tuileries; the queen with her children had come to the entrance to receive him. "I share all the sentiments of the king," she said to the deputation; "I join heart and soul with him in this act, to which affection for his people has just prompted him." And pointing to the dauphin, she added, "I shall neglect nothing which shall teach him early in life to imitate the virtues of the best of fathers; and I shall keep alive within him a love of public liberty, of which I hope he will be the firmest support."

In the evening Paris was illuminated; on the motion of Clermont-Tonnerre, the president of the Assembly and sixty members went to thank the king and the queen. "Guard well this precious offspring, Madame," he said, pointing to the dauphin, "that he may have the sensibility, affability, and courage which characterize yourself; your vigilance will assure his glory, and France will feel the worth of the happiness which you have secured for her, in remembering that she owes it to the virtues of your Majesty." The queen replied, "Messieurs, I am keenly alive to your testimonials of affection. You heard this morning an expression of my feelings; they have never varied toward this nation, which I am proud to have adopted by my union with the king; my title of mother secures the bonds between us for all time."

On the following day, Bailly, in his turn, came with a delegation from the Commune to congratulate the king, and on the next Sunday a solemn *Te Deum* was sung in Notre Dame. But this burst of enthusiasm was of short duration. The step taken by Louis XVI. did not disarm his enemies; it displeased a large number of Royalists, and Gouverneur Morris — a sincere patriot, but also a friend to the French monarchy, whose cause was, in his eyes, inseparable from that of liberty — wrote, " If this step of his Majesty has any effect upon reasonable minds, it must be to prove clearly the feebleness of his ministers."

A fortnight later a thoughtless proceeding, from which it was impossible to escape, further compromised the royal family and revived distrust. Two days after the death of Favras, one of his friends, Monsieur de la Villeurnoy, *maître des requêtes*, conceived the unfortunate idea of presenting Favras's wife and son, dressed in mourning for the heroic victim, at the public dinner of the king and queen. The queen, despite her deep sympathy, remained outwardly cold and unmoved; but one can judge of the painful self-control which she must have exercised, in order not to betray her feelings to the bystanders. The National Guards were watching her; and the officer of the day, who throughout the entire repast stood behind the royal armchair, was Santerre. As soon as she could escape after the dinner, she ran to Madame Campan's apartments, and throwing herself, exhausted, upon a chair, exclaimed, after assuring herself that they were alone: "One is doomed to perish, when one is attacked by men who unite all talents and all crimes, and is defended by men who may be very estimable, but who have no

just conception of our position. They have compromised me
in the eyes of both parties, in presenting to me the wife and
son of Favras. If I had been free in my actions, I would have
taken the child of this man, who so lately sacrificed himself for
us, and placed him at table between the king and myself; but
surrounded as I was by the executioners, who had only just put
the father to death, I dared not even cast my eyes upon the
son. The Royalists will blame me for not appearing to notice
the poor child; the Revolutionists will be incensed in believing
that my friends thought to please me in presenting him."

The queen, nevertheless, to show that she was deeply sensible of the devotion of the Marquis de Favras, and of the misfortune of his family, sent some rolls of fifty louis to the
unfortunate widow, and the king assured her of a pension of
four thousand livres, which was paid until the downfall of the
throne. Even this act of gratitude, however, had to be wrapped
in mystery.

Some days later, a nearer affliction overtook Marie Antoinette. A letter from her brother Leopold, dated February 27,
announced the death of the emperor, Joseph II., deceased on the
20th at Vienna. The unfortunate sovereign, who had for two
years suffered from water on the chest, and who for eighteen
months had been languishing, so Leopold wrote, had succumbed
to grief caused by the victorious insurrection of the Belgian
provinces. "Your country has killed me," he had said to the
Prince de Ligne. He left a heavy charge to his successor, —
a divided empire, a war with the Turks, another with the
Netherlands, Austria's most loyal provinces, which had been
stirred up by imprudent philosophical reforms. The difficulties
against which he had to contend probably did not permit him
to interfere actively in the affairs of France; but he still retained a certain influence, and he loved his sister sincerely, despite his occasional unjust observations and chiding tone. One
of his last letters to his brother had been a warm tribute to this
sister, and a protest against the calumnies which pursued her, —
a protest which was all the more conclusive because not destined for publication : —

"I, like you, have been grieved at all the horrors which have been
circulated against the queen of France," he wrote on Oct. 8, 1789;
"but what is to be done with insolent rascals and fools? They cannot
overcome the idea that my sister has secretly sent me millions, while I

neither know how nor why I should have asked for them, nor how she could have conveyed them to me; I have never seen a sou from France."

In him Marie Antoinette lost, if not a real supporter, at least a counsellor, and, above all, a devoted friend. Some days before his death Joseph had written to her "a most affectionate, touching letter, assuring her that one of his keenest regrets in dying was to leave her in so cruel a position, and to be unable to give her some efficient proofs of the affections which he had always felt for her."

Whatever Madame Campan may say, the queen's sorrow was deep, but she was obliged to suppress it, only revealing it to a few friends; she wrote to the Duchesse de Polignac, "I have been very unhappy over the loss which I have just sustained; but at least the strength which he whom I mourn manifested in his last moments forces all the world to do him justice and admire him, and I dare to say that he died worthy of me."

This was one of the last letters which the queen wrote to Madame de Polignac, or rather that she received from the queen. Constantly spied upon, she was obliged most of the time to relinquish a correspondence which was a consolation, but which might become a danger. The name of Polignac was one of those watchwords which on days of tumult the party leaders threw as fuel to the passions of the mob to arouse and irritate them. A few days later, the publication of the "Livre Rouge," by order of the Assembly, furnished fresh food for recriminations against the court and the favourites of the queen, especially against the Polignacs, whose name figured therein for large sums, to be explained, however, by the vast outlays they were obliged to make to uphold the dignity of their offices. The Committee of Pensions, who had determined upon this publication, made themselves the echo of these malevolent rumours, in a notice which served as introduction; and while feigning to exclude the king from the affair, they awakened concerning the close friends of the sovereign, the "avidity of those in favour," the "depredations of the ministry," the extravagance of the queen and royal family, who were represented as the "true source of the immense State debt," suspicions which soon took form in violent and odious pamphlets, and which were not long in expressing themselves in riots. Although the queen forced her face to look calm, she could not force her heart to be so. "One cannot tell how far the malcontents may go," she said; "the danger grows from day to day." It was not, however, for herself, but for her husband, and, above all, for her children, that she was fearful. On April 13, the meeting of the Assembly had been stormy; there had even been some excitement in the street, and Lafayette himself feared an attack on the palace. During the night guns were fired on the terrace of the Tuileries. The king, awakened with a start by the noise, rose and flew to the queen's apartments; he did not find her. More and more alarmed, he ran to the dauphin's room, and found the child in the arms of his mother, who pressed him convulsively to her bosom. "Madame," he said to her, "I have been searching for you; you have caused me great uneasiness." "I was at my post," the heroic woman replied simply.

Meanwhile spring was approaching. The royal family, accustomed to the broad stretches and extensive forests of Versailles, were suffocating in the palace of the Tuileries, in which they had been confined since the 6th of October. They longed to breathe the pure air, and more especially to taste again a little tranquillity, to escape from the curious and often hostile mob, who in its familiarity showed no respect for their privacy, and whose cries attacked their honour. Moreover, it accorded with the plans of the leaders of the Revolution that the royal family, whom public rumours represented as prisoners in Paris, should not at the moment of federation, which was to take place on July 14, appear to enjoy less liberty than the rest of France, and especially that first of all liberties, — the right to go and come as they wished. Versailles was too far; the people wished to lengthen the chain, not to break it. St. Cloud was proposed and adopted. On May 29 the queen wrote to her brother Leopold : —

"Our health continues good ; it is a miracle, amid such mental sufferings and such frightful scenes, of which we daily hear the recital, and of which we are sometimes witnesses. I believe that we are to be allowed to profit by the fine weather and go for a few days to St. Cloud, which lies at the gates of Paris. It is absolutely necessary for our health to breathe a purer, more invigorating air, but we shall often return here. We must inspire confidence in this unfortunate people, malcontents make such untiring efforts to excite them and turn them against us. Nothing but excessive patience and the purity of our intentions can lead them back to us."

They set out, in fact, on Friday, June 4, — after having participated on the preceding day in the long and fatiguing procession of the Fête Dieu to St. Germain l'Auxerrois, — for St. Cloud, the country, the open air, freedom, solitude, all the blessings of which they had been deprived for eight long months; what joy, what a relief for the royal family!   Nothing had been prepared to receive the august guests: they were lodged as they could be.   All participants in the journey were admitted to the royal table; and this informality, this absence of etiquette, added still greater charms to the sojourn.   To make use of the witty sayings of Madame Elisabeth, they found Paris beautiful from a distance; and at least they no longer heard "all those curious wretches, who, not content with standing at the gate of the Tuileries, overran the garden, that no one might remain ignorant of their infamy."   The weather was beautiful and the sky clear.   The king resumed his ride, accompanied by a single aid-de-camp, belonging to Monsieur de Lafayette; after dinner he played billiards with his wife and sister.   Madame Elisabeth went to St. Cyr; when she did not go for a walk outside, she passed her time in a small and closed garden, which was her delight.   "It is not so pretty as Montreuil," she wrote; "but at least I am free here; I breathe good fresh air, which makes me forget somewhat all that is around me. And you will agree that one has frequent need of that."   The dauphin sported with light-heartedness in the park, and even went sometimes as far as Meudon.   His health, which had been somewhat impaired by confinement at the Tuileries, regained its vigour; his mind developed in a surprising degree.   The queen made occasional excursions in an open carriage, walked with her children, assisted at their studies and at their games; and despite the presence of the National Guards of Paris, who had been sent more for the purpose of surveillance than as an honour, she could there, at a distance from the great city, more easily receive those persons whose society was agreeable to her, — Madame de Fitz-James and Madame de Tarente, or even political men like Mirabeau, who wished to talk with her of their plans.   In the evening the queen received; a few intimate friends were admitted.   Monsieur came with Madame from the little country house which they had hired near St. Cloud. One day a noise was heard in the court of the palace under the windows of the queen; at her command Madame Campan

raised the curtain, and perceived some fifty people, old chevaliers of St. Louis, Knights of Malta, priests, and country
women. The queen appeared on the balcony; and a few of the
women drew nearer and said to her in a low tone, "Have courage, Madame; the true French people suffer for and with you;
they pray for you. Heaven will grant their prayers. We love
you; we respect you; we revere our virtuous king." Marie
Antoinette burst into tears; but fearing to compromise those
who manifested so touching an interest in her, she re-entered
her chamber with moistened eyes and expanded heart. There
was, then, still some love for her in France.

Amid this apparent calm and comparative relief, however,
the sorrows of the present revived with greater bitterness the
memory of the happy days of 1786. Did not the very date of
their establishment at St. Cloud recall the anniversary of the
death of the poor prince for whose benefit the château had been
purchased? The queen could not shut her mind to these remi-
niscences of the past. One day, seeing round her the Parisian
militia, which was made up in part of the French Guards who
had deserted, she could not refrain from remarking bitterly,
"How astonished my mother would be if she could see her
daughter — the daughter, wife, and mother of kings, or at least
of a child destined to be one — surrounded by such a guard!"
Then evoking the most melancholy memories of her childhood,
she recounted to her ladies-in-waiting the sombre forebodings
of her father as he had quitted her. "I should never have
remembered them again probably," she continued, "if my
present position, in recalling the circumstances, did not show
me for the rest of my life a series of misfortunes which are
only too easy to foresee." Poor woman! Did she foresee them
all? And she added sadly, stopping at the end of the gallery,
from which her gaze embraced the panorama of the capital,
"Formerly this view of Paris was my delight. I often longed
to live there. Who would have said then that the accomplishment of this desire would be steeped in bitterness, and that
the king and his family would be the captives of a revolted
people?"

The king himself, although less impressionable than his wife,
could not refrain from writing to the Duchesse de Polignac, —

"I am just returned to the country. The air has done us good; but
how changed does our sojourn appear to us! How gloomy was the

breakfast-room! None of you were there! I do not lose hope that we may all meet there once again. When? I do not know. How much we shall have to say to each other! The health of your friend continues good, despite all the troubles which weigh upon her."

This visit to St. Cloud extended through the entire summer. From time to time the royal family returned to Paris; for Paris wished to see its king, and the queen herself judged it expedient to respect their demand. "We must not yield to their cries," she said; "but it is well to prove that we are not averse to going there when there is something to be done." Therefore they went almost every Sunday to dine at the Tuileries. They returned for holidays, for important meetings; and, above all, they came back for the grand ceremony of the federation.

The Assembly had decided by the decree of May 27 that the anniversary of the taking of the Bastille should be celebrated with great pomp by a solemn federation of all the representatives, and of all the troops of the kingdom. The Champ de Mars had been chosen as the meeting-place; the king, with his suite, the deputies, the National Guards, the delegates from all the departments, were to take the oath of allegiance to the nation, the law, and the Constitution. The news of the ceremony had been received with enthusiasm. A veritable madness prevailed; every one esteemed it an honour to lend his aid in the preparations for the national *fête*. Women of the best society, priests, monks, politicians, even convent attendants, were to be seen coming with pickaxes or spades in their hands to assist in the transformation of the Champ de Mars; all classes were mingled together, and often in the evening these improvised workmen would return in bands to the sound of the drum and singing, "Ça ira!"

Despite the infatuation of the mob, people beheld with apprehension the approach of July 1. Both parties had, or feigned to have, fears. The partisans of the Revolution circulated the report that the court would take advantage of the enthusiasm of the confederates to dissolve the Assembly and restore absolute power. The Royalists, with more reason, dreaded a popular uprising, always easily provoked in a vast concourse of men; and the unexpected return of the Duc d'Orléans, who had suddenly arrived from England on July 9, lent some credence to the possibility of such a demonstration. The queen received the duke pleasantly, but she was by no means reassured.

"It is very necessary, especially during the month of July, to have some of our own followers with us," she wrote on July 12. "I cannot think of this celebration without a shudder. It will concentrate for us all that is most cruel and painful, and yet we must be present. One will have need of a supernatural courage for that moment. Things go from bad to worse: the ministry and Monsieur de Lafayette force us every day to false measures; we yield in every point, yet far from contenting these monsters, they become more insolent at every instant, and in the eyes of upright men we demean ourselves just so much the more."

All of these fears were not realized. On the contrary, there was a gleam of brightness in the darkened heavens. "On the eve of the federation," Madame de Tourzel relates, "the king passed in review the confederates of the department. They defiled before him and the royal family at the foot of the grand staircase of the Tuileries. The king asked the name of every deputation, and spoke to each of its members with a graciousness which increased their devotion. The queen presented her children, and addressed a few words to the confederates with that charm which added a new force to all that she said. Transported with joy, they entered the Tuileries amid cries of "Vive le roi, la reine, Monseigneur le Dauphin, et la famille royale!" The king walked about with his family without guards, in the midst of an immense throng, and surrounded by the confederates, who were so entirely under the domination of the malcontents that not one of them dared to do his duty.

On the morrow, Wednesday, July 14, the confederates from the provinces, drawn up under eighty-three banners, set out from the Bastille in the teeth of a driving rain; the delegates of the infantry, of the navy, and of the Parisian militia accompanied them. While awaiting the beginning of the ceremony after their arrival at the Champ de Mars, they amused themselves by forming in circles and dancing *farandoles*, — a singular sight, and one which did not give a high idea of the discipline of these improvised soldiers. Three hundred thousand spectators, it is said, were packed together in the vast enclosure, seated on tiers of grass, and trying in vain to protect themselves with parasols from the torrents of water which deluged them. An altar in antique form had been raised in the middle of the Champ de Mars; the bishop of Autun was to celebrate mass here, assisted by three hundred priests, robed in white albs crossed by broad tri-coloured sashes.

An immense platform had been erected for the king, the ambassadors, and the deputies. Louis XVI. had desired that his family should surround him; the Assembly would not allow it. It decided, on July 9, that the king should be alone, with the president on his left. The royal family should be placed at the windows of the École Militaire, where a drawing-room had been arranged for them, adjoining but distinct from the tribune for the Assembly. This was a fresh mark of distrust toward the royal family, toward the queen especially, whom they thus sought to separate from her husband, and from the representatives of the nation.

"You know," Madame Elisabeth gayly wrote to her friend, Madame de Bombelles, "that I have the good fortune to be acquainted with one of the members of this august family of bygone days. Well, let me inform you that this is a matter of indifference to them; they are only grieved on the queen's account, for whom this is a blow given with full force, and the more effectually dealt because aimed from afar, and also because until the last moment the king was told that the contrary was to take place."

Louis XVI. repaired to the École Militaire at an early hour; while waiting until everything was ready, he remained with his family, showing himself from time to time at the queen's window, and greeted at each appearance with cries of "Vive le roi!" with which were mingled shouts of "Vive la reine!" "Vive le dauphin!" Marie Antoinette, touched, held her son up to the crowd; and as the rain wet the child, she wrapped him in her shawl; the acclamations redoubled, cheering both the mother and the queen.

During this time the deputations, one after another, arrived. When the entire procession had entered the enclosure, the king took his place on the throne, in the midst of the deputies, near the president. After the mass, the bishop of Autun blessed the eighty-three banners, and intoned the *Te Deum*, which was sung by twelve hundred musicians. Lafayette went up to the altar, and in the name of the army swore fidelity to the nation, the laws, and the king. The president of the Assembly, the Marquis de Bonnay, repeated the oath; and a loud cry of "I swear it!" broke forth from the throats of three hundred thousand people, crowded together on the Champ de Mars. Cannon roared, flags were waved, hats thrown in the air, the caps of the grenadiers raised on the ends of sabres and bayonets. The king rose, and in a loud voice swore to uphold the Constitution. The queen took the dauphin in her arms and presented him to the people, saying, "He joins, and I also, in these sentiments." "This unexpected act," says Ferrières, "was rewarded by repeated cries of 'Vive le roi!' 'Vive la reine!' 'Vive Monseigneur le Dauphin!'"

For several days universal rejoicing prevailed. These worthy delegates from the provinces, still filled with the traditional respect and love of the French people for royalty, were delighted to approach so near to the royal family. From the early morning they thronged the court and the garden of the Tuileries, crowding under the windows, especially eager to see the dauphin. The young prince appeared on the balcony, and did them the honours of his small garden, distributing to them flowers and leaves from his trees. Loud cheers greeted him. "Come into your province of Dauphiné," the federates of Grenoble said to him; "we shall know how to defend you well." "Do not forget," replied the Normans, "that you have borne the name of our province, and that the Normans always have been and always will be loyal."

Four days later, the king held a review of the National Guards at the Porte de Chaillot. The queen, with her children and Madame Elisabeth, attended in an open calash without emblazonry. Her carriage was immediately surrounded by federates, with whom she conversed familiarly, answering and even inviting their questions. They desired to kiss the hand of the little dauphin. She presented him to them herself; these good people were enraptured. At that moment the arm of the queen chanced to rest on the carriage door; one of the federates seized it hastily and pressed his lips to it. The example was contagious; and affection silencing respect, three hundred mouths had in an instant covered with kisses the arm which the queen, greatly moved, did not think to withdraw. The poor woman, touched by this expressive sympathy, to which she was unaccustomed, wept with emotion.

"That day," an eye-witness relates, "was truly a day of happiness for the king, the queen, and for those who were devoted to them. There was an intoxication of feeling; it was the queen's last bright day."

"The deputies of the provinces were heart and soul for the king and queen," writes another witness; "they overwhelmed them with touching marks of respect, love, and loyalty; and their Majesties treated them with marvellous condescension. They were captivated by the queen, who received them with all the graciousness and affability of which she was capable."

If Louis XVI. had wished to profit by this enthusiasm; if, as the Duc de Villequier entreated him to do, he had mounted his horse and declared that, finding himself for the first time at the head of the chosen of the nation, he considered it right to explain to them that he could not with propriety swear fidelity to an unfinished Constitution; above all, if, as Madame de Tourzel advised him, he had set out at once to visit the provinces, where he would probably have been welcomed with the same acclamations,— he would have been able, supported by the veritable majority of the country, to put a stop to the encroachments of the Assembly, and to resume the rightful exercise of his royal power. The Assembly feared him; the attitude of the federates made them for a moment question their success and the approval of the nation; and Barnave acknowledged this to Madame Elisabeth in one of those conversations on his return from Varennes, from which the young deputy came away won over to the cause which he had so violently attacked. As the princess complained of the designs which the Assembly had entertained in decreeing the federation, Barnave replied quickly, "Ah, Madame, do not complain of that event; for if the king had known how to profit by it, we should have been lost."

The king, however, did not know how; he drew back before the fear of a conflict. The lost opportunity did not present itself again. The federates went back to their departments, delighted with the welcome which they had received, imbued with sentiments of love and respect for all the royal family, but without direction, without instructions, with no understanding among themselves or with the court, abandoned in their distant provinces, without defence, to the unwholesome influences from which they had escaped only for the moment. Louis XVI. and his household returned to St. Cloud, somewhat calmed, and with a glimmer of hope reviving within them; but, alas! for how long? Hardly had they arrived at their summer residence, when a wretch named Rotondo forced his way into the château to assassinate the queen. He had penetrated as far as the outer gardens; the rain, which prevented the queen from going out on that day, alone saved her from his dagger.

Almost at the same time a plot to poison her was discovered. Marie Antoinette knew of it, and did not appear in the least affected by it. Nevertheless, her physician, Vicq d'Azyr, and her first waiting-woman, Madame Campan, decided that the powdered sugar which the queen was in the habit of taking to put in her glass of water, should be renewed in the queen's sugar-bowl several times a day. One day the queen surprised Madame Campan as she was busy making the change agreed upon. She smiled sadly and begged her to spare herself useless trouble. "Remember," she said to her, "no one will employ a grain of poison against me. The Brinvilliers are not of this age; there is calumny, which is a better weapon for killing people, and it is by it that I shall be destroyed."

A few days later, the attitude of the Assembly justified these presentiments. The Châtelet had been charged to open an investigation of the events of October. The queen, when interrogated by the commissioners, had observed a generous silence. "I will never be the accuser of my subjects," she had replied. "I saw all, knew all, and have forgotten all." The investigation continued, notwithstanding, and on Aug. 7, 1790, Monsieur Boucher d'Argis, the judge-advocate, came to the Assembly to give information concerning the inquiry. His summary, written in a clumsily emphatic style, concluded with the arraignment of Mirabeau and the Duc d'Orléans, and was the subject of a report by Chabroud. This work by Chabroud, which was a monument of hypocrisy and lies, full of malevolence toward the body-guards, and of hateful insinuations against the queen, seemed to have for its aim to make light of the outrage, accuse the victims, and vindicate the guilty. This end was accomplished. Chabroud's conclusions were adopted, despite the protestations of the Abbé Maury and Montlosier, and on October 2, after a vigorous tirade by Mirabeau, who adroitly shifted his ground, and in place of the accused, posed as the accuser, the criminal attempts of October 6 were only "misfortunes" designed to "furnish a lesson to kings." Mirabeau, the Duc d'Orléans, Théroigne de Méricourt, and even Jourdan Coupe-Tête were released from all charges; and the real culprits, held up by the report to the fury of the galleries and the blows of the populace, were the defenders of the crown, transformed into enemies of the Constitution.

The queen's indignation was aroused, less perhaps by the

decision which exonerated Mirabeau and the Duc d'Orléans than by the glorification of crime and the odious perversion of facts. "I say nothing of the judgment which has just been passed on the affair of the 5th and 6th of October of last year. It was to be expected; but in my opinion it defiles the soul as the deeds themselves profaned the palace of the king last year. As to the rest, it is for Europe and for posterity to pronounce judgment upon these events, and to render justice to me, and to those brave body-guards with whom I am proud to be named."

Meanwhile, at this very time — so entirely did her duties as queen dominate her antipathies as woman — she had entered into negotiations with one of the men whom public opinion had most deeply incriminated in the events of October, and who under all circumstances had shown himself one of her most violent adversaries; namely, with Mirabeau.

CHAPTER VII.

MIRABEAU, who had been thrown into the revolutionary party through pride, resentment, ambition, the dissoluteness of his private life, and the necessities of his needy condition, and had been placed in the first rank among its leaders, not because of his authority, — he did not exercise an important influence until the second year, — but because of his talent and the passionate nature of his eloquence, was not long in perceiving the abyss into which the inexperience and impetuosity of his friends were about to precipitate France. Passion had made him a Revolutionist; reason maintained him a Royalist. The very nature of his temperament made him an upholder of authority, and he did not hesitate in the secrecy of his intimate circle to deplore the dangers of the monarchy which he was willing to attack, which he even consented to weaken, but which he did not wish to destroy. At the end of May he had offered Necker through Malouet his co-operation in saving "the monarchy and the monarch from the tempest which was gathering;" these were his own words. The very cold reception given by Necker, who detested him, but did not yet fear him, had thrown him back into the opposition. "Monsieur," the minister had dryly and contemptuously said to him, "Monsieur Malouet tells me that you have some propositions to make to me; what are they?" "My proposition," Mirabeau replied abruptly, "is to wish you a good day." And he went away furious, vowing to place his bold spirit and the force of his talents at the service

of what was then called the "popular party." Although on
certain occasions he had shown monarchical sentiments and had
proved himself an enlightened statesman, anxious for pure conditions of constitutional monarchy, and for the true liberty and
greatness of France, the year 1789 had seen him among the
fiercest detractors of the government; and he had been vehemently, although according to Monsieur de la Marck, unjustly,
suspected of having been one of the promoters of the bloody
deeds of October. Little in sympathy, however, with the
leaders of the Left, with Lafayette, whose presumptuous ineffi-
ciency irritated him, with the Duc d'Orléans, about whom he
expressed himself in the strongest terms; hostile to the ministers, yet at bottom attached to the monarchy; an aristocrat by
instinct and frightened at the progress of democracy, which he
saw advancing with threatening mien,— he did not relinquish the
thought of an alliance with the court, even during his fiercest
attacks upon it, and he disclaimed in private the violent language into which he allowed himself to be betrayed in public
through passion, and perhaps through calculation. "Let it be
known," he said at the end of June to his friend, the Comte de
la Marck, one of the former *habitués* of Trianon,— "let it be
known at the palace that I am more for than against them." He
was appalled at the dangers which his far-seeing genius showed
him were imminent. "What are those people thinking about?"
he repeated continually in his rude manner of speech. "Do
they not see the abysses which are opening in their path?"
And one day near the end of September, when he was more
alarmed than ever and more exasperated by the incapacity of
the ministers, he exclaimed, "All is lost. The king and queen
will be killed, and you will see the populace trample on their
bodies; you do not sufficiently understand the peril of the
situation, yet they must be made to recognize it."

Two weeks later, on the very day following the mournful
return to Paris, he resumed his efforts. "If you have any way
of making yourself understood by the king and queen," he said
to Monsieur de la Marck, "convince them that they and France
are lost if the royal family do not leave Paris. I am engaged
on a plan to render their departure possible." And he submitted this plan to his friend on October 15.

La Marck, however, hesitated; he was aware of the horror
with which Mirabeau inspired the queen, and it must be ad-

mitted that for a man who solicited the honour of becoming the counsellor of the royal family, Mirabeau had a strange manner of defending his clients.   His attitude in the Assembly during October had revolted those who were the sincerest friends of liberty; and on the 5th he had hurled against the unfortunate Marie Antoinette herself one of those perfidious insinuations which the populace was on the morrow to translate into such bloody language.   Monsieur de la Marck had even been forced to make excuses to the queen for his relations with this hot-headed tribune, giving as pretext that he might some day prove useful to the cause of the Royalists; and the queen, who was little able to conceal her antipathies, had replied, "We shall scarcely be so unfortunate, I think, as to be driven to the painful extremity of having recourse to Mirabeau."   Not daring therefore to communicate Mirabeau's plan directly to the queen, he confided it to Monsieur.   But this plan depended, above all, upon departure from Paris and a retreat into some loyal province like Normandy, or to a safe city like Beauvais.   It demanded a positive decision, and Monsieur had no faith in his brother's firmness.   "The king's weakness and indecision," he said, "are beyond all description.   To give you an idea of his character, imagine oiled ivory balls, which you vainly endeavour to hold together."   Even the queen's energy could not overcome her husband's vacillation.

Despite this discouraging answer, the project was not abandoned.   Monsieur maintained connections with Mirabeau; the queen was informed of it; and it does not appear that she disapproved, although she chose to take no part in the matter. Soon, however, an inexpedient measure, adopted on November 7 by the Assembly, on the motion of Lanjuinais and with the ill-considered support of the Right, forbidding deputies to become ministers, deprived Mirabeau of some of his resources. No longer able to be of the cabinet himself, he at least wished to appoint Monsieur, who at that moment accepted his counsels, as its chief; but this new combination failed, and it is certain that the queen, who had little love for her brother-in-law, had not regarded it with favour.   Moreover, Mirabeau soon quarrelled with Monsieur, as he had already done with Necker, Lafayette, and the Duc d'Orléans.

Monsieur de la Marck, feeling discouraged, had, on December 16, left for his estate of Raismes, whence he had passed into

Belgium, where his private affairs and the interest which he took in the Netherlands, then in revolt against Austria, called him, when about the middle of March a letter from the Comte de Mercy summoned him back to Paris. Negotiations had been resumed, and the king had at last determined to treat with Mirabeau. The queen still retained some doubts concerning the violent tribune's participation in the events of October; these doubts were removed, and after a first interview between Mirabeau, Mercy, and La Marck, and a long conversation between La Marck and the king and queen, it was decided that the powerful orator should prepare a note, which should be delivered to the queen by La Marck and by her to her husband. Absolute secrecy should be observed toward the ministers until a better ministry had been formed, which could be put into communication with the new counsellor of the monarchy.

An understanding between the king and the tribune on the subject of reforms would be easy. "Louis XVI. was far from cherishing the idea of reconquering his former absolute authority; he was perfectly resigned to the fact that the Revolution had taken from him the power and rights of his predecessors. I should say," adds La Marck, from whom we borrow this judgment, "that in this respect Mirabeau was less resigned than he."

Mirabeau acquiesced with alacrity in the plan thus fixed upon. On the 10th of May he wrote a letter, in which he protested his monarchical views, and promised the king "loyalty, zeal, activity, energy, and courage." The king and queen were gratified by this declaration, and the queen wished to assure the Comte de la Marck of the fact. "She confirmed what the Comte de Mercy had told me of the satisfaction which the king had experienced in reading Mirabeau's letter; she repeated to me again that the king had no desire to recover his authority to the full extent of former days, and that he was far from believing this necessary for his personal happiness or for that of his people." The poor woman at that moment seemed full of hopefulness and almost joyful; and in the course of a two hours' conversation with La Marck she began to evoke memories of the past, as if, looking henceforth upon the future with greater calmness, she was already throwing off the anxieties of the present. It was agreed that the king should pay Mirabeau's debts — and they were numerous — and guarantee him a salary of six thousand livres a month and a million at the close of the Assembly. This was the price of the services expected of him. Mirabeau was overjoyed; and his delight at being freed from the cramped, adventurous existence which he had until then led, inspired him with an overflowing enthusiasm for the royal family and for the queen.

"I professed monarchical principles," he said at the opening of his first memoir, "when I saw the weakness of the court, and when acquainted neither with the soul nor the thoughts of the daughter of Maria Theresa. I could not then count upon this august ally. I fought for the rights of the throne when I inspired naught but mistrust, and when all my proceedings, poisoned by malice, appeared so many snares. I served the monarch when I knew well that I could expect neither benefactions nor rewards from a just but deluded king. What shall I not do now that confidence has restored my courage, and recognition has transformed my principles into duties? I shall be what I have always been, — the defender of monarchical power, restricted by law, and the apostle of liberty guaranteed by monarchical power. My heart shall follow the path which reason alone had marked out for me."

Negotiations, once begun, were vigorously carried on, through the medium of the Comte de la Marck, the Comte de Mercy, Monsieur de Fontanges, archbishop of Toulouse, and former confessor to the queen, and later, through the medium of Monsieur de Montmorin. Notes followed one another in rapid succession. Mirabeau insisted on the necessity of restoring the authority of the crown, of weakening Lafayette's dictatorial influence, of maintaining agents in the provinces to win over the inhabitants, and of tightening the bonds of discipline in the army, which would be needed to restore the monarchy. "The king," he said, "has only one man near him, and that is his wife. There is no safety for her except in the re-establishment of the royal authority. It is my belief that she would not wish for life without a crown; but I am very sure that she will not preserve her life unless she preserves her crown. The moment will come, and soon, when she will have to try what a woman and a child can do on horseback. For her it is a family custom; but meanwhile she must prepare herself, and not fancy that she can, by the aid either of chance or of intrigue, weather an extraordinary crisis by means of ordinary men and ordinary measures."

Mirabeau, knowing the king's weakness and the queen's

strength, was convinced that this princess alone would have sufficient influence with her husband to overcome his indecision. This high opinion of Marie Antoinette's character made him desire an interview with her, that he might acquaint her more thoroughly with the perils of the situation, explain to her in detail his plan of action, and by winning greater confidence from her, imbue her, to a certain degree, with his spirit. "It is essential," he wrote to La Marck on June 26, "that I should see your man, and, above all, that I should see *Her.*" It was by this word that he designated the queen. The queen, however, felt an extreme repugnance to such an interview. Despite Mirabeau's assurances of devotion, she could not forget that she had, for more than a year, been used to regard him as a "monster," and that at that very hour the Châtelet had marked him out as one of the accomplices in the events of October. However, urged by the Comte de Mercy and the archbishop of Toulouse, she overcame her natural instinctive aversion for the sake of the king, her children, and the country, and finally consented to the conference asked for. It only remained to choose the day and a suitable place. St. Cloud, where the court was passing the summer, offered greater facilities than Paris, but even at St. Cloud the royal family were watched. After some searching, Marie Antoinette found a spot "not convenient, but which would serve to receive him, and which overcame the disadvantages of the garden and the château." The audience, at first fixed for Friday, was postponed until Saturday, the 3d of July, at half-past eight in the morning. The better to cloak his actions, Mirabeau left Paris on the preceding evening and slept at Auteuil in the house of his niece, the Marquise d'Aragon. The next morning he started forth in a cabriolet with two horses, accompanied only by his nephew, the Comte du Saillant, who was disguised as a courier, and drove the carriage. He alighted at the small gate of the park, and moved by a sentiment of distrust, of which he soon repented, he handed a letter to his nephew before entering, saying, "If in three quarters of an hour I have not returned, depart and deliver this note without the loss of an instant to the commander of the National Guards." Then he knocked at the gate, and was admitted to the park, through which he was conducted to the queen's apartments. Despite the control which Marie Antoinette exercised over herself, she was overcome by such deep emotion on perceiving the "monster" that on the following day she suffered a slight indisposition as the result of it. She recovered herself, however, and advancing toward the violent tribune, said with her sovereign graciousness, "With an ordinary enemy, with a man who had sworn the ruin of the monarchy, without perceiving the benefit which it is to a great people, I should at this moment be committing a most unbecoming act. But when one is speaking to a Mirabeau . . ." Mirabeau was captivated. Marie Antoinette's appearance alone had dazzled him. Her serene dignity, the incomparable charm which pervaded her whole person, the melancholy smile which played upon her lips, her affability when he accused himself of having been one of the chief causes of her suffering, —all concurred to arouse his enthusiasm. "Madame," he remarked, on withdrawing, "when your august mother admitted one of her subjects to the honour of her presence, she never dismissed him without giving him her hand to kiss." The queen extended her hand. Mirabeau, bowing respectfully, kissed it, and rising, said, "Madame, the monarchy is saved."

When he again crossed the threshold of the park gates, at the end of three quarters of an hour, his breathing was laboured, his speech broken. He listened as if with regret to the final crunching of the sand under the feet of those who were returning. Then, approaching his nephew, he hastily took back the letter which he had confided to him, and pressing his arm violently, exclaimed, "She is very great, very noble, and very unhappy, Victor, but I will save her."

"Never had my uncle's voice been shaken by a similar emotion, by an emotion so true," Monsieur du Saillant adds.

Despite the care with which the secret of this interview was guarded, despite the precautions taken by the queen to disarm suspicion, or at least to fix it upon some one else who would be less compromising and less compromised, such as the Comte de Ségur, a vague rumour, I know not what, was whispered about among the people, and anonymous letters denounced to the Committee of Inquiry that which had been called, on a preceding occasion, the "great treason of the Comte de Mirabeau."

These clamours, however, intimidated the powerful orator now as little as they had intimidated him on May 22. Illumined by the queen's bounty, touched by the king's resignation, and the moderation of his views on the re-establishment of royalty, he ardently pursued the end which he had set for himself. "Nothing shall stay me," he said; "I will die rather than fail in my promises." Unfortunately the perfect union which the interview at St. Cloud seemed to have established between the tribune and the royal family was short-lived. The king, vacillating as ever, hesitated to place entire reliance upon him; he sought advice in every quarter, and ended by following none. This division of confidence exasperated Mirabeau. Having once dedicated himself to the cause, he wished to have his counsels followed exclusively; he was jealous of all those to whom the king and queen seemed to accord some credit, as De Ségur, De Rivarol, and De Bergasse. On July 9 he complained that he was not told all, and that Louis XVI. did not carry out the decisions agreed upon with his wife. "The queen must always give the impetus to the king," — and that which he did not add, but which lay at the bottom of his thoughts, was that the queen should always accept Mirabeau's direction, — "otherwise the king and queen will only be timid people, constantly obliged to make terms with their jailers, . . . constantly at the mercy of insurrection, of ambition, of demagogy."

But even Marie Antoinette, intrepid as she was, shrank at times from the plans proposed by her new ally. On the 13th of August, Mirabeau presented the well-known memoir, the beginning of which has been so often quoted: "Four enemies are approaching with rapid strides, — taxation, bankruptcy, the army, winter. It is necessary to take some decided step. I mean by that, we must prepare ourselves for events by directing them. In two words, civil war is certain and perhaps necessary." And he concluded by demanding another interview and laying stress upon the necessity of organizing in the army a solid nucleus of-resistance.

The queen was terrified. This brutal calculation of danger, which she felt strongly enough, but which she preferred, without doubt, to believe less pressing; the very tone of the note, a tone to which the polished and obsequious phrases of her ministers had little accustomed her; the "extraordinary" style (the word is hers), that disjointed, abrupt style, which smelled of powder and sounded the charge, — all this awakened her anxiety and fears; she was almost tempted to consider her audacious correspondent mad. Civil war, especially, inspired in her, and continued to inspire in her to the end, an insurmountable aversion. "How can M. or any other thinking creature," she wrote to Mercy, "ever, but, above all, at this moment, believe that the time has come for us, *us*, to stir up a civil war?" As to another conference with Mirabeau, that was impossible. The first had been suspected, and this simple suspicion had almost wrecked everything. What would happen if the second should be discovered?

Mirabeau was probably informed by Mercy of the impression produced by his memoir. He was more saddened than astonished, and at the same time discouraged. He wished the king to assume an active part, and the king could not bring himself to other than a passive rôle. He wished to stir up the people by adroit agents, to arouse, if need be, the discontent which the reforms of the Assembly must inevitably awaken in the provinces, and the king was waiting for this discontent to germinate and grow of itself; he left all to time, and there was not a day to lose. Even the queen, in whose courage he trusted, drew back, as if dazzled by the sinister light which he had thrown upon the situation. She also took refuge in a passive rôle. "Time and patience are the true remedies for our ills," she wrote a little later to her brother; "I believe that there will come a time, however, when we shall have to aid public opinion, but we are not yet there." The nearer the moment for action approached, the more obvious the necessity for energetic action became, the more she sought to delay it, as if terrified by the consequences. And Mirabeau repeated sadly: —

" I shall continue to give my services, so far as the nature of things will allow, even despite the passive rôles to which the royal family condemns itself, despite the repugnance I feel for this order of things ; and this repugnance is such that if I have abstained here from unfolding all the dangers, it is only to spare your imagination or your feelings a picture the hideousness of which would distress you to no purpose. Since you must believe yourself powerless to do anything for the common weal or for yourself, I lament that so good a prince and a queen so gifted by nature should be useless to the restoration of their country, even by the sacrifice of consideration and of their safety. I shall be loyal to the end, because such is my character ; I shall limit myself to temporary and circumstantial measures, until they wish to lend themselves to others. . . . Beyond this, I shall wait until a peal of thunder break this deplorable lethargy which I can only bemoan."

A month later he wrote again, —

"I confess, not without regret, that I am little useful; but my clients impose upon me the duty of serving the more as they deprive me of the power to do so. They listen to me with more kindness than confidence; they manifest more interest to know my counsels than to follow them; and, above all, they do not sufficiently realize that the passive rôle of inaction, were it preferable to all others, does not consist exactly either in doing nothing, or in allowing only those who hurt the cause to act."

Then, referring to the revision of the Constitution, decreed by the Assembly, he added, —

"I shall give my ideas on this subject if they are solicited. I shall give my opinion on other plans if one deigns to consult me; for since the initiative, which has been allowed me, has so far produced only hesitation and embarrassment, it might perhaps be wise to try if I could not be more useful in changing my policy."

In the unreserve of intimacy, his complaints were livelier and even brutal; he allowed himself to give way to gross expressions, for which he asked pardon later; he went so far as to call his august clients "cowards" and "royal cattle." "It is pitiable," he wrote. ". . . One would say that the house in which they sleep might be reduced to ashes without hurting or even arousing them." Then, estranged by the subterfuges of the Court, irritated by the hostile attitude and the interruptions of the Right, he gave way in the tribune of the Assembly to outbursts of anger, to "worse than that," as La Marck expresses it, which, in awakening doubts of his fidelity, only increased the hesitation of the king and queen. At other times, recovering himself and realizing, not without remorse, how well founded at bottom was the repugnance of the royal family, he exclaimed bitterly, "Ah, that the immorality of my youth should thus harm the commonwealth now!"

This was indeed the secret of the queen's doubts and the real cause of Mirabeau's impotence. In vain did he write, on October 24, three days after one of his most virulent outbreaks:

"My zeal has never been more pure, my devotion more boundless, my desire to be useful more constant, — I venture to say, more persistent. It was not for myself, it was to attain greater success, that I coveted the prize of confidence; and those who shall succeed in depriving me of it will tear from my heart neither gratitude nor the oath which I have sworn to defend the authority of the crown, if I must fight alone, and succumb in this illustrious struggle in which I shall have Europe as witness and posterity as judge."

The queen could not be convinced that the man who had so rudely shaken the throne, who was still led into attacking it from time to time with such passion and violence, was sincerely resolved to uphold it; and she asked herself anxiously what secret motive these overtures might conceal, — if Mirabeau had not in view his own private interests, rather than those of the monarchy; if he did not justify that hard saying of his father, "Whether he be monkey, wolf, or fox, it matters not to him; he minds nothing." Or this other, no less hard, "The conversion of Saint Paul might make another man, but could not revive this one."

Justly angered by his revolutionary discourse of October 2, upon the proceedings of the Châtelet, she wrote to Mercy: "He has sent me his address; if I could see him, there are several points about which I would ask an explanation; and with all his cleverness and cunning, I think that he would have some difficulty in proving that he delivered it to serve us."

The archbishop of Toulouse, who was otherwise so devoted and disposed to uphold Mirabeau throughout this entire negotiation, said on his part after another and no less brutal outbreak, "How can you expect that confidence, which is so necessary under the circumstances, should spring up after such blunders as those of day before yesterday?"

The queen was mistaken. Mirabeau honestly and seriously desired a monarchical government, tempered by liberty; and since the interview at St. Cloud, his devotion to Marie Antoinette, in particular, was inspired by a sentiment of chivalry; it was not only the queen, it was also the woman whom he desired to serve. But he, who complained so frequently of the indecision of the royal family, often merited the same reproach. Torn, as he was, between his reason and his passion, between his eagerness not to endanger his popularity and his wish to save the crown, his very efforts to reconcile the irreconcilable rendered his course of action vacillating, and gave to his conduct an appearance of falseness which revived suspicion and reawakened the prejudices which had with such difficulty been lulled to sleep. He was sincere; he was not straightforward. He was faithful; he was not constant, and did not seem logical.

The danger grew from hour to hour; and the enemies of the crown, who, like Mirabeau, felt that the queen alone of the royal family was a serious obstacle to their desires, showed no less ardour in attacking her than the eloquent tribune in defending her. The tactics employed against her were skilful; her enemies had begun, in writings prompted by the leaders, by speaking in loud praise of the king, while maintaining silence about the queen; then the silence was changed into hostile insinuations, and soon after into open attack, which concurred with unfriendly reports circulated among the people, with perfidious intrigues plotted in the dark, with odious schemes audaciously avowed. "A portion of the public," says La Marck, "had finally let themselves be imposed upon in the matter, and stupidly believed in the atrocious calumnies which had been spread abroad against this unfortunate princess." All the decisions of the Right, even those which she condemned, all the proceedings of the monarchists, even those to which she was most alien, — such as the duel of the Duc de Castries with Charles de Lameth,— were imputed to her. The ministry had finally been dissolved through their own impotence. Necker, who had fallen under the weight of public indifference, had left on September 4; he had departed without hearing one charitable expression of regret or having the satisfaction of being attacked. "He is regretted by no one," said Fersen, "not even by his own circle; and his departure will produce no effect." Two months later, the other members of the cabinet tendered their resignations. New ministers succeeded the old, creatures of Lameth for the most part, and chosen, of course, outside of the Assembly. Monsieur de Montmorin alone remained, supported by Mirabeau, for whom he was to serve as intermediary with the court ; and he alone also dared to defend the queen, even against some of his new colleagues. For it was always the queen whom the Revolutionists pursued; it was she who must be separated from the king and made to disappear, voluntarily or by force.

Once, not long after the return to Paris, the Constitutionalists had proposed to her, through her friend, the Duchesse de Luynes, to retire from France for a time, that the Constitution might be completed without the patriots accusing her of opposition to it. The Duchesse de Luynes, who knew in what great danger the person of Marie Antoinette stood, had consented to communicate the proposition to her; but she must set out alone. The queen replied "that she would never abandon the king and her children; that if she believed herself the only object of the popular hatred, she would at that very instant sacrifice her life; but that they had designs on the throne, and that in abandoning the king she would only be committing an act of cowardice, since the only advantage which she saw in it was to save her own life."

Persuasion having failed, menace was resorted to. Her enemies talked of assassination, of a trial. The rumour was circulated — about the end of 1790 — that the plan which had failed on October 6 was to be again essayed. Monsieur de Montmorin, alarmed by these reports, begged his colleagues to take measures to prevent the accomplishment of so heinous a crime. The keeper of the seals, Duport du Tertre, addressing the meeting, declared coldly that he would not lend himself to a murder, but that he would feel otherwise if it were a question of bringing the queen to trial. "What!" replied Monsieur de Montmorin, indignantly, "you, the king's minister, — you would consent to such infamy?" "But," Duport answered calmly, "if there is no other way?"

In default of assassination, in default of a trial, or perhaps as a consequence and end of the trial, divorce was proposed; and Monsieur de Lafayette, in an interview with the queen, had the shameless indecency to say to her that to accomplish it they would accuse her of adultery. The queen met this insulting threat with her habitual dignity and courage; but what self-control she must have had, not to have ordered the forcible expulsion of her insolent interlocutor from the palace! And is not here in this affront of Lafayette to be found the cause of the insurmountable antipathy which Marie Antoinette retained to the end for this "hero of the two continents," and which made her declare that she would rather perish than owe her salvation to him? Madame de la Motte was at this time in Paris, called thither by the leaders of the Revolution, and ready to begin again her secret and infamous intrigues against her royal victim. Mirabeau sprang up, exclaiming, "I will snatch this unfortunate queen from her executioners, or die." And seizing his pen, he wrote, —

"It is impossible to exaggerate the sentiment of bold devotion which the discovery of so much bold iniquity and treachery arouses in me, and if I name other abettors [he had proposed that Fréteau or D'Ailly should demand the arrest of the conspirator] it is because the vague rumours of my relations would militate against me if I should speak first ; but he who doubts that I would not perish in the breach for such a cause and for all that concerns this august and interesting victim, whom so many rascals covet, does me the cruellest wrong, and also makes a most pitiable miscalculation in this matter."

The malcontents aimed not only at the queen, but at the king, through his wife. Mirabeau felt this.

" In this project," he wrote, " the queen, whose disposition, sound judgment, and firmness they know, will be the first object of their attack, as the chief and strongest guardian of the throne, and the sentinel who most closely guards the safety of the monarch. The great art of the ambitious, however, will be to hide their purpose ; they wish to appear to be impelled by events, not to direct them. After having utilized the trial of the woman La Motte as a destructive poison for the queen ; after having transformed the most absurd calumnies into legal evidence capable of deceiving the king, — they will bring up, one by one, the questions of divorce, of the regency, of the marriage of kings, of the education of the heir to the throne. . . . But," he added, " if this country should perish from end to end, I would yet be the defender of the queen and of the king."

Those who had summoned Madame de la Motte, being frightened by the disturbance which the affair had created, and by the turn it had taken, judged it more prudent to send her away again; and for this time, at least, the conspiracy miscarried.

Unfortunately, on the very day following that on which the great orator composed these eloquent notes and signed this declaration of unalterable devotion, he was again in the Assembly betrayed by his passion into the use of violent language, into an apology for the insurrection, which threw his friend La Marck into despair and dissipated the fresh confidence which the notes had awakened in the queen. Mirabeau apologized; but he was incorrigible, and a fortnight later, in the discussion on the civil Constitution of the clergy, he fell back into his former ways and delivered an address of extraordinary violence. What was his true purpose in acting thus? Did he wish by his vehement attacks the better to dissimulate his real intentions? Did he hope, as he claimed to, that the very exaggeration of the measures proposed would render them illusory? Did he consider that he could not better make himself heard by

his colleagues than by adopting their tone, by exceeding them
and redoubling the severity of their decrees? Did he, as he
boasted, entertain the thought of "hurting" the Assembly
and of bringing it into discredit, by making it tyrannical? Did
he believe in the efficacy of that theory, so often extolled in
times of revolution and so rarely crowned with success, which
claims to evolve good from an excess of evil? Whatever may
have been his real intentions, the effect produced was deplorable. In indulging in such invectives against the clergy and
the Catholic religion, he wounded not only the political views,
the prejudices, if you will, of the royal family, but also his own
conscience. All the objections formerly urged against him
were revived. Mirabeau multiplied his memoirs without avail;
they no longer had any weight; and La Marck himself scarcely
dared approach the queen, so discouraged and estranged did he
know her to be with regard to his friend. The eloquent and
capricious tribune, to regain the confidence which he felt
escaping him, set to work anew, and on December 23 sketched
out an elaborate scheme of defence and safety by the reconciliation of public liberty with royal authority. It was not a plan of
counter-revolution: he looked upon this as neither possible
nor desirable; it was a plan of counter-constitution.

"I regard," he said, "all the results of the Revolution and all
that must be retained of the Constitution as conquests so entirely irrevocable that no upheaval short of the dismemberment of the kingdom can destroy them."

Moreover, these reforms, according to him, were not so un-
favourable to the royal power as old prejudices would lead people
to fear.

"The perfectly even surface required by liberty also renders
the exercise of authority much more easy; this equality in
political rights, about which so much stir is made, is also an
instrument of power."

Without doubt these reforms had often been excessive, pre-
mature, and ill-considered; they should be corrected. "The
Revolution in its spirit," and "the Constitution in the majority
of its fundamental principles," should be accepted. "To labour
for a better Constitution is the only aim which prudence,
honour, and the true interest of the king, inseparable from that
of the nation, permits us to adopt."

The present Assembly was, however, incapable of accomplishing the necessary improvements; it should, therefore, be ruined in the opinion of the public and forced to dissolve. To this end, the Royalists should acquire influence over the minds of the people and over the future electoral assemblies, who must be persuaded themselves to demand the revision of certain articles of the Constitution, and — this was the chief thing — the meeting of the future Legislative Assembly in any other place rather than at Paris; for, he said, "no deliberative body, and I do not except the National Assembly, is to-day free beside the redoubtable power which has been given to the people."

The minds of the people must be won over, both at Paris and in the provinces; the Assembly must be controlled by a coalition of deputies from the Right and from the Left, of which Monsieur de Montmorin should be the accredited correspondent and Mirabeau the secret instigator. There must be a sure and united cabinet, both agreeable to the masses and devoted to the authority of the crown.

The king and queen must also win popularity.

"It is essential that no one be able to question their adhesion to all changes beneficial to the people and to all principles which may assure liberty; to show themselves often in public; to take the air, sometimes, even on foot, in the most frequented localities; to assist at the reviews of the National Guard; to appear in the president's tribune at some of the meetings of the Assembly; to visit the hospitals, public asylums, the large workshops, and distribute offerings there. Such acts, alike becoming to the queen and king, would undoubtedly prove of more advantage to them than close seclusion."

And Mirabeau terminated by the following urgent appeal and dramatic picture: —

"One may hope all things if this plan is carried out; and if it is not, — if this last chance of safety escapes us, — there is no calamity, from individual assassinations to pillage, from the fall of the throne to the dissolution of the kingdom, which one may not expect. Beyond this plan, what resource remains? Is not the ferocity of the people gradually increasing? Is not the resentment against the royal family constantly fanned by the malcontents? Do they not openly talk of a general massacre of the nobility and clergy? Is not a man banished for difference of opinion only? Are not the people led to hope for an equal division of property? Are not all the large cities of the kingdom in frightful tumult? Do not the National Guards take the lead in all popular acts of vengeance? Do not all administrators tremble for their own safety, without having the slightest power to provide for that of others? Finally, could folly and fanaticism be carried farther in the National Assembly? Unhappy nation! Behold where a few men, who have substituted intrigue for talent, and deeds for ideas, have brought you! O king good but weak, O unfortunate queen, behold the frightful abyss to which your wavering between blind confidence and exaggerated mistrust has led you! One effort still remains for both, but it is the last. If this is abandoned, if this fails, a funeral pall will cover the kingdom. What will be the sequel of her destiny? Where will the vessel drift, shattered by the thunder, beaten by the storm? I know not. But if I myself survive the public shipwreck, I will always say with pride, in my retreat, 'I exposed myself to ruin to save them all; they did not wish it.' "

Never had the powerful orator been clearer, more precise, or more sagacious. Never had he drawn a darker or a truer picture of the situation. Never had he more distinctly pointed out the remedy. Never had he drawn up a more elaborate plan, or one embracing more completely every part of the administration and of the kingdom. Never had he been more eloquent, more touching, or more touched. The queen, deeply impressed by this note, entered with ardour into the views of her counsellor. The king was more difficult to arouse; the dangers appeared to him exaggerated, and energetic action was antipathetic to his disposition. He ended, nevertheless, by accepting Mirabeau's plan, and the execution of it was begun. The queen, overcoming her personal dislike, consented to employ as intermediaries Montmorin and Talon, against whom she entertained a strong prejudice. With Talon she showed herself full of intelligence and tact, yet added to the charm which was natural to her a reserve which commanded the situation. With Montmorin she manifested more openness and confidence. The king organized, or rather let others organize, some of the governmental machinery recommended by Mirabeau: a bureau of police was founded to work upon public opinion; journalists were won over, and certain good effects were already felt. Paris appeared better disposed toward the king; the queen was less talked of. The provinces were for the most part still friendly; calumnies against Marie Antoinette were less current there, and her presence would have sufficed to win the confidence of the people. This had been evident at the federation. A weighty argument could be found in this.   La Marck set out for Metz to arrange with Monsieur de Bouillé the royal family's departure from Paris, which was the basis of the whole scheme of restoration.

The Royalists were then trying to do something; but it was still very little, and further efforts were necessary.   Besides, was not this plan of Mirabeau too vast and too complicated to succeed?   Even the august clients for whose salvation it had been contrived were not the least of the obstacles to its satisfactory and prompt execution.   The king, though he permitted others to act, remained inert, each day meditated on the life of Charles I., whose portrait hung in his room, but it was to learn to suffer and to die rather than to learn to resist.   When people talked to him of his own affairs and of his position, he acted, one of his most faithful servants sadly remarked, as if they spoke of things relative to the emperor of China.   The queen, more energetic and active, saw her energy paralyzed by her husband's inaction; she struggled without hope against her lamentable destiny.   "As woman, she is joined to an inert creature; as queen, she is seated upon a tottering throne," wrote La Marck.

She herself, moreover, ill-prepared for the struggle, did not unite with her strength of character experience of affairs or perseverance in her ideas.

"The queen," wrote La Marck on another occasion, "has certainly sufficient intelligence and resolution for great actions ; but I must confess that in matters of business, or even in conversation, she does not show that degree of attention and that logical sequence which are indispensable if one would learn thoroughly all that it is necessary to know in order to prevent errors and to assure success."

There was, however, one ground upon which Mirabeau and his friends would have with difficulty come to an understanding with the royal family; this was the question of religion, which the first judged by the principles of rational philosophy, and the second by the light of faith and delicate susceptibility of conscience, to which, in the case of Louis XVI., had been added, since the fatal sanction given to the civil Constitution, godly pangs of remorse.

As to the agents of this vast plan, could they be relied upon absolutely?   Montmorin was weak and without initiative; Talon and Sémonville, open to suspicion; several others, of an extremely uncertain fidelity. There remained La Marck and Mirabeau himself. La Marck was energetic, capable, and sincerely attached to the cause; but Mirabeau, despite his ardent protestations, did not give himself wholly up to it. His intimate friend, his correspondent, La Marck, himself makes this observation. With him the execution was often very different from the project and the reality from the promise. "He wished to reconcile an apparent desire to serve with inaction; to push others forward and himself hold back; to have the credit of success *without putting his popularity to too great a test.*" Hence his vacillation, his occasional inactivity, and his intermittent attacks of demagogy, which spoiled all.

It must be admitted, moreover, that his position was a singularly critical one. As Fersen wrote, "He had not so many resources for doing good as for doing evil." The very mystery in which he enveloped his conduct made it more difficult to uphold it. The secret, if guarded, exposed him to the ill-will of the Right; if discovered, or even suspected, it deprived him of all credit with the Left.

In any case, however, it was necessary, if Mirabeau's plan was to come to anything, that he who had conceived it should be there to execute it. It was necessary that the powerful man who had disposed all the batteries and held all the springs in his hand should continue to direct them. Whereas, at that very moment Mirabeau's days were numbered; his life, which he had so ill used, was about to slip from him at the hour when he would consecrate what remained of it to the defence, to the salvation, perhaps, of what he, more than any other, had helped to destroy. Toward the close, however, his attitude was honourable. On February 24 he asked that the municipality of Arnay le Duc be commanded to allow Mesdames to continue their journey, which had been illegally interrupted. On the 28th, he opposed with his most glowing eloquence the passage of a law against the refugees; and despite the ardour of the Left, he succeeded in obtaining its defeat. "If this law is passed," he exclaimed, "I swear that I will not obey it." And it was then, when he had been violently interrupted by the partisans of Lameth and their friends, that he gave utterance to that scornful cry, "Silence to the thirty voices!" In the evening he appeared again at the Jacobin Club to combat the chiefs of the Revolution, who were angered by his attacks and by what they called his defection. On March 23, in the debate on the regency, he sided with the supporters of true monarchical principles in advocating an hereditary regency.

This was the death-song of the swan. On March 27, 1791, Mirabeau was taken ill; on Saturday, April 2, he died, after having several times asked for his friend, the Comte de la Marck, the confidant of his last projects, and murmuring those words which have become famous: "I carry with me the ruin of the monarchy; after my death the malcontents will quarrel over the fragments."

Would he have saved this monarchy? The conditions under which he attached himself to it, and which we have described farther back, make us doubt it. Madame Elisabeth gave a less political reason for this doubt, but one more in accord with her rather narrow religious ideas. when she wrote on April 3 to Madame de Raigecourt, —

"Mirabeau has decided to go to the other world to see if the Revolution is approved of there. *Bon Dieu!* what an awakening will be his! Many regret his death; the aristocrats are very fearful of the consequences of it. During the last three months he had shown himself to be for the right cause; much was expected from his talents. For myself, although a thorough aristocrat, I cannot but regard his death as a stroke of Providence for this kingdom. I do not believe that it is through unprincipled and immoral men that God intends to save us."

Madame Elisabeth's thought was a true one under a mystic form; in troublous times, it is rare that those who shake the foundations are able later to fix them, — that those who have torn down know how to build up again. This is the logic and also the justice of revolutions.

CHAPTER VIII.

WHATEVER may have been the chances of success for Mirabeau's great plan, it was evident that it was to disappear with its author; the keystone of the arch having fallen, the whole edifice was crumbling. A few pygmies might dispute the inheritance of the giant; no one of them was powerful enough to succeed to it in its entirety.

Meanwhile, the situation was becoming daily more critical; riots were in a way ordinary occurrences. When a measure adopted by the Assembly, or when the administration displeased the Jacobins, the people, or rather the populace of Paris, rose and expressed their opinion after their own manner, by shouting, pillaging, and hanging. The Assembly was no freer than the royal family. The street was sovereign ruler; and it was by right of this that Malouet could with truth write that the Terror in France dated from July 14, 1789. The saying was still truer after the government and the king had been brought back to Paris by force. The list of popular movements, after Oct. 6, 1789, only, would be a long one to enumerate. We shall not attempt to do it, but shall limit ourselves to the most memorable riots.

On Sept. 2, 1790, at the news of the suppression of the revolt at Nancy by the General de Bouillé, forty thousand men rushed to the Tuileries and to the Assembly, vehemently demanding the dismissal of the monsters. For a moment it was

even feared that this mob might march to St. Cloud, where
the royal family then were, and repeat the scenes of Versailles.
On September 4, Necker, overcome with fear, had quitted the
cabinet and France.   Two months later, the hôtel of a member
of the Assembly, the Duc de Castries, was sacked, to punish
him for having wounded one of the popular heroes, Charles de
Lameth, in a fair duel.   On Jan. 27, 1791, a band of men
went to mob Clermont-Tonnerre, assaulted him in his own
house, and with the cowardly co-operation of Bailly, closed by
force the Impartial Club, of which he was president.   "We
have had no disturbance for a week," wrote Madame Elisabeth
to Madame de Raigecourt on February 5.   This unaccustomed
calm, however, did not last long.   Less than two weeks after,
the news of Mesdames's departure furnished fresh food for a
popular demonstration.   A deputation from the sections repaired to the Tuileries, and wished to force the king to forbid
his aunts to go away.   Louis XVI. refused.   Mesdames set out
on February 19.   The two princesses, arrested by the municipality of Arnay le Duc, were only able to continue their journey
through a decree of the Assembly, after an unseemly jest by
Menon, for whom the aunts of the monarch were no more than
two old women, so far had respect for authority and for the
royal family in less than two years disappeared, both from the
language and customs.

The report was circulated that this departure of Mesdames
was only a prelude; that the king, queen, and Monsieur would
soon follow Madame Adélaïde's and Madame Victoire's example.   Seven or eight hundred individuals, dregs of the
people, prostitutes of the Rue St. Honoré, and their supporters in crime, rushed in confusion to the Luxembourg, forced
Monsieur and Madame to go to the Tuileries, and did not leave
them until they had assured themselves that they had entered
the palace.   On the 24th, a confused mass of courtesans, of
emissaries from the Jacobins, and of men disguised as women
invaded the Tuileries gardens, and demanded, with loud
clamours, that the king order his aunts to return.   At the
injunction of the mob, the soldiers removed their bayonets, and
Bailly proposed that they open the doors and admit to the palace
some twenty of the delegates, desirous of seeing the dauphin,
who was said to have gone with Mesdames.   Fortunately the
guard was more resolute than the mayor; the crowd was ordered

to disperse, and at the first roll of the drum, it fled like a flock of birds.

On February 28, things were more serious. The Commune of Paris was at that moment having the château of Vincennes repaired. The rumour was circulated that the reparations were only an artifice to favour the escape of the king, who would go by an underground passage from the Tuileries to Vincennes, and from there to the frontier. Bands of workmen from the faubourgs, armed with pickaxes and pikes, started for Vincennes to demolish the prison. Lafayette and the National Guards followed, and succeeded in dispersing them. The news of this popular demonstration, however, had spread. A certain number of courtiers, fearing an attack on the Tuileries in the absence of the Parisian militia, gathered there. They numbered about three hundred; most of them carried weapons to defend the royal family, and if need be, to defend themselves; the purpose which had led them to the palace rendered this necessary. Once there, were some of the young men guilty of imprudent actions, as Madame Elisabeth seemed to think? Did they make a show of hostility, or did they give utterance to remarks which wounded the guards on duty? Or, as Hue claims, had brandy been served to the National Guards to excite them? All that is known positively is that a conflict broke out; and the report spread that the friends of the royal family were come to carry off the king and effect a counter-revolution. Lafayette, only just returned from Vincennes, hastened to the palace, addressed the courtiers, and wished to disarm them. They resisted; but the king, anxious to avoid a struggle at any price, himself besought his defenders to leave their arms in his cabinet, promising that they should be returned on the following day. The nobles obeyed; an hour after, the National Guards requested that the arms be carried to the house of the mayor-general, Monsieur de Gouvion; at the foot of the stairs they were stolen.

And the loyal servants of the king who had already suffered from this humiliating request, as they came out of the Tuileries at eight o'clock in the evening, were searched, hooted, maltreated; and several were taken to the Abbaye. Even old men like the Maréchal de Mailly were not spared insults and blows.

On the next day, Lafayette had a proclamation posted on the walls of the capital to notify the National Guards that he had given orders to the "chiefs of the domestic service" — it was by this name that he designated the gentlemen of the chamber — that they were to admit to the palace no more men, "of a justly suspected zeal," thus by these words confirming the false rumours of conspiracy, and authorizing, by his popular prestige, the absurd and fatal legend of the "chevaliers du poignard."

"It has been extremely quiet since that time," wrote Madame Elisabeth — who was always quick to reassure herself, or rather to reassure her friend — on March 2; "and I believe that the trouble is over, because the wrong-doers have obtained all that they desired, and we others, good-natured fools, do not see farther than the end of our noses, and fall headlong into every trap set for us."

The princess was mistaken; nothing was over. The affair of February 28 had aggravated the dissension between the Monarchists and the Constitutionalists, and had weakened the king's authority by just so much as it strengthened that of Lafayette. It was, however, on the whole, only an incident and an indication. A more serious question, upon which the king could not come to an understanding with the Assembly, was that of religion. Louis XVI. was strongly imbued with the tenets of Catholicism. He had, it is true, in a moment of weakness given his sanction to the civil Constitution of the clergy, and to decrees which exacted from the bishops and priests an oath at variance with their conscience; but the very remorse which he felt rendered his attachment to his creed the more steadfast from henceforth, and no human force could have constrained him to listen to the ministration of a priest who had taken the oath, and who in his eyes was the same as a schismatic. Marie Antoinette was no less firm. Montmorin and Mirabeau, who did not understand their scruples, in vain urged them to attend the ceremonies at which members of the constitutional clergy officiated, and to appear to propitiate the democratic sentiment by attending mass on Sunday in their parish church. Neither the king nor queen would consent; and the king flatly refused to admit into his chapel any ecclesiastics who had taken the oath.

Meanwhile Easter was approaching. Louis XVI., deprived of the exercise to which he was accustomed, and indisposed since the painful scenes of February 28, felt the need for breathing a purer air than that of Paris. He resolved to go to pass Holy Week at St. Cloud, where he would also be freer to perform his religious duties. The preparations were made with perfect openness. The mob-leaders, however, circulated the report that the journey announced concealed another; that it was not to St. Cloud, but to Metz that the king intended going, and that in any case he was impelled to this journey by scruples unworthy of a constitutional monarch. The enemies of Catholicism became every day more intolerant. On April 3, curates who had taken the oath were installed in every parish of Paris. The faithful, taking advantage of their privilege of non-attendance at offices, celebrated by schismatics, had rented the church of the Théatins for their services. When, however, they appeared there on Palm Sunday, April 17, a riotous mob molested them; the women were insulted, the young girls scourged, and in the evening the Club of the Cordeliers agreed to stir up a demonstration at the palace on the following day, in order to force the king to discharge the priests of his chapel, and receive the Easter sacrament at St. Germain l'Auxerrois. On the same day the National Guards had wished to prevent the royal almoners from saying mass at the Tuileries. In view of this agitation, the king, who wished to give no ostensible ground for the disturbances, had, it is stated, renounced his plan of departure; he returned to it again only at the entreaties of Lafayette and Bailly, who believed themselves competent to maintain order. The event soon proved to them that the members of the Club of the Cordeliers were the true masters of Paris.

In fact, on the following morning, the Monday before Easter, April 18, the mob rushed in a body to the Tuileries. When the king and queen appeared at eleven o'clock to step into their carriage, they were assailed with hostile cries. Nevertheless they took their seats in a berlin with their children, Madame Elisabeth, and Madame de Tourzel; but departure was impossible. The National Guards, in league with the rioters, barred the gates, surrounded the carriages, and addressed the king and queen in the most insulting language. "Down with the lackeys! Down with the horses!" they cried. "No one shall leave Paris until the Constitution is finished." Lafayette harangued his troops in vain; the troops refused to obey him. The king vainly remarked to Bailly, "It would be remarkable if, after giving liberty to the nation, I myself were not free."

For two hours the royal family sat in their carriages, exposed to the insults of the populace. For two hours Lafayette tried in vain to restore order among the agitators, and discipline among his troops. Neither commands, entreaties, nor threats were heard. The tumult grew from hour to hour; the mayor refused to proclaim martial law. The king's servants were maltreated; the grand almoner was aimed at; and Monsieur de Duras was struck with such violence that the dauphin began to cry. To avoid further excesses, the royal family were obliged to abandon the journey. The National Guards, satisfied with their victory, protested their devotion. "Do not be alarmed; we will defend you," the soldiers said to the queen, as they crowded around her. "Yes," the princess replied ironically, "we count upon you; but you will admit now that we are not free." Then, taking the dauphin in her arms, she proudly re-entered the Tuileries. In the evening the National Guards insisted again upon searching the apartments, even the king's chamber, the attics, the stables, on the ground that they might find refractory priests there; and at ten o'clock a man on the Carrousel read aloud a paper full of horrors against the king, exhorting the people to storm the palace, to throw everything out of the windows, and, above all, not to miss their opportunity as they had missed it at Versailles on October 6.

The next day, the king went to the Assembly and delivered a vigorous protest against the violence which had been done him. The president, Chabroud, gave as sole reply, "that a restless agitation was inseparable from the progress of liberty." As this agitation continued to increase, the king invited his first almoners, Monseigneur de Roquelaure and Monseigneur de Sabran, the priests of his chapel, the first gentlemen of the chamber, Monsieur de Duras and Monsieur de Villequier, to withdraw from his service; the queen addressed the same invitation to her first maid of honour, Madame de Chimay, and her lady of the palace, Madame de Duras; and on Easter Day, April 24, Louis XVI. and Marie Antoinette were forced to go to St. Germain l'Auxerrois, the parish church of the Tuileries, to assist at high mass chanted by the intruder who had replaced the venerable curé, dismissed for having refused to take the oath. Madame Elisabeth alone, although threatened with the most terrible outrages, was able to absent herself from this service, which so justly offended her conscience. This was undoubtedly what Chabroud meant by the progress of liberty.

The week was a sad one for the prisoners at the Tuileries; the mourning of the church during Holy Week accorded too well with the mourning in their own hearts for them to be unaffected by it.

"The loneliness of the Tuileries," Madame de Tourzel observes, "the sight of the king deprived of his first officers, and all of us on the eve of being forced to abandon him; the church services, which we attended regularly, and which offered such striking analogies to the situation; the tomb of Holy Thursday, a sort of cenotaph surrounded by cypresses and surmounted by a crown of thorns, so true an emblem of that which the king wore,—all contributed to intensify the deep sadness which overwhelmed us, and which we were forced to conceal within ourselves, that we might not communicate it to our poor little dauphin."

This treatment was more than the king could endure. The man had generously pardoned the outrages which his enemies had unceasingly heaped upon him; the king had abundantly sacrificed his authority; but at the violation of his conscience, the Christian rebelled. Louis XVI. resolved to leave this Paris which was for him only a prison.

For a long time the oldest servants of the monarchy, as well as his more recent counsellors, had looked upon the departure of the king as indispensable to the preservation of royalty. Even on the day following that on which the victorious rioters had carried him back to the capital, statesmen who were really worthy of the name had judged it impossible for him to remain there, because he did not have the necessary liberty. Projects of flight were constantly proposed. Despite the mystery in which the death of Monsieur de Favras has enveloped his plans, it is certain that their fundamental aim was the departure of the royal family, either voluntarily or by force. A little later, in March, 1790, a deputy from the nobility, the Comte d'Hinnisdal, had organized a complete scheme for abducting the king; the National Guards on duty had been won over, the men were at their post; relays had been stationed along the route; everything was ready; the consent of Louis XVI. alone was wanting. Monsieur Campan was delegated to sound the prince in the evening while he was playing whist with the queen and his family. The king at first turned a deaf ear to the proposition; then, pressed to give a definite answer, he replied, "Say to Monsieur d'Hinnisdal that I cannot consent to allow myself to be carried off." "You understand clearly,"

added the queen: "the king cannot consent to an abduction."
Did she hope that no account would be taken of this ambiguous
refusal, which might conceal a tacit acquiescence? The fact remains, according to Madame Campan, that she was occupied
until midnight in arranging her jewel-casket. No sound, however, came to break the silence of the night. Monsieur
d'Hinnisdal, displeased by the king's equivocal response, and
unwilling to act without the positive consent of those for whom
he was compromising himself, had abandoned the enterprise.

If departure from Paris was difficult, it was more practicable
from St. Cloud, where the royal family passed the summer
of 1790. The king was there without guards, accompanied
only by one aid-de-camp, belonging to Lafayette; the queen also
had only one man-servant with her. Often they both went out
early and returned late, and no one concerned himself about
them. It was still possible to travel in France unmolested; it
was easy to leave St. Cloud and thence to reach a safe
province. Madame Campan states that a plan of escape was at
that time sketched out; the king was to proceed alone to some
woods four leagues distant from the château, where the royal
family should rejoin him. On the other hand, Madame de
Tourzel relates — and this seems to refer to the same affair —
that Monsieur de la Tour du Pin, minister of war, besought the
king to take advantage of his sojourn in the country to escape,
promising to station loyal troops to guard the route, and declaring — the future justified his statement only too well — that if
this opportunity was lost, another would not be found. The
truest servants of the monarch, the royal family themselves,
eagerly desired him to accept the proposition. Madame Elisabeth hoped for it; she thought she saw from certain indications
that, to give her own enigmatical language, "recovery was
nearing." For a moment, in fact, after the debate on the events
of October, they believed that the king, who was incensed by
the resolutions adopted by the Assembly, would yield to Monsieur de la Tour du Pin's counsels.

If the Comte Esterhazy is to be believed, Louis XVI. one
day gained the heights of St. Cloud and went out by a gate
in the park which was fastened, and which he ordered his
attendant to break open. He was accompanied by the Duc de
Brissac, Messieurs de la Suze, de Tourzel, and Esterhazy.
They descended by the plain close to Rueil; and after hav-

ing passed the bridge of Chatou, they entered the forest of
the Vesinet.   There the king turned to the right and started
his horse along the road to Maisons.   The queen, on her side,
had driven out with Madame Elisabeth and her son.   Everything pointed to the supposition that they would push farther on
their way; they would have found a boat to traverse the Seine,
and on the other side, carriages to proceed to Chantilly, where
the horses of the Prince de Condé, still in the stables, would have
served as relays to carry them to the army.   Suddenly the king
stopped, and they returned to St. Cloud.   Their hopes were
once more deceived.   The Comte Esterhazy could not, on his
arrival at the château, restrain himself from expressing his disappointment to the queen, and dwelt on the pressing necessity
of escaping the vigilance of the jailers.   The queen replied
that she thought as he, — she had already made the same statement to Madame Campan.   But she despaired of obtaining the
king's consent before it would be too late; as for herself, she
was determined never to leave her husband, and to follow the
fate which destiny had prepared for her.

At that moment, however, negotiations with Mirabeau were
in full progress; and Mirabeau's plan depended above all on
departure from Paris.   Only — and it was in this that the able
orator differed in opinion from La Tour du Pin and Esterhazy
— Mirabeau did not approve of flight.   "A king, who is the
sole safeguard of his people," he said, "does not fly from
them; he does not put himself in a position where he cannot
return to the heart of his States except armed, or where he is
reduced to beg for foreign succour."   And he wrote to La
Marck, "A king withdraws in open day only when it is for
the purpose of remaining king."   This was his conviction even
on the day following the events of October.   He wished the
royal family to retire to Rouen, where, being in the heart of
Normandy, a faithful province, near Brittany and Anjou, which
were no less so, it would be easy to surround themselves with
trustworthy troops.   The succeeding year it was to Fontainebleau that he asked to transfer them, but always openly, after
an official notification to the Assembly, and under the protection of the National Guards, to whom would be added a regiment of infantry, the Royal Comtois, then stationed at Orléans,
and imbued with an excellent spirit, and two hundred cavaliers
from the regiment of Lorraine, which should come from Ram-

bouillet. Later, when the revolutionary sentiment had made further advance, it was no longer a question of Fontainebleau, which was an undefended town at the mercy of a *coup-de-main*, but of some fortified city nearer the frontier, like Compiègne or Beauvais, whence they could proceed still farther under the protection of Monsieur de Bouillé's army. The great obstacle to the execution of the plan, however, was the king's indecision. Louis XVI. manifested the same aversion to departure presented under any form which he had so unfortunately shown during the inauspicious days of October; and without positively refusing, he brought to bear the most fatal of all opposition,— the force of inertia. The queen was more resolute in the matter. "We must in the end resort to flight," she said one day to Madame Campan. Madame Elisabeth was even firmer, but she was seldom called into council; and her letters to her friends are full of lamentations over her brother's inaction. After so many alternations of hope and deceptions, she wrote on October 24, soon after the abortive attempt recorded by the Comte Esterhazy, to Madame de Raigecourt, in the figurative style which she used in her correspondence : "I have seen the man who is so handsome; he is somewhat in despair. My patient still suffers from numbness in the legs, and he fears that it may affect the joints so seriously as to render a cure impossible."

The queen carried on negotiations in various directions, despatched courier after courier, and letter after letter, to her brother and to Monsieur de Mercy, asked advice, aid, money. The king held aloof, as if he had no interest in his wife's schemes or in his sister's hopes. At the end of October, 1790, however, he determined to enter into correspondence with the general in command at Metz, the Marquis de Bouillé. Mirabeau had himself mentioned him; his services and his talents recommended him still more. The Marquis de Bouillé, formerly famous for his brilliant exploits in the Antilles during the war in America, more recently for the energy with which he had suppressed the insurrection at Nancy, highly esteemed by the army, loved even by the National Guards, a true Royalist, and yet extremely popular, possessing great strength of character and admirable moderation in his views, even inclining, it was said, to a constitution modelled on that of England,— such was the man designed to be the supreme defender of royalty in its extremity. He was in command at Metz; and this situation, in placing under his orders all the strongholds along the frontier, permitted him to assure the royal family of a refuge there. He himself had already thought out a plan of departure for the king, for this was the vital question which justly occupied the minds of all the Royalists, as the essential basis of any restoration of the monarchy. He was not, therefore, in the least surprised, when at the end of October, 1790, the bishop of Pamiers, Monseigneur d'Agoût, came to make known to him the king's project. The king's plan, however, differed intrinsically from that of the general.

Monsieur de Bouillé, like Mirabeau, advocated an open departure, upon the demand of the departments and of the troops, to which he thought the Assembly would offer no opposition. Louis XVI., influenced by his natural weakness, which made him regard with horror any energetic measure, preferred flight. Moreover, the details of his plan were as yet unsettled, and its execution was not to take place before the spring. The general made some objections; they gave way before the royal will, and nothing remained but to name the town which seemed to offer the safest refuge. After an extensive interchange of letters, the king decided upon Montmédy. The date of departure was fixed for the end of March.

Affairs had reached this point, and Monsieur de Bouillé, although regretting Louis XVI.'s resolution, was preparing to carry it out, when in the month of February he received the Comte de la Marck's visit. The prince had finally determined to accept Mirabeau's plan, and Monsieur de la Marck was come to confide the details of it to the commander of the army at Metz.

The king would leave Paris in broad daylight and go to Compiègne, where Monsieur de Bouillé should meet him and surround him with loyal troops, either to remain with him there, or to proceed farther if circumstances rendered it necessary. Once at liberty, he would issue a proclamation to the country, and no one doubted but that the general discontent coming to the aid of the sovereign's protest would force the Assembly to modify the Constitution, or enable the king to convoke, outside of Paris, a new Legislature, which would effect the reforms demanded by the public, and would restore to the royalty the lawful exercise of its authority. Mirabeau believed that he could count upon thirty-six departments; Monsieur de Bouillé upon six, and besides, the majority of the departmental administrations were royalistic. Monsieur de Bouillé approved of the plan, which he found much wiser than the withdrawal to Montmédy, and begged Louis XVI. to follow out the execution of it, while continuing to employ his adroit and able counsellor. Unhappily Mirabeau died, and the king relapsed again into his vacillating mood.

Moreover, the situation became every instant more serious. If it was possible at the beginning of February to go out of Paris in broad daylight, was it possible, two weeks later, after the adventure of Mesdames? If the aunts of the king had had so much difficulty in passing, would the king himself be allowed to pass? Was not the riot which had forced Monsieur to come to the Tuileries to spend the night a sign of what the Parisian populace could and would do? Two months later every illusion on this subject, if any still remained, was dispelled; the National Guards, who, despite Lafayette and Bailly, refused to allow the royal family to go even to St. Cloud, would allow them still less to go to Compiègne. The impossibility of a public departure was manifest, and this attack on his liberty, which irrevocably determined the king to leave Paris, left him nothing but the chances of flight.

The original project proposed by Louis XVI., the flight to Montmédy, was again adopted. On April 20, the queen wrote to Mercy: "The event which has just occurred strengthens us more than ever in our designs. The guard which surrounds us is what threatens us the most. Our very life is not safe. . . . Our position is horrible; we must absolutely have done with it by next month. The king desires it even more than I."

This letter and those which follow reveal the plan of the royal family: until departure was possible, Louis XVI. should resort to absolute passivity, should accept without resistance the laws, which his lack of liberty would later stamp as null, and while waiting, he should make every effort to procure resources and win for himself supporters.

It was necessary to secure fifteen millions; they hoped to find them in Holland. Spain and Sardinia could, by the manipulation of troops on the frontier, exercise a moral pressure which would assist the outbreak of discontent in the provinces.

Prussia and Austria, if they succeeded in coming to an agreement, would take up the claims of the princes who possessed Alsatia, and would protest, "not," remarked the queen, in making herself the mouthpiece of Mirabeau's thought, "in order to stir up a counter-revolution, or to create strife, but as guarantees of all treaties, of Alsatia and of Lorraine, and because they judge as most reprehensible the manner in which France treats her king." If Prussia, whose conduct was extremely suspicious, and whose agent, the Jew Ephraim, furnished gold to the Revolutionists, if England, whose neutrality the Royalists sought with little success to obtain, if Holland showed herself hostile to the restoration of order in France, — the powers of the North, Russia and Sweden, would act as a counter-force and intimidate them. In the mean while, the demonstrations which Austria was to make in the Netherlands would permit Monsieur de Bouillé to concentrate troops and provisions in Montmédy.

Unhappily, the more the royal family delayed, the greater became the difficulties. The disposition of the troops, which was still friendly at the close of 1790, had since the beginning of 1791 been terribly corrupted, especially since Portail — a creature of the Lameth faction — had replaced the loyal La Tour du Pin as minister of war. At his request the Assembly had authorized the soldiers to go to the clubs; and their constant attendance there, so deplorable in its results, was not long in demoralizing the discipline. At the opening of May, Monsieur de Bouillé could count on six or eight battalions only, either German or Swiss, and some thirty squadrons of cavalry; almost all the infantry and artillery had gone over to the Revolutionists.

The spirit of the civil population had undergone the same modifications as that of the army. The threats of the refugees, the rumours of intrigues among the aristocrats, of treachery among the officers, which had been adroitly circulated and perfidiously employed to advantage, had both frightened and exasperated the inhabitants along the frontier, and had aroused their resentment against the king, whom they supposed in league with the French refugees. A struggle was therefore possible; and in anticipation of this, Louis XVI. had solicited aid from the Swiss Cantons, whose cause was bound to that of France by the Secular Capitulations, and he had also demanded for the first moment, if needful, a body of eight or ten thousand Austrians. Not that he desired the direct intervention of foreign powers in the affairs of the country, — the queen had distinctly repudiated this in her letter of June 12, 1790, to Monsieur de Mercy, — he only asked their moral support; or if he was forced to call upon the ten thousand men belonging to his brother-in-law, he accepted them only as auxiliaries, meaning to make them march by the side of the French troops, under the royal standard, as Henri IV., who had likewise been obliged to reconquer his kingdom, had had under his orders soldiers belonging to Elisabeth, and *reitres* from Schonberg, and as frequently still German or Swiss regiments served in the French army by the side of the national militia. Louis XVI. would, moreover, only resort to this measure as a last extremity; he still hoped to avoid a struggle, although Mirabeau, before dying, had proclaimed more loudly than ever its near approach and its necessity.

It was most important, however, to pacify public opinion, and to do this, the enterprises of the refugees must be arrested. This was the object toward which all the queen's efforts tended; her instructions to her agents, her correspondence with her brother and with Mercy, are full of the most urgent entreaties that the emperor oppose by his counsels, or if need be, by the force of his authority, the imprudent proceedings of the Comte d'Artois. "Our safety and our glory," she wrote, "depend upon our withdrawal from here; I do not wish to leave the merit of it exclusively to others."

After their departure from Paris, what was to be done? Marie Antoinette's letters, the correspondence of the Marquis and Marquise de Bombelles, the recently published Memoirs of Madame de Tourzel, even the disclosures of Louis XVI., enable us to reconstruct the plans. The king, arrived at Montmédy, in a French town, surrounded by Monsieur de Bouillé's troops, would summon to him all faithful subjects; he would command the refugees to return to France; and supported by these forces, to which could be added, if need be, the ten thousand men of his brother-in-law, aided still more by the reaction which could not fail to take place in the provinces so soon as they knew the sovereign at liberty and could find in him a centre of action and a support, he would address a manifesto to the country. He would protest loudly against the proceedings of the Assembly, who in the most vital matters had exceeded the instructions of their constituents; he would declare null, "because of absolute lack of liberty," all the acts which had been extorted from him since Oct. 6, 1789; and he would announce that he would not re-enter Paris until the government should be re-established on a firm footing, and that, through its decrees, the property and estate of every citizen should be left unmolested; that the laws should not be infringed without punishment, and that finally liberty should be planted on a fixed and immovable foundation.

Would this Constitution have been a return to the old *régime?* Assuredly not; the very word "constitution" excluded such a thought. Louis XVI. had never — the fact is so self-evident that the statement of it is trite — Louis XVI. had never coveted absolute power, and in 1791 he coveted it less than ever. The Marquise de Bombelles, who must have been thoroughly acquainted with the intentions of the royal family, since her husband and the Baron de Breteuil were the accredited agents of the court abroad, wrote on July 13, —

"The king wished to return to the declaration of June 23, in which he fulfilled the wish which the nation had expressed through its delegates at the meeting of the States-General; he limited his power, but at the same time he rendered it secure, and reassured the minds of the people; for despotism can never again exist in France, and (one must be just) *it is not desirable that it should.* The king, therefore, did not wish to conquer his kingdom with the aid of foreign forces; he wished to overawe his subjects and treat with them."

To meet all debts and dispel the idea of impending bankruptcy, he would have guaranteed the payment in full of contingent annuities, reduced stock-jobbing and burdensome loans to a reasonable rate (of interest), and in restoring to the clergy their property, would have forced them to reimburse the assignats. This was possible, Fersen declared; and the property of the clergy, realized by the king as he proposed, would have brought about results which could not be effected by the confiscation decreed by the Assembly. Thus capitalists, who had done all for the Revolution, and whose interests were at that moment threatened by the Revolution, would have been reassured, and would have declared themselves in favour of a return of royal authority, which they dreaded much less than bankruptcy. Was this sufficient? It is doubtful.

It is worthy of remark, nevertheless, that after the defeat of Varennes, and when people found themselves face to face with the imperfect Constitution which the Assembly had substituted for the king's propositions, many of those even who had applauded the arrest of Louis XVI., who had perhaps abetted it, began to regret — this is affirmed by an unprejudiced witness — that which was known as the *plan of Montmédy;* for, it was said, it promised France a constitution equally distant from the two extremes.

The queen shared her husband's opinion. She had at the beginning of 1790 declared that she had no wish for a "counter-revolution;" she had repeated it on June 12 ; and on Feb. 3, 1791, she wrote again to Mercy, "We have determined to adopt as the basis of the Constitution the declaration of June 23, with such modifications as circumstances and events may render expedient."

What would these modifications have been? We cannot say; but it is certain that Marie Antoinette, like Louis XVI., was decided to satisfy the demands of the *cahiers* of 1789, and to allow France at last to enjoy a just and wholesome liberty, "such," she said, " as the king had always himself desired for the happiness of his people, free from license and anarchy, which would precipitate the most prosperous kingdom into every possible misfortune."

The queen, while awaiting the accomplishment of this plan, was watched more closely than ever. If a compatriot, a friend of her childhood, or an envoy from her brother — as the Prince de Lichtenstein — came to visit her in her prison of the Tuileries, she was obliged to dismiss him immediately, and charge him to tell no one that he had seen her alone.

"Although I have seen him — the Prince de Lichtenstein — only once in my apartments, and for ten minutes only," she wrote to her brother Leopold, "I feel that every Austrian of distinction owes it to me not to be here at this time." And she added sadly, "Our health continues good, and it would be still better if we could only perceive one ray of happiness round us ; for us, it is forever at an end, whatever may happen. *I know that it is the duty of a king to suffer for others ; but then let us do it creditably.*"

CHAPTER IX.

AT the beginning of June, 1791, all preparations for the
departure had been made. Of the two routes between
Paris and Montmédy, Louis XVI. had preferred that which
went by way of Varennes, notwithstanding the inconvenience
which Monsieur de Bouillé pointed out in connection with it;
but the other passed through Rheims, the coronation city, and
the king feared that he might be recognized there. A body of
troops was to be stationed at Montmédy, and detachments placed
along the route starting from Châlons, to assure unobstructed
passage from it; the Austrian battalions were to have taken up
their post at Arlon on June 12. A million in assignats had
been forwarded by Fersen, addressed to the Comte de Contades.
The queen had ordered an outfit of linen for herself and her
children sent to Arras, and her travelling-case to Brussels; the
barber Leonard was to carry away her diamonds. The departure, at first fixed for the end of May, had, despite the entreaties
of Monsieur de Bouillé, who begged them not to delay longer
than June 1, been postponed until June 12, then until the 15th,
then until the 19th, and finally until the 20th, because of one
of the dauphin's waiting-maids, who was justly suspected, and
who was not to leave his service until the morning of the 19th.
This last delay, only decided upon on the 13th, was fatal; for it
was in large part the cause of the failure of the plan.

"There are only two persons in the secret, — Monsieur de
Bouillé and Monsieur de Breteuil," the queen wrote to her
brother on May 22, 1791, — "and a third person who has been
charged with the preparations for the departure."

This third person was a Swede, whom we have already encountered in this history, the Comte Axel de Fersen. Possessing a heart full of warmth, and great nobility of character, he

had in the hour of adversity felt his devotion wax doubly strong for this royal family, who had welcomed him in the days of their prosperity.

"I am attached to the king and queen," he wrote to his father in February, 1791, " and I owe it to them in return for the great kindness with which they have always treated me when it has been in their power ; and I would be base and ungrateful .if I abandoned them when they can do no more for me, and when I have the hope of being useful to them. To all the bounties which they have continually heaped upon me, they have just added another flattering distinction, — that of confidence ; this is all the more flattering as it is limited and centred in three or four persons, of whom I am the youngest."

Louis XVI. and Marie Antoinette had realized that there was in the young man an unfaltering devotion upon which they could count, a disinterested and pure attachment which would ask no return.   Disgusted with the services of hirelings, with the counsels of the ambitious, with enthusiasts and with incompetent men, they opened their hearts to Fersen in perfect confidence; and if they could have desired as counsellor a more adroit politician and a shrewder diplomat, more open to modern ideas, they could not have found a more chivalric and trustworthy servant.   At the beginning of 1791 Fersen had become their acknowledged confidant, the guardian of their thoughts, and the agent of their correspondence.   He wrote their letters in cipher and sent them; he received and deciphered the despatches addressed to the royal family; he transmitted their instructions to the Baron de Breteuil and the Marquis de Bouillé, — the first, the diplomatic agent, the second, the military agent, in the project of flight.

It was Monsieur de Fersen who took charge of the preparations for the departure from Paris.   He solicited and obtained, through the intervention of the Russian minister, Monsieur de Simolin, a passport for a great Russian lady, — the Baroness de Korff; he superintended, at the shop of the carriage-maker Louis, the construction of the roomy berlin which was designed to shelter the entire royal family.   This berlin, which would surely arouse suspicion by reason of its size, had alarmed Monsieur de Bouillé's prudence; he made certain remonstrances through his son Louis, and proposed that they substitute two lighter carriages for the large single one, — one to contain the king, Madame Elisabeth, and Madame Royale; the other the queen and the dauphin; but the queen refused to be separated from her husband, and replied that if their friends wished to save them, it must be all together or not at all. Monsieur de Bouillé had also requested that they take with them the Marquis d'Agoût, former major of the body-guards, a man of brains and of heart, whose co-operation would have been valuable in case of accident or hindrance. The king had thought of Monsieur de Saint-Priest; the Chevalier de Coigny had proposed a commander of the *gendarmerie*, a retired post-master, Monsieur Priol, who was sincerely attached to the royal family, and who knew all the roads throughout the kingdom. At the last moment they took no one, either from scruple of etiquette or to avoid admitting other confidants into the secret. The king would not even — and it was deeply to be regretted — allow Fersen, who was thoroughly acquainted with all the details of the project, to accompany him.

Be that as it may, after all these discussions and vacillation, the plan was definitely settled on June 13. The king, the queen, their children, Madame Elisabeth, Madame de Tourzel, and two waiting-women (Madame de Neuville and Madame Brunier) should set out during the night of the 20th and 21st, — the first six in the famous berlin, the other two in a cabriolet, which should precede the berlin. In the absence of Monsieur d'Agoût, three body-guards — Monsieur de Valori, Monsieur de Moustier, and Monsieur de Maldent — were to accompany the carriage in the capacity and costume of couriers, two upon the box and one galloping ahead. From Pont-Sommevesle to Montmédy, guards should be ranged at every relay station, to escort the travellers, and if need be, to protect them. Fersen would have preferred to do away with these detachments, or at least to station them only after Varennes.

"No precautions are necessary from here to Châlons," he wrote to Monsieur de Bouillé; "the wisest of all would be to take none. All depends upon despatch and secrecy; and if you are not very sure of your detachments, it would be better not to station any, or at least to station them only from Varennes, in order not to excite remark in the country. The king should pass in all simplicity."

Circumstances showed that Fersen's view was a just one. Monsieur de Bouillé himself had urged as objection, so he

said, "the great disadvantage which would result from station-
ing a chain of guards along the route." But the king unfortunately desired it; and it is very certain that the superabundance
of precautions, this show of etiquette, this anxiety to preserve
in flight a remnant of royal grandeur and princely comfort, did
much to injure the success of the enterprise. Such extensive
preparations could not be made without awakening mistrust,
which had been continually on the alert since the departure of
Mesdames. "All would be lost if the least suspicion of the
project should be aroused," wrote the far-seeing Fersen to the
Baron de Breteuil. Nevertheless, indiscretions, imprudent
acts, and denunciations held public opinion in suspense. Rumours of attempts at flight on the part of the king were in the
air. They were spoken of in the papers, talked about among
the people, and discussed in the meetings of the committees.
The preparations had been too long and too elaborate to be entirely hidden; those who had been employed in making them
had not always been discreet. On May 21, the woman of the
wardrobe, who had been suspected with cause, and whose services the queen had unwisely continued to accept, had given information of a plan of departure. If the Marquis de Raigecourt
can be believed, Monsieur de Bouillé's followers showed a want
of reserve, and the general, "prudent and reticent as he was,
sometimes forgot himself." The circle of refugees whom the
queen had so often and so wisely recommended to refrain from
interference, were informed, if not of the whole plan, at least
of the intention of an approaching departure. At London it
had been spoken of openly at the house of Lord Randon, before
the Prince of Wales, who was the intimate friend of the Duc
d'Orléans. At Brussels it was gossiped about in Monsieur
de la Quenille's drawing-room, upon a word from Monsieur,
who had urged Madame de Balbi to remain in Belgium instead
of returning to France. At Paris one of the body-guards,
Monsieur de Maldent, had the imprudence to confess it to his
mistress, and she had nothing better to do than to recount it to
her sister and her servant. The attention of the public was so
aroused that, on June 11, Lafayette wished to double the sentinels and examine all the carriages at the palace.

All this, however, it must be said, did not go beyond a vague
uneasiness. People had their suspicions, because such a desire
on the part of the king was too natural for a project of depar-

ture not to be in the expected order of things; but no one knew anything definite.

The appointed day at last dawned. Everything proceeded at the palace as usual. The dauphin went out to his garden at half-past ten. At eleven o'clock the queen repaired to the chapel with her attendants; she ordered her carriage for five in the afternoon to take her children for a drive. Meanwhile, Madame Elisabeth had been to Bellevue; she returned at one. At half-past one the family dinner took place. During the day Fersen came, conferred with the king and queen respecting the final preparations, and determined upon the course of action in case of arrest. "Monsieur de Fersen," the king said to him, "whatever may happen, I shall not forget what you have done for me." The queen wept copiously; at the approach of danger, her heart, although it did not fail her, softened. At six o'clock, Fersen went away, and Marie Antoinette, following the order given in the morning, drove out with her children to Monsieur de Boutin's garden at Tivoli, where the children had a luncheon. During this time she tried to prepare her daughter's mind for the events about to take place. On returning from the drive, about six or seven o'clock, the dauphin was taken to his governess, then to his own apartment, and ate his evening meal, served by his valet, Cléry, who did not leave him until nine o'clock, when he was in bed. Madame Royale retired at ten, according to her usual habit.

The queen had her hair dressed, and afterward went to the drawing-room, where she found Monsieur, who remained with her until nine. At that hour the king, queen, and Madame Elisabeth passed into the dining-room. Everything was done with the habitual ceremony, and at about ten the royal family withdrew to their apartments. The undressing of the queen took but little time; when she was in bed, the doors of the corridor were closed, and the orders for the following morning were given, as usual, to the *valet-de-chambre* and the officer on duty. The undressing of the king was accomplished with the usual formality. Lafayette and Bailly assisted at it, and conversed with the king for a while. Despite the secrecy which the august travellers had observed toward their most faithful attendants, and even toward the members of the royal family, — Madame Elisabeth was notified only at noon of the very day, and Madame Brunier and Madame de Neuville at bedtime only,

—vague rumours had been whispered about; for several days the surveillance had been more lively. The number of guards had been increased; in the after-dinner watch on the 20th, it had even been tripled; and in the evening a grenadier slept across Madame Elisabeth's door. For some time, however, the king had adopted measures to ascertain the facilities of exit from the palace. In the month of January, secret communications between the various apartments of the royal family had been arranged, and doors cut in the wainscoting with such cunning skill that it was impossible to discover them. Besides, the king had, for two weeks before, taken the precaution to order the Chevalier de Coigny, whose figure resembled his, to leave the palace by the main gate. At about a quarter or half past ten, the queen rose, went to the dauphin's chamber, and led him with his sister down to the *entresol.* Madame Brunier and Madame de Neuville dressed the children. Madame Royale wore a reddish-brown calico, figured with blue and white flowers; the dauphin, a little girl's dress. "He was lovely," Madame Royale relates: "he was so heavy with sleep that he did not know what he was doing. I asked him what he thought we were going to do; he replied that he thought that we were going to act in a play, since we were in costume." They passed into the queen's cabinet, then from there, by the secret passages of which we have spoken, into the Duc de Villequier's unoccupied apartment, whence they reached an unguarded door opening into the Cour des Princes. It was a quarter past eleven.

A carriage had been waiting for an hour in the court; Monsieur de Fersen, after having in the evening attended to the final details of the departure, had disguised himself as a coachman, in order to drive in person the august fugitives at the outset of their journey. The queen herself brought the children and Madame de Tourzel and placed them in the carriage; Monsieur de Fersen then started, drove several times up and down the quay, to baffle the guard, then returned and drew up near the smaller Carrousel. Lafayette passed several times, but noticed nothing. At the end of half an hour according to Monsieur de Fersen, of three quarters of an hour according to Madame Royale, who found the time long during her anxious waiting, Madame Elisabeth arrived, escorted by a boy belonging to her suite; then near midnight the king, and finally the queen. She had wished to be the last to leave; and having perceived Lafayette's carriage, she had, in her fear of being recognized, turned into the labyrinth of lanes which surrounded the Tuileries, and had for a time lost herself there, with the body-guard who accompanied her. As soon as she had taken her place in the carriage, the king, who had felt great uneasiness at this delay, embraced her tenderly, repeating several times, "How glad I am to see you here!" The queen was in a morning dress, with a hat and a short black cloak; the king wore a round hat, a wig, a brown frock-coat, and carried a stick in his hand. Madame de Tourzel was to play the part of the Baroness de Korff; the queen was the children's governess, and was called Madame Rochet; the king, the *valet-de-chambre*, Durand; Madame Elisabeth, the lady's companion, Rosalie; the dauphin and Madame Royale, the two children of Madame de Korff, under the names of Amélie and Aglae.

At the barrier of St. Martin, they met the berlin, which had been brought there by Monsieur de Moustier and Monsieur de Fersen's coachman, Balthazar Sapel. The two carriages were placed side by side, that the royal family might go from one to the other without stepping to the ground. Fersen climbed to the box by the side of Monsieur de Moustier. "Now quick; drive fast!" he said to his coachman, who drove mounted on one of the horses. They started, and the four horses, vigorously spurred on, arrived at Bondy in half an hour. Here Monsieur de Valori had ordered a relay of six horses to be ready; they were hastily harnessed. Fersen took leave of the travellers, calling out to them, "Adieu, Madame de Korff!" which was designed to deceive the postilions; and the carriage, preceded by the body-guards as couriers, drove off along the road to Clay, where they met Madame de Neuville and Madame Brunier. During this time Fersen rode back to Paris, taking the cross-roads, and on the same day left for Belgium. At six o'clock on the morning of the 22d, he arrived at Mons; and on the following day, at Arlon, he learned from Monsieur de Bouillé's lips the sad result of the flight.

The royal family remained alone, left to their own counsel, and with no other guides than those three young men, who were undoubtedly sincerely attached to them, but who were without authority and without experience. Valuable time had been lost in quitting Paris; still more was lost at various stages along the journey; and unfortunately no one realized the necessity of making it up.

"When we had passed the barrier," Madame de Tourzel relates, "the king, encouraged to augur well for his journey, began to talk of his projects. First, he would go to Montmédy to decide upon the most suitable policy; he was firmly resolved not to go out of the kingdom unless circumstances rendered it necessary for him to pass through some town on the frontier, that he might arrive more quickly at that of France where he wished to fix his residence, for he was unwilling to remain even for an instant in a foreign land."

"Here I am," the good prince exclaimed, "outside of that city of Paris where such bitter humiliations have been heaped upon me. Be assured that I shall be very different from what you have seen me. Lafayette," he added, in looking at his watch, "is at this moment sadly troubled in his mind."

The august fugitives, overjoyed at feeling themselves free, grew careless about the smaller precautions, a strict observance of which was indispensable, and to which Fersen or D'Agoût would have unfailingly recalled them. The nights are short at that season of the year; and owing to the delays at the outset, the journey from Paris to Châlons, which should have been made in the darkness, or at least during the early morning, was made in broad daylight. The king, without anxiety alighted at the relay stations, and at the risk of being recognized, talked with the people, peasants or post employees, who surrounded the carriage. He barely escaped recognition at Etoges. At Châlons he was recognized. A man notified the mayor, who, being little of a Revolutionist, saw fit to reply to the informer that if he was perfectly sure of his discovery, he had only to make it generally known, but that he would be held responsible for the consequences. The man, frightened, said nothing; and if Madame Royale and Monsieur de Bouillé are to be believed, "many praised God to see the king, and said prayers for his flight."

After Châlons they entered Monsieur de Bouillé's military command, and were to meet at every relay escorts disposed in *échelons* by the general, nominally for the purpose of protecting a convoy of money addressed to his troops. The first detachment was at Pont-Sommevesle, under the command of the Duc de Choiseul, accompanied by Monsieur de Goguelat.

But the delays occasioned at the departure, and increased still more by the slowness of the journeying, foiled the plan agreed upon; the royal carriage was expected at three o'clock; at half-past five it had not arrived, nor had the couriers which preceded it. The prolonged halt of the troops in this place, where there seemed to be no reason for their presence, awakened apprehension among the inhabitants. Monsieur de Choiseul, alarmed by the hostile attitude of the crowd, gave the order to withdraw. When the august travellers finally arrived at Pont-Sommevesle, the troops had been gone for an hour. The king was surprised, but continued his journey notwithstanding; he hoped to meet the promised escort at the next halting-place. At Orbeval, there was nothing. "The same silence, the same uneasiness," Madame de Tourzel writes. At Ste. Menehould, they found thirty dragoons under the command of Monsieur d'Andoins, but also a nervous population in great excitement over the presence of the troops. Monsieur d'Andoins, approaching the berlin, said in a low tone to the false Baroness de Korff, "The plans have been badly carried out; I withdraw, in order not to arouse the least suspicion." "These few words," Madame de Tourzel adds, "pierced us to the heart; there was, however, nothing to do but to continue our journey, and we did not allow ourselves to give way to the slightest hesitation." Mistrust had been awakened; the postmaster Drouet had thought that he recognized the queen, whom he had seen while serving in the dragoons of Condé. His suspicions were confirmed when he compared the face of the supposed *valet-de-chambre* with the portrait of the king engraved upon an assignat. Proud of his discovery, and of the importance which it gave him, he hastened to notify the municipality, who ordered him and a former dragoon of the queen, named Guillaume, to run after the carriages and stop them, if they could overtake them. In the mean time, to facilitate his enterprise, he had recommended the postilions not to hurry too fast.

The royal family, however, who had not perceived the commotion, pursued their journey with the same feeling of security, and alas! with the same slowness. The delay at the outset continued and increased at every halt. At Clermont, as at Ste. Menehould, they arrived four or five hours after the appointed time. Monsieur de Damas, chief of the detachment, became anxious, the population agitated, and the fidelity of the dra-

goons singularly shaken by contact with the inhabitants. The
change of horses was, nevertheless, accomplished without hindrance; but when Monsieur de Damas commanded the troops
to move on, the National Guards protested, and the dragoons
refused to mount their horses.

Drouet and Guillaume had galloped off at full speed. Having
learned from the postilion of Ste. Menehould that the royal
family had gone in the direction of Varennes, they struck out
through the cross-roads to arrive before them. They did, in fact,
arrive first, found, despite the lateness of the hour, a few young
men in an inn, gave the alarm, and ran to notify the authorities.
The procurator of the Commune, Sauce, in the absence of
the mayor, who was detained at Paris by his duties as deputy,
assumed direction of the affair. The tocsin was sounded; the
inhabitants were awakened by children who ran through the
streets crying fire; the bridge which connected the two portions of the town of Varennes, and which the carriages must
necessarily cross, was barricaded, and a guard of determined
men, armed with guns, took up their post there ready to dispute
its passage by force.

The king's enemies had everything ready; his friends, nothing. The unfortunate delays along the journey, and the mis-
understanding which had resulted from them, had troubled their
minds and disarranged the measures which had been taken.
At the entrance to Varennes, no relay was found; the postilions, the body-guards, the king, and even the queen lost precious time in searching for it. The drivers refused to go farther
with the same horses; they argued, they treated with them;
when they were finally persuaded to cross the city at least,
it was too late. Sauce, Drouet, and their friends were waiting
under the little arch which joined the upper with the lower
town. The cabriolet containing the waiting-women came first;
it was stopped. Passports were demanded; one of the travellers
replied that they were in the second carriage. Sauce went
to the berlin and repeated his request. The king held out
the passport; the procurator observed that it was rather late
to visit, — it was half-past eleven, — that they would have to
alight, and in the morning he would see. The Baroness de
Korff protested loudly and tried to force a passage, but the
National Guards threatened to make use of their fire-arms; they
were obliged to submit and alight.

The travellers were taken to Sauce's house, which was at a stone's throw from the bridge; and while two rooms on the first floor more fitting to receive the unexpected guests, whose greatness was surmised, were being prepared, the travellers were introduced into a low room, where Sauce served them a frugal repast. The children, especially the dauphin, were heavy with sleep; they were put to rest on a bed. The queen had retired into an obscure corner of the apartment and drawn her veil over her eyes. Despite the invectives of the municipal officers, despite the declarations of Drouet and of a physician of the district, named Mangin, who claimed to know the royal family, Louis XVI. continued obstinately to deny his identity. At one moment the queen very nearly betrayed herself: shocked by the offensive tone which Drouet assumed in his discussion with the king, she raised her veil and exclaimed with spirit, "If you recognize him as your king, show him proper respect." But decisive proofs were still wanting. The procurator, uncertain, wavering, both fearing to let the prisoners escape if they were indeed those whom he supposed, or to make himself ridiculous by an arbitrary and vexatious arrest if his suspicions were unfounded, ran, after he had "deposited" — the word is his — the strangers in a back chamber, to the house of the tribunal judge, Monsieur Detez, who had seen the king and queen several times during a visit to Paris. Monsieur Detez returned with Sauce and recognized the royal family. After this formal declaration, further denial was useless. "Yes," Louis XVI. replied in a loud tone, "I am your king; this is the queen and the royal family. Placed in the capital between poniards and bayonets, I am come to seek, among my faithful subjects of the provinces, the liberty and peace which they all enjoy; I cannot live at Paris without dying, neither my family nor I. I come to live in the midst of you, my children, whom I will not abandon." The prince was moved, and his listeners no less so. "The tenderness, the emotion, of all those present awakened in response to that of the king," relates the first *procès-verbal* drawn up by the municipality; "and the monarch and his august family deigned to embrace all the citizens in the room, and to receive the same token of their lively and unconstrained feeling."

This emotion was of short duration; the municipality renewed their entreaties that the travellers return to Paris. The king refused; he urged as objections the series of humiliations to which he had been subjected in the capital, and the dangers to which his return exposed his family. "The queen, who shared his anxieties, expressed them by extreme agitation." The king, with his customary good-nature, explained his plans, swearing not to pass the frontier and to proceed to Montmédy, even allowing the National Guards to escort him there. "The sight was a touching one, but it did not shake the Commune in their resolution and courage to retain their king." Sauce, at bottom a worthy man, but intoxicated by the unexpected part which circumstances had allotted to him, moved by the touching picture which he had before his eyes, yet frightened by the big words and loud cries of the patriots, desirous to satisfy the king, yet not wishing to displease the people, was torn between his lifelong respect for the monarchy and his vanity, seconded by his fear. Fear mastered him and also his wife, from whom the queen could indeed draw forth tears, without, however, being able to conquer her naïve egotism. "*Bon Dieu!* Madame," she replied, "they would kill Monsieur Sauce. I love my king sincerely, but, *dame!* listen, I love my husband sincerely also. He is responsible, you see." The procurator's grandmother, a venerable octogenarian, asked to see the unexpected guests whom the accident of revolutions had introduced into their family. Still full of respect and of the traditional love of the French for the dynasty, she approached the bed on which the children were sleeping, and dropping on her knees, begged the favour of kissing their hands. Then she blessed these unfortunate little ones, whom her grandson in his weakness was to give over to captivity and death, and withdrew, deeply moved.

Meanwhile, Monsieur de Choiseul and Monsieur de Goguelat had arrived with the hussars of Pont-Sommevesle. Perhaps at that moment, when the crowd was not as yet formidable, and the National Guards of the neighbouring communes had not been mustered, it would have been possible, with a little effort, to force the way. "*Eh, bien!* when do we start?" the king inquired of Goguelat, as he saw him enter the room. "Sire, we await your orders," the aid-de-camp replied. But to ask for orders from a prince of so vacillating a character as Louis XVI. was to thrust him back into his habitual irresolution. Monsieur de Damas, who had in his turn just arrived, proffered energetic counsel; this was to dismount seven hussars, have the king, queen, and their attendants mount the horses of these hussars, and with the remaining soldiers force their way through the crowd. Marie Antoinette would not have recoiled from this hazardous scheme. "But," the king said, "can you promise that in the uneven conflict a ball may not strike the queen, my sister, or my children?" As if to confirm his fear, the populace muttered complaints under the windows of the little house; the expedient was abandoned as too perilous. When later, about two o'clock in the morning, Goguelat attempted to push through a reconnoitring party in the direction of Dun, the National Guards of the vicinity were assembled; resistance had been organized through the efforts of Monsieur de Signémont, commander of the militia of Neuvilly; barricades had been erected, cannons mounted. When the aid-de-camp wished to get possession of the royal carriage, in order to hold it in readiness for any emergency, he was struck down by a bullet fired by the major of the National Guards of Varennes; and the hussars, already wavering, shaken by the overtures of the patriots, frightened by the fall of their chief, began to fraternize and drink with the National Guards.

When, at five in the morning, Monsieur Deslon, the commander of the detachment from Dun, having galloped hither post-haste with sixty horsemen, pushed his way into the house of Sauce and asked for the king's orders, the unhappy monarch replied with bitterness, "My orders! I am a prisoner, and have none to give."

One thing remained: to gain time and wait until Monsieur de Bouillé, notified by his son, should march upon Varennes with his troops.

Two other actors, however, who were to add to the gravity of the situation, and destroy the last hopes of the royal family, arrived upon the scene before Monsieur de Bouillé; these were the emissaries of the Assembly.

When, on the morning of the 21st, Paris had discovered the flight of the king and his family, the first sensation had been that of stupor; then to this stupor had succeeded a lively anger; and the Assembly, sharing in the popular exasperation, had issued a decree ordering the king's arrest. One of Lafayette's aids-de-camp, Monsieur de Romeuf, especially attached to the service of the queen, who had on many occasions loaded him with favours, set out to make known the decree of the Assembly. At Châlons he met a major of the National Guards named Bayon, who, with Palloy, had started in advance of him, the bearer of similar orders from the mayor of Paris. They continued their journey together, Bayon quickening the zeal of Romeuf, who, because of his personal relations with the royal family, found the accomplishment of his mission especially painful. They reached Varennes at six in the morning; and Bayon, proceeding the first to Sauce's house, said in a voice broken by the breathless haste of the journey: "Paris is in a state of massacre! . . . Our wives, our children — the interest of the State —" Romeuf then approached, and with tears in his eyes handed to the king the decree of the Assembly. "There is no longer a king of France," the unhappy prince remarked with sadness. The queen took the decree, read it, and exclaimed, "The insolent wretches!" and threw the paper angrily from her; it fell on the bed where the dauphin lay; she flung it violently to the ground, saying, "I will not have it contaminate my son's bed."

Outside, the riotous mob muttered threats, and shouted, "To Paris, to Paris! Force them to start. . . . We will drag them by the feet if they will not go otherwise." In vain did the ill-fated monarch exhaust every means of delay. The dauphin and Madame Royale slept; their rest must be respected. Madame de Neuville, one of the waiting-women, comprehending the purpose of her masters, threw herself upon a bed writhing in a violent convulsion; the queen declared that she could not leave her without assistance, but the populace, secretly stimulated by Bayon, and openly by Palloy, did not trouble itself about the sleep of the children or the real or feigned maladies of the travellers. The shouts grew more and more furious. The king conferred with his family for an instant; and recognizing, without doubt, the impossibility of longer resistance, he sorrowfully yielded.

The carriages already stood before the house of Sauce; the horses were brought and quickly put to them; the National Guards formed the escort. The unhappy captives sadly descended the narrow, dark staircase, which led from the first to the ground floor; the queen leaned on the arm of the Duc de Choiseul, Madame Elisabeth on that of Monsieur de Damas. As they appeared at the door of the house, the street rang with shouts of "Vive le roi!" "Vive la nation!" Not one cry of "Vive la reine!" For the inhabitants of Varennes, as for those of Paris, she was always "the Austrian."

They took their places in the carriages; Monsieur de Choiseul closed the door, and the horses dashed off along the road to Clermont. It was about half-past seven in the morning.

When Monsieur de Bouillé, who had been delayed in his departure by the inconceivable slowness of the commander of the Royal German, finally came in sight of Varennes at the head of the regiment upon which he counted, the mournful procession had been gone for nearly two hours. It was too far in advance for him to be able to overtake it with horses tired out by a forced march of nine leagues. The general gave the order for retreat; and with downcast mien and a broken heart, he returned to Stenay, and from there immediately crossed the frontier.·

Meanwhile, the melancholy train pursued its march to Paris, under the escort of five or six thousand National Guards, and in the midst of an immense throng of people. At Clermont the municipal officers of Varennes left them to return to their town. Drouet remained with Bayon; as to Romeuf, he had stopped at Varennes to protect Monsieur de Choiseul and Monsieur de Goguelat, and had himself been arrested.

The carriage advanced slowly amid clouds of dust, and under a scorching sun; the heat was overpowering, the air parched. The children were prostrated with fatigue; the queen gazed at them sadly, thinking of her vanished hopes and of the sombre realities of this return. At Ste. Menehould, they were forced to submit to an insulting address by the municipality, and to show themselves to the crowd from the windows of the Hôtel de Ville; the queen, holding the dauphin in her arms, was greeted with cries, evidently hostile, of "Vive la nation!" But fallen as she was from power, she still preserved the sweetest and most cherished of all her rights, that of charity. Before leaving this little town, which had been so ill-disposed toward her, she, herself a prisoner, ordered five louis to be distributed to the prisoners there.

A horrible tragedy marked the journey from Ste. Menehould to Châlons; a gentleman from that part of the country, the Comte de Dampierre, having joined the multitude, was recognized, denounced as an aristocrat, assaulted by the National

Guards, thrown from his horse, and killed by a shot from a gun.
"What is the matter?" asked the king, startled by the noise
of the report. "Nothing," replied the crowd; "they are only
killing a fool;" and the murderers came back to the carriage,
"bearing the head in their blood-stained hands."

They arrived at Châlons toward half-past eleven at night.
This town was royalist, and the reception of the prisoners
differed from that which had heretofore been accorded them.
"The municipal bodies," says the official *procès-verbal*, "held
it as one of their first duties to see that the respect due royal
majesty was preserved." The king was received at the gate
of the city by the municipality, and conducted between two
lines of National Guards to the intendant's residence, which
had been prepared to receive him. This was the same hôtel at
which the beautiful dauphiness, then radiant with happiness,
had stopped, amid clamorous cheers and popular *fêtes*, when
twenty-one years before she had come to France, to encircle
her brow with the royal crown. At Châlons, at least, the population did what they could for their involuntary visitors to relieve the bitterness of their situation. As in 1770, young girls
presented flowers to Marie Antoinette; several among them
eagerly hastened to serve her; and when the royal family had
retired to their apartments, after a supper partaken of in public,
the procurator of the department, Rozé, even proposed to the
king to help him escape by a private staircase unknown to the
public. Louis XVI. declined, because no one but himself could
be saved.

This rare devotion and sympathy, shown by an entire town
almost without exception, had deeply touched the prisoners;
they met with no further example of it on their journey. About
ten o'clock on the following morning, the 23d, day of the Fête-
Dieu, while they were hearing mass in the chapel of the intend-
ance, the Rheims volunteers, who had arrived during the
night, broke into the court and rushed toward the chapel; the
mass was not ended; the king and queen were obliged, nevertheless, to go out and show themselves on the balcony. It was
necessary to hasten their departure, lest these volunteers, who
were made up of the dregs of the populace of Rheims, might stir
up a riot. The queen, as ever gracious, and sincerely touched,
replied "that she regretted the circumstances which prevented
the king and herself from passing a few moments more among

good citizens." A dinner had been hurriedly prepared for the travellers; but "their emotion," says the *procès-verbal*, "prevented them from eating anything." At noon they set out in such haste that the king left at Châlons a small casket containing thirteen hundred louis.

The nearer they approached to Paris, the more hostile became the attitude of the inhabitants. At Épernay, where they arrived at half-past four in the afternoon, their reception was unfriendly. The president of the district delivered an harangue full of reproaches; gross insults were hurled at them, and the very life of the august captives might not have been respected had it not been for the loyal devotion of the young Gazotte, who, having hurried hither at the head of a band of peasants, stood at the door of the carriage and restrained the crowd. A wretch was heard to say to his neighbour, "Conceal me well, that I may aim at the queen without any one knowing whence the shot is fired."

The throng pressed so closely round the fugitives that Marie Antoinette's dress was torn by their feet; it was necessary to mend it on the spot. The daughter of the landlord, at whose house they had alighted, performed this slight service for the unhappy sovereign with a respect and affection which did her sad heart good. During this time, the municipal officers addressed insulting remarks to the king. "Despite your errors," they said to him, "we will protect you; do not be afraid." "Afraid!" the prince replied in a surprised tone; and he set to work to explain to his interlocutors that he had had no intention of quitting France, but that he could not remain at Paris, where his family were in danger. "Oh, yes, indeed, you could," replied one of the by-standers.

They started again about five o'clock, amid an insurgent multitude. "Be off, my pretty little one; you will be shown many more," was the biting adieu called out to Marie Antoinette by one of the shrews of Épernay. Again, when the queen wished to give a piece of *bœuf-à-la-mode*, which she had in the carriage, to a National Guard who complained of hunger, one of his fellows cried out: "Do not touch it! Do you not see that she wishes to poison you?" The queen immediately ate some of it, and made her son eat some. This cry of insulting mistrust, however, pierced her to the heart, and of all the many outrages, this wounded her the most keenly.

A short distance beyond Épernay, the royal family were joined by the commissioners whom the Assembly had delegated to "bring the king back to Paris, to assure his safety, and to see that the respect due his Majesty was observed." They were Barnave, Pétion, and La Tour-Maubourg. The last-named did not wish to take his place in the royal carriage; declaring that the august travellers could be sure of him, but that they must win over the other two, he got in with the waiting-women. Pétion and Barnave took their places in the berlin, where thenceforth eight persons were packed together, choking with the clouds of dust and the suffocating heat; the children were held on the knees of the others. Barnave showed himself eminently decorous and respectful. The sight of this great misfortune, and the queen's charm, made a deep impression upon this hot-headed but true-hearted young man; a Revolutionist and almost a Republican when he entered the carriage, he left it a Royalist. As to Pétion, the account which he has written of his journey is the most notorious monument of brutality and pretence which the brain of a fop without education or tact could produce; it gives the measure of the man, in whose sight Madame Elisabeth's purity even did not find favour, of the vain and impertinent personage of whom the Revolution has made a hero, and who was only a dolt.

As he took his place in the carriage, he declared that he was well aware that the fugitives had near the palace taken a hack-cab driven by a Swede; and feigning not to know his name, he asked it of the queen. "I am not in the habit of knowing the names of cab-drivers," the princess replied dryly. A little later, when the king, having joined in the conversation, said that his flight had no other aim than to give to the executive the force necessary in a constitutional government, since France could not be a republic, Pétion insolently answered, "Not yet, because the French people are not ripe for that; and I shall not have the good fortune to see it established in my life-time."

At Dormans, they were obliged to stop at a simple inn. "I was not sorry," remarked Pétion, with his envious affectation of austerity, "that the court had occasion to learn what an ordinary inn was like." During the night the National Guards and the inhabitants of the surrounding country, who had flocked in troops to the town, sang, drank, and danced under the win-

dows of the hostelry; and it was amid this uproar and shouting that the exhausted travellers were forced to snatch a moment's rest. The poor little dauphin had frightful dreams, and began to sob; the attendants could only quiet him by taking him to his mother.

They set out again at five o'clock; Pétion placed himself on the back seat between the king and queen, and took the dauphin on his knee. The conversation began; the king was embarrassed, according to Pétion's account, who, nevertheless, deigns to admit "that it was rare that an objectionable opinion escaped him, and that he did not hear the king make one foolish remark." The queen was less restrained; she talked of the education of her children. "She spoke as the mother of a family, and as a well-informed woman. She set forth most excellent principles on education." But, the grotesque narrator hastens to add, as if to excuse himself for this involuntary homage to the queen, ".I have since learned that this is the jargon in vogue at all the courts of Europe."

At La Ferté-sous-Jouarre, the sympathetic and reverential reception of the mayor, Monsieur Regnard, furnished a momentary diversion from the insults of the mob. They found at his house a fresh apartment and a simple but well-prepared dinner. The wife of the mayor, not wishing, out of delicacy, to eat with the royal family, had dressed herself as cook to serve them. The queen, however, recognized her and said to her, "You are, without doubt, Madame, the mistress of the house." "I was a moment before your Majesty entered it," the excellent woman replied with a courtesy.

On leaving the town, there was a slight disturbance. It was caused by a deputy, Kervelegan, who had an altercation with the National Guards and attempted to gain access to the prisoners, whom he grossly insulted. "That is a very ill-mannered man," the queen could not keep from saying.

As they were nearing Meaux, a priest endeavoured to push his way to the carriage; the mob broke out in threats, and prepared to murder him, as they had Monsieur de Dampierre. The queen saw it and uttered a cry; Barnave thrust himself half out of the door and shouted, "Frenchmen, nation of valiant citizens, do you wish, then, to become a nation of murderers?" His indignant tone and powerful intervention saved the ill-fated priest from death.

They reached Meaux at rather an early hour, and slept at the house of the constitutional bishop. The king ate little, and retired at once to his apartment. The grandson of Louis XIV. had no more linen, and was obliged to borrow a shirt of an usher! In the evening Barnave had a long conversation with Louis XVI. and Marie Antoinette. He spoke with force; they listened to him with attention and kindliness. "Evidently," said the queen, "we have been deceived as to the real state of public sentiment in France." Barnave left them, Monsieur de Beauchesne says, "with the determination to die loyal to the throne and devoted to the cause of liberty."

They set out again at six in the morning; this was the last stage of the journey to Paris, a long march of thirteen leagues. The heat was excessive. The nearer they approached to the capital, the more hostile was the attitude of the mob, the more odious became the exactions of the guardians; despite the burning sun and terrible dust, they were not allowed to lower either curtains or blinds. The queen was grossly insulted, and several times there was reason to fear an attempt on her life. The poor woman could not restrain her tears, nor the dauphin a cry of terror.

Instead of entering by the Porte St. Denys, they skirted the walls to come in by the Porte de la Conférence. The Champs-Élysées were thronged with people; the barriers, the trees, the roofs of the houses, were covered with men, women, and children. They all kept their hats on their heads; the deputy Guilhermy alone had the courage to bow to the prisoners. Instructions had been given; placards had been posted everywhere bearing the words, "Whoever applauds the king shall be flogged; whoever insults him shall be hung." The cry of "Vive la nation!" alone broke the silence, like an insult and a threat.

As soon as the carriage had entered the garden of the Tuileries, the swivel-bridge was closed. The garden, however, like the Champs-Élysées, was full of National Guards; some of the deputies came out of the Assembly hall to enjoy the sight. As the berlin arrived at the palace, there was a movement in the crowd; the mob wished to cut the body-guards in pieces; the active intervention of the deputies was necessary to rescue these unfortunate victims from the fury of the populace. As the king stepped from the carriage, there was universal silence;

when the queen's turn came, murmurs arose on all sides, and it was amid the noise of insults that this ill-fated sovereign, under the protection of the Vicomte de Noailles and the Duc d'Aiguillon, entered, with uplifted head and haughty bearing, but with despair in her soul, this palace which she had quitted five days before full of hope.

Throughout this scene the king preserved his coolness and apparent calmness. "He was as unmoved and composed," Pétion writes, "as if nothing unusual were happening. . . . He acted as if he were returning from a hunting expedition."

The queen, however, more spirited, exhausted by so many shocks, prostrated by fatigue, grief, humiliation, and anger, had only the strength to address to the Chevalier Fersen these simple words, to write which she was forced to hide herself, "Do not be uneasy about us; we live."

CHAPTER X.

The Royal Family under Strict Surveillance at the Tuileries; their Life in Captivity. — The Queen is interrogated by the Commissioners of the Assembly. — July 17. — The Red Flag unfurled on the Champ de Mars. — The Constitutionalists.

FRANCE had *reconquered* her king; such was the official formula used in the congratulatory addresses sent to the National Assembly from all parts of the country. It was in truth a conquest; and the prince who entered Paris on June 25, 1791, amid general silence, broken only by cries of hatred, was nothing more than a humiliated and dethroned captive. The resolution of the Assembly, adopted on the motion of Thouret, was equivalent to a decree of forfeiture. The king, queen, and dauphin were to be surrounded by a guard, which was responsible for their persons; "the minister of justice continued to affix the State seal to the decrees of the Assembly without the need of royal sanction, and the ministers were authorized to discharge, each in his own department, the functions of executive power."

This decision was carried out to the letter; the royal family, reinstated at the Tuileries, was kept under strict surveillance. Its members could not communicate with one another except under the eyes of their jailers, and there were always several officers of the Parisian militia with them. A large company was quartered in the courts, a veritable camp (this is the expression employed by Madame Elisabeth), a numerous and noisy camp, stationed under the windows of the king and queen, lest, ironically adds the princess, who never even in the most painful circumstances loses her mirthfulness, — "lest they may jump into the garden, which is hermetically sealed, and filled with sentinels, two or three of whom stand under these same windows."

There were sentinels on every staircase of the interior, to the very roof.   No one could enter the palace without a note from Lafayette or Bailly; even members of the Assembly were refused admittance.   All the apartments of the royal family had been searched with the greatest care; the officers of the National Guards held the keys of them in their pockets; and if Madame de Tourzel can be believed, Lafayette had pushed the precautions so far as to send chimney-sweepers to examine and see if the captives might not be able to escape through the chimneys. All of the outer rooms of the queen's apartments had been transformed into guards' rooms.   Two National Guards were stationed permanently in her bedchamber with the order not to lose sight of her by day or night, even in the most private details of life.   During the first days, the unhappy sovereign was obliged to rise, dress, and retire before her jailers.   Only after long negotiations did she succeed in having them lodged elsewhere than in her very chamber; but they remained near her bed during the night, and one of them, leaning his elbow on her pillow, had wished to dismiss her first woman, Madame de Jarjayes.   The chapel seeming too far removed from the lodgings of the prisoners, an altar was arranged in a room on the ground floor.   Here the royal family heard mass.   When the queen went to the dauphin's apartments, she was escorted by two officers; she always found the door closed; one of the officers would tap on it, saying, "The queen!" and it was only at this signal that the guardians of the young prince and of his governess would consent to open to this mother who came to see her son.

After a time, however, either because Lafayette finally realized the indecency of his orders, or because the queen made complaints, certain modifications were effected.   The guards remained in the queen's chamber so long as she was up.   They retired when she went to bed; but during the night, one of them was stationed in a kind of lobby formed by the thickness of the wall between the two doors in such a manner that when the chamber door was left open he could see all that passed within.   Weber even relates an anecdote apropos of this, which will illustrate the state of the public sentiment and the confusion of ideas at this epoch.   One night, Marie Antoinette, being unable to rest, lighted her candle and began to read. The guard who was watching her perceived this, and entering the room, pushed back the curtains, sat down with a familiar manner on her bed, and said to her: "I see that you cannot sleep. Let us have a talk together; that is better than reading." The queen, adds the narrator, "restrained her indignation, and gently made him understand that he must leave her to herself."

In appearance, the royal family had resumed the regularity of their habitual routine,—"their life of vegetation," writes the Cardinal de Bernis: the domestic functions were performed as usual; the persons attached to the court continued at their posts. They went to mass at noon; they dined at half-past one; at half-past nine they took supper. As the king, who was accustomed to active life, was no longer able to walk or ride, the royal family played billiards after dinner and after supper, in order that he might have a little exercise. The rest of the time the prince remained shut up in his cabinet reading and studying; neither he nor his wife left their apartments. Not wishing to expose themselves as captives to the eyes of the mob, they did not even go to take the air in the dauphin's little garden. The queen occupied herself with her children — these were her only moments of diversion and consolation — and passed her days in reading, writing, and doing needle-work. At seven o'clock she received the ladies of the palace. At eleven every one retired to his own apartments.

But how gloomy this existence! How irksome this regularity, and despite the apparent tranquillity, how frequent the secret rebellion against this enforced monotony! With what restrained emotion they welcomed sympathetic faces, the deputies who passed under the windows of the château that they might greet the prisoners in passing, and the few friends who dared to cross the threshold of this suspected palace. One day, soon after the return from Varennes, Malouet had the courage to do this:—

"I found the king, queen, and Madame Elisabeth more calm than I had expected," he writes. "As I entered, the queen said to the young dauphin, 'My son, do you know Monsieur?' 'No, mamma,' the child replied. 'It is Monsieur Malouet,' the queen continued. 'Never forget his name.' It was the hour for mass; the attendants entered. The king said but one thing to me, 'We were well pleased with Barnave.'"

On June 26 the Assembly appointed three of its members, Adrien Duport, D'André and Tronchet, to receive the depositions of the king and his family. That very evening the three commissioners repaired to the Tuileries and were admitted to the king's chamber. The king protested against all idea of examination. He declared that the outrages which had been committed against his family, and which had gone unpunished, had alone determined him to quit Paris, but that he had never intended to go out of the kingdom. The commissioners next went to the queen's apartments, but as she had just entered her bath, they returned on the following day at eleven o'clock. Marie Antoinette received them alone, and by her statements confirmed those of Louis XVI. "I declare," she said, "that since the king desired to go away with his children, nothing in the world could have kept me from following him. I have given ample proof on several occasions during the last two years that I would never leave him; and I was especially determined to follow him, because of my confidence and conviction that he would not quit the realm. If he had wished to leave it, I would have made every effort to prevent him." In addition, the king and queen assumed the entire responsibility of the escape, and exonerated all those who had concurred in the plan or in its execution. The Assembly did not accept this policy, and refusing to bring the king and queen to trial, choosing to regard the departure as an abduction rather than a voluntary flight, it referred Monsieur de Bouillé and his accomplices to the high court of Orléans.

The Jacobins, however, went further than the Assembly; they attacked the king; it was he whom they reviled in their speeches at the clubs, and in their articles in the newspapers. Thanks to cunning intrigue and frequent distribution of money, the popular fermentation did not diminish; the streets were hung with gross caricatures; foul songs and cruel satires against the king, and especially against the queen, were sold on every square; orators retailed the most odious calumnies in the public resorts. The addresses received from the departments were "veritably infamous," so an impartial observer affirms. A former soldier, Achille Duchatelet, took the initiative in an insolent address in which he demanded the forfeiture of the crown; and on Sunday, July 17, the people were summoned to the Champ de Mars to sign this document. In the early morning a disorderly crowd gathered in the place named; incendiary resolutions were passed; the rioters talked of proceeding in a body to the Assembly. The National Guards interfered; the mob pelted them with stones. The mayor, Bailly, then ordered the red flag to be unfurled, and declared martial law. One discharge of powder scattered the mob; but soon, seeing that there were no dead or wounded, the fugitives rallied and began afresh to assault the National Guards. A second discharge brought down some thirty of them, — "a dozen or two of heroes in tatters," remarks Gouverneur Morris. The rest fled as fast as their legs could carry them. As to the leaders, those who had not gone into hiding on the preceding evening hastened to do so, or to quit Paris; but they did not forgive Bailly for this strenuous measure, and made him cruelly expiate it later.

The unexpected energy displayed by the municipality and the National Guards re-established tranquillity in Paris, and for the moment terrified the malcontents. This might perhaps have furnished a starting-point for a new era, if this attitude had been maintained; but that would have been too much to ask of the Assembly, and the weakness of which it gave proof a few days later, in the debate on the law regarding the clubs, revived the courage of the insurgents.

The affray on the Champ de Mars, however, had enlightened the leaders of the Constitutionalists as to the designs of the Jacobins. Separating themselves abruptly from these last, they founded the club of the Feuillants; and the principal men among them sought a reconciliation with the king and queen. The journey from Varennes had formed the connecting link between Barnave and Marie Antoinette; the reserved and re-spectful bearing, the elevated mind, the generous sentiments, the distinguished manners of the young deputy from Dauphiné, contrasting with Pétion's vulgarity and ill-breeding, had in-spired the queen's confidence as the dignity and graciousness of the queen had captivated the young deputy. The relations which had been formed in this sad drive were continued at Paris; and the reply made by the king to the delegates of the Assembly was even attributed to Barnave. Less personal, but no less forcible reasons — fear of the Jacobins, dread of an-archy, and perhaps Barnave's eloquence — determined his friends, who had until then been so hostile toward the king, and espe-cially toward the queen, to make efforts to re-establish the throne, which they had done so much to undermine. A sort of triumvirate was formed, and communications were opened with the Tuileries, and particularly with Marie Antoinette, through the medium of Monsieur de Jarjayes, who had already on various occasions performed confidential missions for the royal family. Barnave, Alexandre de Lameth, and Duport made up this triumvirate. The queen listened to their counsels, and apparently accepted their ideas; but she refused to place entire confidence in men some of whom had, according to their own avowal, no fixed plan, and lived from day to day, and others of whom seemed to have no other aim than to retain the power in their hands. From this time begins a double and secret policy, the agents of which constantly contradict and disclaim one another, amid complications in which the diplomatists of that period must have had great difficulty in threading their way, and which the historian of our day does not always succeed in unravelling,— a policy which for a long time remained unknown, although suspected, and upon which the recent publication of Monsieur de Fersen's paper has at last thrown new light.

We shall attempt to give an outline of it.

CHAPTER XI.

AMONG all the foreign princes, the eyes of the queen and of her new allies, the Constitutionalists, most naturally turned toward the emperor. We have already described the kind of aid which Marie Antoinette expected from her brother: the manœuvring of troops on the frontier, to explain Monsieur de Bouillé's movements, the concentration of about ten thousand men at Luxembourg; then, if it were in the first moment necessary, the temporary support of this company. On June 20, Leopold was not in Germany, but at Padua in Italy; he had at first believed in the success of the escape. He had indeed been told that the royal family had been arrested in their flight; but to this news had been added the information that Monsieur de Bouillé had unexpectedly arrived at the head of his army, had delivered the prisoners, and carried the king to Metz under the protection of his troops, while the queen had reached Luxembourg. On July 5, the emperor wrote to his sister, —

"If I had consulted my heart alone, I should have set out at once to come to you to embrace you; circumstances, however, prevented me. I envy the lot of my sister Marie, who will have this satisfaction. I charge her, and also the Comte de Mercy, to arrange everything to suit your present pleasure. I trust that you will be assured that in my domain you are as in your own, and that you will lay aside all ceremony with a brother who is so tenderly and sincerely attached to you as I.

"As to your affairs, I can only repeat to you, as I have already done to the king, that all that I have is yours, — money, troops, in short, everything. My sister and the Comte de Mercy have all necessary orders to issue any manifesto or proclamation, or effect any movement or disposition of troops which you may command. I am only too happy if I can serve you in any way."

And on the same day he wrote to his sister, Marie Christine, governor of the Netherlands, —

"At this moment the king is free; the king has protested against all that has been done. I am certainly not wiser in the matter than the king; I am his relative, friend, and ally, and desire to help and second him with all my might and power."

Unfortunately, on the same day he learned, through the elector of Trèves, of the positive arrest of the royal family; he was deeply affected by it; and on the next day, displaying, says Vaudreuil, "the tenderness of a brother, the greatness of soul of a true monarch, and the resolution which great men show in great emergencies," he addressed a circular to the chief powers — Spain, Russia, England, Prussia, Sardinia, Naples — for the purpose of organizing a concerted intervention in favour of the prisoners. It was necessary, he said, to draw up a forcible manifesto, which would overawe the French Revolutionists. The powers should boldly demand, in the name of the public right of Europe, the liberation of the king of France, and at the same time "leave the way open for an honest resipiscence, and the pacific establishment of an order of things in France which would at least save the honour of the crown, and the conditions essential to the general tranquillity." They would pledge themselves to recognize as constitutional laws, legally established in France, only those which were adopted with the voluntary consent of the sovereign. The manifesto of the powers should be upheld by "sufficiently forcible means," and they would not shrink from the most rigorous measures. "I am pleased to forewarn them, the Revolutionists," Leopold writes to Marie Christine; "but if I do not succeed, I will inflict a merited punishment upon them."

The king of Sweden, more passionate than the emperor, a military sovereign, eager to play a military part in the coalition, had, on June 27, broken with the Assembly; on the 30th, he had conveyed to Louis XVI. and Marie Antoinette the assurance of his sympathy and support. At the same time he opened negotiations in various directions, and like Leopold, made efforts, but with more ardour and less prudence, to unite all the powers in a league, of which he should be the armed member. Fearing the emperor's coldness and temporizing ideas, he addressed himself on July 9 to Catherine II., and some days later, on July 16, to the king of Spain, to make known to them his plan, and to solicit their co-operation. According to his scheme, the imperial troops, thirty-five thousand strong, should enter France by way of Flanders, while twelve thousand Swiss soldiers should invade Franche-Comté, fifteen thousand Sardinians, Dauphiné; the princes of the Empire, Alsace and Brisgau, and twenty thousand Spanish soldiers should cross the Pyrenees. He hoped to have the assistance of Hanover and Prussia and the neutrality of England.

"As soon as the emigrant princes find themselves on French territory," Gustavus continued, "they will gather around them the peers, grand officers of the crown, archbishops, bishops, magistrates of Parliament; and then, after having proclaimed the regency, Monsieur will give a warranty to preserve the ancient laws of the realm, and the rights of the different orders, and to reinstate Parliament. There is no doubt that the terror and confusion, dissension and disorder, added to the delays and the lack of secrecy, — which it is impossible to preserve in the deliberations of a body, — will aid the attack of the princes; and it is to be believed that success will attend their enterprise."

He himself would set out at the head of sixteen thousand Swedes, to which he entreated the empress to add seven or eight thousand Russians. These troops, transported by the combined fleets of Russia and Sweden, should disembark at Ostend, and proceed to Liège to form, with the Hessian and Palatine troops, "the centre of the line, the right of which should extend toward Dunkirk, and the left toward Strasburg," or following out a subsequent plan, they should embark at Ostend, to sail round and land in Normandy with the purpose of marching on Paris.

The North would thus have a preponderant influence in this great undertaking; and in case of need it would be there to check the rapacity of the other powers, who might be tempted to profit by the misfortunes of France and dismember it. Gustavus added that pecuniary aid from Russia would not be amiss to equip the Swedish army. Catherine was "certainly rich enough to pay for her own glory and that of her allies."

At the same time, the impetuous sovereign urged Monsieur to proclaim himself regent, and to form a government which would be the true government of France, since the king must be considered as the prisoner of his revolted subjects. "This name of regent," he said, "will free Monsieur and all Frenchmen faithful to their duty from the imputation of revolt, with which the Assembly will without fail try to sully them. It will not be Frenchmen fighting against France, but loyal subjects attacking rebels to deliver their oppressed sovereign."

This impatience of the king of Sweden was in complete accord with that of the emigrants, who had, since June 21, greatly increased in number and importance. The failure of the attempt at flight which had been planned by the king and queen, unknown to the princes and their friends, seemed to give to these last unquestioned power. What could be henceforth the authority of Louis XVI., surrounded as he was by spies, and manifestly a captive in his own palace? Consequently, in the counsels of the emigrants, what weight could his agent, the Baron de Breteuil, have, — one of the authors of the plan which had so miserably failed? Did it not devolve upon those who had systematically been kept in ignorance of the projects, the melancholy issue of which had just been seen, — upon the Comte d'Artois and upon Calonne, — to assume henceforth the direction of affairs? Their partisans grew more numerous every day. A great many noblemen, who had only remained in France in order to place themselves at the disposition of the king, in case he might wish to undertake some enterprise, considered that all effort had been rendered vain by the new situation which had been brought about by the unfortunate adventure of the royal family. It cost them much, without doubt, as one of them wrote, "to leave the king behind them;" but "a rallying-point being no longer possible in France, that which the princes offered at Coblentz was the only one which honour and duty seemed to designate." What means remained to the king to combat the tyrannical resolutions of the Assembly and of the clubs? If before Varennes he had been unable to spare his faithful servants the humiliation of February 28, after Varennes what could he do? Could they not best aid him by going where they could organize resistance? Monsieur de

Bouillé must have understood the matter thus, since he had taken refuge in Luxembourg with all his staff, and Monsieur de Bouillé was no hot-headed youth, no counter-revolutionist; he was a wise, patriotic man, partisan in a large measure of the reforms demanded by the public. So soon as the former commander of the army of Metz had left France, after having written to the Assembly a threatening letter in which he took upon himself the sole responsibility of the king's flight, and swore to avenge his arrest, he had addressed an urgent appeal to all faithful officers, and many had responded to this appeal, bringing to the emigrants their devotion, their swords, their flags, and in some cases, their wealth, — whole regiments, as the hussars of Berchiny. The regiment of Beriack, the larger part of the Royal Germans, had followed the example of their officers. These were powerful reinforcements for this nucleus of an army, which was being formed under the orders of the Maréchal de Broglie and the Prince de Condé.

Finally, June 21 had given to the emigrant party what it had until then lacked, an undisputed leader. Monsieur the Comte de Provence had succeeded where Louis XVI. had failed; he had not surrounded himself with the luxury of relays and detachments which had everywhere drawn attention to the passage of the king, and had thus succeeded in reaching Mons and Brussels unmolested. The authority of the Comte d'Artois, the last-born of the royal family, might be disputed; that of Monsieur, the first prince of the blood, the regent of France in the event of the minority or the imprisonment of the sovereign, could not be; and if he refused to parade a title which the evident captivity of the king appeared to give him, and which Gustavus III. urged him to claim, it at least devolved upon him resolutely to assume the direction of affairs. In truth, this was a singular piece of good fortune for the emigrants, who were at last called to play a part. If the Comte de Provence, although possessed of a fine and cultivated mind, well informed and elegant in his discourse, lacked the charm and brilliancy of the Comte d'Artois, he also lacked his lightness and improvidence; he was even regarded as an able politician. Unfortunately he had not then acquired that maturity and wisdom which twenty-five years later made his reign one of the most healthful ever known in France. Although he passed for a liberal, and affected the appearances, he shared in many points, and continued to share for a long time, the prejudices and illusions of the emigrants. He especially shared the hostility felt by some among them — and by Calonne in particular — against the queen, whose tardy maternity had dissipated his dreams of grandeur. The queen reciprocated his feeling in full; she had had more than one war of epigrams and words with him. Adversity had not destroyed this mute rivalry, and Marie Antoinette retained for her brother-in-law, who had been more fortunate than she in his flight, a distrust which finds expression in the following letter to Madame de Lamballe: —

"Rest assured that there is in his heart more personal ambition than affection for his brother, and certainly for me. It has been a lifelong sorrow to him that he was not born master; and this wild desire to usurp the first place has grown even stronger since our misfortunes, which give him the opportunity of pushing himself forward."

In the beginning, however, it seems that Monsieur, while reserving for himself the first rank, abandoned the first rôle to the Comte d'Artois, who, although his junior in age, was his senior in emigration, and for that reason was better acquainted with the resources and the aspirations of the emigrants, and who had, moreover, already participated in all negotiations with the powers. The Comte d'Artois, impetuous, light, passionate, "always talking, never listening, being sure of everything," allowed nothing to deter him, and desired immediate action, — no negotiations with members of the Assembly; force only; at most they might seek to work upon Paris with money, and guarantee safety and oblivion of the past to Lafayette and his companions. Monsieur, more cautious than his brother, but, according to Fersen, at that time completely under his subjection, lent himself to these schemes and accepted almost entirely the direction of the Comte d'Artois's man, the fatal Calonne. The emigrants of Belgium were organized under six leaders, — Messieurs de Frondeville, de Robin, de Jaucourt, the Marquis de la Queuville, the Duc d'Uzès, and the Duc de Ville-quier. At Coblentz, a regular government was formed: a council of State was instituted, composed of the Prince de Condé, Monsieur de Vaudreuil, with the bishop of Arras — a prelate more political than religious — as chancellor, and Calonne as prime minister. Breteuil, the queen's man, was excluded. At the same time, the Baron de Roll was sent to Berlin, the

Baron de Flachslanden to Vienna, the Baron de Bombelles to St. Petersburg, and Calonne himself to London.

It was this double action of the princes and of Gustavus III. on the one hand, and of the emperor on the other, which the leaders of the constitutional party were endeavouring to neutralize. They had already tried, but without success, to establish connections with the Comte de Mercy, through the mediation of Monsieur de la Borde; repulsed on one side, they addressed themselves to the queen, with whom they were in frequent communication, and the queen consented to write, at their instigation and almost at their dictation, the following letter to the emperor: —

"July 30, 1791.

"It has been requested that I should write to you, my dear brother; and those who desire it have undertaken to transmit my letter to you, for I myself have no possible way of sending you news of my health. I shall not enter into details concerning that which preceded our departure; you already know all the motives for it. During the events which attended our journey, and in the situation which followed our return to Paris, I experienced many deep emotions. When I had recovered from the first agitation incident upon them, I began to reflect upon what I had seen, and I sought to discern what were the king's interests in the present state of things, and what the line of conduct which they prescribed for me. My ideas were fixed by a combination of reasons, which I shall explain to you. . . . The condition of affairs here has greatly changed since the circumstances which occasioned our journey. The Assembly was divided into a multitude of parties. Far from appearing to re-establish order, every day beheld the power of the law diminish. The king, stripped of all authority, did not see a possibility even of regaining it at the end of the Legislative Assembly, through the influence of the Assembly; for the Assembly itself was daily losing the respect of the people. In a word, it was impossible to see a limit to the great disorder.

"To-day circumstances give much more hope. The men who have most influence in affairs have united, and openly declared themselves for the preservation of the monarchy and of the king, and for the re-establishment of order. Since their reconciliation, seditious efforts have been repulsed with great superiority of strength. The Assembly has throughout the realm acquired a consistence and an authority which it apparently desires to employ to insure the execution of the laws and to bring the Revolution to a close. The most moderate men, who have constantly heretofore opposed its operations, have now become its allies, because

they see in it the sole means of enjoying in security that which the Revolution has left them, and of putting an end to the troubles, a continuation
of which they dread.   Finally, all things seem to unite to assure a termination of the agitation and of the disturbances to which France has
been delivered over for the past two years.   This natural and possible
conclusion will not give the government the amount of power and authority which I deem necessary for it; but it will save us from greater
misfortunes; it will place us in a more tranquil situation; and when the
public has recovered from this madness in which it is at present plunged,
it will perhaps realize the expediency of giving greater latitude to royal
authority.

"In the course which events are of themselves taking, such is what
can be discerned of the future.   I compare this result with that which a
line of action opposed to the wish manifested by the nation would produce.   I see an absolute impossibility of obtaining anything otherwise
than by the employment of superior strength.   In this last supposition I
will say nothing of the personal danger which the king, his son, and
myself might run.   But what an enterprise is that, the issue of which is
uncertain, and the results of which, whatever they may be, present misfortunes impossible to look upon!   Every one here is determined to
resist.   The army is in bad condition through lack of leaders and of discipline; but the realm is covered with armed men, and their imaginations
are so inflamed that it is impossible to foresee what they might do,
or how many victims would be sacrificed before the foreign army could
penetrate into the heart of France.   It is difficult to calculate, moreover,
when one sees what passes here, what would be the consequences of
their despair.   In the contingencies which such an attempt offers I see only
doubtful success and the certainty of great evils for all factions.   As to
the part which you, my dear brother, could take in the matter, you would
make great sacrifices to our interests, and they would be just so much the
more dangerous as the people supposed us influential in actuating them."

What, then, should the emperor do?   Cease all protestation,
all threats, be the first to recognize the Constitution when it
had been accepted by the king, and thus bind himself closely to
regenerated France.   By this course he would dispel "all uneasiness, which was the more unfortunate for every one because
the chief obstacle to the re-establishment of public peace."
Such an attitude could not but draw the public back to the king,
to whom it would unfailingly attribute a preponderant part in
this determination of his brother-in-law; the leaders of the
Revolution, "who had upheld the king in the last event, and
who wished to insure him the consideration and respect neces-

sary to the exercise of his authority," would find in that "a means of reconciling the dignity of the sovereign with the interests of the nation, and thereby of consolidating and strengthening a Constitution of which they all agreed that the royal majesty was an essential part."

"I do not know," the queen added in closing, "whether the king will not, by this course of action, find in the dispositions of the nation, as soon as it has grown calmer, more deference and more friendly feeling than he could expect from the majority of French subjects at present outside of the realm." As to these last, the emigrants, whose menaces exasperated the nation and compromised the pacific interior policy, the essential thing was to hold them in check; and the simplest way to hold them in check was to make them re-enter France.

Some days later, at the beginning of August, the leaders of the Constitutionalists, wishing to confirm the thought contained in this letter and give it greater weight by verbal explanations, sent out, with the consent of the king and queen, two emissaries,—one, the Chevalier de Coigny, to Coblentz, to deliver despatches to the princes; the other, the Abbé Louis, to Brussels, to meet Leopold's minister, the Comte de Mercy, who, for a long time the confidant of the queen, had not lost his interest in France.

The Chevalier de Coigny, formerly one of the inner circle at Trianon, a faithful visitor at the Tuileries since the return to Paris, and, it is said, one of the confidants of the journey to Varennes, was a loyal follower of the royal family, and would, it was thought, inspire confidence in the king's brothers. The Abbé Louis, Duport's intimate friend, was rather a man of the constitutional party. Both had an interview with Louis XVI. and Marie Antoinette before their departure; but Monsieur de Coigny saw them only in the presence of the ministers, and it was before them that the letter for the Comte d'Artois was given to him and read. The king added a sealed letter for Monsieur and Monsieur de Montmorin,—a memoir which should be communicated only in case the princes appeared well disposed. In his open despatch Louis XVI. urged his brothers to return to France with all the emigrants. The Constitution had the sympathies of the nation; it was therefore impossible to oppose it; it was wiser to yield submission to it. In the letter to Monsieur, the king added that the princes should have no regard for what concerned them or their family personally, but should consult only the happiness and welfare of the nation; that, in addition, they could have perfect confidence in the Chevalier de Coigny. When the chevalier arrived at Coblentz, the princes, after examining the two letters, asked if it was indeed the king's wish that they should take no action whatsoever. The chevalier replied that he did not think so; but that the king desired that if they did act, they should take all necessary precautions for his safety and that of his family and of those in the kingdom who were attached to him. This response of the Chevalier de Coigny, whether it was the expression of Louis XVI.'s thought or not, accorded too well with the inner feeling of the princes for them not to hasten to shape their conduct in conformity to it. Urged on by the king of Sweden, flattered by the empress of Russia, invested since July 1 with full and absolute power sent by the king, freed, in consequence, from the control of the Baron de Breteuil, the queen's agent, they were less than ever inclined to return, and more than ever determined to act.

The Abbé Louis, in his turn, had had a conference of some length with Marie Antoinette before setting out. He had shown her that three courses were open to her,—to favour the enterprises of the princes; to throw herself into the democratic party; or to wait for time and an adroit and wise policy to effect a return of the people to moderate ideas, the necessity of which would be forced upon them by the misfortunes of anarchy.

"The queen," Staël writes, " being on close terms with the leaders of the Assembly, and evidently holding instructions from them, rejected the first course with great energy, repeating many times that the princes wished to be heroes at the expense of France, of the king's safety, and of her own; that she had always been averse to their designs, and that she had only conceived the plan of Montmédy that they might owe nothing to foreign aid, but all to the sentiment which would be formed and manifested in France in favour of the monarchy. She also expressed a strong repugnance for the exaggerations of the democrats; and she found that party preferable which permitted the king to take advantage of every opportunity to win back the affection of his people. The Abbé Louis suggested to her that one way of inspiring confidence in the people would be the line of action adopted by the emperor; that if he was the first sovereign to effect an alliance with France and to expel from his domain the French emigrants, who were known through their hostile projects, the people would believe that the queen was truly determined to seek for no other reform in France than that which time and past experience might suggest."

The queen, apparently sharing the abbé's views, gave him a letter of recommendation to De Mercy, and urged the count to return to Paris on her behalf, and also because it was the desire of the Constitutionalists, adding that she feared that she had been mistaken in the course which she ought to have taken, and that she stood in great need of his wisdom and advice.

The queen, however, only outwardly favoured the plans of her new allies; and although she listened to their projects, and transmitted their memoirs to her brother in rendering them justice for their good intentions, she in no wise accepted their policy.

"I am well enough satisfied in that quarter," she wrote, — "that is, with Duport, Lameth, and Barnave, — the only three," she said on another occasion, "with whom one can attempt anything. Although they always hold to their own opinions, I must do them the justice to acknowledge that I have never seen aught in them but great frankness, resolution, and an earnest desire to restore order, and consequently royal authority. . . . But," she added almost immediately afterward, "despite the good intentions which they manifest, their ideas are exaggerated and can never be in harmony with ours."

This instinctive distrust was only too easily explained. Were not these men who now made pretensions to save the monarchy the very ones who had struck the first and fiercest blows against it? Was not this people, in whose goodness she was urged to confide, the people of July 14, of October 6, of April 18, who every day insulted the royal family under the windows of the palace, and threatened their most faithful servants? Did not the queen know that it was easier to loosen the torrent than to arrest it, and that those who are skilful in destroying are seldom capable of reconstructing? The intentions of Barnave and his friends were honest; the queen believed them to be so; but are not politics paved with good intentions? Would the perspicacity of the Constitutionalists, so often at fault, be more felicitous to-day, and, furthermore, would their power be as great as their good-will? Had not this Assembly of which they believed themselves the rulers, and which they represented as so eager to restore the royal authority, but lately committed a gross outrage against the majesty of the king, in publicly voting a recompense to those who had arrested him, and dealt a mortal blow to his power and safety in removing from his person the Swiss Guards, and the most faithful defenders of the monarchy?

What had Barnave or Lameth done to spare the king these insulting measures, or if they had wished to do anything, what was their influence? And what, then, was the worth of their support, and of the ideas which they claimed to promulgate?

Therefore, on the day following that on which the queen had written the letter prompted by the leaders of the Left, and had had the conference with the Abbé Louis, she hastened to retract what she had said and disavow her agents: —

"On the 29th I wrote you a letter, which you will easily perceive was not in my style," she wrote to Mercy on the 31st. "I considered it expedient to accede to the desires of the leaders of the party here, who themselves gave me the rough draft of the letter. I wrote another to the emperor yesterday, the 30th. I should be humiliated by it if I did not expect that my brother would understand that in my position I am obliged to do and to write all that is exacted of me."

On the following day, she returned to the charge, —

"The Abbé Louis is soon to join you; he will say that he is accredited by me to talk with you. It is essential that you appear to listen to him and to be apprised of his mission, but do not be influenced by his ideas."

Mercy, who was more inflexible than the queen, — inflexible even to injustice, it must be admitted, was full of contempt for these ancient enemies, now repentant. In his eyes, Barnave and the Lameths were nothing but "dangerous rascals," Duport, "the most resolute anti-royalist and intrepid malcontent."

Marie Antoinette herself was convinced that the Constitutionalists had only sought a reconciliation with her through ambition and resentment; that the attachment for the royalty, which they paraded, was only a means of regaining the power which was slipping from them; and that if through their coalition with the Royalists, they again became the masters, they would be no better than their more advanced adversaries. If she feigned to listen to them and to follow them, it was to lull them to sleep, to prevent them from joining the Jacobins, and founding with these a republic; she also hoped, by this division, to bring discredit on the new government, to render it in a way impossible, and thereby prepare the minds of the people for a discontent from which would result the re-establishment of the throne; but she had not full confidence either in the frankness or the disinterestedness of her new allies. It is the misfortune of revolutionists, who desire to return to more wholesome ideas, that no one believes in the sincerity of their conversion. It is also their punishment.

CHAPTER XII.

IF Marie Antoinette did not adopt the ideas of the Constitutionalists, nor accept those of the emigrants, what did she
intend to do? What was her plan? This plan, at the date which
we have reached, was not and could not have been more than
mapped out. After the arrest at Varennes, which had so completely foiled their carefully arranged and ripened projects, the
queen, a prisoner, and isolated from her friends, needed a little
time to collect her thoughts, to digest a course of action, and
to combine the previously matured scheme with the new exi-
gencies of the situation. A letter of July 8 to Fersen, nevertheless, gives the first idea and, as it were, the first outlines of
that plan which has been for so many years unknown, but which
certain recent publications enable us to reconstruct with some
exactness. What the king and queen desired above all, what
they requested with the utmost energy, was that their partisans
should not resort to force.

"The king thinks," wrote Marie Antoinette on July 8, "that it is
through negotiations alone that their aid — that of the foreign powers —
can be of service to him and to his kingdom; that the display of force
must be a secondary measure only, employed in case the people here
close the way to all negotiations.

"The king thinks that open violence, even after a first declaration,
would be of incalculable danger, not only to himself and his family, but
to all Frenchmen in the kingdom not in sympathy with the Revolution.
There is no doubt but that a foreign force could succeed in entering

France; but the people, armed as they are, would, on fleeing from the frontier and from the foreign troops, instantly turn their arms against those of their fellow-citizens whom the Revolutionists have for two years constantly pointed out to them as their enemies. . . . All that has been done during the past two years should be considered as null so far as the will of the king is concerned, but impossible to alter so long as the great majority of the nation are eager for the innovations. We must turn all our efforts to change this spirit.

"Summary: He desires that the king's captivity be certified and well known to the foreign powers; he desires that the good-will of his relatives, friends, allies, and of those other sovereigns who may wish to lend their support, be manifested by a kind of congress, in which the means of negotiations be employed, — it being understood that there be a commanding force to uphold them, but always kept far enough in the background not to provoke the people to crime or massacre."

It is easy to see, by this simple account, how much this plan differed from that of the Constitutionalists, who desired the inaction of the powers; how much more still it differed from that of the emigrants, who wished to enter upon an immediate campaign. It was this last project which the queen opposed especially with the greatest energy. All her letters to the emperor, to Mercy, to Fersen, her private and her semi-official, if not strictly official letters, were full of entreaties to restrain the emigrants, to reduce them to inaction, if not to impotence. Her distrust of the leaders of the emigrants, above all, her antipathy for Calonne, whose summons to the side of the Comte d'Artois had appeared a sort of personal insult to her, and whom she saw triumphant and more active than ever, seemed to have acquired strength from the humiliation of her failure. It had been especially strengthened by the news which she received from Coblentz, of the little value which the leaders of the emigrant party set upon the king's authority, and of the little respect they had for his person. She could, indeed, scarcely be ignorant of the fact that at Brussels and at Coblentz they behaved ill toward her most faithful servants,— Breteuil, the Maréchal de Castries, Monsieur d'Agoût; that she herself received little better treatment, and that it had required some courage on the part of Monsieur de Vaudreuil to defend her against their burning accusations; that the Comte d'Artois's party was openly opposed to that of the queen, and that certain emigrants had pushed their indecency to the point of rejoicing

publicly over her arrest.   At Coblentz had they not gone so far
as to say that "the king, when his brothers had restored his
crown to him, should never have the power to dismiss, on any
pretext or in any case, one of the ministers who formed a part
of the council named by the princes, without the wish and consent of the other members of this council"?   Not, assuredly,
that these reproaches of personal ambition should be applied to
all the emigrants; the larger part of them had only been led to
enlist in the army of the princes through devotion to the royal
family, and because, after Varennes, they saw no other way of
serving them.   Many brave noblemen from the provinces had
hastened from the heart of their estates ready to shed their
blood, simply, unassumingly, as at Fontenoy, as at Claster-
camps, because they regarded it as their duty, and because, in
their loyal enthusiasm, to fight for the king was always to fight
for France, — short-sighted politicians, perhaps, but large-
hearted servants, possessed of a boundless devotion.   For them,
to borrow Madame Swetchine's felicitous words, "royalism was
patriotism simplified."

Unfortunately, however, it must be acknowledged that certain
chiefs of the emigrant party, the leaders, those who gave the
tone at Coblentz, "those red heels and light heads," as the Cardinal de Bernis somewhat contemptuously calls them, did not
have such disinterested views or such naïve expectations.   It
was their own cause as much as the king's which they were
upholding; it was their own power still more than that of the
king which they were seeking to defend and to perpetuate,
whoever might be the reigning sovereign, — whether it was, as
Gustavus III. had written to Stedingk, Louis XVI., Louis
XVII., or Charles X.   In 1790, had not an emigrant, the Baron
de Castelnau, "one of the best informed and most loyal," according to Mounier, said at Vienna that "even if in a counter-
revolution the king, queen, and the children should be sacrificed,
the Comte d'Artois would remain and the monarchy be saved"?
Was not this all the more true now that besides the Comte
d'Artois, Monsieur, the heir-presumptive to the throne after
the dauphin, was also outside of France?

Who can say that this prospect of a change in the person of
the royalty had not entered into the designs of some (though not
into those of the king's brothers, despite Marie Antoinette's
distrust of the Comte de Provence), but into those of some of

their counsellors, who hoped to have greater influence with the princes than they could ever have with the king and queen?

Madame de Bombelles was right, therefore, when she wrote that "the little regard which they — the princes — have shown for the queen would always make her dread their dominion." And it can be conceived that the unhappy princess could have angrily exclaimed one day, when informed of this attitude, "They think themselves heroes! What will these heroes do, even with their king of Sweden?" And that at another time, she should have allowed herself in a moment of bitterness and unreserve to say, "If our brothers did succeed in rendering us some assistance, gratitude for it would be a heavy burden, and we should have in them, besides, the most intolerable and imperious masters."

Her political judgment, then, as well as her resentment as outraged sovereign and offended woman, led her to reject the armed co-operation of the emigrants. "It is essential," she wrote to Mercy on August 7, "that the princes and all the French refugees be held in check. I dread any action on the part of Calonne, and one false step would ruin everything."

On August 16 she is still more urgent. Why should she trust to the princes? They had no serious design; they would do no good; they could only do harm.

"And even if they have a real advantage, — which is not presumable, — we would, under their agents, fall into another bondage worse than the first, because, seeming to owe them something, we should be unable to free ourselves from them. They already prove this to us in refusing to concert with those who have our confidence, on the pretext that they have not theirs ; whereas they wish to force us to place ourselves in the power of Monsieur de Calonne, who can in no way be agreeable to us, and who, I fear, in all this pursues only his own ambition, his private animosities, and his characteristic levity, while always believing all that he desires to be possible, and even accomplished. I even believe that he can only do harm to my brothers, who, if they acted according to their own hearts, would assuredly be all for us."

Was she ignorant of the hostile designs entertained against her at Coblentz? Were they not thinking of proclaiming Monsieur regent, the Comte d'Artois lieutenant-general of the realm? They wished to annihilate the king, after having deprived him of his defenders. For was it not these perpetual summons to the emigrant camp which had created around the captive sovereigns an insulation under which they were sinking, and which was forcing her to demean herself and stoop to dissimulation? And the queen, indignant at this thought, feeling her wrath rise, reopened her letter of August 20, to insist again in the most explicit and harshest terms upon the necessity of rejecting the co-operation of the emigrants.

" It is essential that the French, above all, that my brothers, remain in the background, and that the allied powers act alone. No prayer, no argument on our part, will obtain this from them : the emperor must demand it ; this is the only way in which he can render me, in particular, a service. You yourself are acquainted with the evil designs and the evil purposes of the emigrants. The cowards! After having abandoned us, they ask that we expose ourselves alone and serve their interests only. I do not accuse the king's brothers. I believe that their hearts and intentions are pure ; but they are surrounded and led by ambitious men, who will undo them after having undone us first."

On the 26th, after the departure of this letter, she wrote further entreaties : "It is vital that, for conditions, he — the emperor — demand that the king's brothers and all Frenchmen, but, above all, the first-named, remain in the background and do not appear."

The emperor, moreover, was very naturally disposed to gratify his sister's wishes; he felt neither confidence in nor sympathy for the emigrants. On July 6, he had addressed an appeal to the electors of Trèves and of Cologne, urging them to prevent the French refugees from taking any imprudent step; and on the 30th of the same month he wrote to his sister, Marie Christine, governor of the Netherlands : —

" Do not allow yourself to be led into anything, and accede to nothing which the princes and the French emigrants ask of you beyond polite attentions and dinners ; but no troops or money. I heartily pity their situation and that of all Frenchmen who have been obliged to expatriate themselves ; but they are surrounded by evil companions ; they think of naught but their romantic ideas, their revenge, and their personal interests, and believe that all the world should sacrifice itself for them."

" In this whole affair," he wrote a little later, "I have seen no one who talks sensibly, and hearkens to reason, except the queen, Monsieur de Fersen, and Bouillé." He himself wished to act only with " the complete co-operation of all the powers."

It was to this purpose that he arranged an interview with

the king of Prussia. The interview took place at Pillnitz in Saxony on August 25; the Comte d'Artois had also gone thither with Calonne, much to Leopold's displeasure. The proclamation which resulted from the long conferences between the emperor, the king, their ministers, the French prince and his counsellors, is known; it will not be amiss, however, to give the text of it here: —

His Majesty the emperor and his Majesty the king of Prussia, having heard the wishes and statements of Monsieur and of Monsieur le Comte d'Artois, declare conjointly that they regard the present situation of his Majesty the king of France as an affair of common interest to all the sovereigns of Europe; they hope that this interest will not fail to be recognized by the powers whose concurrence is solicited; that, in consequence, they will not refuse to employ, with their said Majesties, the most efficacious means relatively to their forces to place the king of France in a position to establish in perfect liberty the basis of monarchical government, which is equally in accord with the rights of the sovereigns and with the well-being of the French nation. Then, and in this event, their said Majesties, the emperor, and the king of Prussia, are resolved to act promptly, by mutual consent, with the forces necessary to obtain the true welfare of all. In the mean while they will issue to their troops proper orders, that they be in readiness to go into active service.

LEOPOLD.

FREDERICK WILHELM.

PILLNITZ, Aug. 27, 1791.

As threatening as this proclamation may have seemed, it was, at bottom, to use Mallet du Pan's expression, only "an august comedy." The five words, "Then and in this event," which had been introduced by one of the Austrian diplomatists, Spillmann, in drawing up the document, had annulled its whole import. The sovereigns should only act in the event of a general concurrence of the powers; and Leopold himself pronounced this occurrence "very difficult," if not impossible. It was, however, a singularly dangerous comedy. The manifesto, sooner or later known by the public, who were ignorant of the mental reservations and the other side of the cards, could not fail to produce a double effect: raise the expectations of the emigrants, who would believe themselves supported, and inflame the passions of the Revolutionists, who would suppose themselves threatened; in every way, then, it would endanger the security of those whom it designed to save.

The queen understood this; she disapproved strongly of the proclamation of Pillnitz:—

"It is said here," she wrote to Mercy on September 12, "that in the agreement signed at Pillnitz the two powers pledged themselves never to permit the establishment of a new French Constitution. There are indeed points in it which the powers have the right to oppose, but in what regards the interior laws of a country each is master in his own, and may adopt those which are pleasing to him. They would therefore do wrong to make such an exaction, and all the world would recognize in it the intrigue of the emigrants, which would destroy all the justice of their cause."

It will be objected, perhaps, that there is in this a strange contradiction, and that the queen, in soliciting the support of the powers, in effect demanded that which by this letter she refused,—foreign intervention in the interior constitution of the country. We believe this to be a wrong interpretation of her thought. The queen desired that, through the menacing attitude, or if one wishes, through the pressure even of the powers, the king be set at liberty; that was all. The king, once more become master of his actions, would himself decide with the representatives of the nation what he should retain and what reject in the Constitution, the defects of which were evident, but which he could not, while a prisoner at Paris, refuse to sanction.

It must not be imagined that it was under the influence of Lameth and Barnave that Marie Antoinette had written the wise and resolute lines which we have just cited. No; this letter of September is distinctly confidential: it is the protest of her patriotism, the cry of her heart, the deep feeling of her dignity as queen and as Frenchwoman. If any one desires to see to what extent she opens her whole soul in it, let him continue the letter to the end and read this:—

"At last the die is cast; at present each one must think of shaping his course of conduct according to circumstances. I heartily wish that every one would shape his actions after mine; but even in our interior we have serious obstacles to overcome and bitter contests to fight out. Pity me; I assure you greater courage is needed to endure my position than to stand in the midst of a battle,—all the more that I have rarely been deceived, and that I see only misfortune alike in the weak energy of the one side and in the ill-will of the other. *Mon Dieu!* is it possible that, born with strength of character, and fully sensible of the blood which flows in my veins, I am destined to pass my days in such a century and with such men? But do not fancy, for that reason, that my courage is forsaking me. Not for myself, but for my child I will bear up, and follow my long and painful career to the end. *I no longer see what I write.* Adieu!"

But some days later she wrote to Esterhazy "that he must not concern himself for her personal safety, but only for the welfare of France."

CHAPTER XIII.

DURING all these negotiations and interchange of letters,
the National Assembly had reached the end of its career.
The Constitution was completed on September 3, and on the
4th was presented for the king's acceptance; but the converted
Constitutionalists who had been abandoned on the day of discussion, through the unintelligent rancour of the Right, had
been unable to effect the introduction of those modifications
which they deemed essential to the dignity of the royal authority. What did Louis XVI. mean to do? Would he sanction a
work which experienced liberals, like Gouverneur Morris, declared "impracticable," which even its authors — the Lameths,
Barnave, Duport — considered full of dangerous errors, and
against which he had constantly protested, either secretly to
the other sovereigns, or publicly, in his message of June 20,
1791, before setting out for Varennes? Would he refuse his
sanction? But what would be the consequences of such an
act?

The queen had for some time been considering this grave
question, and had untiringly sought counsel concerning it from
Mercy and her most faithful friends. "The charter will be
presented to the king at the end of the week," she wrote on
August 21; "this moment is a terrible one." But did Mercy,
did Leopold, did the counsellors beyond the frontier, exactly
understand the situation?

"The Assembly will wish to compromise," wrote Mercy on July 28;
"the king must have the resolution to say that he will never consent to
anything until he, the queen, and the dauphin enjoy perfect liberty. It

is only by the greatest courage that he will overawe them. . . . He must not omit reasonable conditions. These would be, — the disarming of the nation, the king's power over the army, his full right to declare war or peace and to act in negotiations, and the right to assemble the next legislature outside of Paris."

But had these conditions, very wise, it is true, in the main, any chance of being accepted by a people as passionate and inclined to prejudices as the French? Who at that time could, without a violent struggle, have deprived the National Guards of their arms, which were to them the palladium of liberty? Had not the experience of Varennes just proved that Paris considered itself the capital only so long as it held the king and the Assembly? Could that have been done in 1791 which was only done eighty years later, after the most terrible revolt, and which even then did not last? The queen did not think so. To speak with resolution, as Mercy wished, it would be necessary to have an abundant force at their disposition, and if necessary support their words by energetic actions. She had not this force.

"What you write of the conditions to make," she answered, "is right, but impracticable for us. We have neither the strength nor the means; we can only temporize." Then, obstinately clinging, despite everything, to an invincible hope, she added, "With time and a little wisdom, I believe still that we shall be able to prepare a happier future for our children." A happier future, — what irony!

Leopold, like Mercy, named, as first condition, the king's departure from Paris, and his withdrawal to some province where, in full liberty, and under the protection of devoted followers, he could without constraint examine the Constitution now submitted to him. Even the place of his retreat was named, — a château belonging to Monsieur de Crouy, called the Hermitage, situated near Condé, or rather near Montmédy; and there the king would be surrounded by his body-guards.

Would the Assembly, however, consent? It was scarcely probable, for it would place the king in precisely the position in which he had wished to put himself on June 20; and it was to prevent him from executing this plan that he had been arrested at Varennes, brought back to Paris, and kept under strict guard at the Tuileries.

Would he even be permitted to go, not to Condé or Montmédy,— that is to say, to a town on the frontier and in the vicinity of foreign troops,— but to a little distance from the capital; to Fontainebleau, Rambouillet, or Compiègne, for example? Despite the opinion of Malouet and of Mallet du Pan, the queen had no belief in this.

"It is desired that we go thither,— to Rambouillet or to Fontainebleau ; but on the one side, how and by whom would we be guarded? and on the other, the people will never allow my son to leave. They are accustomed to look upon him as their property. Nothing will make them yield ; and," she added with the touching abnegation and legitimate apprehensions of maternal love, " we could not leave him alone."

It was easy enough for Burke to write from England: "If the king accepts the Constitution, you are all lost. . . . Not cleverness, but firmness alone can save you. . . . Your salvation consists in patience, silence, and refusal."

Patience,— the queen had exercised it for a long time; but silence, how observe that? How refuse the sanction, which was demanded, and in a way exacted? Did not one hear throughout Paris, and under the very windows of the Tuileries, the incessant murmur of insurrectionary threats? Were not the people, not only in the capital, but even in the provinces, — it had been clearly seen on the journey from Varennes, — carried away by an unreasoning but irresistible enthusiasm for this Constitution, which they did not know, but which in their naïve credulity and with that need inborn in France of always seeking a deliverer, they regarded in spite of Malouet's sinister prophecies as the dawn of cloudless day? Resist this popular impulse, but with what? What army, what authority had they?

" We have neither troops nor money," wrote the queen. " All that we can do for our honour and for the future is to make observations which will, of course, not be heard, but which, with the protest made by the king six weeks ago and modelled after it, will serve as basis of action for the moment when the enemy, misfortune, and a return to mental calmness will give play to reason."

Mercy himself, so strong a partisan at first of an energetic policy, came round to totally different opinions, and in sending the queen Burke's counsels, of which we have already spoken, and which urged resistance, he was careful to add: " Such is the idea of Mr. Burke and of the friends of the queen; but this idea, true in theory, is dangerous in practice. . . . Therefore we must undertake nothing rashly, but employ all our resolution in an effort to gain time."

The more the days advanced, the more the terrible necessity of accepting the Constitution pressed upon Marie Antoinette, however hard it might be for her pride. On August 26 she wrote again to Mercy: —

"In view of the situation here, it is impossible for the king to refuse his acceptance. *Believe that this must be true, since I affirm it.* You know my character well enough to believe that it would incline rather to a noble and courageous measure, but it is not one to incur a danger which is more than certain."

The queen, face to face with this evident necessity, endeavoured solely to gain time, as Mercy said, in order to wait a favourable opportunity to correct the more than imperfect work which they were being forced to accept. To accomplish this, they must before everything inspire confidence; nothing, either within or without, must occur to check the return of public favour or furnish food for the revolutionary passions. "It is only in this way," the queen wrote to the emperor, "that the people, having recovered from their madness, either through the misfortune which they have undergone in the realm, or through the fear of those outside, will come back to us, and desert the authors of their evils."

If we may believe an observer, — a friend, it is true, of the Constitutionalists, — a certain reaction was already being manifested in the public. A more sympathetic mob gathered about the Tuileries; the queen, taking her son in her arms, held him up to the people. She was cheered. On September 4, the mass at the château was extraordinarily brilliant; Louis XVI. and his family in going to it were, according to the report of a trustworthy witness, greeted with acclamations. Royalist sentiment was making perceptible advance; people were beginning to venture its defence in the cafés, at the Palais Royal even, that centre of the Revolution; and the leaders of the popular factions professed it among themselves. The majority were convinced that the Constitution, such as they had sketched it out, was impracticable. Barnave went so far as to say that future Assemblies should have no more weight than a council of

Notables, and that all the power should be vested in the government. Still more, many of those who had applauded and perhaps shared in the king's arrest, had come to lament openly that he had failed in his enterprise; they regretted that which was called "the plan of Montmédy," for, they said, this plan promised France "a good Constitution equally distant from the two extremes." The queen herself, so bitterly maligned, enjoyed a share in this return of popular favour; and sixteen thousand National Guards, it is said, wore rings bearing this motto, "Domine, salvum fac Regem et Reginam." It was therefore important to profit by this unexpected reaction, and even if the aristocrats should accuse her — as they did, to punish her for her antagonism to the emigrants — of sacrificing the welfare of France to her pride, was it not better to submit, in appearance at least, to a Constitution the defects of which were so glaring as to be obvious to the eyes of all so soon as they should even attempt to put it into practice?

It was then necessary to accept the constitutional act; but how, and in what terms? Here, again, opinions were divided. Malouet, La Marck, and Gouverneur Morris begged the king to make some reservations; and this was the policy to which Louis XVI. and Marie Antoinette manifestly inclined at first. The Constitutionalists, however, insisted upon an unreserved and simple acceptance; and the king, desirous not to alienate these counsellors of recent date, or awaken distrust in the sincerity of his adhesion, determined to follow their advice.

"To refuse would have been nobler," the queen wrote to Fersen; "but that was impossible under the existing circumstances. I should have preferred the acceptance to be simple and shorter; but that is the misfortune of being surrounded only by scoundrels. Yet I assure you that this is the least evil project that has passed. The follies of the princes and of the emigrants forced us into these measures; we were obliged, in accepting, to dispel all doubt as to our good faith."

On the very day on which the Assembly had put the finishing touches to its work, Lafayette, in order to take away all appearance of constraint from the king's deliberation and acceptance, had come to remove the guard placed round the royal family. The palace was again free, and the gardens were again reopened to the public. On the following Sunday, mass was celebrated in the chapel. The people repaired to it in a body, and manifested great joy in seeing the august prisoners once more.

They shouted on every side, "Vive le roi!" But a voice from the crowd, taking upon itself to state at what price the popular acclamations were given, called out, "Yes, if he accepts the Constitution."

On September 4, a deputation, led by Thouret, came in great pomp to present the constitutional act to the king; the king took it from the hands of the president and replied. that he would examine it. On the 13th he wrote to the Assembly that he accepted, and would go on the following day to take a solemn oath to uphold it; he demanded also that "the accusations and prosecutions to which the events of the Revolution had given rise should be cancelled in a general amnesty." The reading of this letter, composed by Duport du Tertre, but entirely written by the king's hand, called forth frantic applause. The amnesty was voted forthwith; there was a general exchange of politeness and good-will. A large deputation carried the decree to the Tuileries. The prince was with his family. "This is my wife, and these my children," Louis XVI. remarked; "they share my sentiments." Marie Antoinette added, "These are my children; we all heartily concur in the king's sentiments."

The king was sincere in his acceptance of the Constitution; he still hoped, through wisdom and patience, to make it fairly practicable, while enlightening the nation on the defects of this immature work, and on the true interest of the country. "He requested the queen and all those about him," says Madame de Tourzel, "to refrain from all reflections on the measures which circumstances had forced from him; to permit themselves no act contrary to the Constitution, and in conformity with one of its articles, to call Monseigneur le Dauphin in the future only by the name of Prince Royal." The queen had not the same confidence as her husband in the result of the experiment which they were about to try, nor in the goodness of the people; she submitted less easily to the sacrifices which the new system imposed upon royalty.

This submission, moreover, was soon to be subjected to a rude test. At noon of the 14th, the king repaired to the Assembly, surrounded by all his ministers. He took his place in an armchair by the side of the president, and pronounced the formula of the oath in a firm voice. The president, Thouret, with a strange disregard of all traditions and all propriety, had obtained a decree that the Assembly should remain seated while the king was speaking; the prince, who had stood in taking the oath, remarked this, and was keenly affected by it. The queen, who had voluntarily joined her husband and assisted at the meeting in a gallery, with her son, her daughter, and Madame Elisabeth, was moved by it still more. The enthusiasm, however, was so general that the public did not notice the singular innovation of the new government, which began by an official humiliation of royalty, or the sovereign's legitimate indignation; the hall and the galleries had united in loud and unanimous acclamations. After the meeting, the entire Assembly accompanied the royal family back to the Tuileries. The queen, on her arrival at the palace, hastily bowed to the ladies of her suite and entered her apartments. The king, pale, and with disturbed features, followed her, and throwing himself in a chair, exclaimed, pressing his handkerchief to his eyes, "All is lost. Ah, Madame, you were a witness of that humiliation. What! you came to France to see —" His voice was choked by sobs. The queen threw herself on her knees before him and clasped him in her arms. Madame Campan was there; Marie Antoinette made her a sign to leave the room, and the husband and wife remained together, mingling their tears and their sad forebodings.

Meanwhile, the enthusiasm outside was no less intense than at the Assembly. People thought the Revolution at an end, and peace and order henceforward assured,— no more dangers for the present, no more menaces for the future; it was a moment of transport, of madness. "The wise," said the Swedish ambassador, "did not share in this joy." But what did that matter to the crowd?

A few days later, the Constitution was proclaimed on the Champ de Mars; the municipality, the department, the public officers, the multitude, pressed thither; and when the constitutional act was read from the altar of the nation, a mighty shout of "Vive la nation!" burst forth from the throats of the three thousand men who were stifling in this enclosure. They laughed; they embraced one another; they congratulated one another. Balloons rose in the air, covered with patriotic inscriptions; there were popular games and distributions of provisions on the squares and public places. In the evening all Paris was illuminated; the boulevards, the Louvre, the Tuileries, the Place Louis XV., the Champs-Élysées especially, were ablaze; garlands of light stretched from tree to tree to the Porte de l'Étoile. The king, the queen, and the dauphin drove about until eleven at night, escorted by the National Guards and cheered by the crowd; shouts of "Vive le roi!" resounded on all sides. A man, however, had attached himself to the royal carriage; and each time that the cry, "Vive le roi!" broke forth, he shouted in stentorian tones in the queen's ear, "No, do not believe them. Vive la nation!" It was the brutal voice of the Revolution proclaiming that it had not abdicated, even before the people's enthusiasm. "The queen," Madame Campan relates, "was struck with terror by it; and when she returned to the palace, she remarked to Madame de Tourzel, 'How sad it is that anything so beautiful should leave in our hearts only a feeling of sadness and uneasiness!'"

The festivities, both religious and civil, continued none the less: the *Te Deum* was sung at the Tuileries; pieces expressing royalist sentiments were played at the theatres. On Sunday, the 25th, there were popular diversions furnished by the king, in the garden of the château.

"We have been to the opera," Madame Elisabeth wrote on that day to her friend, Madame de Raigecourt; " to-morrow we go to the Comédie. *Mon Dieu!* what pleasures! I am quite enraptured by them. And to-day we had the *Te Deum* at mass. There was one at Notre Dame. Monsieur, the intruder, was most anxious that we should attend; but when we have one sung at home, we can be excused from going to sing others, you will admit. We therefore remained quiet. We have another illumination this evening; the garden will be superb, all in lamps and little glass affairs which we have not been able for the last two years to mention without horror."

On Tuesday, the 20th, at the opera, and on Monday, the 26th, at the Comédie Française, their reception was excellent; there was "inexpressible applause." A few days later, at the Comédie Italienne, the enthusiasm was no less clamorous. "You can form no idea of the uproar which there was at the Comédie Italienne on Saturday," wrote Madame Elisabeth again to Madame de Raigecourt. "But," added the princess, sadly, "it remains to be seen how long this enthusiasm lasts."

On September 30, the king went to the Assembly to dissolve it. The president, Thouret, declared that the National Assembly had accomplished its mission; and Lafayette, radiant with happiness, set out for Auvergne, joyfully announcing that the Revolution was over.

CHAPTER XIV.

WHAT had been the impression created abroad by the solemn act of September 14? The princes, even before its official recognition, had, on the 10th, issued a protest against it, declaring that since the king's acceptance could not be voluntary, and was besides proscribed by his duty and the oath taken on his accession to the throne, it was null and void. They added that no order would keep them from following the course which their consciences marked out for them, and "that they were obeying the true command of their sovereign in not submitting to the interdictions which had been extorted from him." On September 11, the Prince de Condé, the Duc de Bourbon, and the Duc d'Enghien declared their adherence to this proclamation.

In the middle of September, and even before he had received this protestation, which was brought to him by the Duc de la Force, Louis XVI. had written a most touching and judicious but unavailing letter to his brothers, entreating them to return to France, and not to complicate the difficulties which assailed him.

"I know," he said, "how much the nobility and clergy are suffering from the Revolution. All the sacrifices which they have so generously volunteered have been repaid only by the destruction of their fortunes and of their existence. Certainly no one could be more unhappy and have deserved it less ; but, for crimes done, must others be committed? I too have suffered ; but I feel the courage to suffer still more rather than make my people share my misfortunes. . . .

"I know," he said further on, "that many among my emigrated subjects imagine a great change in the minds of the public. For a long time I believed that it was to come; but to-day I am disillusioned. The nation loves the Constitution because that word suggests to the lower class of the people nothing but the independence in which they have been living for the last two years, and to the class above, equality. They are ready to censure this or that decree individually; but these are not what they call the Constitution. The common people see that they are taken into account; the *bourgeoisie* sees nothing beyond. Their vanity is gratified; this new delight has caused all others to be forgotten. . . . Time alone will teach them how much they have been deceived.

"We must therefore wait, and, above all, carefully guard against everything which could make the people believe that we wish to destroy the Constitution, which they regard as the charter of their liberty; its application (and this cannot be deferred) must prove to them its unfitness."

And the king closed with these lines, in which he could not conceal his bitterness of soul : —

"I was just finishing this letter when I received the one which you had sent me. I had seen it printed before receiving it, and it was circulated everywhere at the same time. You cannot imagine what pain this step has caused me. . . . I will make you no reproach; I cannot find it in my heart to do so. . . . I will only call your attention to this: that in acting independently of me, he [the Comte d'Artois] only thwarts my movements as I foil his. You tell me that public opinion has reacted, and you assume to know more about it than I, who am enduring all the evils of it. I have already told you that the people bore their privations because their leaders constantly held out to them the promise that they would end with the Constitution. Only two days ago was it terminated, and you desire that public opinion be changed! I have the courage to accept it, in order to give the nation time to taste this happiness with which they have been led on, and you desire that I renounce this useful experiment! You fancy that you will overawe me by declaring that you will proceed despite me; but how convince me when that proclamation of the emperor and the king of Prussia was drawn up at your request? Will any one ever believe that my brothers will not execute my orders? Thus you will make me appear to the nation as giving my acceptance with the one hand and stirring up the foreign powers with the other. . . .

"I say nothing to you of my personal position. No one probably concerns himself about that outside of France; but I am concerned about that of my brothers. . . . I understand that others no longer consider my sufferings or my perplexities, but you should spare me those which regard you."

In vain did Louis XVI., a few days later, fearing lest this letter might appear an official and enforced message, address another and strictly confidential note to his brothers, in which he renewed his entreaties and besought them to conform their policy to his, and not deprive him of his last defenders; for he said, "I have great need of some of them near me." All his prayers were unavailing. The princes, as sole response, circulated in profusion at Paris and in the departments a new protest against the Constitution, and wrote the following note to their brother, which was found after August 10 in the king's writing-table, "If we are addressed in the name of those men, we shall not listen; if in your name, we shall listen, but shall go our own way."

In vain did Madame Elisabeth, who was held at Paris by a devotion worthy of admiration, but who was often drawn in heart to Coblentz, try, through the medium of her friends, Madame de Bombelles, and especially Madame de Raigecourt, to allay the dissensions which divided the royal family. In vain did she write to them in that enigmatical style which was employed in their correspondence.

"They will ruin all if they have other views for the future than confidence in and submission to the orders of the Father. Every opinion, every idea, every sentiment, should give way before them. . . . You will tell me that this is difficult even if it is in the heart ; but the more I feel it to be difficult, the more I desire it. . . . The Father has almost recovered ; his affairs have revived ; but now that his head has returned, he will wish in a short time to resume the administration of his estates, and that is the moment which I fear. The Son, who sees advantages in leaving them in the hands in which they are, will insist upon it ; the stepmother will not permit it ; and this must be avoided, while at the same time the young man must be made to feel that even for his personal interest he must not pronounce an opinion in this matter. . . . The young man must also be persuaded to show a little more favour toward his stepmother, — only a little of that charm which a man knows how to employ, and by which he will convince her that he wishes to see her as she has always been. . . . People will speak ill of the stepmother, but I believe it to be exaggerated."

Madame Elisabeth's expostulations were listened to no more than Louis XVI.'s prayers. It has been seen by the note cited further back, what value the princes set upon the king's authority; their followers were more violent at Coblentz. The queen was daily spoken of as "Democrat;" the king as "poor man" and "small joist." The "Journal des Princes," published by Suleau, was so full of insults against Leopold and Marie Antoinette that the princes were obliged to suppress the paper, to discharge Suleau, and dismiss the censor, Christine, Calonne's secretary. Madame de Bombelles, the echo of these reports, indignant at these outrages, was driven to write to Madame de Raigecourt on November 3, —

"How could the queen ever trust Monsieur le C. D. when she knew the infamous things which those about him have said and still say against her and against the king? I cannot, thank God, be reproached for having brought to her ears *all that I have heard;* but I know enough to feel that if she is as well informed as I she will not run the risk of intrusting her fate to men who owe her much and who are her deadliest enemies. I except Monsieur le Comte d'Artois from the qualities of which I speak; his soul is upright, noble, and frank, and I am inwardly convinced of the purity of his intentions; but being weak, like most princes of the blood, he allows himself to be blindly led by his associates."

The dissension between the Tuileries and Coblentz grew in intensity every day. Apart from the rivalry between Breteuil and Calonne (the first the authorized agent, the second the personal enemy of Marie Antoinette), the differences of opinion between the princes and the king, and more especially the queen, became daily more marked, each wishing to control the proceedings, — the princes desiring to rush ahead and destroy the Constitution, sword in hand; the king endeavouring to temporize, and better matters; and the queen opposing, above all, any action on the part of the princes, which she thought, with reason, would have no other result than to "irritate the malcontents without frightening them," and would, through this, imperil the success of a plan with which she had been occupied since the return from Varennes, and which every day assumed a more definite form.

The powers, like the royal family, were divided; as their own private interests prompted them, they leaned toward the princes or toward the king. Whereas Gustavus III. broke with the Assembly, returned to Louis XVI., unread, the note in which the French king notified him of his acceptance of the Constitution, and accredited the Comte d'Oxenstiern with

Monsieur; whereas the empress of Russia declared that the king's acceptance should be considered void because it had been forced; and that if Louis XVI. and Marie Antoinette were sincere in their acceptance, so much the worse for them, and that "in that case, the king must be regarded as a nonentity [*sic*];" while the king of Spain ordered his minister at Paris to make a journey to Nice,—Leopold, delighted with a circumstance which accorded with his procrastinating inclinations, proclaimed that all idea of counter-revolution was henceforth useless and dangerous, and that since Louis XVI. had announced his adherence to the constitutional act, there was nothing more to do but to wait and observe the turn that events might take. "The king and queen," he said, "have no other resource than to allow the Legislative Assembly time to bring itself into discredit. They should in the mean while conform strictly to the laws, build up around them a party, and take advantage of circumstances. That swarm of French bees," he added, in speaking of the emigrants, "should at last think of withdrawing; they will be a heavy burden for the country." And the king of Prussia on his side exclaimed, "At last I see the peace of Europe assured."

And Fersen, the zealous Fersen, returned from Vienna, where his master had sent him, to Brussels, where he established himself in order to keep up a correspondence on behalf of the king of Sweden with the king of France,—Fersen, who had remained for two months without direct news from the Tuileries, and had already been misled by Louis XVI.'s language, was still more so on receiving this letter from Marie Antoinette:—

"I believe that the best way to disgust the people with all this is to appear to be wholly in favour of it; this will soon show them that it is in nowise practicable. Besides, in spite of the letter which my brothers wrote to the king, and which, by the bye, has not produced in the least the effect here which they hoped it would, I do not see, judging from the declaration of Pillnitz, that foreign aid is so prompt. This is perhaps fortunate, for the more we advance, the more will these scoundrels here feel their misfortunes; perhaps they will themselves come to desire the foreigner."

Fersen, dumfounded by this unexpected resignation of his royal correspondent, put to her directly the three following questions:—

"1st. Do you intend to place yourself sincerely on the side of the Revolution; and do you believe that there is no other resource?

"2d. Do you wish to be aided, and do you wish that all negotiations with the courts be discontinued?

"3d. Have you a plan, and what is it?"

The queen, however, hastened to undeceive her chivalric servitor:—

"Do not be alarmed; I am not going over to the *enragés*, and if I see and have communications with some of them, it is only to make use of them; they inspire me with too great horror for me ever to go over to them.

"Be undisturbed; I shall never go over to the *enragés;* I am obliged to make use of them to prevent greater evils; but as for good, I know that they are incapable of doing it."

They must dissimulate; they must gain the confidence of the people: this was the only way of arresting or at least of deferring the evil, and of preparing the good. For, said the queen, "If public sentiment does not change, no human force could steer in an opposite direction." Therefore, to change the sentiment, it was better to appear to yield to it at first in order to convert it, and the passive attitude formed a part of the plan the execution of which Marie Antoinette was endeavouring to accomplish through the medium of her former counsellor Mercy, and of the faithful Fersen.

Convinced that there was nothing for the moment to be accomplished within the realm, that the discontent which the application of the Constitution could not fail to arouse would be unfruitful and inefficient if the malcontents did not feel themselves supported and if necessary incited by an imposing force outside; convinced, on the other hand, that the emigrants could not form this force because their threats would only serve to exasperate the French; galled herself, moreover, by their attitude and the little respect which they showed for the king's wishes, even when formally and distinctly expressed,—she asked that the emperor take the initiative in what she called an armed congress. The powers should assemble at Aix-la-Chapelle their ambassadors to Paris, and all other plenipotentiaries. There, taking in hand the threatened peace of Europe, especially instancing the occupation of Avignon, the infringed rights of the German princes in Alsace, the guarantee of the treaties passed with France and compromised through the change of government; supporting their claims, if need be, by the presence of the heads of the armies on the frontier, who would be able at the same time to overawe the "more enraged party of the malcontents," and "of affording the more reasonable means of doing good;" studiously avoiding, however, all mention of the Constitution, even announcing loudly that they wished in no way "to interfere in the interior government of France,"— they would, "in reasonable language," address to the French government an injunction, the first article of which would be that Louis XVI. should have the power to leave the capital and go where he chose. Meanwhile, — for this could not be the work of a day, and "the nation must be allowed to breathe after so many shocks," and be given time to "resume its habits and customs before judging of what circumstances might require and permit,"— the king should endeavour to win the confidence of his people, should secretly combat the Assembly while striving to bring it into discredit, but should enforce a strict application of the Constitution, that the nation, perceiving through experience the evils of this misbegotten work, be led itself to desire its alteration. The proclamation of the powers, coming at that moment, would restore courage to honest people in giving them armed support and a rallying-point, and would terrify the rebels; and the king, once more free, could join the congress and act as mediator between his subjects and the allies. "This is the only expedient course for him," wrote the queen, in a letter she acknowledged to be the exact expression of her thought; "both from love of his people and in order to intimidate the seditious emigrants, who, by the tone which they take, and which would become more aggressive if they should contribute to the establishment of a new order of things, would replunge the king into a new bondage." Having recovered his full authority, without in any way wishing, however, to reinstate the old government, "free to make such a Constitution as he might wish," he would, in concurrence with the representatives of the country, accomplish all necessary reforms, as he had intended to do if he had reached Montmédy on June 20. All rational citizens of the nation would come to the aid of the sovereign in the execution of these reforms; and the Revolutionists, having everything to fear from the resolute attitude of the powers, would be glad enough to submit to justice tempered with mercy. Thus order would be re-established without bloodshed, through the simple accord of the powers and the initiative of the king. "The Revolution would be effected in the interior of each town, but would be achieved by the approach of war, and not by war itself."

So far as one can make it out from the innumerable despatches interchanged between Paris, Vienna, Brussels, Stockholm, and St. Petersburg, such was the plan upon which the queen had fixed,—the plan the realization of which she pursued with indefatigable perseverance until the declaration of war rendered a pacific solution impossible, and for which she condemned herself to incessant correspondence, writing letters upon letters, memoirs upon memoirs, she who, as she said, "did not know how to write them;" the plan which Mercy, after some hesitation, had finally adopted, and in which the king had been able to concur without being accused of duplicity; for in accepting the Constitution, he knew that it was impracticable, and although he obeyed it scrupulously himself, he could not render possible that which was by its nature impossible; the plan, in fine, to which the chivalric Fersen, still the confidant of the Tuileries, dedicated himself heart and soul. Here are the touching lines by which he protested his absolute and disinterested devotion, for calumny had not spared him; the Swedish and Spanish ambassadors had ventured to accuse him of ambition:—

"They are right," he wrote to the queen: "I am ambitious to serve you, and all my life I shall regret that I have not succeeded; I wished to discharge toward you a part of the obligation which it is so pleasing to me to owe you; and I wished to show them that one can be devoted to persons like yourself with no ulterior motive. The rest of my conduct would have proved to them that this was my sole ambition, and that the glory of having served you was my sweetest recompense."

But was this plan practicable, and was it not founded upon an illusion? The accord of the powers, which was its essential basis,—how obtain it from former adversaries, who were jealous of each other, and who at bottom had but one common aim: the weakening of France, a natural consequence of the anarchy to which the country seemed condemned. This universal alliance, dreamed of by the queen, in behalf of the monarchical principle attacked in France, was only a "snare," said the Comte de Metternich to the Baron de Breteuil. Prussia regarded

Austria with distrust. Austria had no more confidence in Prussia, and turned at times toward England; meanwhile she shut herself up in her egotism. Spain, in her feebleness, England saw with joy, was perhaps secretly stirring up a revolution which promised to reduce her eternal rival to impotence for some time to come. Russia urged the others to throw themselves into the fray on the condition of doing nothing herself, and of being allowed a free hand in Poland. Sweden alone was honest in her desire to act; but what could she do alone, and had not the ill-fated Louis XVI. the right to say to Fersen some months later, "I was abandoned by every one"?

However, even if this unattainable agreement had been realized, even if this "armed mediation" which the worthy and wise Mounier coveted as much as the queen, and which the Constitutionalists themselves at last perceived as the remedy, had been effected, would it have succeeded? Many truly liberal minds — we have just cited some examples — thought so. They had so often seen a handful of malcontents terrorize a well-meaning crowd that they believed that fear would be an effectual means of restoring all, as it had been of destroying all. This was a mistake. They reckoned without that excitability of the national sentiment which rebelled against any show of intervention, and which would respond to threats of force by a seizure of arms. The king and queen were sincere in their desire to avoid war, and in their conviction that they would avoid it; but without wishing it, they were inevitably marching toward it.

CHAPTER XV.

MEANWHILE, in France, a second legislature had succeeded the first. The Constituent Assembly, by a fatal resolution, in which the animosity of the Right unhappily joined with the animosity of the extreme Left, had decided, before breaking up, that none of its members could be re-elected. This was yielding up the destinies of the country to all the blunders of inexperience and the follies of impetuosity. The old Assembly, whatever may have been its faults, contained in its midst great talents, great fortunes, great names; three years of practical experience in affairs had tempered the ardour and modified the prejudices of many of its members. The new Assembly was composed for the most part of unknown men without personal position, and without distinction, — small provincial noblemen, insignificant country lawyers, petty municipal officers, and procurators of districts, intoxicated with vague theories, fed on hollow phrases, without knowledge of politics, and without ideas of government. "It was scarcely more," Staël jestingly remarks, "than a council of the lawyers from all the towns and villages of France."

"It is believed," added the ambassador, "that the majority will be good." Staël was mistaken, and one of the new deputies, Hua, attorney to the Parliament of Paris, saw more correctly when he wrote: —

"The Right is composed of one hundred and fifty Constitutionalists; the Left counts one hundred and fifty Jacobins; and the Centre presents a mass of more than four hundred deputies, which are called the Impartials, — a phalanx immovable for good, and only impelled by fear; it gives the majority, and it will give it, not to the Right, which it esteems, but to the Left, which it fears."

From the start the Assembly manifested the spirit which was to control it. The king having announced that he would come in person to take the oath of obedience to the Constitution, the question of the formalities to be observed in receiving him was immediately raised. The Jacobins noisily opposed all form, not only that which would recall the old *régime*, but that which would express a simple deference on the part of the legislative power for the monarchical authority. The Assembly, yielding to their clamours, and to the domination which was already passing into the hands of the most violent, decided that the title of Sire or of Majesty should be no longer given to the king; that the prince's armchair should be placed on the same line as that of the president; and that when the monarch had arrived, the deputies could take their seats and resume their hats. On the following day, it is true, the decree was revoked; but the Left had shown its strength and the Assembly its weakness.

It had been obliged, however, to give way before an irresistible reaction of opinion in the capital. The Parisian *bourgeoisie*, who were sincerely attached to the Constitution, had been indignant at the attacks of this new legislature; the National Guards had vigorously protested, hence the repeal of the decree. The royal family experienced in this a last revival of popularity. On Saturday, October 8, they went to the Comédie Italienne. When they appeared, cheers greeted them; applause mingled with sobs was heard, and the shout of "Vive la reine!" was once again associated with the cry of "Vive le roi!"

A few days later, on November 2, a deputation from St. Domingo came to solicit the protection of Louis XVI. against the disorders which were desolating their island. The expiring colonies saluted the royalty which was so soon to die.

"Madame," the leader of the delegation said to the queen,

"in our great misfortune we needed to see your Majesty to find both consolation and a noble example of courage."

Marie Antoinette, choking with emotion, was unable to reply at once; she met the delegates again on coming from mass. "Messieurs," she said to them, "it was impossible for me to answer you; my silence will tell you more than any words."

The putting into practice of the Constitution had occasioned trouble at the court; the so-called honours and prerogatives which were attached to it had been suppressed. Several of the ladies of the palace had resigned their positions; they were not replaced, and the civil household was not formed. The king and queen could not bring themselves to it; they shrank from thus sanctioning officially the annihilation of the old posts by nominations to the new ones; they felt that the household without knights and maids of honour would be but a melancholy entourage. Besides, who would consent to enter an organization which had been thus modified and, as it were, abased? "If this constitutional household were formed," remarked the queen, "there would not remain one nobleman with us; and when things were again changed, we should be forced to dismiss those whom we had put in their places."

They occupied themselves solely with the military household, which was organized a little later under the command of the Duc de Brissac; but its existence was short.

In this critical position of affairs, counsellors abounded. Spain accepted the idea of a congress, but she wished first that the king be free, and prove it by openly leaving Paris. Leave Paris! No one desired it more than Marie Antoinette; but was it possible under the conditions mentioned by the king of Spain? Obviously not. "It will always be said here," replied the queen, "that he — the king — is at liberty to go where he chooses, but he cannot, in fact, because, aside from his departure from here, which would be hazardous, and to effect which he would be obliged, perhaps, to leave his wife and his son, his personal safety would be nowhere greater than here, since there is not a town or a troop upon which we can count."

A project of flight was indeed formed in the beginning of October; the attempt which had been so unsuccessful in the month of June was to be repeated toward the middle of November, and, it would seem, under nearly analogous conditions. Who were the originators of this plan? What were the details of it? With the concurrence of whom was it to be realized? The queen does not tell us, and we find no trace of it elsewhere. Why was it given up? Was it through the remembrance of the defeat at Varennes, or in consequence of that sad statement that they could not count upon one town or one troop? This last reason seems to us the most probable one. That which is definitely known is that the idea, announced in a letter of October 19, seems abandoned twelve days later, on the 31st. The report of it, however, had got about among the people, spreading uneasiness and distrust of the royal family. It was talked of at Paris; it was known at Coblentz in October. The date was even fixed, the 27th of the month; and by a strange coincidence, at the very time named by Marie Antoinette for the execution of the project, the news suddenly spread among the emigrants that the king had succeeded in happily quitting the capital, and had arrived at the house of Monsieur de la Marck at Raismes near Valenciennes, so ill-guarded were the secrets of the court, even those which were known to the fewest confidants.

The queen, deceived in her hopes of flight, returned to her original plan,—to efface herself as much as possible, and allow the powers assembled in a congress to act; then only could the king recover his liberty to some purpose, that he might go to defend the interests of France in this European assembly. "If we ever gain this point," wrote Marie Antoinette, "it will end all troubles, and it is for this goal that we should strive." To do this, it was essential to silence mistrust, and to win back public opinion. On this every one was agreed,— Mercy, La Marck and Fersen; but was it necessary for the king and queen to submit entirely to the revolutionary party, to adopt without comment their ideas and their measures, to have no share, even, in the choice of the ministers? Neither Mercy nor La Marck thought this; they would have liked a cabinet which was homogeneous and able, enlightened and loyal, eminently constitutionalist, but also very royalistic and resolute, determined to create for itself in the Assembly a government majority.

It was not even attempted. The queen was convinced that neither good ministers nor loyal deputies could be found; she prevented Monsieur de Moustier from entering the cabinet, and even regretted having called Bertrand de Molleville to it; she wished to reserve these men for better times. Meanwhile, everything was adrift; and the ministry, which, if judiciously composed, might have secured a predominant position in opposition to an Assembly discredited at the outset, became the humble servant of the legislative body.

This species of abdication distressed La Marck, who could not understand it.

"The queen," he wrote to Mercy, — "the queen, despite her spirit and tried courage, loses every opportunity which presents itself of seizing the reins of government and surrounding the king with faithful men, eager to serve him and to save the State with her and through her.

"If one attempt to search out the causes of the indecision and inaction which reign at the Tuileries, one finds that the king and queen, through indolence of mind and of disposition, and perhaps also through prostration, which often follows prolonged misfortune, have no hope except in the chances of the future and in foreign intervention, — of which the announced congress gives a vague glimpse, — and they think that in the interim only a few private measures are required on their part to assure their personal safety.

"In joining this policy to the frantic agitation of eighty million fools, how can one foresee any result but the most deplorable future?"

Malouet and the Abbé de Montesquiou, two of the usual counsellors of the court, discouraged like La Marck, left Paris, — the first to go to England, the second to withdraw into the country, to the home of Monsieur du Châtelet.

Did the queen succeed at least in winning the favour of the people by this passive attitude? At the beginning it was believed so. Either because of fatigue from past agitations, or confidence in the future, there was a momentary pause, if not a reaction, on the part of the Parisian public: it craved order and peace; it felt no need of new upheavals, since the chief leaders were overthrown and the king seemed to submit to his rôle of constitutional monarch. For many politicians of Lafayette's school, the goal was reached; they wished to go no farther. But one cannot easily arrest his course in the path of revolution; behind the satisfied stand the starving, and like a turbulent sea, one wave drives the other on. The queen felt this; and however reassuring appearances might be, she saw clearly, through the painful experience which she had gained in ten years of calumnies and three years of revolution, that this was only a lull between two storms, and that the hateful pack of hounds which were tracking her would not relinquish their pursuit.

"All is tranquil in appearance for the moment," she wrote on October 19; "but this tranquillity holds by a thread only, and the people are still what they were, — ready to commit horrors. We are told that they are loyal to us; believe nothing of the sort, — not at least, to me. I know the price of their loyalty; most of the time it is paid, and they only like us so long as we do what they wish. It is impossible to continue long in this way; there is no greater security in Paris than formerly, — and perhaps even less, — for the people are becoming used to seeing us dishonoured."

This respect, moreover, with which the people affected to surround Louis XVI. and his family, was only feigned; in reality they treated them like criminals. Every night a guard slept across the door of their apartments. Once even, a corporal had taken upon himself to confine the king and queen in their chambers from nine o'clock in the evening until nine in the morning; and this had continued for two days.

Devoted members of the Jacobin Club wormed their way into the service of the palace, and the unhappy prince, warned that they wished to poison him, dared not touch the dishes upon his table; a faithful servant, the steward of the small apartments, Thierry de Ville d'Avray, was obliged himself to bring him the bread and wine. The destitution of the august prisoners was extreme; they had even on one occasion remained nine days without a sou, and the queen had been on the point of borrowing from a deposit which the Prince de Nassau had made for her. "Not being sure of my ability to repay it," she had said, "I do not wish to do injury to those who are devoted to us." And the archbishop of Aix, who had just passed some days at Paris, said to this same Prince de Nassau : —

"Whatever idea one may form of the misfortunes of the king and queen, no imagination can compass them. One must have undergone the anguish of witnessing them to conceive all their horror. And those which the Jacobins and the Republicans are preparing for them surpass these. However, it is more than probable that their intention is to end them only with their life."

But what were these physical privations beside the moral tortures? The queen saw herself alone in the struggle of at-

tempting all that she felt "so necessary for the general good."
The emigrant party had taken from her her surest supports. In
vain had she tried to arrest the current which carried the nobles
across the frontier; they paid no heed either to her admoni·
tions or to her prayers. Outside the princes were arming,
despite her and almost against her, thus furnishing fresh ground
for the suspicions of the Assembly, and fresh food for the
passions of the populace. And to allay these suspicions, she
was forced, ardent and proud woman, to stoop even to duplicity,
to beg, as it were, the suffrage of the Assembly, — a horde of
scoundrels, idiots, and beasts, for whom she felt nothing but
contempt; to speak contrary to her thoughts, to flatter people
whom she despised, to discourage those who possessed her con·
fidence. "Do you comprehend," she wrote to Fersen,— "do you
comprehend my position and the part which I am obliged to
play all day? Sometimes I do not understand myself, and am
obliged to reflect to make sure that it is indeed I who speak."

Even in her family — and this was the explanation of that apparent apathy which La Marck called indolence of character, and
which was only enforced inaction — she felt herself isolated.
Neither her husband nor her sister-in-law shared in her way of
thinking. Louis XVI. realized the evils which were over-
whelming him and the dangers which threatened his family; but
he resigned himself to the one, and made little effort to fight
against the other. Insensible to his wife's expostulations,
scornful of death, and too unmindful of life, possessed of a real
but purely passive courage, without vigour and without initiative, he had only strength to suffer. Madame Elisabeth, who
was more passionate than her brother, would have preferred
energetic action; she would not have recoiled from civil war;
she would gladly have mounted a horse; and it was not the
queen's diplomatic plan which appealed to her, but the attitude of the emigrants, of the Comte d'Artois and the Prince de
Condé especially, who were rallying round their white plumes
the soldiers of the monarchy. An heroically accepted duty
retained her at the Tuileries, but her thoughts and her heart
were at Coblentz. On the subject of the emigrant party, there
was too marked a difference of opinion between the two sisters·
in-law for their intercourse not to be at times troubled by it;
and I do not wonder that the unhappy queen, in a moment of
discouragement, between the king's inertia and Madame Elisa-

beth's sympathies for the princes, should have exclaimed, "Our domestic life is a hell!"

In her public life she was no happier: her intentions were traduced; the diplomacy of the emigrants thwarted her own, and the better to thwart it, they pretended to represent her as a Democrat. In vain did the queen write to Catherine II. to explain her policy, to show her the necessity which forced her to accept in appearance that which she disavowed in secret, and to invoke the aid of Russia for the congress in which she had put her last hope; she reaped but her own vain tears, and that disdainful note in which I know not what hidden gratification of feminine jealousy could have inspired the irony of the all-powerful aristocrat, "How unhappy is a man when he is brought so low as to cling to a reed as his sole hope! But what can be expected when people act continually from two different and exactly contrary motives?"

The emperor himself showed little more readiness to act. The queen had vainly urged her brother to do something. Leopold resorted perpetually to evasion, heaped pretext upon pretext for not bestirring himself, and did not even seem to be concerned about the terrible dangers to which his sister, brother-in-law, and nephew were exposed. Since the acceptance of the Constitution, which he had advised, he had become more and more indifferent. Even on the question of the armed congress, which seemed nevertheless to involve him so little, he held back, used every circumstance as an excuse for not interfering, which was tantamount to frustrating the entire plan; for it was well known that without him nothing could be done. At bottom, he thought only of his own interests, and feared, in the event of a conflict with France, a revolt of the Netherlands, ill pacified since the time of Joseph II., excited, moreover, by the proximity of the Parisian Revolutionists, and stimulated by their emissaries. Mercy himself, Marie Antoinette's old counsellor, who, however, had never been a warm advocate of a congress, — Mercy, faithful interpreter of his master's wishes, distressed the queen by his theories: —

"Our position becomes daily more embarrassing," wrote the unhappy sovereign on November 25, "yet the Assembly is so incompetent, and all honest men so weary of all these troubles, that with wisdom I believe that we shall be able to triumph; but for this I still insist on the armed congress, as I have already described it. This alone can check the follies of the princes or of the emigrants; and I see from all quarters that such a degree of disorder will develop here, before long perhaps, that, with the exception of the Republicans, every one will be delighted to find a superior force, in order to arrive at a general adjustment."

To all these urgent entreaties, Mercy only replied, "We believe a congress to be useless and impossible. We have taken into account the reasons which were opposed to a congress. Many other political reasons would render this congress more prejudicial than useful to France."

And growing indignant with those who wished to drag the emperor into dangers while themselves remaining under cover, he enumerated the disbursements which had already been made by Austria for the king of France. This was enough. Leopold was not disposed to prolong sacrifices for which he was so ill repaid, and the marching orders given to the troops were countermanded.

Thus all Marie Antoinette's hopes vanished; everything conspired against her,—her husband's weakness and her brother's coldness; the armed congress, her last resource, the keystone upon which her scheme of defence rested, was tottering to its fall like all the rest, through the fault of her own family. She could no longer bear it; and although she had hitherto carefully veiled her innermost sadness with silence, she could not now keep the bitterness of her heart from overflowing in her letters.

"I will not make reproaches for the past," she wrote on December 16; "I will not say that if the emperor had done what I asked of him in the month of July and since, the congress would have already met, or at least would be announced, and we should be in another position. . . . At this moment the armed congress could still be of the greatest use; but there can be no delay. This is the moment to serve us; if it is missed, all is said, and the emperor will only have the shame and the reproach, in the eyes of the entire universe, that he allowed his sister, his nephew, and his ally to languish in degradation when he might have rescued them. My view is perhaps a harsh one; but how can it be otherwise when all my interests are involved?"

With Fersen, her most devoted and most intimate confidant, she was still more explicit and severe:—

"What a calamity," she wrote to him, "that the emperor should have betrayed us! If he had served us well since the month of September only, as I wrote him in detail, the congress might have been instituted next month, and that would have been indeed fortunate, for the crisis advances here with rapid strides, and it may out-distance the congress; then what refuge shall we have?"

She no longer knew whom to trust, and one day when she had gone to St. Cloud to allow her children to breathe a purer air, she took Madame de Tourzel and Madame de Tarente aside and said to them, "I feel the need of pouring out my heart to persons so trustworthy as you, upon whose attachment I can count. I am wounded to the quick. On arriving in France, I put my trust in Monsieur de Mercy. . . . I looked upon him as a father; and I have the sorrow of seeing, by the little concern he has for my melancholy situation, how greatly I was deceived. Monsieur de Breteuil, on his side, always considers his own interests, and does not inspire us with entire confidence. The king is extremely displeased with Monsieur de Quenille, who writes his letters in a most peculiar style."

"We are watched like criminals," the unhappy woman wrote to the friend of her heart, the Duchesse de Polignac, "and such restraint is indeed horrible to endure. To be in constant dread for one's family, not to approach a window without being heaped with insults, to be unable to take the poor children out for the air without exposing these dear innocent creatures to the shouts of the crowd! Then, again, if one had only one's own troubles! But to tremble for the king, for all that is dearest in the world, for present friends, for absent friends, — this is a burden too heavy to bear; but as I have told you, my friends alone uphold me. Let us hope in God, who sees our consciences, and knows whether or not we are animated by true love for the country."

But why credit her with this true love? The journals railed against her untiringly, and Prudhomme published, in the "Révolutions de Paris," these threatening lines:—

"Antoinette, we do not demand of thee civic virtues; thou wast not born to have them! But abstain only from doing harm, and envelop thyself in thy purple mantle. So long as the hyena of the mountains remains in her lair, no one molests her; but when she descends into the plain to stain it with blood, the civic crown awaits the hero of humanity who, at the peril of his life, will deliver the country from this wild beast."

The allusion was obvious, and neither the queen nor the assassins could mistake it. In this painful situation the year 1791 came to a close, and the year 1792 began.

CHAPTER XVI.

THE queen had reason to say that the situation was becoming daily more alarming. The Legislative Assembly was directing a vigorous attack on the throne and the Constitution. A violent minority ruled the Assembly and inaugurated the reign by aggressive measures of which, by a just turn of events, it later became the victim. On November 9 a decree declared the proscription of the emigrants, pronounced the confiscation of their property, and decided that those who had not returned before Jan. 1, 1792, should be liable to death. On the 29th, another decree imposed severe penalties upon those priests who had not taken the oath prescribed by the civil Constitution. The king, encasing himself in his rights as constitutional monarch, and officially solicited, moreover, by the Directory of the department of the Seine, put his veto upon these two decrees; but at the same time, to propitiate public opinion, which had been aroused to indignation by the arming of the princes, he wrote to his brothers, urging them to return to France.

Louis XVI. and Marie Antoinette had neither of them ever approved of the emigration; they had tried to keep their most faithful followers from departing; they would have liked to retain, or at least recall, the body-guards. They despatched letters upon letters, agents upon agents, Viomesnil after Coigny, Goguelat after Viomesnil; they obtained nothing, on the ground that the sovereign being a prisoner, the princes were forced to act con-

trary to his instructions.   To the official letters the princes replied that they refused to obey "orders which were evidently
extorted by violence."   To agents like Goguelat they answered
by raillery, and an injunction to quit Coblentz immediately,
but not without having witnessed the little respect with which
the members of the inner circle of the little court at Schonburn-
lust spoke of the king and queen, designating the king as
"weakling," and the queen as "Democrat."

How painful was Louis XVI.'s position!   He saw the popular agitation increase round him; he felt that nothing excited
the passions in France more than the attitude of the emigrants
beyond the frontier, and that, as Pellenc discerningly wrote,
"if hatred of abuses had been the cause of the Revolution, hatred
of persons had almost immediately replaced hatred of abuses."
He knew that the populace had loudly applauded the decree
against the emigrants, because it gratified their rancour, and that
in putting his veto upon it, he had furnished his enemies with a
powerful weapon.   And during this time, his brothers refused
to obey both his confidential and official letters.   Do what he
would, he struggled unavailingly; neither on the one side nor
on the other did they believe in his sincerity.   The Assembly
suspected him of connivance with the emigrants; the princes
accused him of complicity with the Revolutionists.   Isolated
in his kingdom, without a party, without defence, he could only
expect an amelioration in pacifying the minds of the people, and
these grew daily more bitter.   The arming of the emigrants provoked the decree of the Assembly, as the threats of the Assembly provoked the attacks of the emigrants, and the king stood
between the two,— sorrowing but impotent spectator of a duel
to the death, of which his crown and his head were the prize.

On November 29, the Legislative Assembly obliged Louis
XVI. to demand from the princes of the empire the dispersion
of the troops of armed Frenchmen near the frontier.   On December 14, an ultimatum was addressed to the electors of
Trèves and of Mainz, summoning them to discharge the companies of emigrants; an army of one hundred thousand men,
under the leadership of Lafayette, Rochambeau, and Luckner,
was to support the summons.   The electors, thus threatened,
invoked the assistance of the emperor; and on December 21,
Leopold replied to the French message by a resolute note, in
which he declared that as head of the empire he would tolerate

no violation of imperial territory.   And to give greater weight
to his words, he commanded Maréchal Bender, then at Luxem·
bourg, to protect, if necessary, the electorate of Trèves against
all aggression.

This was not as yet war, but the harbinger of it.   The em·
peror, despite his disinclination, found himself forced to act.
The emigrants were overjoyed, despite the momentary disper·
sion which Leopold required of them, because they saw in this
the beginning of a conflict, in which they counted surely upon
playing a part; and the queen's counsellors were also delighted,
because they thought that the emperor, once involved, could
not draw back, and that he would necessarily be driven to resort
to an armed congress, which his inaction alone had prevenied
hitherto.   Mercy himself, the temporizing and prudent Mercy,
was beginning to believe that matters could not end without a
war, civil or foreign, perhaps both.   Nothing was ready yet, but
preparations were being made.   Leopold, the pacific, was be·
coming bellicose.   "The French desire war," he had said;
"they shall have it, but they shall pay the cost of it."   The
effective force of Austrian troops in Belgium was already aug·
mented, and orders given that all be in readiness by March 1.
The king of Prussia had, on January 14, declared his determina·
tion to assist at the armed congress; Catherine II. had also
announced her concurrence; and the king of Sweden was all
eagerness.

The Jacobins pressed this war with all their force, because
they dreaded the congress above everything.   On the otner
hand, the Constitutionalists feared it, because they felt that
amid the shock of armies and the tumult of passions, the frail
edifice which they had reared would perish in the tempest.   They
therefore drew up a memoir, to try to dissuade the emperor
from it, pointing out to him the fatal consequences which a
conflict would have for France, and for the safety of the royal
family, and citing the deleterious effect which the order given
to the Maréchal Bender had, according to them, already pro·
duced.   The queen, loyal to the principle of accepting every·
thing without objection, consented to send this memoir to
Vienna by a secret emissary, but in procrastinating on the pre·
text that she had no sure means of corresponding with her
brother.   And she was very careful to inform him that this was
the exclusive work of her temporary counsellors; that they had

not in any way expressed her own thought; and that it was of
the utmost importance to distinguish clearly her real interest
from all that she was obliged to do and say for her personal
safety and that of the king. She, on the contrary, gloried in
the resolute language to which Leopold for the first time had
given utterance, and in the fear which he had aroused among
the Constitutionalists,— a fear attested by the step which they
had taken at Vienna; and she concluded from this that a declaration of the powers, supported by imposing forces, would produce the same effect upon the entire country, and force the Assembly at last to come to terms with the sovereign.

This two-sided diplomacy, this contradiction between official
proceedings and secret sentiment, obliged the king and queen
to have outside of France authorized agents, commissioned to
make their real intentions known to the foreign courts. At
Berlin, it was the Vicomte de Caraman; at St. Petersburg,
the Marquis de Bombelles; at London, the bishop of Pamiers
and Mr. Crawford; and most important was the Baron de Breteuil, who was empowered to act for the king, and Count Fersen, the queen's correspondent. Then, besides these agents,
there were emissaries, sometimes French and sometimes foreign,
because these last, by reason of their very nationality, aroused
less the attention of the spies of every sort which were attached
to the Tuileries. And when among these foreigners the queen
met a man of trustworthy character, tried loyalty, and at the
same time of recognized authority, who, having had a near view
of things, could show her how they really stood, she did not hesitate to confide to him the delicate mission of picturing to her
friends and her allies the true situation of France and the
private sentiments of the sovereigns.

Such a man at the beginning of 1792 was Jean de Simolin,
Russian minister to Paris since 1784, who after the Comte de
Mercy's departure had in a measure taken his place in Marie
Antoinette's confidence. Simolin was to take a leave of absence
for some weeks; the queen begged him to come to see her,
received him in her sack without ceremony in her chamber,
where the king soon joined her; and there, after carefully slid-
ing the bolt of the door, she opened her heart to Simolin without
reserve, was profuse in expressions of gratitude for the czarina,
but did not conceal her dissatisfaction with the emperor's conduct, who, she observed, retained upon the throne the same way

of thinking as a petty Duke of Tuscany, took no interest in his relations, and did not even answer her letters. Emotion overcame her. Her eyes were wet; but forcing back her tears, she unfolded her entire plan to the Russian minister, explained to him the reasons for her policy, depicted the situation in strong terms, and charged him to represent it exactly in all its horror to Leopold and Catherine; and when Simolin, himself moved to tears, urged as objection the dangers which the interventions of the powers might create for the royal family, she replied:

"Say to the emperor that the nation has too great need of the king and of his son for them to have any cause for fear; it is they whom it is important to rescue. For myself I fear nothing; provided they are safe, all else is of no concern to me, and I prefer to run all possible dangers rather than to live longer in my present state of degradation and unhappiness."

The queen, in her letter to the emperor, entered into no details, but contented herself with recommending Simolin, of whose wisdom and frank, straightforward manners she spoke in warm praise, and left to the Russian minister the task of communicating at length the ideas of the prisoners of the Tuileries.

Marie Antoinette was more explicit with Mercy, although Simolin was charged to "use some reserve" in talking to him. The letter which she wrote to him on this occasion was too important, and expresses too well the true sentiments of the unhappy princess, for us not to consider it our duty to reproduce it here in full:—

"February, 1792.

"M. de S., who is to join you, Monsieur, is kind enough to undertake my commissions. He purposes making a little journey to see Prince Galitzin; and following your advice, I have begged him to carry a letter from me to my brother. My total ignorance of the designs of the cabinet at Vienna daily renders my position more distressing and more critical. I do not know what attitude to assume or what tone to take. All the world accuses me of dissimulation and falseness; and no one can believe, with reason, that my brother concerns himself so little for his sister's frightful position as constantly to expose her to danger without saying anything to her. Yes; he exposes me to danger, and a thousand times more than if he took some action. Hatred, distrust, insolence, are the three springs of action at present in this country. They are insolent through excess of fear, and because at the same time they believe that no step will be taken by those beyond the frontier. That is clear. One need only observe the moments when they believed that the powers were really about to assume the tone befitting them; namely, at the emperor's office of December 21, — no one dared speak or move until he had been reassured. Let the emperor, then, once feel his own wrongs; let him show himself at the head of the other powers with an army, — an imposing army, however, — and I assure you that every one here will tremble. There is no cause for being uneasy about our safety: this country is provoking the war; the Assembly desires it; the constitutional course taken by the king protects him on the one hand, and, on the other, his existence and that of his son are so necessary to these scoundrels about us that this guarantees our safety, and I say there can be nothing worse than to remain as we are. There can be no help expected from time or from interior efforts. The first moment will be a difficult one to pass, but we must use great prudence and circumspection. I think, with you, that we should have adroit and trustworthy men, informed of everything; but where find them?"

Monsieur de Simolin, bearer of these letters and these instructions, left Paris on February 7, arrived at Brussels on the 9th, had an interview with Messieurs de Breteuil, Fersen, and de Mercy, and continued his journey to Vienna. Two days later, on February 11, Count Fersen on his side set out for Paris.

Of all the sovereigns who were concerned for the situation of the king of France, Gustavus III. was beyond doubt the most sincere and disinterested. He had accepted the congress; he was even disposed to go further; but he was, with reason, fearful of the tumult which the first threats of the powers could not fail to create at Paris, and of the dangers which the royal family would then run. The rumour had already spread abroad that in the event of war the king, queen, and their children would be carried to the south, probably into the Cévennes, under the protection of an army of Protestants. To avoid a double peril of a popular insurrection or of an abduction, Gustavus deemed it "imperative," and in this he was agreed with the empress of Russia, that Louis XVI. should, whatever might be the risks of a new flight, make every effort to elude the hands of his jailers. Two ways were open: to reach the sea and escape on a small English vessel, which would land at Ostend, or to take the land route, cross through the "Hunting Forests," avoiding the villages, and proceed under the guidance of smugglers to within about ten leagues of the frontier, where a detachment of light troops would meet the fugitives and protect them in leaving the realm. The king, queen, and dauphin should set out alone, in order not to complicate the preparations; Madame Elisabeth and Madame Royale should remain at Paris, where it seemed they would have nothing to fear. Whatever details there may have been of the plan, as it was urgent it be kept secret, and it would have been imprudent to trust it to the post, Fersen was commissioned to go and propose them to the prisoners, and arrange with them upon the spot.

This was not, moreover, the first time that projects of this kind had been presented to the royal family. Another faithful friend in misfortune — an Englishman, Mr. Crawford, who succeeded in residing at Paris incognito from December, 1791, to April, 1792 — had, in concert with the king of England, proposed to the queen to leave France with the dauphin, and had made all arrangements for the flight. The queen had refused. Her duty was to remain at the side of her husband; she was unwilling to abandon him.

By a strange coincidence, however, at the very moment when the counsellors of the king of Sweden were maturing a plan of escape, the rumour of another flight of the royal family was circulated about Paris. The public gossiped about it; the journals discussed it. They went into the details; the departure was to be effected by Calais; they even fixed the date, the night of January 12 and 13. The Assembly and municipality were roused; the new mayor of Paris, Pétion, doubled the guards at the palace; and the Assembly, after having on January 11 declared every Frenchman dishonoured who should take part in a congress designed to change the Constitution, decreed that no one should travel in France without an individual passport. The queen, informed of the intentions of her confidant, and alarmed at the dangers which he, the author of the journey to Varennes, would have to run if he were recognized, wrote to him to delay; and it was only after the king had refused his sanction to the decree concerning the passports that she permitted him to come.

Fersen therefore left Brussels on February 11 at half-past nine in the morning in a post chaise, without a servant, and accompanied only by a Swedish officer, by the name of Reuterswaerd. Both had a courier's passport for Portugal, under assumed names; and Fersen, the better to disguise himself, wore a wig. Despite their fear of the annoyances which travellers were then made to endure, they encountered no obstacles. Everywhere the people were polite; at Péronne, where an accident to their carriage detained them four hours, they had every reason to be satisfied with the kindness of the municipality and the National Guards. On Monday, February 13, at half-past five in the afternoon, they entered Paris unmolested. Fersen left his fellow-traveller; and the same evening, after having made arrangements with Goguelat, whom he had apprised of his arrival, he went to the Tuileries by a circuitous way, was only able to see the queen for an instant, but returned at midnight on the 14th, and found both the queen and the king.

One can surmise without difficulty what were the emotions of this first meeting after eight months of separation; what confidences exchanged between the prisoners and this defender, who had consecrated his fortune and his life to them without reservation; what memories revived, what tears shed! First came the ineffaceable memories of Varennes, the agonies and the outrages of that painful journey back; then the miseries of the present, and the brighter outlook, perhaps, for the future. They talked of the projected flight; they argued that it would offer great advantages in giving the stronger impetus to affairs, and facilitating the good intentions of the allies.

The queen appreciated this fully, and it was not the failure of the first attempt which discouraged her from a second. But the difficulties were very great; Fersen himself, who had his heart so fixed on flight, was forced to declare it impossible. The royal family were under direct surveillance; all vessels on the point of sailing were rigorously visited; and on the other hand, a large number of municipalities, especially those in the country, ignoring the king's veto, executed the decree concerning passports as if it had been sanctioned. The vigilance was so great that flight was physically impossible. To the material obstacles was added the moral obstacle, even more insurmountable, perhaps, — the king's conscience; having so often promised to remain, he felt scruples about leaving. He acceded, however; he even requested that one of the first acts of the congress should be to demand his departure from Paris, in order to assent in perfect freedom to the measures to be adopted, and to ratify the agreements made with the powers.   If this liberty were denied him, then he could attempt to flee through the woods by the route which Fersen advised and declared possible; and if this attempt failed, he gave full consent to the powers to act without regard to him.   "I must be put entirely out of the question," he said, "and left to go my own way."   This was a confirmation of what the queen had said to Simolin.

As to the measures taken by him and the approbation which he seemed to bestow on the acts of the Assembly, the powers must not be astonished at them, or deceived by them.   Such a policy on his part was rendered necessary by his precarious situation and his desire to avoid greater evils.   He had only sanctioned the decree of the confiscation of the property of emigrants to save it from plunder and fire, but he would never consent to its sale.

"Ah, so," he said, with his brusque good-nature, "we are among ourselves, and can speak freely.   I know that people charge me with weakness and irresolution; but no one has ever been in my position.   I know that I missed my opportunity; it was on July 14.   I should have gone away then, and I wished to; but how could I, when Monsieur himself begged me not to leave, and the Maréchal de Broglie, who was in command of the army, replied to me, 'Yes, we can go to Metz; but what shall we do when we get there?'   I missed the right moment, and I have never found another since.   I have been abandoned by every one."

The king and queen began to recount in detail, without recriminations, but with an emotion which also overcame Fersen, all the instances of ingratitude and desertions to which they had been and were daily victims, having in the cabinet only one man, Bertrand de Molleville, who was truly devoted to them; betrayed by those who owed them the most, and only able to look for help from those who owed them nothing.   In the extremity to which they were reduced, with the advance of revolutionary sentiments, the attacks of the Assembly, and the insults of the street, there was nothing to hope from within the realm, not even from an excess of evil, which, the queen asserted, "could not beget good;" there would be no serious and complete reaction of public opinion; they could only count upon the intervention of the powers.   This was not only the belief of the king and queen, but of their constitutional advisers,

Alexandre de Lameth and Duport, who constantly repeated to them that such a condition of things could not last; but there was no redress except through foreign troops, and without these all was lost.

"Altogether," wrote Fersen, in describing his interviews with the royal family to Gustavus III., "I found the king and queen firmly determined to bear anything rather than their present position; and from a conversation which I had with their Majesties, I believe that I can assure you, Sire, that they feel strongly persuaded that any compromise with the rebels would be useless and impossible, and that there is no way of re-establishing their authority except by foreign troops and foreign assistance."

However sweet this interview may have been, despite its sadness, Fersen did not consider it expedient to repeat it. The vigilance was so strict, and it would have been so disastrous for them, still more than for him, if he had been recognized! It was already a great deal that he had been twice able to gain admittance to the palace, in spite of the watchfulness of the jailers. He therefore set out again on the 15th; and to disarm suspicion went as far as Tours, and returned by way of Fontainebleau. On the 19th he re-entered Paris at half-past six in the evening, but he did not dare to return to the Tuileries. He was content to write to know if the king and queen had not further orders to give him, and remained in hiding two days. At one o'clock on the morning of the 21st, he again left Paris with his friend Reuterswaerd, having taken the extra precaution of providing himself with the courier's passport; and after some trouble in a little village near Marchiennes, he arrived at Brussels on the 24th.

If Fersen had not been held back by such great prudence; if he had been able to show himself at Paris, — he might have enjoyed a momentary consolation before quitting France.

On February 20, the queen went with her children to the Théâtre Italien; "Les Événements Imprévus," by Grétry, was given. When it came to the duet of the valet and the waiting-maid, Madame Dugazon, who was as strongly a Royalist as her husband was a Democrat, bowed in the direction of Marie Antoinette as she sang, —

"Ah, how I love my mistress!"

This was a signal for a frightful tumult. "No master! No mistress! Long live liberty!" shouted the Jacobins in the pit. "Vive le roi!" "Vive la reine!" replied the occupants of the boxes; the public became divided. Jacobins and Royalists dragged each other by the hair; but the Royalists were the stronger, and, as Madame Elisabeth said, "The Jacobins were well beaten." Tufts of black hair flew about the hall. The guards interfered and restored order. The audience made them repeat the duet three or four times, and when Madame Dugazon came to the line,—

" We must make them happy," —

people cried out on all sides, "Yes, yes!" Amid all this uproar the queen maintained a calm and noble bearing. As she left the theatre, she was overwhelmed with acclamations.

"This nation of ours is a queer one," wrote Madame Elisabeth to her friend, Madame de Bombelles, in relating this incident. "One must admit that it has charming moments." Alas! these moments were rare, and these plaudits fleeting. Four days after, two of the queen's pages were recognized at the Vaudeville, maltreated, and dragged in the mud. As for the queen herself, she was unwilling to run the risk of furnishing a pretext for quarrels in which her friends probably would not always be uppermost, and February 20 was the last day on which she went to the theatre.

CHAPTER XVII.

DESPITE the failure of his plan of flight, Fersen returned
from Paris "rather well content with his journey." He
was now acquainted with the real intentions of Louis XVI. and
Marie Antoinette; he knew what end to pursue, and this end
seemed in large measure attained. Harmony had been established between the king and the powers. The king consented
to let them act; the powers appeared determined to act. The
king of Prussia and the king of Spain, as well as the king of
Sweden and the empress of Russia, proclaimed the necessity
for it. Republican Switzerland united with monarchical Europe
for this purpose; even the emperor, that "Florentine" whose
slowness and silence had so often distressed his sister, seemed
disposed, despite the counsels of Kaunitz, who called the
queen's complaints "commonplaces," to rely no more upon
"declarations." "I have never seen him so animated," remarked Colloredo to Simolin. And Mercy, who had become
bellicose, laid his hand upon his sword, exclaiming, "There
remains no other means of saving France and all Europe."

An unforeseen blow, however, was about to overturn all this
scaffolding which had been erected with so much labour. On
March 1, 1792, Leopold died suddenly, carried off by a violent
disease of the bowels, which had lasted only two days. Despite her grievances against the emperor, Marie Antoinette
was deeply affected by his death; and in the first moment of
her affliction she exclaimed — the rumour had, moreover, got

about — that her brother had been poisoned by the Jacobins. But she had not the leisure to weep; she must consider the changes which this unexpected loss would make on the political chess-board.

Leopold's successor was a youth of twenty-four years, weak and sickly; the empire remained for the moment without a head, and the chief scene of the political drama was transferred from Vienna to Berlin. Doubtless the young king of Hungary declared that his intentions were the same as his father's; the high chancellor, the Prince von Rosenberg, without doubt wrote to the sister of the Marquis de Raigecourt, "I hope that my new master will continue faithful to all the promises contracted by his deceased father, and that he will be the restorer of the throne and of the royal authority in France." But the diplomatic Kaunitz affirmed at the same hour "that they could make only vague assertions, and that if they were working for a concurrence of the powers, it was impossible to know when and how this concurrence might be established." The queen, uneasy over these uncertainties and delays, hastened to send Goguelat to Vienna, under the name of Daumartin, to request a definite answer. "There is no time to be lost," remarked the poor woman, sadly, "for our enemies lose none."

It seemed as if misfortune followed these ill-fated sovereigns, to undo all their plans. On March 16 Gustavus III., the most ardent and devoted chief of the coalition, was struck during a masked ball by a bullet, fired at Stockholm, but aimed, perhaps, from Paris.

"This," said the wounded king to the Baron des Cars, "is a blow which will delight your Jacobins." The excitement in France was indeed intense when it was learned that the prince had on March 29 succumbed to his wound. Among the Jacobins there was a shout of triumph. Ankerstroem and his accomplices were styled Brutuses and Mucius Scævolas, and they proclaimed that the dagger was the final judgment of the people. At the court there was a cry of astonishment; the king and queen were struck with consternation; they had lost their best support. On the very eve of his death, Gustavus sent word to them "that one of his regrets in dying was to feel that his loss might hurt their interests." When Madame de Tourzel, who had been informed in the dauphin's apartment of the fatal event, rushed down with agitated countenance to the queen, the unfortunate sovereign said to her, "I see by your face that you know the cruel news which we have just received. It is impossible for us not to feel grief-stricken; but we must arm ourselves with courage, for who can be sure that he will not experience a similar fate?" And the young Madame threw herself into her mother's arms and burst into tears.

They had indeed reason to weep, unhappy victims, for their situation became daily more critical. All the miseries which a revolution invariably entails, anarchy which springs from the absence of government, and which all the writings of the time attest too clearly (spontaneous anarchy, as a famous historian has called it), the diminution or loss of private fortunes, the depreciation of the public funds, threatened bankruptcy, the high price of grains, the impossibility of transporting them from one department to the other, prospective famine, the total lack of specie, the little confidence in paper money, the attacks of orators in the Assembly or in the clubs on the royal family, the instigations of the newspapers, the calumnies of the journalists, — all this kept the Parisian populace in a constant state of feverish excitement. The Jacobins were all hatred; the Republicans did not conceal their hopefulness. The king himself was sinking into a discouragement which amounted to physical prostration. He remained whole days without uttering a word, and only aroused himself from this torpor when his wife threw herself at his feet and made the most heart-rending appeal to his affection and courage, going so far as to say that if they must perish it should at least be honourably and without waiting for the people to come and strangle them on the floor of their apartment.

The Revolutionists were preparing the downfall of royalty in broad daylight, amid a flood of ignoble insults. They manufactured hooked pikes to tear out, they said, the entrails of the aristocrats; and the Assembly accorded the privileges of the meeting to those who carried them. Regiments of women were being armed, and it was purposed to have them defile before the queen. The red cap, that hideous emblem, made its appearance under the king's windows; threatening motions were proposed in the garden of the Tuileries, and the insults of the populace were assuming the grossest and most disgusting character. The plan of the conspirators was matured during a supper at Condorcet's house. Their object was to suspend the king, take into their hands the education of the dauphin, and give him Condorcet as tutor. As to the queen, they were undecided whether they would simply send her back to Austria, as Siéyès wished, or confine her in a convent or at the Val de Grâce, or arraign her before the high court of Orléans under nineteen indictments. The queen knew this; she was prepared *for anything;* and when she one day expressed her views to Madame de Tourzel, the governess remarked, "But the king will never tolerate the accomplishment of so atrocious a design." "I would prefer it," replied the brave woman, "rather than imperil his life, if his refusal were to entail such a consequence." Anxious, however, above all, to compromise no one, she passed several nights with Madame de Campan in going over her papers and burning those which might be dangerous.

Her inmost feelings were outraged; her grief even was not respected. On the death of her brother no one was permitted to wear mourning in public. An officer, who had appeared in the garden of the Tuileries with a crape band on his arm, was insulted and maltreated, and a head representing Leopold was stuck on the end of a pike under the balcony of the château.

"It — the emperor's death — has had its effect. Elisabeth went to confession that very evening, and Marie Antoinette, despite her reputation as a strong-minded woman, received a severe mental shock from it. Leopold is dead; but the most redoubtable enemy is full of life, and dwells in our midst. The defunct entered the tomb alone; he has left us a sister!"

At the Assembly the orators echoed the calumnies and threats of the press. On March 10, when the queen was mourning her brother's death, Vergniaud, during the memorable and stormy debate which ended in the sending of Lessart before the court of Orléans, exclaimed: —

"From this tribune whence I speak to you, I perceive the palace where perverse counsellors mislead and deceive the king whom the Constitution has given us, forge the irons with which they wish to enchain us, and prepare the schemes which are to deliver us over to the House of Austria. I see the windows of the palace where the enemies of the people are plotting the counter-revolution, and contriving means to replunge us into the horrors of slavery, after having made us pass through all the excesses of anarchy, all the fury of civil war.

"The day has come when you may put an end to such audacity, to such insolence, and at last confound the conspirators. Alarm and terror have often, in ancient times, proceeded from this famous palace. Let them return to it to-day in the name of the law; let them penetrate all hearts; let those who inhabit it know that our Constitution declares *only the king* inviolable; let them know that the law will overtake the guilty without distinction, and that there will not be a single head convicted of guilt which will be able to escape the sword."

The allusion was obvious. In the state of public feeling at that moment, to denounce the queen was to mark her out for popular vengeance and the assassin's dagger; the bloody threats of June 20 and the scaffold of October 16 were contained in germ in these venomous words of the Girondist orator.

Marie Antoinette, it is said, shed torrents of tears at the account of this terrible meeting. "Tears of hate," remarks Monsieur E. Quinet. Could one expect them to be tears of love?

Who will be surprised after this that the queen, thus driven to save her own head and that of her husband and of her children, placed by the outrages, of which she was the object, in a position of justifiable defence, should have sought from without the support which she no longer found within, and have demanded of the powers, of her relatives, of her allies, the succour which Constitutionalists like Duport and Lameth, Monarchists like Mounier and Mallet du Pan, Royalists like Breteuil and Bombelles, declared alone capable of wresting the royal family from assassins and France from anarchy?

On March 16 Dumouriez was appointed minister of foreign affairs in the place of Lessart. Former agent of the secret diplomacy of Louis XV., a writer and a soldier, pliant and insinuating under a show of frankness and brusqueness, he soon attained a marked influence over Louis XVI., but he could not win Marie Antoinette's confidence. In vain he made the most ardent protestations of devotion to her; in vain he threw himself at her feet, assuring her that he was not and never could be a Jacobin; in vain did he one day seize her hand and kiss it with transport, saying, "Madame, let yourself be saved." He thought he had convinced her; he had not shaken her. The queen has been reproached for this obstinate mistrust; it has been said that Dumouriez, with his political adroitness and

military talents, could have restored the monarchy. Perhaps;
it is easy to argue and criticise afterward. However, given the
character and attitude of the person in question, Marie Antoinette's refusal is easily explained. Which should she believe
sincere, his protestations of fidelity to royalty or his protesta·
tions of devotion to the Jacobins? And was it possible for her
to accept blindly a co-operation which a few days before Dumouriez had offered to Robespierre and Collot d'Herbois?

On March 24, Roland and Clavière in their turn entered the
cabinet, which was completed a month later by the nomina·
tion of Servan. The Gironde was at last gaining the power to
which it had so long aspired,— the Gironde, the party which
had shown itself most implacable to Marie Antoinette, whose
most eloquent orator had poured out against her the odious
denunciation which we have cited, and whose acknowledged inspiration, Madame Roland, a woman of lofty intelligence and
firm character, but of an envious nature and malicious heart,
pursued the queen with a feminine hatred, and wrote to Bosc
on July 26, 1789, "You are only children; your enthusiasm is
a straw fire; and if the National Assembly does not legally
bring to trial the two illustrious heads, or if some generous
Decius does not overthrow them, you are all fools."

Easter was approaching. Since the queen's director, the
curé of St. Eustache, had taken the oath to the civil Constitution, she had chosen another confessor; but she was forbidden
to perform her religious duties publicly. To satisfy her con·
science and fulfil the great Christian laws, she asked one of
her chaplains to say mass for her on Easter day at five o'clock
in the morning, which she could hear privately. It was on the
8th of April; the dawn had not broken. Madame Campan, with
a candle in her hand, accompanied her mistress as far as the
chapel and left her there alone. The princess remained for a
long time absorbed in her prayers and sad meditations; the dawn
had already broken when she returned to her apartments.

Eight days later, on April 15, despite Gouvion's indignant protest and André Chénier's passionate strophes, Paris celebrated
a *fête* in honour of the Swiss Guards belonging to the regiment
of Châteauvieux who had been condemned to the gallows for having, at the insurrection of Nancy, in 1790, plundered the treasury
of their regiment and fired at the National Guards and French
troops. It was a *fête* of disorder, robbery, and murder. Freed

convicts were carried about in triumph; the Assembly conferred upon them the honours of the session, and in the evening the city was illuminated.   Madame Elisabeth, in her letters, made merry over this grotesque procession of three or four hundred patriots heated with wine, yelling, "Vive la nation!" and "Down with Lafayette!" and over "Dame Liberty shaking on her chariot."   This ceremony, however, which revived the remembrance of Monsieur de Bouillé, was an occasion for redoubled insults to the queen.   The "P. Duchesne" of course distinguished itself by an overflow of infamies; we will cite some lines from them only to show to what depths the rage of the pamphleteers had stooped: —

"Ah! f——, what joy, what happiness to see her eat cheese on this beautiful day.   I can see her through her window-blind as on the day of the Voltaire celebration at that time ; f——, she roared like a caged lion because she could not drink our blood.

". . . Your pikes! f——, brave *sans-culottes;* sharpen them, to exterminate the aristocrats if they dare act amiss.   May this fine day be the last of their reign!   We shall only have peace when the last aristocrat's head is laid low."

Amid these melancholy experiences and fatigues — for upon her rested the care and trouble of the voluminous correspondence which she kept up in every direction, and of those memoirs, "very long" for her "who did not know how to compose them" — one supreme consolation was left Marie Antoinette, her children; and she wrote to Fersen: —

"For myself, I bear up better than one would expect, considering the prodigious mental fatigue to which I am constantly subjected and the little I leave my apartments; I have not a moment to myself between the people whom I must see, letter-writing, and the time which I pass with my children.   This last occupation, which is not the least, is my sole source of happiness, and when I am very sad I take my little boy in my arms, embrace him with all my heart, and in a moment this consoles me for everything.   Adieu."

The young dauphin was indeed an extremely pretty and fascinating child, with his long, curly hair, large blue eyes, precocious mind already ripened by misfortune, and a heart full of tenderness.

"It was not possible," remarks Madame de Tourzel, "to find a more engaging child, or one possessed of more intelligence and with so charming a way of expressing himself. He grasped every opportunity to say agreeable things to those round him. He was sincerely attached to the king; but the king overawed him, and the boy was not so much at ease with him as with the queen, whom he adored, and to whom he expressed his feelings in the most touching manner, always finding something tender and amiable to say to her. His gayety and amiability were the queen's sole diversion from the daily troubles with which she was weighed down. She was bringing him up admirably; and although she always showed him the greatest tenderness, in justice to her I must say that she never spoiled him, and that she always sustained the just reproofs made to the young prince."

He, on his side, had for his mother delightful cajoleries, delicate sentiments, and adorable outbursts of affection. He brought her flowers from his garden; he devoured her with caresses.

One day, soon after the return from Varennes, when the lessons, which had been interrupted by the strict surveillance to which the royal family had been subjected, had been resumed, the queen assisted at them.

"If I remember rightly," said the dauphin's preceptor, the Abbé d'Avaux, to his pupil, "the last lesson was upon the three degrees of comparison, — the positive, comparative, and superlative; but you have probably forgotten it all?" "You are mistaken," the child replied; "as proof, listen to me. It is positive when I say, my abbé is a good abbé; the comparative when I say, my abbé is better than any other abbé; it is the superlative," he continued, looking at his mother, "when I say, mamma is the loveliest of all mammas." The queen took her son into her arms, pressed him to her heart, and could not restrain her tears.

She was proud of her child, the poor mother, and she showed it willingly to all who came near her.

"While the queen was talking with me," Bertrand de Molleville relates, "the little dauphin, beautiful as an angel, amused himself by singing and jumping about in the apartment, with a little sabre and a shield which he held in his hand. Some one came to fetch him for supper, and in two bounds he was at the door. 'What, my son,' the queen said to him, 'you are going out without bowing to Monsieur Bertrand!' 'Oh, mamma,' replied this charming child, while continuing to jump, 'Monsieur Bertrand is one of our friends. Good-night, Monsieur Bertrand.' And he darted out of the room. 'Is he not lovely?'

remarked the queen to me, when he had gone. ' He is very fortunate in being so young ; he does not feel our sorrows, and his gayety does us good.' "

The unhappy queen could not enjoy even this last consolation in peace; the possession of her son was contested. The dauphin would soon attain his seventh year, — the age when, according to the monarchical tradition, he should be taken from the hands of women and pass into those of men. The Assembly did not forget it ; and eager to encroach upon the rights of the father as they had encroached upon those of the sovereign, they had the presumption to force upon Louis XVI. the choice of a preceptor. They had already drawn up lists from which the king should select a governor for his son ; in them one read the names of the principal leaders of the Left, — Pétion, Siéyès, Condorcet ; Robespierre had even been placed at the head. It was to these philosophers without faith that the Assembly wished the most Christian king to surrender his child's soul. The queen was more distressed than she could say. A motion was even made that the Assembly itself should appoint the governor of the prince royal, but a lingering sentiment of decency restrained the deputies ; the motion was rejected. The king took advantage of this to write the following letter to the president : —

" April 18, 1792.

" I beg you, Monsieur le Président, to notify the National Assembly that my son having reached the age of seven, I have appointed Monsieur de Fleurieu his governor ; his uprightness, universally recognized intelligence, and also his loyalty to the Constitution determined my choice."

This decision, which disconcerted the plans of the Gironde, produced no evil results.

As a matter of fact, Monsieur de Fleurieu never took possession of the post to which an august confidence had called him. The king and queen continued, as in the past, to direct the education of their son. Louis XVI.'s prompt action had averted this danger. Oh that it had also been able to exorcise those dangers which threatened the crown, his family, and his life !

CHAPTER XVIII.

ON April 20 Louis XVI. declared war against the king of
Hungary; he had only decided upon this step in the last
extremity, and when he announced it to the Assembly, there
were tears in his eyes, but he was forced to yield to the denunciations of the Gironde, to the pressure of public opinion, and
to the unanimous advice and *written agreement* of his ministers.
The queen did not regard it with the same repugnance as the
king. Since the disappointment of all her hopes, she saw in
war a last resource, and it seemed to her less dangerous if the
Assembly took the initiative in it; the royal family could not
be accused at least of having urged on the powers. This might
occasion a reaction of public opinion; but it was essential
that nothing be done to exasperate this opinion. So on April
30, the queen wrote to Mercy: —

" War has been declared. The court of Vienna should endeavour to
separate its course as much as possible from that of the emigrants; to
announce this in its manifestos, while at the same time it should employ
the natural influence which it has over the emigrants to moderate their
claims, to bring them to reasonable ideas, and to join, in short, with all

those who will defend the king's cause. It is easy to imagine the ideas which should form the basis of the manifesto of Vienna ; but while calling the world to witness the intentions of this power, her efforts to maintain peace, her constant desire still to settle everything amicably, her unwillingness to uphold private claims or any individual against the nation, it should avoid saying too much of the king, of making it too strongly felt that it is he whom it is supporting and whom it is designed to defend. Such language would embarrass, would compromise him ; and in order not to appear to connive with his nephew, he would be forced to exaggerate his hostile actions, and through this to debase himself, or give a wrong impulse to public opinion. It must speak of tne nation, and say that Austria has never desired to wage war against France. An equally important observation is to avoid any appearance of wishing at first to interfere in the internal affairs of the realm, or even to effect a settlement. People here have already sought to foil Leopold's good intentions, by spreading the report that he wished to bring about a compromise among all the parties. It is undoubtedly desirable that the step which the court of Vienna is to take should carry with it the French ; but this purpose should be carefully hidden, for any previous manifestation of it would render its execution impossible. The French would always reject all political intervention of foreigners in their affairs, and the national pride is so bound to this idea that it is impossible for the king to disregard it if he desires to re-establish his kingdom."

Three weeks later a friend of Malouet, Mallet du Pan — one of the wisest and most far-seeing men of that epoch, and a writer who had defended the cause of the monarchy with untiring energy and moderation — was deputed to go and urge the plan traced in this letter before the powers and explain the details of it. He especially insisted on the necessity of pledging the princes and the French emigrants "not to let a hostile and offensive concurrence on their part take from the present war the character of a foreign war waged by a power against a power." It was not less urgent that the co-allies should, in the manifesto which they were to address to France, endeavour to "separate the Jacobins and the malcontents of every class from the rest of the nation, to reassure every one who might be turned from his error,—all those who, without advocating the present Constitution, feared the return of great past abuses; all those whom mental aberration, the contagion of example, and the first intoxication of the Revolution had involved in this criminal cause, but who, meriting reproach only for errors, enthusiasm, and weakness, would show themselves disarmed and penitent, so soon as they were shown an issue free from ignominy and personal danger." The powers should also "insert in their manifesto the fundamental truth that they had no intention of impairing the unity of the realm, and that the fear of a dismemberment was an unworthy artifice, by which the usurpers were seeking to misrepresent the veritable and only aim of the powers; that they were warring against the anti-social faction, and not against the French nation."

Finally, they must "not impose or propose any system of government, but declare that they were arming to re-establish the monarchy and the lawful authority of the crown, such as his Majesty himself saw fit to limit it."

Such were the objects of Mallet du Pan's mission, the kind of aid which the king and queen demanded of the powers, the programme which they meant to lay out for them and also for themselves, and the result which they expected from the struggle which they were about to begin.

Strange fact! war was declared. The Assembly had desired it for several months; the powers knew it; the queen had herself notified them; and neither the one side nor the other was ready. The Austrian troops in Belgium were scattered and in no condition to fight; they were, moreover, under the domination of Jacobin emissaries, and their fidelity could not be relied upon. It would need at least six weeks for important reinforcements to arrive; and if the French generals had pushed matters vigorously, they could have reached Brussels almost without striking a blow. But they also were not in marching order. The French army, deprived of its most illustrious leaders, who had emigrated, and of a part of its regiments, who had followed their leaders over the frontier, was disorganized; this was apparent in the first engagements, when it was disbanded without resistance. Theobald Dillon's company assassinated their general; Biron's company disgracefully fled before a charge of Uhlans; Lafayette was obliged to fall back, and Rochambeau tendered his resignation.

There was a moment of panic at Paris; some cast the blame on the king, others on the cabinet, a larger number on the queen. The agitation was intense among the Parisian *bourgeoisie;* and Monsieur de Vaublanc claims that if a resolute leader had appeared at that moment, they would gladly have rallied round him to restore the royal authority. Was it this thought which determined Lafayette to come to the capital in May? Did he fear that the Assembly in its alarm and hatred might carry off the royal family? It is positively known that he proposed to the king through Malouet, and to the queen through Monsieur de Gouvernet, to withdraw to his army, for which he answered. A division of this army was to be stationed at Compiègne, and from its detachments would, with the assistance of the Swiss Guards and the loyal portion of the National Guards, facilitate the departure of the royal family. The king and queen declined, — the king with kind words for the general, the queen with some bitterness. Neither wished to exchange the tyranny of the Assembly for Lafayette's guardianship. Perhaps they remembered that on the occasion of Monsieur de Narbonne's dismissal the general had in his anger exclaimed to the keeper of the seals, "We shall see which of us, the king or myself, will have the majority of the kingdom." Perhaps they still retained in mind that last warning of the mighty tribune, whose genius was so much needed by them at this moment, "In case of war Monsieur de Lafayette would seek to hold the king prisoner in his tent."

For the Revolutionists in the Assembly and in the press, however, these first military reverses served as a pretext for fresh diatribes against the queen. They accused her of being the cause of the defeat and of having given secret orders to occasion the panic. The populace rose in arms; and on May 1 a Greek, who resided in France, and who had greeted the beginnings of the Revolution with enthusiasm, wrote to his friends, "Do not be astonished if I write you in a few days to inform you of the murder of the unfortunate king and of his wife." Two weeks after, a friend of the Girondists, Carra, denounced, in the "Annales Patriotiques," a so-called Austrian committee, who, he said, held meetings in the Princesse de Lamballe's apartments, and was preparing with the queen a second St. Bartholomew of patriots, while the king, taking flight, should surrender the fortified towns and the army to the emigrants. Carra was prosecuted; and in the discussion which arose, he declared that he had his information from three deputies of the Left, — Merlin of Thionville, Bazire, and Chabot. The justice of the peace, Larivière, who had conducted the examination, issued a warrant against the three deputies, for-

getting that they were inviolable. The Assembly harshly reminded him of it by sending him to the high court of Orléans,
the antechamber of the scaffold.

The king became alarmed; perhaps he feared that the Assembly sought in these malevolent allegations a pretext to put into
practice the plan so often ascribed to the Jacobins, to carry the
royal family to the south to deliver them into the hands of the
rioters of Marseilles and the murderers of the Glacière. He considered that "the interest of the State and its internal tranquillity did not permit such calumnies to be passed over in silence,"
and directed the keeper of the seals to arraign the authors of
them before the court, that "this whole affair might be clearly
explained." The Girondists replied to this letter of the king
by openly repeating in the Assembly the odious accusations
pronounced by their friend Carra. Brissot, the great denunci-
ator, attacked Monsieur de Montmorin in violent terms; but
this time he overshot the mark, and despite Gensonné's support,
the attempt miscarried. At the same time, Pétion, whose appointment as mayor of Paris the queen had unadvisedly fur-
thered against Lafayette, and who made use of his position only
the better to overthrow royalty,— Pétion communicated to the
commander of the National Guards, feigned apprehensions of a
near departure of the king during the night, apprehensions,
he said, based upon probabilities and indications, and gave an
order to increase the patrols, thus keeping the inhabitants in a
perpetual state of alarm.

Some days later, on May 29, there was a new alarm, a new
muster of National Guards, another armed march round the
palace to watch the king.

A more serious disturbance, however, occurred to excite the
public and aggravate the situation. Toward the beginning of
1792 Madame Campan had been warned that Madame de la
Motte had composed a new lampoon against the queen and had
sent it into France. The informant added that it was more
than anything else an affair of blackmail, and that probably the
bearer of the manuscript would give it up for one hundred
louis. Madame Campan acquainted Marie Antoinette with
this proposition; but the queen rejected it, saying that she
had always treated such libels with scorn, and that, moreover,
if she was weak enough to buy one to prevent its appearance, she would not escape the vigilant espionage of the Jaco-

bins, and would thereby furnish them new weapons and new pretexts.

The reasoning was wise, and, besides, so many unclean calumnies flooded the streets that one more or less was of little importance. Louis XVI., however, was not so indifferent as his wife; he dreaded for her the painful memory which the name of Madame de la Motte awakened, and he instructed Monsieur de la Porte to buy up the entire edition of the "Memoirs." Instead of destroying it at once and in secret, Monsieur de la Porte only locked up all the copies of it in a closet of his hôtel. But events continued to march on; the violence of the Assembly and of the populace augmented from hour to hour; Monsieur de la Porte, himself denounced, feared lest a search of his house made unexpectedly might bring the pamphlets to light and give them the publicity dreaded. He determined to dispose of them; but through a blunder or inexplicable blindness, he had them transported in a cart by broad daylight to the Sèvres manufactory, where they were burned in a great fire lighted expressly for this purpose before two hundred workmen who were strictly forbidden to approach. This excess of precaution and imprudence, by exciting without satisfying the curiosity of the public, only nourished their suspicions. The incident was denounced by the workmen; and despite the explanations of the director of Sèvres and of Monsieur de la Porte, summoned to the bar of the Assembly, people persisted in seeing in these burned pamphlets the papers of the famous and imaginary Austrian committee. Girondists and Jacobins united in decrying the plot, and faithful to their method of breaking down one by one the last supports of the monarchy, that they might the more easily overthrow it, they took advantage of the agitation created to deprive the king of his constitutional guard.

This guard, organized on March 16, and composed of one third infantry and two thirds National Guards, under the superior command of the Duc de Brissac, who had under his orders Monsieur d'Hervilly and Monsieur de Pont l'Abbé, was sincerely devoted to the king, and would in case of riot have been, with the Swiss Guards and the uncorrupted part of the National Guards, an important centre of resistance. It was also hostile to the new institutions, and full of deference for the citizen's militia; it had on many occasions given proof of it. There existed between the two bodies an ardent desire to live on good terms. "Let us stand united," said the king's guards; " it is the way to be strong." But this very accord excited the mistrust and hatred of the enemies of the crown. Threatening bands were formed at the Tuileries; they surrounded the guards, insulted the officers, accused them of harbouring in the barracks of the École Militaire a white flag; they denounced them to the Assembly, which at once declared itself " in permanence," as if it were in the face of a great danger. Bazire, going straight to the point, demanded the disbanding of the constitutional guard, composed, he said, "of refractory priests, emigrants, and Arlesian aristocrats." And after a long session, in the middle of the night, Bazire's proposition, sustained by Brissot, was adopted. The constitutional guard was dissolved, and its commander, the Duc de Brissac, sent to the prisons of Orléans; he left it only to be massacred at Versailles on September 9.

While the Assembly thus deliberated, the second commander of the guard, Monsieur d'Hervilly, came to Malouet and Montmorin, and said, " Whatever the decree may be, I am sure of my company, and if the king will permit it, with eighteen hundred men I will drive out the Assembly to-morrow."

But the king did not permit it. Vainly did Malouet and Montmorin beseech him not to sanction the decree of suppression. In vain Monsieur d'Hervilly with most earnest entreaties repeated the proposition to fall upon the Jacobins and the factious members of the Assembly. "The scoundrels," he said, " are weak when they meet resistance, and this could be made a mighty day for the defence of the royal cause. If we succeed, we shall secure the welfare of France; if we succumb, disclaim me, accuse me, and let the wrath of the Assembly fall upon me."

In vain was the king shown that this vanguard of Monsieur d'Hervilly could be reinforced by six thousand Royalists enrolled at Paris by Monsieur de Clermont-Tonnerre. The king, as ever, frightened at the prospect of a conflict, refused; and the queen, to whom any energetic resolution was agreeable, but who was forced to bend to her husband's will, could only say to Madame de Tourzel, " Monsieur d'Hervilly's proposition is noble and honourable; but the king cannot bring himself to accept it; and in this position it would be reprehensible of me to influence his decision."

Louis XVI. was disarmed; all support failed him at once; his guards were disbanded, and the Constitutionalists, impotent and without authority, abandoned him. Barnave, in his turn, had gone away after having begged of the queen as a last favour the honour of kissing her hand. The queen had accorded him this grace; and deeply moved herself, she had seen him depart with tears in his eyes, this counsellor of the last hour, whose noble sentiments she appreciated without accepting his ideas, and who was to pay for his tardy devotion with his life.

The Assembly, however, did not disarm. On May 26 it had by a decree sentenced to deportation all nonjuring priests, who were denounced by twenty active citizens. On June 8 it determined that a camp of twenty thousand men, composed of five men to each canton, should be formed before the following 14th of July, for the purpose of repeating the *fête* of the federation, and of drawing closer by this means the bonds of fraternity between the departments and the capital. In reality this meant the mustering of a force of twenty thousand Revolutionists under the walls of Paris, at the disposition of the clubs, to prepare soldiers for all the riots, and to form for the Assembly the guard which had been denied the king. The project had been decided upon at the Jacobin Club, and Servan, the minister of war, had presented it to the Assembly without having spoken of it in council, or even notified the king. The two decrees insulted the dignity of Louis XVI., threatened his power, and offended his conscience; he refused, or at least deferred, his sanction. The three Girondist ministers, Roland, Clavière, and Servan, who since their entrance into office had not ceased to plot almost publicly against him, whom they should have counselled and defended, achieved the downfall of the ministry. On June 10 Roland crowned his attacks by writing to the king, under the inspiration and through the medium of his wife, an insolent letter, which by a singular breach of etiquette he read in full council, after having sworn to keep it secret. In this letter, which Dumouriez called an "impudent diatribe," and which the latest editor of Madame Roland's Memoirs has termed "an unnecessary violence and an abominable action," Roland brutally censured the policy of Louis XVI. and Marie Antoinette, gave the monarch notice of the order to change his confessor, and was carried so far in his passion as to call him a perjurer. He commanded him to execute the wishes of the Gironde, and warned him that if he refused to sanction the decrees, he would arouse "the implacable distrust of an afflicted people, who would thereafter look upon their king only as the friend and accomplice of the conspirators." This was too much;

on June 13 Louis XVI. dismissed the three ministers, and instructed Dumouriez to choose others to succeed them. The Assembly responded to this vigorous measure by declaring that the discharged ministers carried with them its confidence, and decreeing the publication of Roland's letter, and its distribution in the eighty-three departments.

Dumouriez remained the head of the cabinet; and Louis XVI. felt himself drawn toward this man of complex nature, who resembled in nothing the ministers whom he had removed; but Dumouriez declared that his continuation in office could only be useful provided the royal sanction were given to the two decrees, promising, moreover, to transfer the camp, which Servan wished to form near Paris, to Soissons. The king, despite his repugnance to assemble, as the queen said, " twenty thousand knaves who might murder him," finally yielded to the minister's demands, at least so far as the decree of June 8 was concerned; but in regard to the decree against the priests, after a moment's hesitation, he remained inflexible, despite the general's urgent entreaties.

On June 15 Dumouriez handed in his resignation, resolved to quit Paris and repair to the army. Before setting out, however, on June 18, he went to take leave of the king; the interview was affecting. Dumouriez made a last attempt to overcome what he called the sovereign's " scruples; " he represented to him forcibly the dangers of a refusal, the unpopularity of the clergy; he pictured to him in pathetic tones the priests massacred, his crown threatened, himself, his wife, his children, a prey to the fury of the populace. " I expect death," the prince replied simply, " and I pardon them in advance." But he persisted in his resolution, not wishing to add to all the sorrows which he was enduring the more poignant grief of remorse.

" Dumouriez withdrew," says an eminent historian, " without having comprehended the grandeur of that scene, nor the import of the rôle which he had played; without having replied that he was there to demonstrate how far the majesty of duty was superior to political considerations."

Some days after he set out to join Luckner's army, of which he was to take command.

On June 19 the king, using his constitutional right, and solicited, moreover, by the Directory of the department of the Seine,

and by a petition covered with eight thousand signatures, officially put his veto upon the two decrees, one of which was the
gravest violation of that liberty of conscience proclaimed by the
Constitution, and the other a perpetual menace against order
and liberty of government.

This was, by a perfectly legal and justifiable act, throwing down
the gauntlet to the Assembly, which had voted the decrees; to the
Gironde, which had presented them; to the Jacobins, who had
framed them; to the populace, which was seething in the faubourgs. The gauntlet was not to remain long upon the ground.
The king knew this; and on the very day on which he refused his
sanction to the decrees, he wrote to his confessor, Monsieur
Hébert, superior of the Eudists, "Come and see me; I was
never so much in need of consolation. I have done with men;
my eyes are turned toward heaven. Great misfortunes are announced for to-morrow; I shall have courage."

CHAPTER XIX.

FOR some time past preparations for an uprising had been maturing; the date had been chosen, the 20th of June, the double anniversary of the oath of the Tennis-Court and of the flight to Varennes. Conclaves were held in the Faubourg St. Antoine, at the house of the brewer Santerre, where, at Danton's suggestion and with the connivance of the mayor of Paris, Pétion, the usual leaders of the Parisian populace met, — Fournier, the American, the Marquis de Saint-Huruge, the butcher Legendre, the Pole Lazouski, Alexandre, chief of the battalion of the Faubourg St. Marcel. The refusal to sanction the decrees and the dismissal of the Girondist ministers furnished the pretexts.

On the evening of the 19th, Paris was astir; the charm of a beautiful night allured the inhabitants out of doors; in the streets, the squares, they gathered in groups to discuss the demonstration planned for the morrow. "At the Tuileries," says a witness, "there were more people than grains of sand." Journals like the "Révolutions de Paris" openly advocated the overthrow of the Constitution and revolt against "the royal individual."

The Directory of the department, which was made up of confident and resolute Constitutionalists, having been apprised by the new minister of the interior, Terrier de Montciel, of what was passing, sent for the mayor and police administrators, and forced them to give the commander-general of the National Guards, Ramainvilliers, a written order to "keep all the posts full, to double those of the Assembly and the Tuileries, to hold reserves of infantry and cavalry, and in case of necessity, to call out the troops of the line." At the same time it admonished them to take *without delay* every necessary measure to prevent all gatherings contrary to law.

Despite these explicit injunctions and formal commands of the law, nothing was done to hinder the insurrection. The municipality, on the contrary, " being informed," it was said, " that a great number of citizens proposed to visit the Assembly, and the king to deliver an address," passed the resolution to order the commander-general to " muster under the flags citizens of every uniform and weapon, who should thus march under the command of the officers of the battalion." This resolution, in disarming authority and bestowing, as it were, the sanctity of legality upon the riot, was rendering the violation of the law legitimate, and discipline impossible.

Ramainvilliers, torn between these contradictory instructions, hesitated, became confused, and finally did nothing. Throughout the day of the 20th, people sought him everywhere, but could not find him.

At five o'clock in the morning the call to arms sounded; at eight o'clock the " faubourgs " began their march; toward noon they arrived at the Rue St. Honoré. Having started from the two banks of the Seine, it was not long before they united to form a compact band, which in marching was swollen by all the idlers and loafers. Santerre's fifteen hundred men thus became twenty thousand. The sappers were at the front; then came the cannon and a wagon bearing the tree of liberty, which was to be planted on the terrace of the Feuillants.

At the gate of the Assembly the column halted, and Santerre sent in a letter to the president.

The Assembly was at that moment deliberating on the reception which it should accord the petitioners. The president, Français, from Nantes, read the letter which demanded their admission to an audience. The galleries applauded. " Let them come in," cried the Left. " No, no! " replied the Right. Remarks flew back and forth across the hall. Some individuals succeeded in gaining entrance; they were forced to go out.

The hall of the Manège, which since the king's return to Paris had served as place of meeting for the Assembly, was a large structure about one hundred feet long, running parallel to the terrace of the Feuillants. A long narrow court, separated from the Tuileries gardens by a high wall, ran along between the hall and this terrace; a small gate cut in the wall gave access to the garden. The mob, not wishing to pack themselves in this court, where they could easily be hemmed in, had congregated at the other end of the buildings. The head of the column was massed at the foot of the stairs which led to the Assembly hall; and pushed by the new hordes which constantly swelled the ranks, unable to advance or to recede, it escaped to the side and spread out in a neighbouring garden belonging to a former Capuchin convent. The sappers, not knowing what to do while the Assembly was deliberating, planted here in this garden the tree of liberty which they were dragging on the cart.

Other bands, meanwhile, after seeking an outlet and finding every place taken, had invaded the court of the Manège. Also pressed by fresh relays, which were arriving from moment to moment, and suffocating in this narrow space, they rushed toward the gate which led into the garden of the Tuileries. The gate was guarded by a detachment of grenadiers, and cannon were pointed to prohibit passage through it. Three municipal officers, — Boucher René, Boucher Saint-Sauveur, and Mouchet, — who had gone to meet the throng, and thus found themselves at the head of the procession, vainly demanded the opening of the gate; the commander of the post referred them to the commander-general. The municipal officers proceeded to the palace, and not meeting Ramainvilliers, applied to the king. One of them, a little dark bandy-legged man, Mouchet, who on that day played the sad rôle of revolutionary busybody, appealed to Louis XVI., and asked that the entrance to the garden be left free to citizens, who, marching *lawfully*, could not but be wounded in finding themselves suspected. "We ourselves," he added, "were excited on seeing cannon pointed at the people. Such measures are better qualified to irritate than to pacify them." "Your duty," the king replied, "is to enforce the law." "If the gate is not opened," answered Mouchet, "it will be broken open." "Very well," said the king; "if you judge it expedient, have the gate of the Feuillants opened. Let the crowd walk along the terrace and go out by the stable gate; but do it in such a way that the public peace be undisturbed. Your duty is to watch over that."

The municipal officers withdrew to transmit the king's response; it was too late. The gate had been forced in, and the crowd had broken through into the garden, from which it still would have been easy with a little alacrity and energy to scatter them. The other half of the column which was thus cut in two, the one which had crowded into the court of the Feuillants, had ended by gaining admittance to the Assembly. The orator of the band, Huguenin, came forward to the bar and read a long and violent diatribe against the king: "Why must free men see themselves reduced to the cruel necessity of steeping their hands in the blood of conspirators? There is no longer time for dissimulation; the plot is discovered; the hour has come. Blood will flow, and the tree of liberty which we have just planted will flourish in peace. . . . One single man should not sway the will of twenty-five million men."

The Left applauded; the Right was indignant. Matthieu Dumas asked the preliminary question concerning the petition; but amid the vociferations of the galleries and the threats of the bands growling outside, the deliberation was not free. The preliminary question was rejected; and the Assembly decided that the citizens of the Faubourgs St. Antoine and St. Marcel should be admitted to defile before it.

A roll of drums recalled the crowd dispersed in the garden of the Tuileries; and the defiling began to the sound of drums and music. Santerre and Saint-Huruge were at the head; they placed themselves at the foot of the tribune, and passed their army in review. Then came a confused medley of women, children, National Guards, and *sans-culottes*, some without weapons, others armed with sabres, pikes, scythes, axes, knives, and even saws. One man carried on the end of a pike an old pair of breeches with these words, "Long live the *sans-culottes!*" another bore aloft the bleeding heart of a calf, under which was written, "The heart of an aristocrat." Gross emblems, insulting signs, threatening inscriptions, floated above their heads : " Down with the Veto! A warning to Louis XVI. ! The people are weary of suffering! Liberty or death!" The band played the "Ça ira," and the crowd now repeated the words of the popular song, now shouted by way of refrain, " Down with the Veto ! " Occasionally the procession stopped and performed patriotic dances in the middle of the hall; and the Assembly, with humble resignation, assisted at this shameful degradation of the national representation.

The defiling lasted nearly two hours. When it was terminated, Santerre thanked the deputies for the friendly feeling which they had been pleased to manifest toward the petitioners, presented to the president a "superb flag" as a token of gratitude, and hurried back to the Place du Carrousel to resume the command of his army. It was half-past three. The Assembly adjourned.

The column, on leaving the hall by the court of the Manège,

instead of returning to the Rue St. Honoré, pushed their way into the garden of the Tuileries, and marching along by the façade of the palace, made their exit by the gate of the Pont Royal. In passing under the windows the mob noisily repeated its favourite cries: "Long live the *sans-culottes!* Down with Monsieur and Madame Veto!" Ten battalions of the National Guards were drawn up there, forming a front of banners, before which the faubourgs defiled. The procession, having arrived at the Pont Royal, seemed to take the line of the quays; and for a moment it might have been thought that the demonstration would be limited to the violent denunciations with which the Assembly had resounded. But such was not the plan of the leaders of the riot. The invasion of the palace formed part of the programme, while perhaps they hoped for something better, and left to chance the task of completing the work. When the band arrived opposite the Place du Carrousel, instead of continuing its march, it turned and passed through the gate.

The Cour du Conseil was invaded; there the procession halted and knocked at the gate of the Cour Royale. "We wish to enter," they shouted; "we have no evil designs against the king." As sole response, the two gendarmes who were on guard crossed their bayonets. The crowd fell back an instant. But the gendarmes and the National Guards had no instructions. Some wished to defend the gate at the point of the bayonet; others hesitated. "What shall we do?" asked a captain of Colonel Rulhière. "I have no orders," Rulhière replied; "but I believe that the troops are here to support the National Guards." The commander-general, Ramainvilliers, chanced to pass; a lieutenant-colonel of the *gendarmerie*, Carle, ran to him and interrogated him. "Remove your bayonets," Ramainvilliers replied. "Why," retorted Carle, indignantly,—"why do you not order me at once to give up my sword and take off my breeches?" Ramainvilliers made no answer, and disappeared.

One of the most devoted officers of the royal family, Aclocque, to conciliate all parties, urged the leaders of the column to choose twenty petitioners, whom he promised to conduct to the king. Some thirty men presented themselves; they were permitted to enter, and the gate again closed.

The crowd murmured outside. Rumours, best calculated to excite the passions of the people, circulated, adroitly disseminated and commented upon. It was related "that twelve or fifteen hundred chevaliers of St. Louis had been seen in the morning at the château; that former members of the king's abolished household had been recognized in the court; that the apartments were filled with persons dressed in black, animated with the most counter-revolutionary intentions; that this day was destined to repeat the *journée des poignards*, etc." All these reports were noised abroad and exasperated the populace, who were already in a state of feverish excitement. The gunners of the faubourgs who were drawn up with their pieces upon the Place du Carrousel joined the crowd. The commander of the battalion of the Val de Grâce, Saint-Prix, tried in vain to make his men, whom he knew to be ill-disposed, return to their quarters. The men refused, and in opposition to their leader loaded their cannon. "We will not leave," a lieutenant said. " We did not come for nothing; the Carrousel has been forced, the palace must be also. This is the first time that the gunners of the Val de Grâce have been in service; they are not j—— f—— ; we shall see." Then pointing to the palace, "Follow me, gunners! Straight to the enemy!" The gunners shifted their position, and turned their pieces toward the royal gate. "If they refuse to open the gate," said Santerre, who had just arrived, "we will shatter it with balls."

It was not necessary, however; two municipal officers — Boucher René and another whose name has remained unknown — gave the order to open. The human tide rushed into the court of the Tuileries; every one entered at once, — people, National Guards, gendarmes. "I shall long bear in mind," writes an eye-witness, "the sight of those sixteen thousand armed men, submissive, believing themselves obliged to yield to two municipal officers, who ordered them in the name of the law to allow twenty thousand men to pass with pikes and axes, scaling the steps of the palace with a terrible rapidity. The waves of an angry sea have never seemed to me so dangerous." A few loyal officers endeavoured to close the gate which separated the court from the great staircase. The National Guards, discouraged by the attitude of the municipality, refused to defend the entrance; and when one of the commanders said to them, "Are you sure that there are not among those who present themselves men capable of making an attempt on the life of the king?" a guard replied, "It is better that one man be murdered than that all of us should be." Thus with these words, which justified every dastardly act and authorized all crime, the last door was broken through, and access to the royal dwelling was thrown open to the invaders.

The mob, meeting no resistance, rushed toward the staircase; it pushed forward in such compact masses and with such impetuosity that one of the cannon of the Val de Grâce was carried as far as the third room of the château,— the room of the Swiss Guards. There the wheels caught in the panel of a door; this unexpected obstacle arrested the invaders for an instant, and redoubled their wrath. The report circulated that it was a cannon pointed by the defenders of royalty to riddle the people; nothing more was needed to cause the massacre of all the inhabitants of the Tuileries. Fortunately, on the order of Mouchet, the sappers disengaged the cannon and carried it down to the foot of the great staircase, where it remained until the close of the day.

The king was in his chamber with his family, when suddenly he heard some one knock at the door. An attendant opened, and admitted one of his faithful servants, the Major Aclocque, who had come to entreat him to show himself to the people. Louis XVI. consented; he passed into the bedroom, and thence into the hall of the Œil de Bœuf. The queen wished to follow him; the king prevented her from doing so. He was hurried away; and she had only time to say to the grenadiers, " My friends, save the king !" Madame Elisabeth, " more fortunate than she," — it is she herself who makes the remark, — accompanied her brother, and with her several ministers and courtiers: Terrier de Montciel, De Lajard, Beaulieu, the Admiral Bougainville, the Maréchal de Beauvau, De Mouchy, and De Mailly; Messieurs de Tourzel, d'Hervilly, etc. " Follow me, grenadiers !" the king said. A certain number of National Guards and the larger part of the Ste. Opportune battalion hastened after him, with La Chesnaye, commander of the sixth legion. " Messieurs, save the king !" Madame Elisabeth said to them with tears in her eyes. They all surrounded Louis XVI., and drew their swords. On a word from Aclocque, however, who showed them that this threatening attitude might expose the prince, whom they wished to defend, they sheathed them again.

An ordinary door separated Louis XVI. from the invaders; the mob roared outside, and shook the door with blows from their axes. The two lower panels had already been shattered, when Aclocque urged the king to have it opened rather than let it be broken in. " I am willing," the prince replied; " I fear nothing in the midst of those who surround me." An usher opened the door; the masses surged in. "Citizens," said Aclocque, "recognize your king; respect him. The law orders you to do so. We shall all of us perish rather than suffer the slightest harm to be done him." These words, pronounced in a loud and firm voice, produced a momentary pause in the invasion; the National Guards profited by it to draw the king into the embrasure of a window on the side of the court. He mounted on a bench; the grenadiers placed themselves before him. "Sire," one of them said to him, "have no fear." "My friend," the intrepid monarch replied, taking the hand of the grenadier and laying it on his breast, — "my friend, put your hand upon my heart and see if it beats faster."

The popular waves continued to mount; the mob, which had for an instant wavered, rushed forward and filled the hall with shouts of hatred and threats of death: "Down with Monsieur Veto, Madame Veto, and all their gang! To the Devil with the Veto! Recall the patriot ministers! He must sign; we shall not leave until he has done so." A wretch among the first to enter, and armed with a long stick at the end of which a sharply pointed sword-blade was fastened, tried to fall upon the king; he was driven back with bayonets. Another, a dark pock-marked man dressed in a greenish frock-coat and linen trousers, carrying a sword in his left hand and a pistol in his right, attempted to break through the crowd. "Where is he, that I may kill him?" he yelled. "Wretch! there he is, thy king," said an usher of the apartment to him. "Dost thou dare look upon him?" The brigand shrank back, as if seized with a sort of terror. There was a moment of silence. The king wished to take advantage of it to speak; but a fresh "inundation" swept in, "with such horrible cries," says one account, "that thundering Jupiter would not have been heard." Among the foremost invaders appeared a brigand by the name of Soudin, the so-called conqueror of the Bastille, whose principal feat at that time was to have washed and carried on the end of a pike the bloody heads of Foulon and Berthier. Farther on gesticulated an individual dressed in a green coat, who, to use the forcible expression of a witness, was reputed to have been a *head-cutter* in 1789. All this rabble filled the Œil de Bœuf, shouting, yelling, adding threat to insult, breaking the furniture, shattering the mirrors, tearing out the bolts, stealing articles of value, acting, in a word, says the report of the Directory, "as if the object of the expedition was to lay siege to and pillage the Tuileries."

"What do you wish?" Louis XVI. asked quietly. "I am your king. I have not swerved from the Constitution."

His voice was lost in the tumult. The butcher, Legendre, approached the embrasure. "Monsieur," he said. At this unexpected appeal Louis XVI. started. "Yes, Monsieur," Legendre continued, "listen to us; it is your duty to listen to us. You are a dissembler; you have always deceived us; you still deceive us. Take care! the measure is full to the brim; the people are weary of being your toy." Then he read a sham petition, which, says Rœderer, "was only a tissue of reproaches, insults, and threats."

"I shall do what the Constitution and the decrees ordain me to do," the king replied simply.

"Down with the Veto! Recall the ministers!" the mob retorted, and this horde of *sans-culottes*, which filled the Œil de Bœuf, grew louder in their insults. Several wretches, armed with swords, attempted to break the line of National Guards to reach the king; the grenadiers drove them back. Louis XVI. remained unmoved; neither the shouts nor the acts of violence could ruffle his incomparable serenity.

"In so terrible a circumstance," says an unprejudiced witness, "Louis behaved with marvellous resolution and truly royal prudence, joined to extraordinary calmness and kindness."

An individual, meanwhile, who bore a red cap on the end of a stick, approached the king and inclined the stick toward him. The municipal officer, Mouchet, understood the sign; he took the cap and gave it to Louis XVI., who placed it upon his head. The crowd applauded. "Vive la nation! Vive la liberté!" it shouted. Some acclamations of "Vive le roi!" were heard, but they found no echo. And the brave grenadier, Bidaut, overheard several wretches murmur in a low tone: "He did well to put it on; for we should have seen what would have happened; and f——, if he does not sanction the decrees we shall come back every day."

In the midst of the throng a woman carried a sword wreathed with flowers and surmounted by a cockade. The king saw it; he made a sign. Mouchet, who was always to be found everywhere, took the sword and handed it to the prince, who brandished it and had the cockade attached to his cap. "Vive la nation!" the crowd shouted; and the king repeated with it, "Vive la nation!"

Mouchet then proposed to him to go out on the terrace. Louis XVI. refused. "I am well enough here," he said. The heat, however, was stifling. A National Guard, to whom a bottle of wine and a glass had been passed, offered the king a drink. "Sire," he said, with naïve familiarity, "you must be very thirsty; for I myself am dead with thirst. . . . If I may make bold to offer you — Fear nothing; I am an honest man; and that you may drink without fear I will drink first, if you will permit it." "Yes, my friend, I will drink from your glass," the prince replied; and raising the glass, he exclaimed, "People of Paris, I drink to your health and to that of the French nation."

Madame Elisabeth was standing in the embrasure of another window; she was seen by some of the crowd. "Ah!" they cried, "there is the Austrian! We must have the head of the Austrian." "That is not the queen," said Monsieur de Sainte-Pardoux, the squire of the princess. "Why undeceive them?" the generous woman rejoined with animation. "Their error might save the queen." Then perceiving near her, in that horde which surrounded her with threats, a young man whose bayonet almost grazed her breast, she pushed the weapon gently away with her hand, saying, with an angelic smile, "Be careful, Monsieur; you might wound some one, and I am sure you would be sorry to do that."

Meanwhile, several deputies, informed of the invasion of the château, hastened thither of their own accord. Vergniaud and Isnard harangued the multitude and sought to reawaken in them respect for authority; they could not make themselves heard. "Down with the Veto! The sanction! The recall!" were the sole responses which their exhortations obtained.

At last the mayor of Paris, Pétion, arrived. After the meeting of the council in which the resolution which had rendered the insurrection lawful had been adopted, he had retired with a few intimate friends to a room of the town-hall. He was sitting there in *perfect calmness and serenity*, so he says; for the news which he received was *excellent*, and the outlook beautiful, full of gladness and gayety. The Directory had appealed several times in vain to his vigilance; he remained unmoved. Toward half-past four, however, he had given the order to put the horses to his carriage; and sacrificing his dinner to his duty, — he has taken care to note this in his report, — he repaired to the Tuileries. He reached there between five and six o'clock. Accompanied by Sergent, he passed through the crowd, who greeted him with shouts of "Vive Pétion!" and approached the king, whom he beheld with admiration, so he says, "crowned with the emblem of liberty." It was by this expression that he designated the red cap. "Sire," he said, "I have just heard this instant of the situation in which you are." "That is most astonishing," the king replied coldly; "it has lasted for two hours." Two grenadiers lifted the mayor upon their shoulders. He spoke to the people and preached to them respect to the law; but he did it so coldly, according to the municipal officer, Champion, that the shouting redoubled. A tall, fair young man of twenty or twenty-five years of age pushed through the crowd, and addressing the king with threatening gestures, said, "Sire, I demand of you, in the name of the hundred thousand men who surround me, the recall of the patriot ministers, the sanction of the decrees, and their execution, or you shall die."

And Pétion, who was there, did not once attempt to impose silence upon this madman. Champion, growing angry at this cowardice and tolerance, exclaimed, —

"Monsieur le Maire, you are responsible for all that may happen." Pétion decided to harangue the crowd a second time. In the face of this violation of every law by these bands of brigands who treated the Tuileries like a town taken by assault, of these persistent outrages against the majesty of the head of the State, he spoke of the dignity of the people. "Citizens, you are come to present lawfully your good wishes to the hereditary representative of the nation; you have done it with the dignity, with the majesty of a free people. Return to your firesides, and give no occasion for censure of your estimable intentions."

Estimable intentions! And some years later, Legendre confessed to Boissy d'Anglas that one of the secret ends of the movement had been the assassination of the king!

"Are the doors of the gallery open?" Sergent asked. "Yes," the king replied. "I have ordered the apartments to be opened; the people in marching at the side of the gallery will have the pleasure of seeing them."

At these words there was a movement in the crowd; the curiosity of some, the lassitude of others, finally determined the rioters to withdraw. Sergent, with his scarf in his hand, sought to organize the retreat; and the procession began amid the sound of shouts, a thousand times repeated, of "Vive Pétion! Down with the Veto!" The wretch who carried on the end of a pike a bleeding calf's heart with the words, "Heart of an aristocrat!" was seen in the midst of the moving bands. "This man," a witness reports, "sought to stick this horrible emblem under the eyes of the king."

The Œil de Bœuf was partially cleared. Aclocque took advantage of this to propose to Louis XVI. to withdraw. What the monarch had not accepted from the suspected Mouchet he accepted from the faithful Aclocque. Surrounded by municipal officers and guards, who opened a passage for him, he crossed to a private door, by which he escaped; and the mob, deprived of its victim, passed out through the apartments murmuring. In going through the royal chamber they yelled, " Is this the bed of the big Veto? Ah! he has a more beautiful bed than we, the big Veto! Where is he, then, this Monsieur Veto?" Amid these vulgar jestings and sarcasms the procession marched on.

While these sad scenes were passing in the Œil de Bœuf, another band, led by a man who must have had a thorough knowledge of the palace, — for he led them through a door the existence of which was only known to the members of the domestic service, — had ascended to the dauphin's chamber, where they hoped to find Marie Antoinette. The queen had just left it. The bandits, disappointed, shattered the door with their axes, searched the beds and closets, ransacked everything. Hideous shrews poured forth ignoble insults against the unhappy princess, swearing that they wanted to have her in their hands dead or alive. A brigand with an axe in his clenched fist and insults on his lips shouted that he had already broken in a good many doors, but he would break in many more to have the Austrian.

The queen had made vain efforts to accompany the king; when he passed into the hall of the Œil de Bœuf, she rushed forward to accompany him. Some one quickly barred her passage. Turning to her children, she said, "Save my son!" The dauphin, frightened at the noise, uttered lamentable cries. Hue seized him and carried him into Madame Royale's apartment, which was farther removed from the tumult. The queen, knowing him in safety, again hastened to join her husband. She was held back. " Let me go," she said; " my place is with

the king. I will go and die at his feet." Two faithful servants,
Monsieur d'Aubier and Monsieur de Rougeville, stopped her
with respectful firmness; and the minister of foreign affairs,
Chambonnas, showed her that, far from saving the king, she
would perhaps expose him to greater danger; that her place
was near her children. Convinced by these arguments, she allowed herself, not without regret, to be led into the dauphin's
chamber, where her son was brought back to her. Soon, however, the rioters were roaring at the door; the queen was dragged
through a secret passage into the king's chamber, then into the
council-chamber. She was sitting in this last room, pale, her
limbs shaking with involuntary trembling, which was concealed
by the table, surrounded by her children and by Mesdames de
Lamballe, de la Roche-Aymon, de Tourzel, de Maillé, de Mackau,
by the minister Chambonnas, the lieutenant-general Wittinghoff,
and by several grenadiers, when the filing across the apartment
began.

Her attendants, hearing the tumult increase and the popular
waves approach, hastily drew Marie Antoinette into the embrasure of a window, and rolled the council-table in front of her;
and about two hundred National Guards, under the command of
Mandat, placed themselves in three rows before this improvised
barricade.

Soon the rioters invaded the hall. Santerre entered first, and
appealing to the grenadiers, said, " Make way, that the people
may see the queen." Then turning toward Marie Antoinette, he
continued, " Madame, you are deceived; the people wish you
no harm. If you desired it, there is not one of them who would
not love you as much as this child," he added, pointing to the
dauphin. " In any case, do not be afraid; no one will harm you."
" I am neither misled nor deceived, and I am not afraid. One is
never fearful of anything when one is with honest men." And
she extended her hand to the National Guards, who seized it with
transport and kissed it respectfully.

The hideous procession moved on. A wretch carried a bundle
of sticks with the inscription, " For Marie Antoinette." Another
raised a small gibbet, to which was suspended a doll with the
words, " To the lantern with Marie Antoinette!" and a third paraded a guillotine, at the bottom of which was to be read the
darkly prophetic phrase: " National justice for tyrants! Down
with Veto and his wife!" Santerre walked with Mandat, guiding

the procession and exhibiting, if I may use such an expression, the royal family to his bands. "Look," he said: "this is the queen; that is the prince royal." The poor little dauphin was seated upon the table. A brigand addressed Marie Antoinette in a hoarse voice: "If thou lovest the nation, place this cap upon thy son's head;" and he handed her a red cap. The queen took the cap and set it upon the head of the dauphin. The heat was frightful. The little prince was smothered under this thick, unclean head-dress. Santerre himself was moved to pity, and said, "Take that cap off the child; it is too warm."

The queen, in spite of her calmness, turned to one of her friends and said, "This is too much; it exceeds all human patience."

The procession moved more slowly for an instant. A woman with flaming eyes and clenched fists halted before Marie Antoinette, and shrieked, "Thou art an infamous woman! We shall hang thee." "Have I ever done you any harm?" the queen replied sorrowfully. "No; but you are the cause of the nation's misfortune." "You are deceived; I married the king of France; I am the mother of the dauphin; I am French; I shall never see my country again. I cannot be happy or unhappy except in France; I was happy when you loved me." Despite herself, the woman was touched by this sorrow and sadness. Moved to pity, she murmured, "Pardon me; I did not know you. I see you are good." "That woman is drunk," said Santerre, whose plans were disturbed by this emotion; and pushing her rudely forward, he ordered the procession to move on.

"If one of those rascals had dared strike the queen at that moment," a witness of these horrible scenes relates, "every one would have followed his example, and all those who were in the room would have been massacred. Happily, the queen's majesty, perhaps her beauty, her noble and proud bearing, her air of assurance, overawed the mob."

At half-past eight the apartments were finally emptied; and the queen, reassured by Madame Elisabeth as to her husband's fate, was able to rejoin the king. As soon as she perceived him, she threw herself into his arms, and burst into tears. Unmoved and erect before the rioters, she was overcome by the emotion of this meeting. The deputies who were present at this interview felt themselves affected; and one of them, Merlin of Thionville, could not keep from weeping. The queen observed this, and said to him, "You weep, Monsieur Merlin; you weep to see the king and his family so cruelly treated by a people whom he has always sought to make happy." "Yes, I weep," Merlin replied brutally; "I weep over the misfortunes of a woman who is beautiful, sensible, and the mother of a family. But do not misunderstand me; not one of my tears is for the king or for the queen. I hate kings and queens; this is the only sentiment with which they inspire me. It is my religion." And the future regicide, who believed himself a great citizen because he had just shown himself cruel, dried his tears.

Another deputy, whose name has not been preserved, accosted the queen, saying to her in a familiar tone, "You were well frightened, Madame; admit it." "No, Monsieur; I was not frightened, but I suffered keenly in being separated from the king at a moment when his life was in danger. However, I had the consolation of being with my children and of fulfilling one of my duties." "Without pretending to excuse everything," the deputy continued, "admit, Madame, that the people were very good." "The king and I, Monsieur, are persuaded of the natural bounty of the people, who are only wicked when they are misled." "How old is Mademoiselle?" continued this stupid person, pointing to Madame Royale. "My daughter," the queen answered coldly, "is at the age when one feels only too keenly the horror of such scenes;" and she turned her back upon him.

Other representatives, more respectful and more kindly disposed, congratulated Louis XVI. on the courage he displayed during the day. "I have only done my duty," the king replied simply.

The Marquis de Clermont-Gallerande remarked to Madame Elisabeth, "Ah, Madame, Heaven will avenge so many crimes!" "Do not let us speak of vengeance," the angelic princess replied; "let us rather hope that God will pardon and transform the malefactors."

Meanwhile, Pétion, on the one hand, and the leaders of the National Guards, on the other, succeeded in clearing the château. The rioters, left without guidance, dispersed without resistance, but with loud complaints over the result of the manifestation. "We were brought here for nothing," they exclaimed; "but we shall return, and get what we wish." "The attempt has failed," Santerre said on his side; "the king was difficult to move to-day. We shall return to-morrow, and make him evacuate."

At half-past ten all was at an end; the palace was empty; and
the royal family, returning to their devastated apartments, could
at last enjoy the repose which had been bought by such terrible
sufferings. Some days later, the queen wrote these simple words
to Fersen: "I still exist; but it is a miracle. The day of the
20th was terrible."

CHAPTER XX.

ON the morrow of this deplorable day, Thursday, June 21,
new mobs collected. Alarm spread through the château;
and the little dauphin, pressing close to his mother, cried out in
tears, " Mamma, is yesterday not yet finished ? "

On the same day Pétion — the Pilate of royalty, as he has been
justly called — had the audacity to reappear at the Tuileries; he
found the king and queen, the procurator of the department,
Rœderer, and several friends. " Sire," he said, " we heard that
you had been warned that a mob was marching on the palace.
We come to inform you that this band is composed of citizens
without arms, who wish to set up a Maypole. I know, Sire, that
the municipality has been calumniated; but their conduct shall be

known to you." "It should be to all France," the king replied coldly. "I accuse no one in particular. I saw everything."

Pétion sought to justify himself and to vindicate the rioters. "Without the precautions taken by the municipality," he resumed, "much more grievous events might have happened,—not against your person." Then fixing his eyes upon the queen, he added, "You must know, Sire, that your person will always be respected."

His manner was irritating. Louis XVI. lost patience. "Be quiet!" he said in a peremptory tone and loud voice. "Is it respecting my person to enter my palace in arms, break down my doors, and force my guards?"

"Sire," the mayor replied, "I know the extent of my duties and my responsibilities."

"Do your duty," the king rejoined imperiously. "You are responsible for the tranquillity of Paris. Adieu."

Two days later, on the 23d, the monarch addressed to the French people a proclamation full of noble sentiment, in which, having denounced to the people the crimes of which he had been the object and almost the victim, he added these beautiful words: "The king opposed to the threats and insults of the malcontents naught but the consciousness of his duty and a desire for the public good. The king does not know to what limit they may go; but he deems it necessary to say to the French nation that violence, to whatever excess it may be carried, will never extort from him his consent to what he believes contrary to the interests of the public. . . . As hereditary representative of the French nation, he has severe duties to fulfil; and although he may sacrifice his peace, he will never sacrifice his duties."

A mighty movement was the response to this noble language. "I cannot tell you how much Louis has gained in the affection and respect of all since the 20th of this month," an unprejudiced witness wrote on June 24. The audacity of the malcontents, the danger run by the royal family, their heroic attitude, a last remnant perhaps of that traditional affection which France had so long felt for the blood of her kings, at last produced a reaction of opinion. Indignant addresses arrived from seventy departments. Twenty thousand signers, both from Paris and the provinces, protested against this high treason against the nation, and vehemently demanded the repression of the riot. The Directory of the department of the Seine, justly angered by Pétion's conduct, and that of the procurator of the Commune, Emanuel, asked of them a strict account of the employment of their time, and the justices of the peace of the capital opened an inquiry.

On the 28th, Lafayette had arrived at Paris, and in the name of the army had demanded of the Assembly the punishment of the rioters, the suppression of the Jacobin Club, and the adoption of vigorous measures for the defence of authority and of the king in particular. The Right welcomed him with applause, the Left with gloomy silence, and before long with murmurs. On coming out of the meeting, the National Guards cheered him; and he might have fancied for the moment that he had recovered his former popularity. If he cherished this illusion, it was short-lived. When it became necessary to go from words to action; when the general wished to profit by the terror caused by his sudden arrival to dissolve the Jacobin Club, — he met everywhere only coldness and apathy, and he was forced to relinquish all active intervention. On the 30th he set out again for his camp, without having dared take the initiative in any measure, and leaving no other trace of a proceeding which does him honour than a haughty letter which irritated the passions, without reviving the courage, of the people.

On the following day, July 1, the Assembly, after a stormy debate and a long night session, resolved upon the immediate disbanding of the staff of the National Guards. This was the Gironde's response to Lafayette's imperious injunction.

On July 4 the queen wrote the following letter to Monsieur de Mercy, the last which reached him: —

"You are already acquainted with the events of June 20; our position becomes daily more critical. There is only violence and rage on the one side, and weakness and apathy on the other. We cannot count on the National Guards or on the army. We do not know whether we should remain at Paris or withdraw elsewhere.

"It is more than time for the powers to speak emphatically. July 14 and the succeeding days may prove an epoch of universal mourning for France, and regret for the powers, because they have been too slow in explaining their position.

"All is lost if the malcontents are not arrested by the fear of near punishment. They wish the republic at any price. To obtain it they have determined to assassinate the king. A manifesto should render the National Assembly and France answerable for his life and the lives of his family.

"Despite all these dangers, we shall not alter our determination; you may count upon it as I count upon your devotion. I flatter myself that I share the sentiments which attached you to my mother. This is the moment to give me a proof of it, in saving me and mine, if there is yet time."

The queen was only too just in her views; the situation grew more terrible from day to day. The attacks of the Assembly joined with the insults of the street and the outcries of the clubs. The same day on which Marie Antoinette wrote this letter, Vergniaud declaimed violently against the pretended treachery of the court, and in an impassioned outburst of eloquence asked if the sombre genius of the Médicis still wandered under the arches of the palace, and if they were about to see a repetition of St. Bartholomew and the dragonnades. Some days later Brissot, no less violent, exclaimed that to strike at the court of the Tuileries was to fell all traitors at one blow. Marat thundered against the palace, where "a perverse queen" fanaticized "an imbecile king," and "was educating whelps of tyranny." And as if to justify these denunciations and encourage the riot, Pétion, the accomplice of June 20, suspended by the Directory on July 1, was reinstated in his office on the 13th.

The populace responded to these appeals to violence and murder by acts of violence. Incendiary pamphlets were circulated in profusion throughout the capital, in the provinces, and in the army. On the squares of Paris, in the streets, and in all public places, insurrection was loudly advocated. Songs were mingled with the speeches; pamphlets and indecent caricatures, aimed against the king and queen, abetted the work of the newspapers. The garden of the Tuileries, closed for a time, was constantly filled with women, who insulted all those who held to the court; they shouted under the very windows an infamous libel — the Life of Marie Antoinette — accompanied by disgusting prints which the scandal-mongers exhibited amid bursts of insulting laughter. They sang in the ears of the queen the odious couplet: —

> "Madame Veto has promised
> To strangle all Paris."

The guards tried to silence these singers. A quarrel ensued; and one of those who accompanied the queen having struck one of these wretches with the flat of his sword, they complained to the Assembly, and the Assembly accorded them the honours of the house. Another time the crowd attempted to shatter the windows with stones; and the guards were obliged again to close the garden, which was not reopened until the end of July. On July 21 a decree decided that the terrace of the Feuillants should be regarded as an annex of the Deliberative Hall, and as such should remain open to the public. It was at once separated from the rest of the park by a tri-coloured ribbon, and the following inscription was posted on the trees which bordered it, " Citizens, respect yourselves. Give to this feeble barrier the force of bayonets." The terrace of the Feuillants was baptized the territory of Liberty; the garden of the Tuileries was the territory of Coblentz. Whoever dared cross this boundary line was hissed and called an aristocrat. One day a young man, not observing this regulation, went down to the garden. He was assailed with yells. The people shouted, " To the lantern ! " The young man at once drew off his shoes, and with his handkerchief wiped off the sand which had clung to the soles. The people applauded, and carried him about in triumph. Despite the closing of the garden, to which only those provided with cards were admitted, the queen and her children, as soon as they appeared, were assailed with such frightful yells from the terrace that they were obliged to retire; at the end of July they were forced to give up taking the air there.

Meanwhile, an investigation concerning June 20 had been ordered; and Marie Antoinette, learning that Hue would be heard in it, sent for him and said to him, " Use as much reserve in your testimony as the truth will allow. . . . All suspicion that the king or I harbour the least resentment for what has passed must be dispelled. It is not the people who are guilty; and if they were, they would always find with us pardon and oblivion of their errors."

The king, according to the account of the ambassador of the United States, still in the midst of this crisis only thought of securing liberty and lasting happiness for France.

It is thus that the people repaid him.

One night, about one o'clock, the queen, not being able to sleep, was conversing with Madame Campan; both heard muffled steps in the corridor which ran along the apartments. It was a servant, who had slipped in there with a purpose only too easy to divine. A footman, notified by Madame Campan, fell upon him, and threw him to the ground. " Madame," he said, " he is a rascal. I know him; I have him." "Let him go," the queen replied. "He came to assassinate me; to-morrow the Jacobins will carry him about in triumph." Then, turning to Madame Campan, she said, "What a position! — insults by day, murderers by night."

The next day Monsieur Septeuil ordered all the locks to be changed. Louis XVI. did more. He requested that his wife should leave the ground floor, where she lodged alone, and where she was insulted at every instant, and should move to the first floor to a chamber off the dauphin's apartment. Madame de Tourzel, who occupied this room, gave her place to the queen, and slept on a pallet which was made up every evening. The blinds and shutters were left open, that the ill-fated sovereign might see the dawn, and thus make her sleepless nights less painful.

The queen consented to this change of lodgings with extreme reluctance; she was loath to show any uneasiness. She was no less unwilling to disturb her faithful servants; misfortune had tightened the bonds which united her to them, and rendered her still more solicitous for their well-being.

"This princess is so good, and so concerned for all those in her service," Madame de Tourzel says in relating this fact, "that she accounted it a serious matter to cause them the slightest inconvenience. Never was a princess more lovable, more sensible of tenderness shown her by others, or more mindful of the pleasure of those about her. Is it credible that a queen of France should be driven to keep a little dog in her chamber to warn her of the slightest noise in her apartments?"

The dauphin, however, who loved his mother passionately, was overjoyed at this new arrangement. As soon as the queen was awake, he ran to her bed, "clasped her in his arms, and whispered the most loving and tender things to her. This was the only moment in the day when the princess found any consolation; her courage alone upheld her."

In the midst of all these alarms and torments, these nights without sleep and days without repose, these physical fatigues and moral sufferings, the queen's health remained good; still better, it grew stronger. During the time of prosperity she had been subject to nervous attacks; in the hour of sorrow these attacks disappeared. "Nervous maladies," she said, with a melancholy smile, "were for happy women."

The 14th of July was approaching; the Assembly had decided that the *fête* of the federation of 1790 should be repeated; this was an indirect way of gathering together the twenty thousand men whose reunion the king had opposed. The federates arrived from all sides. They had been carefully chosen from among the most hot-headed and fanatic Revolutionists. Those from Marseilles and Brest were distinguished for their violence and boldness. Enthusiastically welcomed by the Jacobins, given free lodging by the municipality, having all expenses paid out of the treasury, intoxicated by wine and speeches, provided with powder and bullets, these men formed an armed force ready at hand for the malcontents. The most upright among them left for the camp at Soissons, where the reserve army was forming for the purpose of supporting that of Lafayette and Luckner. But they were few, — about fifteen hundred; and despite the decree of the Assembly, which on July 11 had declared the country in danger, the others remained at Paris to make a last assault on the monarchy, insulting the royal family, abusing their friends, and quarrelling with those National Guards who belonged to the faithful companies.

"There is no day," Montmorin wrote to La Marck, "that I do not tremble for the life of the king and queen ; and when evening comes, I thank Providence that they still live, and, in truth, to him alone are thanks due."

It was with veritable terror that the Royalists saw the date of July 14 arrive.

Louis XVI. and Marie Antoinette were to assist at the federation; and no one doubted but that the plan which had failed on June 20 would be revived on that day, and that assassins would be found in this tumultuous and hostile mob. Regicide was publicly preached; and there was scarcely a day when some busybody did not come to warn the queen to be on her guard. The poor woman had not a moment of peace. To reassure herself a little, she insisted that the king should have a breast-plate made, which, by parrying the first blows, would at least give his friends time to arrive and defend him. The breast-plate was made ; and the prince, in order to quiet his wife's fears, consented to wear it. "It is to satisfy her; but they will not assassinate me. Their plan is altered; they will put me to death in another way." "That is true," remarked the queen, when Madame Campan repeated to her these words of Louis XVI. "I begin to fear a trial for the king. As for me, I am a foreigner; they will assassinate me.

What will become of our poor children?" and she burst into a
torrent of tears. But it was in vain that Madame Campan urged
her to wear a corselet of the same fabric as the king's waistcoat.
"If the malcontents assassinate me," the poor woman answered,
"it will be a blessing: they will deliver me from this most
painful existence."

Resigned to die, but not wishing to involve in her ruin all those
who had remained loyal to her, she had for some time before
never gone to bed without burning all papers compromising her
friends. In this critical and well-nigh desperate situation offers
of service poured in; it seemed as if peril fanned the devotion of
her followers. The constant preoccupation of all the faithful
friends of these last hours was to rescue the royal family from
this prison of Paris, which meant for them perpetual riot and
danger of death. The Landgravine Louise of Hesse-Darmstadt,
one of the queen's early friends, appalled at the horrors of June
20, had sent her brother, Prince George of Hesse, to France, expressly to try to save her. What was the prince's plan? What
were his resources? We do not know; but it is probable that this
plan aimed at saving the queen only. The friend had only
thought of the friend; she had reckoned without the wife and
mother. Despite all these urgent entreaties, Marie Antoinette refused; but when Prince George returned, she gave him for the
Landgravine the following letter, full of affectionate gratitude and
sorrowful resignation: —

"Your friendship and solicitude, Madame, have touched me to the
bottom of my heart. The person who is about to set out will tell you
the reasons which have detained him so long; he will tell you also that
even at present I dare not see him in my apartments, yet it would have
been sweet to me to talk to him of you, to whom I am tenderly attached.
No, my princess, while appreciating the full worth of your offers, I cannot accept them. I am bound for life to my duties and to those dear
ones whose misfortunes I share, and who, whatever may be said, merit
all consideration for the courage with which they endure their position.
The bearer of this letter will give you the details about the present
moment and the spirit of the place in which we live; it is said that he
has seen much and sees justly. May all that we do and suffer some
day make our children happy! This is the sole wish which I allow myself.
Adieu, princess. They have taken everything from me but my heart,
which I shall keep to love you. Never doubt it. That is the only misfortune which I could not bear."

And the queen, disclosing this project to the confidante of her days of sadness, Madame de Tourzel, said, " My determination is fixed; I should regard it as the most arrant cowardice to abandon the king and my children in danger. Besides, what would life be to me without these precious objects which alone bind me to so unhappy an existence as mine? Admit that, in my place, you would have chosen the same course of action."

Madame de Staël's project was more extensive and complete than that of the Prince of Hesse, for it embraced the whole royal family. An estate — the estate of La Motte, near Dieppe — was for sale. Madame de Staël proposed to buy it; to take with her there a trustworthy man, having about the same size and figure as the king, a woman of the age and shape of the queen, and her son, who was of the dauphin's age. After two or three journeys these persons should cede their places to the royal family; and through the favour which Necker's daughter found among the patriots, whose opinions she had held, but whose illusions she no longer shared, they could leave Paris, and reach the château of La Motte, where they would be in safety. Malouet was charged to communicate this plan to the king and queen, but received only the following discouraging reply, " That the august prisoners were most sensible of what Madame de Staël wished to do for them, but that they would never accept any service from her."

Malouet was not discouraged, however. Together with Montmorin, Lally-Tolendal, Malesherbes, and Bertrand de Molleville, he was always in search of means of saving the royal family; he appealed to the Duc de Liancourt, who since 1790 was in command at Rouen; and the duke, who had four regiments under his orders, promised to carry them to Pontoise, to which the Swiss Guards could conduct Louis XVI. From there the royal family could gain Rouen; a yacht, prepared under the supervision of a commander of the navy, Monsieur de Mistral, should receive them and transport them to Havre, or in the last extremity, to England. Malouet transmitted to the king through Monsieur de la Porte a letter in which he developed this plan, laying great stress upon the danger of remaining in Paris. The king read the letter without comment, and communicated its contents to no one; but he could not conceal his extreme agitation; and when the queen asked him the cause of it, he said, " It is a letter from Monsieur Malouet; but his anxiety is exaggerated, and there is little certainty in his means. . . . We shall see; nothing obliges me as yet to choose so hazardous a course. . . . The affair of Varennes is a lesson."

The queen said nothing, and Monsieur de la Porte withdrew; but Montmorin, when he heard this response, could not help exclaiming, "He must come to a decision; we shall all be massacred, and that before very long!"

The danger, indeed, was becoming so imminent that it struck the most casual observers. Lafayette once again offered his aid, and together with Monsieur de Montciel, minister of the interior, Lally-Tolendal, and the ambassador of the United States, the wise and loyal Gouverneur Morris, sketched out a plan. They were to take advantage of the *fête* of the federation. Lafayette and the old Maréchal Luckner, who was completely won over to the cause, had asked to assist at it in the name of the army. On the 15th, the king and the royal family, placed between these two, and escorted by one hundred loyal cavaliers, should leave Paris in open day. The National Guards would protect their departure, and the Swiss Guards, posted along the route between the capital and Compiègne, would support their march. The king, once at Compiègne, where fifteen squadrons and eight cannon would insure his liberty, freed from the encroachments of the Assembly and the pressure of the clubs, could act as mediator between the powers and France, and resume his authority in revising the Constitution. If the Assembly and the Jacobins opposed his lawful departure, the two generals would consider themselves authorized by this unconstitutional measure to march upon Paris at the head of their troops.

The project was examined in the council of the ministers; it was unanimously approved of. Louis XVI., despite his reluctance to quit the capital and to place himself in the hands of the Constitutionalists, upon whom he laid the blame of his deplorable situation, seemed disposed to lend himself to this plan. The preparations had already been begun. The Swiss Guards had received orders, when suddenly the prince declared that he had determined not to leave, that he preferred to expose himself to every danger rather than give the signal for civil war. It was, it is asserted, the queen's counsel which at the last moment thus modified the king's determination; she felt for Lafayette an insurmountable antipathy, and she said to Madame Campan that it was better to perish than to owe their safety to the man who had done

DE LA FAYETTE

them the greatest harm, and to place themselves under the necessity of negotiating with him.

Marie Antoinette has been bitterly reproached for her fierce opposition to the project. She has been accused of sacrificing the monarchy and the very life of those belonging to her to blind prejudice. Without doubt it would have been more politic to forget past wrongs and to see only present devotion, but the queen did not believe in the disinterestedness of this devotion. Lafayette was always in her eyes the man who had dealt the royal authority the rudest blows, who had inflicted upon her the cruellest wrongs, — such wrongs as a woman does not pardon. The great orator, Mirabeau, her neglect of whose counsels she then regretted, had always warned her against the blundering ambition and presumptuous incapacity of this person, whom he contemptuously called Julius Cæsar; and at that very moment were not her most intimate confidants, Mercy and Fersen, enjoining her in their letters never to appeal to Lafayette if necessity or favourable circumstances determined her to quit Paris, but to solicit the aid of faithful provinces, like Picardy?

Moreover, was this plan so sure of success as it was claimed? Would the National Guards have concurred in it? An event occurring at about that time made it seem doubtful. During the night of Wednesday, the 11th, and Thursday, the 12th, of July, the report had got about among the guards on duty at the palace that the queen had escaped. The commander could not calm his men except by waking the king at two o'clock in the morning and begging him to show him the queen. Were these dispositions favourable either for a flight or for a public departure? Montmorin, who transmitted these details to his friend De La Marck, arrived at this painful decision regarding the matter: —

"Since the king disbanded his guard, I believe it impossible for him to leave Paris and very dangerous for him to remain." And he concluded thus: "The king, and especially the queen, have positively rejected every proposition to leave Paris; and despite the danger I see in their remaining, I believe that they have done well."

Despite these sombre prognostications, the federation passed tranquilly; but the alarm was great. The king with all his family were at the École Militaire, awaiting the *cortége* which was to lay the first stone of a column on the site of the Bastille. When the *cortége* appeared and defiled under the balcony where the royal family stood, portentous shouts of "Vive Pétion!" burst forth on every side; some few cries of "Vive le roi!" replied to them. Louis XVI. descended and went on foot from the pavilion of the École Militaire to the altar erected at the end of the Champ de Mars. His powdered head stood out amid the black hair of the deputies, and his gold-embroidered garments contrasted with the sombre costume of the common people who surrounded him. "When he mounted the steps of the altar, he looked like a holy victim offering himself for the sacrifice." The queen, throughout this long and painful march, did not lose sight of him among those men, who, remarks an eye-witness, "had more the air of being assembled for a riot than for a *fête*." For an instant she saw him disappear in the crowd, and uttered a cry; but it was only a false alarm. Soon after the king returned to his place near his family. "The expression of the queen's face," says Madame de Staël, "will never be effaced from my memory. Her eyes were disfigured from weeping; the splendour of her toilet, the dignity of her bearing, contrasted with the company by which she was surrounded. A few National Guards only separated her from the populace." When the king returned to the École Militaire, she descended to meet him; he clasped her in his arms with tender emotion, and his children embraced him in tears.

When the ceremony was terminated, the royal family returned to their carriage and drove back to the Tuileries. The grenadiers who surrounded the carriage, happy in seeing them alive after the anxieties aroused by this day, shouted uninterruptedly, "Vive le roi! Vive la reine!" "They were all heart and soul," writes Madame Elisabeth; "it did us good." But what were these isolated cries in comparison to the mighty acclamations that had greeted the mayor of Paris, the true hero of the day, — that foppish, wretched Pétion, who had abandoned royalty on June 20, and who was to betray it on August 10?

The agitation at Paris continued. The report circulated more widely than ever that the Assembly wished to abduct the royal family and carry them to the south. To facilitate the execution of this project, and to isolate the king more and more, the three regiments of infantry which remained at the capital, and two battalions of Swiss Guards, were sent to the camp at Soissons. At the château there was no longer an instant of peace. The most absurd rumours received credence so soon as they were hostile to the royal family, and furnished a pretext for popular demonstrations. On July 20 the federates passed the night in orgies on the Place de la Bastille; some of the insurgents came and recounted to them that the court had caused the assassination of the patriot deputies and held eighteen thousand guns stored at the château. They at once snatched up their arms to go " and exterminate the traitors." At five in the morning the rappel was beaten; four thousand National Guards marched to the Tuileries. For this time, at least, the danger was averted; Pétion himself calmed the agitation. But this day nevertheless exercised a sinister influence upon the future; while the royal family were assembled with the ministers in the king's cabinet, awaiting the insurrection and deliberating upon the course of action to pursue, it had been decided that if the malcontents should approach, the king and his family, having no means of defence, should withdraw to the Assembly, — a fatal resolution, which was only too well carried into execution on August 10.

Some days later, during the night of the 24th and 25th of July, Madame Campan was informed that the faubourgs were preparing to march on the Tuileries; they had determined, it was said, to carry off the king and imprison him at Vincennes. The tocsin was already sounding at St. Roch. Madame Campan ran to the queen's apartments; the unhappy woman, prostrated with fatigue after so much wakefulness, was asleep. The king, who came in at that moment, would not allow her to be wakened. They had, besides, just learned that the demonstration announced had miscarried; Pétion, not finding himself quite ready, had opposed it. The queen, however, when she awoke, bitterly reproached her first waiting-woman for having respected her sleep; and when Madame Campan represented that she needed to renew her exhausted energies, she replied, " They are not exhausted; misfortune increases them. Elisabeth was with the king, and I slept, — I, who would wish to perish at his side; I am his wife, and I would not have him run the smallest risk apart from me."

She was forced to this passive rôle. If she had listened to her courage only, she would not have submitted so easily. She would have remembered the words of Mirabeau as to what a woman and a child could do on a horse. If they must perish, she would have preferred to die with weapons in her hand, rather than patiently await death from a poniard or on the scaffold ; but she was paralyzed by her husband's inactivity. "The king," she said, " fears to command, and dreads above everything to speak to a gathering of men. A few emphatic words addressed to the Parisians would increase a hundred-fold the strength of our party; he will not speak them. . . . For myself, I could indeed act, and mount a horse if it were necessary, but if I acted, I would furnish the king's enemies with new weapons. There would be an universal outcry in France against the *Austrian*, against the domination of a woman, and, besides, I would ruin the king if I appeared. A queen who is not a regent should under these circumstances remain inactive, and prepare herself for death."

One day when the Abbé de Montesquiou submitted to her a plan which required much policy and resolution, she replied sadly, " It is useless to advise any such policy as you propose to me ; he who has not the necessary spirit to conceive it would not know how to follow it out."

The queen, thus forced to inactivity in France, had little hope except from abroad. Her correspondence with Fersen became more frequent, — Fersen, whose father had wished to recall him to Sweden after the assassination of Gustavus III., and who had nobly refused to abandon his august clients, even were he reduced to want. She had recourse to most ingenious manœuvres to hide this intercourse. The letters were almost always written in cipher, or at least in a conventional style ; they were sent sometimes by trustworthy men; sometimes, and especially at this epoch, in boxes of biscuits, in packages of tea or chocolate, in the lining of a hat or coat, in the shape of advertisements in a journal. Note followed note with extraordinary rapidity and frequency; every week there were at least two, either from Marie Antoinette or from the faithful Goguelat. At the end of July they were little else than cries of alarm, of desperate appeals. The queen wrote on July 24 : —

" In the course of the week the Assembly is to decree its removal to Blois and the king's suspension. Every day brings fresh scenes, but tends ever toward the destruction of the king and his family; petitioners have declared at the bar of the Assembly that they would murder him. They have been accorded the honours of the meeting. Say, therefore, to Monsieur de Mercy that the lives of the king and queen are in the greatest danger ; that the delay of one day may produce incalculable misfortunes ; that the manifesto must be sent immediately ; that it is awaited with extreme impatience ; that it will necessarily rally a large following around the king and place him in safety ; that otherwise no one can answer for his security for twenty-four hours. The troop of assassins is constantly growing larger."

Eight days later, another and more urgent appeal. On July 28, D'Éprémenil had been almost beaten to death on the terrace of the Feuillants. On the 29th the Marseilles troops had made their entrance into Paris. A collection of brigands and vagrants, a cosmopolitan rabble escaped from the galleys of Genoa, Spain, and Toulon, they brought to the Parisian populace a powerful reinforcement, less through their number — they counted scarcely six hundred — than through their boldness and their experience in riots and crimes. It was to wait for them that Pétion had postponed the riot of July 27. The very next day after their arrival, the 30th, they met on the Champs-Élysées some grenadiers from the battalion of the Filles St. Thomas, who were having a mess dinner at the restaurant of Dubertier, picked a quarrel with them without reason, killed one of them, wounded fifteen, and the others only escaped the same fate by taking refuge in the garden of the Tuileries, and from there in the château, where every attention was lavished upon them. The comrades of the victims demanded justice from the Assembly in vain: the Left received them with murmurs, the gallery with hisses. They were transformed into the guilty ones; and the queen and ladies who had cared for the *assassins* of the brave federates were held up for popular vengeance.

On August 1, Marie Antoinette requested Goguelat to write the following despairing letter to Fersen, the last which her chivalric correspondent received from her; her agony even rendered her at times unjust toward the loyal grenadiers of the Filles St. Thomas: —

"The king's life and also the queen's have evidently been threatened for some time. The arrival of about six hundred Marseilles troops, and of a number of other deputies from all the Jacobin clubs, greatly increases our fears, which are unhappily only too well founded. Every precaution is taken for the safety of their Majesties; but assassins prowl continually round the palace. The Revolutionists excite the people; one part of the National Guards is ill-disposed, the other is weak and cowardly. The only resources available with which to oppose the enterprises of the scoundrels are the regiment of the Swiss Guards and a few persons resolved to make a rampart of their bodies for the royal family. The affair of the 30th, after a dinner on the Champs-Élysées, between

a hundred and eighty grenadiers — the best of the National Guards —
and the Marseilles federates, showed the cowardice of the National
Guards and the little reliance that can be put on these troops, who can
overawe only by their numbers. The hundred and eighty grenadiers fled ;
two or three were killed, and some twenty wounded. The Marseillais
patrol the Palais Royal and the garden of the Tuileries, which the
National Assembly has ordered to be opened. . . . For the moment,
we must think of avoiding the poniards and of foiling the conspirators
who swarm round the sinking throne. The malcontents have not for
some time taken the trouble to conceal their intention of destroying the
royal family. During the last two night sessions of the Assembly, the
deputies have only disagreed on the means to employ. You were able
to judge from my preceding letter how vital it is to gain even twenty-four
hours ; I will only remind you of it to-day, and add that if some one does
not arrive, Providence alone can save the king and his family."

At this date of August 1, the allied armies were in movement.
The Duke of Brunswick had set out on July 28 ; he expected to
be at the frontier in eight or ten days, to leave there companies
enough to cover the fortified towns, and prevent their garrisons
from opposing his operations, and then to proceed himself directly to Paris. Yielding to the importunities of the emigrants,
he had, at the moment of entering the campaign on the 25th,
issued from Coblentz a threatening manifesto. After having set
forth the demands of the emperor and the king of Prussia for the
German princes holding possessions in Alsace, and their desire
to see anarchy cease in France, without wishing to enrich themselves by conquest, or " interfere in the government of France,"
he urged the sane portion of the nation to return to the paths of
justice, and promised to protect those who would yield obedience
to the king; but he threatened with mortal punishment all those
who might resist his arms, declaring that if the least insult was
done the king or queen, the city of Paris would be delivered over
to military execution and total destruction.

By what ill-timed adroitness did Fersen succeed in substituting
this manifesto, due to the pen of an emigrant, — Monsieur de
Limon, — for the wise and moderate text proposed by the authorized agent of the king and queen, Mallet du Pan, and origi-
nally adopted by the powers? By what blindness could he who
knew France, who had just recently passed through it, and who
had written, " One cannot count upon the National Guards or
upon the worthy citizens of Paris, who fear to come to the front

lest they may receive a scratch, while the scoundrels act," adding, " My anxiety for you is extreme; I have not a single moment of peace,"—by what blindness could he believe that this haughty and irritating declaration would revive the courage of the friends of the royalty and terrify their adversaries? How was it that he did not see that to inflict capital punishment upon all the partisans of the Revolution was to swell their numbers, drive them to desperation, and that the first victims of this desperation would be the unfortunate sovereigns whom they wished to save? Yet he himself wrote to his friend Taube, in sending him the manifesto, " This is a critical moment for them; God preserve them!" And at his request the Baron de Breteuil sent the bishop of Pamiers to London to obtain of Pitt the intervention of England in favour of the unhappy hostages whom imprudent threats were to expose to the popular rage.

On the other side of the Rhine, however, even the wisest harboured strange illusions. The emigrants had so often reiterated that the war would be only a military promenade across France, that the Duke of Brunswick imagined that he would meet with no resistance; and Mercy himself, who through his age and experience was little disposed to exaggerated hopes, wrote to Marie Antoinette on July 9, " In a month you will be free." The halting-places along the march of the allied armies were already specified: they would be on such a day at Verdun; on such another at Châlons. The queen herself, momentarily reassured by Mercy's words, confided to Madame Campan, during one of her nights of wakefulness, " that she would be loosed from her chains when she saw the moon the next month." And the Baron de Breteuil was already forming the cabinet which should take the direction of affairs after the return to Paris.

Despite all this, the result of this manifesto was not what its authors expected. " It rallied no one, because it offered no rallying-point; it terrified no one, because it announced extravagant claims; and, finally, it obtained nothing, because it demanded the impossible. A part of France remained mute at the appeal; the other replied by cries of fury and vengeance."

At this supreme moment, however, the Girondins were not quite ready for a republic; they felt that they would not have the support of the army, — even of the army of the south, upon which they counted most securely. There was a moment's hesitation in the advance of the enemies of the royalty. The National

Guards wished to preserve the king as a safeguard against the reprisals of the allies, and certain leaders of the Revolution had already arranged means of flight to America. The plan most pleasing to Brissot and to his friends was to proclaim Louis XVI. deposed, and to place the dauphin on the throne, with Condorcet as governor and Pétion as regent. The Girondins, however, were already beaten; and in order not to be left behind, they were obliged to join the ranks of the Jacobins.

On August 3, Pétion presented himself at the bar of the Assembly, and in the name of forty-six out of the forty-eight sections of Paris demanded the king's deposition. The Assembly, without discussion, sent a petition to a special committee to make their report on August 9. Meanwhile all was being made ready for a last assault on royalty. The insurrectionary committee sat in permanence at the tavern of the Cadran-Bleu. The Mauconseil section, without awaiting the decision of the Assembly, voted the deposition. The section of the Théâtre Français, under the presidency of Danton, declared itself in a state of insurrection. The Marseillais, quitting their distant barracks, removed to the centre of the capital, — to the Poissonnière and Théâtre-Français sections, where they were incorporated into the revolutionary battalions; the malcontents lavished wine and money upon them. Westermann was chosen to take command of the bands in the place of Santerre, whose incapacity was too manifest; and Panis and Sergent distributed among the federates the cartridges which they refused to the National Guards. On all sides the Revolutionists raised recruits upon whom they could count. Jourdan and the murderers of the Glacière were at Paris. "Jourdan and his companions have joined Santerre," Malouet wrote to Monsieur Mallet du Pan; "the parading and hooting in the streets are horrible. The hand-bills and placards are of the colour of blood. Never was this city of mud so noxious, so pestilential."

At the same time, the last defenders of the Crown were removed from the capital. At the end of July, a Swiss officer wrote: "They have succeeded in sending the whole armed force out of Paris. Consequently the five regiments of infantry and the two thirds of the regiment of Swiss Guards, whom they feared, can no longer trouble the malcontents. We are soon to see the tragedy begin." The troops of infantry, in fact, whose friendly spirit the Assembly dreaded, had been sent to the army. Three hundred Swiss Guards had been led into Normandy under the pretext of protecting the transportation of grain, and those who remained at Paris had had their twelve cannons taken from them.

To complete the disorganization of the opposition, the municipality determined that the guard on duty at the palace should each day be composed of citizens from every section, all ready to rush in arms to the Tuileries and depose the king. The day only was as yet uncertain. Successively fixed for the 4th, then for the 6th, it was finally set for the evening of the 9th, when the Assembly should have deliberated upon the petition of the sections of Paris. If justice had not been rendered the people by the legislative corps before eleven o'clock on that day, "the tocsin would sound at midnight, a general call to arms would be beaten, and the whole city would rise together." Meanwhile, terror reigned at the capital; those deputies who still dared, we will not say to favour the king, but simply not to follow servilely the will of the clubs, were insulted and maltreated. The gloomiest reports circulated: it was announced that the queen would be paraded in an iron cage before conducting her to La Force; that the king would be imprisoned at the Hôtel de Ville, then at the Temple. On August 2, a printed sheet was sold in the streets, which was nothing more than the programme of the day predicted; and the physician Brunier gave a copy to Madame de Tourzel. Frightful agitation reigned among the people; and a woman who was on intimate terms with the Revolutionists wrote this sinister phrase, " It will rain blood. I am not exaggerating."

What had the royalty to oppose to these direct and public threats? Nothing but vague promises, fragile hopes, and, alas! obstinate illusions; the still distant march of the Duke of Brunswick; money given to the leaders of the malcontents, Pétion, Danton, Santerre, to prevent the insurrection, and which only served to pay for it; and at the palace nine hundred Swiss Guards, a few faithful National Guards, and a hundred courtiers. What were these against the bands led by Barbaroux and Westermann?

In vain the faithful friends of these last days — the Malouets, the Malesherbes, the Morrises, the Lally-Tolendals — presented, on August 7, a final project of flight. In vain they offered to conduct the royal family to Pontoise, or to Compiègne, under the protection of Aclocque's grenadiers, and Courbevoie's Swiss

Guards, setting out in broad daylight, at eight in the morning, from the Pont Tournant, and notifying the president of the Assembly that they were going to Compiègne in virtue of the Constitution. The king refused; and Madame Elisabeth replied that the predicted insurrection would not take place; that they had as guarantee the word of Pétion and of Santerre, who, in consideration of seven hundred and fifty thousand livres, had promised to bring the Marseillais back to his Majesty's party.

Despite this apparent and strange confidence, perpetual alarm prevailed at the château. If the Royalists had for a time believed, as Morris says, that the National Guards and the Parisians would preserve Louis XVI., "as the most effectual protection against the pillage and insults of the enemies," they could scarcely retain this confidence after June 20: they only sought to gain time; but the royal family were under direct surveillance. To prevent flight, the report of which had again spread abroad, the federates patrolled the Tuileries day and night. Pikemen, before going with red caps on their heads to make incendiary motions at the Assembly, defiled near the château, singing offensive couplets. "One would have said that they came to reconnoitre the ground before attacking it." The queen was insulted even under the windows of her small rooms which opened on the court; and Madame de Tourzel, whose apartments were on the ground floor, dared not bring the dauphin into them. A Marseillais soldier, with a sabre in his hand, cried out to the Swiss Guards on guard at the gate of the Carrousel, "Wretches, this is the last time you will mount guard; we are going to exterminate every one of you."

Every day, every night, there were fresh alarms. The king burned his papers. The queen retired to rest one night out of every two; and she was compelled, as we have seen, to keep a little dog in her chamber, to warn her in case of danger. All during the night of August 4 and 5, they expected to be murdered. Louis XVI. remained up. "Ah! may they come soon!" the unhappy prince exclaimed, resigned to his fate. "I have been ready for a long time; but," he added with touching solicitude, "do not allow the queen to be wakened."

On Sunday, August 5, the royal family went to the chapel of the Tuileries to hear mass for the last time. As they crossed the gallery, some of the National Guards greeted them with shouts of "Vive le roi!" But instantly others answered with threatening hoots: "No king, down with the Veto!" And in the evening at vespers, the musicians, in singing the *Magnificat*, gave one another a signal to "triple the sound of their voices in a frightful manner, when they chanted, *Deposuit potentes de sede!*"

This was the last outrage. Five days later this sinister prediction of the musicians of the chapel was fulfilled.

CHAPTER XXI.

THE day of Thursday, August 10, had been relatively quiet, despite the alarming reports which circulated. The king after dinner had played billiards with Madame Elisabeth, and the pious princess had written to her friend, Madame de Bombelles, " This day, which was to be so exciting, so terrible, is as calm as possible." In the evening there was a sudden change. I know not what sinister agitation reigned in the capital. The ladies of the palace did not dare come to the court for fear of being insulted.

At midnight the tocsin rang out from the belfries of the churches. Soon with the sound of the tocsin was mingled that of drums, some of which were beating a general call to arms, and others the rappel; the sections shouldered their arms. The faubourgs bestirred themselves and began to move. At the Tuileries there were about nine hundred Swiss Guards, two hundred gentlemen, and a few companies of faithful National Guards. It was not much; but this little band was under the orders of a resolute and loyal leader, Galiot de Mandat, former captain of the French Guards. In the morning he had taken most energetic measures for defence: the bridges were guarded, and it would be easy to prevent the faubourgs from coming together by cutting off the communications, and instructing the columns to disperse them. The Swiss Guards occupied the court of the palace, the chapel, the royal gate, and the foot of the grand staircase of the king and queen, while the grenadiers of the Filles St. Thomas were drawn up in line opposite the main gate. Unfortunately the soldiers had no cartridges, scarcely three shots to a man. The Swiss Guards themselves had not thirty, and the commander was without orders.

Toward eleven o'clock, Pétion, yielding to Mandat's repeated importunities, came to the palace. The king questioned him sternly. "Monsieur," he said, "you are mayor of Paris. It appears that there is a great deal of excitement; do the people wish to repeat the 20th of June?" "Sire, the fermentation is great, but I will hasten to the Hôtel de Ville to restore peace." "No, Monsieur," replied the queen, who divined Pétion's intentions; "everything has been organized under your eyes; you must sign as mayor an order to repel force by force. You will remain by the person of the king." Pétion, disconcerted, signed the order; then he slipped away, and after a short visit to the Assembly, returned to his house, where, following the plan agreed upon with his friends, he had himself confined for the rest of the day.

The inhabitants of the château had been somewhat reassured during the early hours; they had confidence in the troops at their disposition, which Mandat had skilfully placed at the most important points, — in the court, in the garden, and at the gates. Reports, moreover, which they believed trustworthy, represented the mob as less dangerous than they had at first supposed. The queen had even sent her son to bed under the care of the faithful Madame de Tourzel; but in kissing him, she had not been able to restrain her tears. "Mamma," the child said, as if divining the danger, "why do you cry? I would rather not leave you to-night." "Do not be uneasy, my son; I shall not be far from you."

Their anxiety, however, soon reawakened; bad news arrived, pressing and unmistakable. The royal family were assembled in the council-chamber; the Princesse de Lamballe, the Princesse de Tarente, Madame de Tourzel and her daughter, the ministers, two municipal officers, Borie and Leroux, the procurator-general, syndic of the department, Rœderer, and a few zealous followers, were with them. In the face of these increasing dangers, traditional etiquette had been set aside: there had been no *coucher* of the king; the queen and Madame Elisabeth were seated upon ordinary stools. A few devoted friends arrived from moment to moment, seating themselves everywhere, on the tables, on the consoles, on the floor.

The queen spoke to every one in the most affectionate manner, reviving their zeal and courage. "Messieurs," she said to the National Guards, who were in the council-chamber, "all that is most dear to you, your wives, your children, depend upon our lives; our interest is a common one." There was not, however, perfect harmony among these defenders of the last hour; some of the National Guards clung to their prejudices against the courtiers. The chief of the La Chesnaye legion desired the removal of the royalist volunteers. The queen opposed this strongly. "You should not," she said, "mistrust these brave men, who will share your dangers and defend you to their last breath. I answer for all those here. They will march before, behind, in the ranks, as you wish; they are willing to do everything necessary, and are trustworthy men."

No one had retired to rest at the château. The dauphin alone slept. About three in the morning, they heard in the distance something like the surging sound of approaching waves. A shot re-echoed in the very court of the Tuileries. "Alas!" said the queen, "that will not be the last one!" She ordered her son to be taken up and dressed; she did not wish the malcontents to find the heir to the throne in bed, and from that moment she kept him always near her. "Mamma," said the poor child, moved at the sight of the trouble which he saw round him, and already familiar with these days,—"mamma, why should they hurt papa? He is so good!"

The night was superb, the sky clear, the air still; the calmness of nature contrasted with the agitation in the street, and the anxiety in their hearts. Through the open casements could be heard the sounds of a great city. The dawn broke; Madame Elisabeth ran to the window. "My sister," she said, "come and see the daybreak." The disk of the sun was just rising above the horizon, red as blood.

Meanwhile an imperious order from the municipality summoned Mandat to the Hôtel de Ville. The commander had already ignored one message. Urged by Rœderer, he dared not resist a second, and set out between four and five in the morning; but a dark foreboding seized him. "I shall not return," he said.

He was not mistaken. When he arrived at the Hôtel de Ville, he found the insurrectionary Commune installed in the place of the lawful Commune. Huguenin, who presided, reproached him violently for the measures which he had taken against the people, called upon him to revoke them, and when Mandat refused, gave an order to transfer him to the Abbey. This was the signal of death. In coming out of the council-hall, some one pierced the head of the unhappy commander with a bullet, and his body was thrown into the Seine. After this, the little garrison at the Tuileries was without a leader, and their resistance was disorganized.

The noise became more distinct; the waves were approaching. The queen implored the king to show himself to his defenders, and to animate them by his presence, by his example, by a word of encouragement. Louis XVI. yielded to his wife's entreaties; he appeared on the balcony dressed in a violet coat, his hair in disorder, his face flushed, his eyes red from lack of sleep. He was greeted with hearty cheers. He crossed through the apartments to reach the court. The queen, her children, Madame Elisabeth, the Princesse de Lamballe, accompanied him. When he passed into the grand gallery, warm enthusiasm was manifested; these old courtiers, recent volunteers, willing to be massacred, acclaimed this royalty so soon to expire. Emotion swelled their breasts; tears bathed their eyes; shouts of "Vive le roi" broke out on every side. The battalion of the Filles St. Thomas occupied the gallery of Diana; the queen spoke to them with the graciousness and heartiness which she put into all that she said, and these good men were transported with joy. "They seemed," said an historian of the time, " to repeat the sublime scene of *Moriamur pro rege nostro.*"

They were less sure of the exterior posts, where Pétion had placed the hostile battalions. The king did not wish to expose his family to a doubtful and perhaps unfriendly reception. Having reached the vestibule of the grand staircase, he requested his wife, sister, and children to return, and continued his last review alone. This was perhaps a mistake. What the somewhat feeble bounty and resigned courage of the king did not do, the more determined attitude of the queen and the more touching beauty of the dauphin might have accomplished.

It was about six o'clock when Louis XVI. descended into the court. Uneasy and troubled, despite his serene bearing, he could not say a word to the National Guards who pressed round him. They still shouted, however, " Vive le roi! Vive Louis XVI.! We shall defend him until death! Let him place himself at our head. Down with the Jacobins! " But the king remained mute. As he went farther from the palace, round which the loyal troops were grouped, his reception became colder. On the terrace at the edge of the water it was hostile. The soldiers cried, " Vive la nation! Down with the Veto! Down with the Gros Cochon! " Some gunners, the worst part of the National Guards, followed the prince, repeating these insulting cries, "as flies," says an eye-witness, "pursue an animal whom they have furiously tormented." On the terrace of the Feuillants, brigands armed with pikes added their threatening yells to these hostile clamours; some of them even descended into the garden, and the faithful servitors who accompanied the ill-fated monarch were obliged to surround him in a double line in order to protect him. "Great God! it is the king whom they are hooting!" exclaimed the minister of the navy, Monsieur de Bouchage. Louis XVI. returned to the palace with despair in his heart; and the queen, who from afar had watched the whole scene, and listened with painful intentness to all these cries, said to Madame Campan, "All is lost; this review has done more harm than good."

It is certain, however, — the most authentic documents, the most trustworthy acts, attest it, — that if even at this moment the king had boldly mounted a horse and resolutely placed himself at the head of his troops, as Marie Antoinette entreated him to do, he could easily have overcome his assailants, and to use Napoleon's forcible expression, " have swept out all this rabble."

The king, however, hesitated; the king feared to shed blood; and the municipal officers present appeared to have no other aim than to disorganize the defence. They walked about in the Court of the Carrousel saying aloud that it would be folly to try to resist so numerous and so well-armed a mob; it was only with reluctance that they read the martial law to the troops, and then they were careful to add, " You are not to fire until you are fired upon." These peculiar instructions threw the National Guards into confusion. Some of the companies wheeled half about; the gunners, for the most part hostile, pointed their pieces on the palace, and the mounted *gendarmerie* who occupied the court of the Louvre fell back on the Palais Royal, thus leaving the way open to the insurgents.

About seven o'clock a rough and compact mob filled the Place Vendôme and the terrace of the Feuillants. The vanguard of the riot debouched upon the Place du Carrousel; some of the bandits were already mounted on horses, on the top of the walls, observing everything and calling to their comrades. The municipal officers tried to parley with them. A loud cry, " Deposition or death ! " was the response. Municipal officers, commander-in-chief, procurator-general, — all were demoralized; they returned to the king. During the night Rœderer had already suggested going to the Assembly. "Monsieur," the queen had replied proudly, "there are troops here; it is at last time to know who is to have the ascendancy, the king and the Constitution, or the factions." The procurator-general had bowed; but he had not changed his opinion. This time the municipal officers took the word.

"Sire," said Leroux, "the only thing to do is to take refuge in the heart of the National Assembly; you must leave at this very instant."

"Do you think so?" Louis XVI. replied.

"Yes, Sire. To say the contrary to your Majesty would be to betray him."

The queen sprang up. Ask shelter of the Assembly, of this Assembly who had done nothing to prevent the riot, and who, while the monarchy was in the throes of death, had the melancholy courage to deliberate calmly on the slave-trade; abandon the palace, give up the struggle, — this was tantamount to signing his deposition, this was abdicating! "Withdraw to the National Assembly," she said in a trembling voice; "have you a thought of it?"

"Yes, Madame; the Assembly is the only thing at this moment that the people will respect."

Toward half-past seven Rœderer appeared, invested with his scarf and at the head of the Directory. "Sire," he said, "your Majesty has not five minutes to lose. There is no safety for you except in the National Assembly." "But," the king said, "I did not see a large crowd upon the Carrousel." "Sire, there are twelve pieces of cannon; and an enormous multitude is arriving from the faubourgs."

The queen's blood boiled in her veins. Turning to her faithful attendants, she exclaimed, "You can nail me to these walls before I shall consent to leave them." A member of the department whom she knew well, for he was a lace merchant, Monsieur Gendret, tried to uphold Rœderer's opinion. "Be quiet, Monsieur," the queen said, with spirit. "Allow the procurator-general to speak. You are the only one who should say nothing here; when one has done the wrong, one should not appear to repair it." Then turning to Rœderer, "But, Monsieur, we have troops." "Madame, all Paris is in motion; action is useless, resistance impossible. Do you wish to render yourself responsible for the murder of the king, of your children, of yourself, — in a word, of the faithful servants who surround you?" "God forbid!" the valiant woman replied. "On the contrary, would that I could be the only victim!" But her emotion was so violent that, an eye-witness relates, "her breast and her face became suddenly streaked."

"Sire," the procurator-general resumed, "time presses; we no longer entreat you; we no longer take the liberty of counselling you. There is only one course for us to pursue at this moment; we beg permission to carry you off by force." The king raised his head, looked at Rœderer for an instant, as if to search his secret thoughts, and finally coming to a decision, said, —

"Very well; since we must, let us give this new evidence of devotion."

"Yes," replied the queen, "it is a last sacrifice; but," she added, pointing to her husband and her son, "you see the object of it." Then, addressing Rœderer, she said, —

"Monsieur, you are responsible for the person of the king; you are responsible for that of my son."

"Madame," Rœderer replied, "we pledge ourselves to die at your side; that is all that we can guarantee."

At about half-past eight the funereal *cortége* was formed. Grenadiers of the Filles St. Thomas and Swiss Guards composed the escort. The king marched alone in front, having at his side the minister of foreign affairs; the queen took the arm of the minister of the navy, and held the dauphin by the hand; then came Madame Elisabeth and Madame Royale, Madame de Lamballe and Madame de Tourzel, and a few faithful followers like the Prince de Poix and the Comte de la Rochefoucauld, the ministers, and members of the department. All those present wept; there was general consternation. "We shall return," the king said. "We shall return," the queen repeated. But neither the king nor the queen had hope; and the spectators felt, as they, that, in Madame de Tourzel's words, "it was the funeral train of royalty" which they saw passing.

The king marched erect; and although his heart was torn and his features discomposed, his bearing was firm. The queen was bathed in tears. She wiped her eyes from time to time, and tried to assume a confident air; but she could not retain it for more than a few minutes. A National Guard, misinterpreting the cause of her tears, said, "Your Majesty need fear nothing; she is surrounded by good citizens." "I have no fear," the queen replied, laying her hand upon her breast.

The *cortége* crossed the rooms, descended the main staircase, went out by the central gate, and entered the garden. The National Guards marched on the right, the Swiss Guards on the left. The crowd which thronged the terrace of the Feuillants greeted the advancing victims with derisive shouts. The king, nevertheless, preserved his impassive attitude. The queen leaned for the moment upon Monsieur de la Rochefoucauld's arm; her heart beat, her hand trembled. The little dauphin, with the heedlessness of his age, amused himself by kicking the dead leaves which encumbered the garden. "How many leaves there are!" remarked the king; "they are falling early this year."

Some days before, Manuel had written in a journal that the monarchy would not survive the fall of the leaves. This prediction was being realized.

As they approached the terrace of the Feuillants the mob became more turbulent; the way was blocked; for ten minutes the *cortége* was obliged to halt at the foot of the staircase of the Passage des Feuillants. Furious cries burst forth from the populace: "Down with him! Down with him! No Veto! Do not let them enter the Assembly." They caught sight of the queen, and their clamours redoubled: "No women! We wish only the king; the king alone!"

A grenadier seized the prince royal, and took him in his arms. The queen, believing that he meant to carry off her son, uttered a terrible cry. The National Guard lifted the dauphin above his head, reassuring the child and the mother.

Meanwhile the Assembly, notified of the royal family's arrival by the president of the Directory of the department, sent a delegation of twenty-four members to meet them. "Sire," said the deputy who led them, "the Assembly offers you and your family a refuge in its midst." The funeral train resumed its march; the members of the Assembly had replaced those of the Directory. Upon the terrace of the Feuillants, however, the cries grew fiercer. The crowd pressed upon them; they were forced to halt. A wretch brandished a pole, and threatened the royal family with it, shouting, "Down with them! Down with them!" A man left the group, and addressing the king said, "Give me your hand; I will conduct you to the Assembly; but as for your wife, she shall not enter. It is she who has caused the misfortune of France." Rœderer rushed forward; with the authorization of the deputies, he ordered the National Guards to mount the staircase. He ascended it himself, and harangued the mob roaring about him. There was a movement; he took advantage of it to open a passage for Louis XVI. and Marie Antoinette. Amid these furious bands, vomiting forth insults, and with difficulty held in check by the escort, the unhappy sovereigns entered the Assembly. The king took his place by the side of the president; the queen and his family behind him, upon the benches of the ministers. The grenadier who carried the dauphin set him down upon the desk of the secretary, amid the cheers of the gallery. The child ran to his mother. "No, no!" a voice shouted; " he belongs to the nation. The Austrian is unworthy of the confidence of the people."

Calm was restored. The king addressed the Assembly, saying, "I am come in order to avoid a great crime; I could not be better off than in your midst."

Vergniaud, who presided, replied, " Sire, you can count upon the firmness of the National Assembly. Its members have sworn to die defending the rights of the people, and of the established authorities."

The Constitution, however, did not permit the Assembly to deliberate in the presence of the king. The Assembly decided that Louis XVI. and his family should be taken into the reporters' gallery.

It was a small grated recess ten feet square, exposed to the heat of a burning sun, so narrow that it could scarcely hold a few journalists, so low that one could not stand erect in it. The king seated himself in the front of it; the queen in a corner; the children, Madame Elisabeth, and Madame de Lamballe, upon a bench, behind which a few devoted friends stood. The iron gratings which separated the alcove from the hall were torn out. It was ten o'clock in the morning; and here in this wretched cell the prisoners, during eighteen hours, witnessed the death-throes of royalty.

Suddenly a spirited firing was heard: there was fighting at the Tuileries. After the departure of the royal family a greater part of the National Guards had returned to their houses. The Swiss Guards had evacuated the court and concentrated in the palace. " Do not let yourself be forced," the Maréchal de Mailly had said to Captain de Durler. The insurrectionary columns arrived and commanded the Swiss to surrender; they heroically re-

fused.   Like that great wounded lion which symbolizes their val-
iance in the rock of Lucerne, they guarded proudly and faithfully
the ancient escutcheon of France, already partially shattered.
The rioters sought to surprise them.   Individuals, armed with
hooks, endeavoured to drag them away by their belts, — vain efforts !   Then suddenly without any one knowing who fired it, a shot
was heard.   The Swiss Guards fired a volley.   The assailants,
without attempting to reply, dispersed in every direction in
confusion, abandoning their cannon, evacuating the court, clearing the palace, not believing themselves in safety until they had
reached their quarters, and showing by this precipitate flight what
their courage was worth, and what might have been done if the
Royalists had attempted to resist.

The king, however, did not wish to continue the struggle ; he
had a horror of shedding blood.   From his prison in the reporters' gallery, he sent Monsieur d'Hervilly with the order to
cease firing and evacuate the château.   The Swiss Guards, obedi-
ent to these instructions, retreated in good order across the garden.   Another message from the king ordered them to lay down
their arms.

The Marseillais, brave against adversaries who did not defend
themselves, returned to the charge, rushed into the palace, plundered, broke everything, venting their fury principally upon what
had belonged to the queen, shattering the mirrors, "in which
Médicis-Antoinette had too long studied the hypocritical air
which she showed to the public."   They put an end to the
wounded, killed with pikes and sabres the servants of the palace
down to the last scullion, fired the barracks of the Swiss Guards
and stables of the king, broke open the cellars, and intoxicated
themselves with wine and blood.   The massacre in the gardens
and the street responded to the massacre in the palace ; the ill-
fated Swiss Guards, disarmed, were assaulted, mutilated, murdered.
Clermont-Tonnerre was assassinated, and the head of Suleau was
carried on the end of a pike by Théroigne de Méricourt.

These conquerors of a royalty who had not tried to defend
itself, covered with blood and drunk from their orgies, appeared
at the bar of the Assembly and requested, or rather demanded,
the king's deposition.   The Assembly bowed to the will of these
new masters of France.   The president, Vergniaud, read a decree
which suspended the king from his functions until the convocation of a national convention, and decided that the royal family

should be transferred to the Luxembourg under the safeguard of the citizens and the laws, and that a governor should be appointed for the prince royal.

Meanwhile, since the king was no longer to be surrounded by National Guards, an order to withdraw was communicated to the faithful attendants who still accompanied and protected him. The devoted servitors retired sadly; but the Comte de Chabot, who belonged to the National Guards, ran, put on his uniform, returned, and took up his post as sentinel at the door of the reporters' gallery.

From his prison the king watched the petitioners succeed one another at the bar with blood upon their hands and insults in their mouths; he saw the spoils of the Tuileries laid upon the desk. He heard them discuss and proclaim his deposition; he remained unmoved and resigned. The queen preserved her proud attitude: her lip curled with a smile of contempt for all these wretches who outraged her before killing her. One provision only of the decree moved her: this was the one which decided that a governor should be appointed for the prince royal. She begged several deputies to try to parry this blow, which was so vital to her; they succeeded the more easily, says Madame de Tourzel, "because the Assembly, contemplating the establishment of a republic, troubled themselves little about giving to Monseigneur le Dauphin a governor." Madame Elisabeth bowed her head; Madame Royale wept; the dauphin, prostrated with fatigue, had fallen asleep upon his mother's lap. The heat was suffocating; the royal party was stifled in this recess without space and without air. The face of the poor child was bathed in perspiration; the queen wished to wipe it, but her handkerchief was already soaked. She asked for that of Monsieur de la Rochefoucauld, who stood near her; the handkerchief which he gave her was stained with the blood of her defenders.

Toward two o'clock in the morning the royal family was transferred to the convent of the Feuillants, situated near the Assembly hall. They set out across the garden surrounded by brigands, whose pikes were dripping with blood, and lighted on their way by smoking candles which, stuck in the barrels of guns, cast a sinister light over the whole scene. For an instant the queen feared for her son. She snatched him anxiously from the hands of Monsieur d'Aubier, who was carrying him, and pressed him convulsively to her heart. The child, reassured, said gayly, " Mamma has promised to let me sleep in her room, because I have been very good with these wicked men."

Four rooms, or rather four cells, uninhabited for more than two years, with brick floors half in ruins, and whitewashed walls, — such was the new palace of the king and queen of France. The architect of the Assembly had hurriedly ordered some furniture to be placed there. The cells all opened upon a long corridor, the issues of which were strictly guarded. The king established himself in the second cell; the queen and Madame Royale in the third; the dauphin and Madame de Tourzel in the fourth. The first served as antechamber; there, a few valiant servants watched over the fallen royalty. An improvised supper was served; the children alone touched it. Outside, the mob growled and demanded the head of the queen. "What has she done to them?" the king asked sadly.

Some wretches pushed their way in as far as the corridor which led to the prince's chamber, yelling that they would murder him if there were the least reaction in his favour in Paris. Others attempted to climb up to the low windows, which were without shutters or grating; they mounted upon one another's shoulders, "to shorten the big Veto." The queen came into her husband's cell for a moment; even at this hour she could not console herself for leaving the palace without having attempted some resistance. "Perhaps," she said, "all would have happened otherwise, if an attack had been made on the Marseillais early in the day." "By whom?" Louis XVI. replied with some irritation. The unhappy woman did not insist; at the end of a few minutes, she returned to her room, — a melancholy refuge, hung with faded green paper, — and threw herself upon her bed, a monk's hard pallet. But alas! sleep scarcely visited her eyelids. It was not until six in the morning that she was able to lose herself in that heavy and unrefreshing sleep which follows a great strain. In order not to awaken her, Madame Elisabeth herself dressed the children. When they were ready, she led them to their mother. "Poor children," the ill-fated sovereign observed, sighing, "how cruel it is to have promised them so beautiful a heritage, and to say, This is what we leave them. All will end with us!"

In the hurry of departure, the royal family had been able to take nothing from the Tuileries, and since then their apartments had been plundered. The unhappy royal family had nothing left, neither clothes nor money. Marie Antoinette's watch and purse

had been stolen on the way from the Assembly to the Feuillants.
A Swiss officer of about the same figure as Louis XVI. sent
some things for the king's use; the Duchesse de Gramont succeeded in transmitting some linen to the queen; the ambassadress
of England, the Countess of Sutherland, whose son was about
the same age as the dauphin, provided clothes for the young
prince; and the daughter of Maria Theresa, absolutely destitute,
was obliged to accept twenty-five louis from one of her women,
Madame Auguié.

In the morning, some of the queen's women, Madame Campan
and her sister among others, were able to rejoin her. She extended her arms to them in tears, saying, "Come, come, unhappy women, behold a woman more unhappy than you, because
it is she who has caused your unhappiness. We are lost," she
added; "we have arrived at the point to which our enemies have
been leading us for three years by every possible outrage. We
shall succumb to this terrible Revolution. The whole world has
contributed to our ruin." The royal family remained for three
days in the convent of the Feuillants. For three days they were
led every morning at ten o'clock into the miserable *loge* which had
sheltered them upon their exit from the palace. For three days
the king saw the petitioners succeed one another at the bar, demanding the heads of the Swiss Guards who had escaped the
massacre, or imperiously exacting his own deposition. He heard
the Assembly accord a recompense to the heroes of August 10
while they arraigned the minister of war, D'Abancourt, and preluded the abolition of the royalty, which still legally existed, by
ordering the overthrow of the statues of the kings. For three
days the monarch submitted to this frightful torture; every evening for three days the prisoners were led back to their prison
under the escort of a numerous guard, who with difficulty defended them from assassination, but who did not defend them
from outrage. One day, in the convent garden, a young man,
well dressed, approached the queen, and thrusting his fist under
her nose, cried, "Infamous Antoinette, thou didst wish to bathe
the Austrians in our blood; thou shalt pay for it with thy head!"
To this atrocious insult the queen replied only by contemptuous
silence.

The Assembly had decided that the royal family should be
transferred to the Luxembourg, but the palace of Marie de
Médicis did not seem sufficiently secure to guard such hostages;

the Luxembourg, it was said, offered means of escape by certain underground passages which it possessed. The Commune of Paris desired to have the prisoners nearer and more dependent upon it. The hôtel of the chancellor, on the Place Vendôme, was proposed; the proposition was rejected. Manuel, in the name of the Commune, signified that it had chosen the Temple; and the Assembly, bowing before the new power which anarchy had raised on the ruins of monarchy, hastened to declare that the royal family should be imprisoned in the Temple. When the queen heard this name, she shuddered; I know not what dark forebodings agitated her; and leaning toward Madame de Tourzel, she said, —

"You will see, they will place us in the tower, and make a veritable prison of it. . . . I have always had such a horror of this tower that I have a thousand times begged the Comte d'Artois to have it destroyed; it was surely a presentiment of all we should have to suffer there. . . . You will see whether I am mistaken."

Alas! She was not mistaken.

The Assembly decided at the same time that all persons not employed in the domestic service of the king should be taken from him. "Ah!" the ill-fated prince exclaimed, "I am, then, a prisoner! Charles I. was more fortunate than I; his friends were left with him until he mounted the scaffold." And turning to those who surrounded him, he ordered them to withdraw.

"Messieurs," the queen said to them with tears in her eyes, "it is only at this moment that we feel the full horror of our position. You sweetened it by your presence and your devotion, and our enemies now deprive us of this last consolation."

Before leaving, the devoted followers deposited upon a table the gold and the assignats which they had in their pockets; they knew that the royal family had nothing. The king perceived it, and gently pushing away this last tribute of loyalty, said, "Messieurs, keep your pocket-books. You have, I hope, a longer time to live."

At six o'clock on the evening of August 13, two large court carriages, each drawn by two large horses, stopped at the door of the convent of the Feuillants. The coachmen and footmen were dressed in gray; it was the last time they were to serve their fallen masters. The king, the queen, their children, Madame Elisabeth, Madame de Lamballe, Madame de Tourzel and her daughter, the mayor, the procurator of the Commune, and a municipal officer got into the first carriage. The king and queen, the dauphin and Madame, occupied the back seat, Madame Elisabeth, Madame de Lamballe, and Pétion the front ; Madame de Tourzel and her daughter were at one of the doors ; Manuel and one of the municipal officers, Collonge, were on the seat opposite ; these two men and Pétion, disregarding common politeness, kept their hats on their heads. Two municipal officers and the suite of the royal family took their seats in the second carriage. The king preserved an impassive countenance ; the queen was gloomy. The dauphin, with the unconcern of his age, turned his eyes in every direction to see the crowd. The National Guards, on foot, with arms inverted, surrounded the carriage ; but thousands of brigands, armed with pikes, mingled with the escort, shouting insults and blasphemies. The obstruction was occasionally so great that the horses were unable to advance. At such times Pétion and Manuel stuck their heads out of the door and demanded passage ; but they did nothing to silence the insults.

On the Place Vendôme the king's carriage halted. The Revolutionists wished the fallen monarch to contemplate at leisure the statue of Louis XIV., which the mad populace had thrown down from its pedestal. " Behold, Sire, how the people treat kings," Manuel remarked. " It is fortunate, Monsieur," Louis XVI. replied, scarlet with indignation, " that their fury is vented only on inanimate objects."

The *cortége* resumed its slow and constantly interrupted march by way of the boulevards. This long martyrdom lasted nearly two hours and a half. The carriages advanced at a walk in the centre of compact and hostile masses shouting, " Vive la nation ! Down with the king ! " The municipal officers charged to escort the prisoners saw fit to join in these shouts, and even to provoke them. " It is impossible," says an unprejudiced eye-witness, " to describe the ignominy of this scene."

Night had fallen when they reached the Temple. In odious irony the windows were illuminated as if for a *fête ;* the drawing-room was lighted by countless candles, and the royal family made their entrance into the court of the palace amid the sinister gleam of little lamps which mocked their downfall. Santerre came first to meet them, and motioned to the carriages to advance to the *perron ;* but a gesture from the municipal officers countermanded Santerre's orders, and the august prisoners were forced to alight in the middle of the court. The officers of the

Commune walked near the king with their hats upon their heads, and addressing him by no other title than *Monsieur;* a man with a long beard, named Truchon, even took occasion to repeat this title at every opportunity.

The crowd howled in the approaches to the palace; to illuminate its clamorous joy, and to bring the defeat of royalty into clearer relief, little lamps were placed on the projecting portions of the exterior walls.

It was half-past eight in the evening; the gates reclosed with a mournful sound, and in this palace, transformed into a dungeon, the royal family were soon to see the realization of that prophetic remark of one of their most faithful friends: " History teaches us that the passage of dethroned monarchs is short from the prison to the grave."

CHAPTER XXII.

THE Temple! What sum of unutterable sufferings the name recalls! All the tortures which hatred can invent, all the insults which brutality can devise, were endured by the royal family. All the bitterness with which the heart of a man and a king can be steeped was tasted by Louis XVI. All the tears which the eyes of a woman and a queen can hold were shed by Marie Antoinette. Of the five prisoners upon whom the gates of the Temple closed on the evening of August 13, three were to recross its threshold to ascend the scaffold; the fourth, a child, — ah! a speedy death would have been sweeter than the long and abominable torture to which his executioners were to condemn him.

The enclosure of the Temple, into which the prisoners had just been admitted, contained two very different structures, — the one a vast hôtel without style, called the palace of the grand prior, former residence of the families of Vendôme and of Conti, and later of the Comte d'Artois; the other a square tower four stories high, surmounted by a pointed roof and flanked at the four angles by round turrets with peaked roofs. Attached to the great tower was a smaller and lower tower, ornamented with two round turrets, and without direct communication with the principal structure. The little door which gave access to it resembled the grated gate of a prison. The stories, which were lower than those of the great tower, each contained scarcely more than two rooms and a closet placed in one of the turrets; the other turret was occupied by a winding staircase which led up to the platform. A broader staircase, which, however, grew narrower as it ascended, rose from the ground floor and connected the stories with one another.

It was to this building, which had served as lodging for the keeper of the archives of the Temple, Monsieur Barthélemy, that the royal family were conducted. They were to remain here until the apartments in the great tower destined for them were ready.

The supper was scarcely ended — a sad supper, which, says Madame de Tourzel, " no one was tempted to touch " — when a municipal officer caught up the dauphin, who was dropping with sleep, and traversing an underground passage, carried him quickly to his room. Madame de Tourzel followed him as rapidly as she could, put the child to bed, and seating herself upon a chair, gave herself up to gloomy reflections. The queen soon rejoined her, and pressing her hand, murmured, " Did I not tell you so? " " Then approaching the bed of this lovable child, who was sleeping soundly, the tears came to her eyes as she gazed upon him. But far from yielding to despondency, she immediately resumed that great courage which never abandoned her, and occupied herself in the arrangement of the rooms of this gloomy habitation."

The queen was installed on the second floor, in the former drawing-room of Monsieur Barthélemy. The furniture, a description of which has been left us by a pious hand, retained some remnants of luxury. It was in blue and white lampas. Madame Royale had a little bed in her mother's room. Mesdames de Tourzel and Saint-Brice slept in the dauphin's chamber; Madame de Lamballe in a dark ante-room, which joined the two apartments. In the turret adjoining the young prince's chamber was the cabinet, for the common use of the whole royal family, the municipal guards, and the soldiers; to reach it, it was necessary to pass through the dauphin's chamber.

The king occupied the third floor; his apartment had been hastily fitted up. Indecent prints were hung on the walls; he removed them himself, saying sharply, " I do not wish to leave such things before the eyes of my daughter."

The little turret was used by him as a study. In a very small recess at the side Hue and Chamilly were lodged. Madame Elisabeth was installed in a former kitchen, which was horribly dirty. She had a folding-bed put up near her for Madame de Tourzel; but it was difficult to sleep. The room adjoining this kitchen was used for the guard-room; and one can fancy the noise which was made there.

The queen's chamber was larger, having formerly served as a drawing-room, and it was here that the company assembled during the day; the king himself came down to it in the morning. The prisoners, however, had not the consolation of being alone; a municipal officer, who was changed every hour, was always in the room where they sat. "The royal family spoke to them all with such kindliness," said Madame de Tourzel, "that they succeeded in softening the hearts of several of them."

At the hour of dinner they went down to the first floor, where the dining-room was situated; next to the dining-room there was a library, which contained from twelve to fifteen hundred volumes. Toward five o'clock in the evening, they walked in the garden, — a painful recreation, during which they were exposed to every possible insult; but the king and queen did not hesitate to face these annoyances in order to give their children the air. From there they could see the men working on their prison.

The works of defence decided upon by the Commune on August 13, and confided to Palloy, the demolisher of the Bastille, were being pushed forward with ardour, although with some indecision. A broad ditch was dug; the walls were raised; the trees near the tower were cut down; the windows, through which one could see beyond the enclosure, were screened. The captivity was growing closer; it soon became still harder through isolation.

During the nights of August 19 and 20 two municipal officers appeared at the Temple, instructed, they said, to carry away " all who were not of the family Capet." The queen tried in vain to retain Madame de Lamballe, alleging that she was her relative. The officers refused to listen to her demands. " In the position in which we were," writes Madame de Tourzel, " we could do nothing but obey." Madame Royale was deprived of every attendant; the queen manifested the liveliest grief, especially in separating from her friend. She could not tear herself from her arms. " Take good care of Madame de Lamballe," she said to

Madame de Tourzel and her daughter. "On all important occasions you must speak, and spare her, as much as possible, the necessity of replying to captious and embarrassing questions." Madame Elisabeth came down in her turn and encouraged her unhappy friends.

"We embraced these august persons for the last time," Madame de Tourzel writes; "and with death in our souls we tore ourselves from the place, which the thought of being of some service to our unhappy sovereigns rendered dear to us."

The municipal officers had promised that the prisoners should return to the Temple after having been questioned by the Commune. Hue came back alone on the following day. Mesdames de Tourzel and Lamballe were confined at La Force. We know how they left there, and under what bloody aspect Madame de Lamballe's beautiful curly head reappeared under the walls of the Temple.

The isolation was complete; and the unfortunate prisoners were forced to inure themselves to the new and henceforth solitary life which the Commune inflicted upon them. Madame Elisabeth descended from the third story to the second, and took the place of the dauphin, whose bed had been removed into his mother's room. Madame Royale joined her aunt. At this time the captives, left alone, sketched out the programme of their day, — a programme which remained the same with but few variations until their removal to the great tower on October 26.

The king rose between six and seven o'clock, shaved himself, dressed, and passed into the turret, where he prayed and read until nine o'clock. The queen and dauphin must have risen still earlier; for when first Hue, and afterward Cléry, came down to their room at eight o'clock, they always found them up. These early hours of the day were the only ones in which the unhappy woman was free. The municipal guards entered with the *valet de chambre*, and did not again leave her. At nine o'clock Marie Antoinette, Madame Elisabeth, and the children ascended to the king's apartment for breakfast. At ten o'clock they returned to the queen's chamber, where they passed the day. The king then continued the education of his son; he taught him Latin, made him recite passages from Corneille and Racine, gave him lessons in geography, and gave him practice in making maps. The precocious intelligence of the young prince responded readily to his father's efforts. The queen on her part occupied herself with her daughter, taught her the principles of religion, and supplemented these serious instructions with lessons in music and drawing. The rest of the day she passed in sewing, knitting, and embroidering, when it was not necessary to repair the king's clothes. At noon the three princesses passed into Madame Elisabeth's chamber to take off their morning costume, — a dress of white dimity, and a simple lawn cap, — and put on a gown of brown linen figured with little flowers.

When the weather was fine, the royal family went down to the garden at one o'clock. Four municipal guards and a chief of battalion of the National Guards accompanied them. They walked in the grand alley of chestnuts, and the young prince played quoits or ball, or ran races. But what torture were these walks, in the midst of hostile faces, derisive shouts, insulting songs, and wretches who remained covered before the royal prisoners? And when they passed through the gate (the arch of which was so low that they were obliged to bend forward in order to walk under it) they were forced to endure the tobacco-smoke and taunting laughter of the jailers, Rocher and Risbey. Rocher, who had risen from saddler to municipal guard, boasted of his insolence. "Marie Antoinette was playing the proud," he said, with a sneer, "but I forced her to come down. Her daughter and Elisabeth make me a courtesy despite themselves; the door is so low that to pass through it they are obliged to bow before me. Every day I blow a puff of smoke from my pipe into the face of this Elisabeth. Did n't she say the other day to our commissioners, 'Why does Rocher smoke all the time?' 'Apparently because he likes it,' they replied."

At two o'clock they returned to the tower. This was the hour for dinner. Santerre frequently came to assist at it. The king occasionally spoke to him; the queen never. After the repast the family repaired to the queen's chamber to play piquet or trictrac. At four o'clock the king took a moment's rest while the princesses read. When he awoke, conversation was resumed. The young prince worked or played. At the end of the day the royal family assembled round a table; the queen or Madame Elisabeth read aloud something amusing or instructive, in the course of which, however, unexpected and painful analogies were more than once met. The king added to this riddles to guess, taken from a collection of the "Mercure de France," which he had found in the library. At eight o'clock the dauphin ate his supper and went to bed; it was always his mother who heard him say his prayers. The child never failed to add special petitions for Madame de Tourzel and Madame de Lamballe; and when the municipal guards were there, he said these two prayers in a low voice.

At nine o'clock the king had his supper; during this time either Marie Antoinette or Madame Elisabeth remained with the dauphin. After supper Louis XVI. quietly shook hands with his wife and his sister, received Madame Royale's caresses, and returned to the third floor. The queen and the princesses shut themselves up in their apartment; the municipal guard remained in the little room which separated the two chambers, and passed the night there.

Such was the life which the august prisoners led, so calm and regular in appearance, so tormented and dreary in reality, divided between manual work and the education of the children: a life of duty and suffering, in which there was but one source of strength, — a clear conscience, — and but one ray of brightness, the joyous frolics of the dauphin.

The days slipped by, bringing their train of painful anniversaries and incessant vexations. Clothing, linen, and table silver were in such small quantities that they barely sufficed for their daily needs. The king had but one coat, which Madame Elisabeth was obliged to mend at night. The dauphin slept between sheets full of holes. The Assembly had decreed that Louis XVI. should receive five hundred thousand livres for his personal expenses. The decree, however, was not executed; and the unhappy monarch was so destitute of money that one day he was forced to borrow six hundred francs of his valet to pay a note of five hundred and twenty-six livres. Journals were denied him; and the faithful Hue could only learn news and communicate it to his masters by lifting himself up to a window, which was partly walled up, and listening to the criers in the street. One day, however, a gazette was left in sight in the prisoners' chamber; this was because on it there had been written these threatening words, which the malcontents had amused themselves by inscribing on the walls, " Tremble, tyrant; the guillotine is in permanence." The new rulers were only generous in their outlays on the works destined for the guard of the prisoners, and for those they spent without counting. The jailers watched everything, even the education of the children. While the queen gave Madame Royale her lessons and prepared extracts for her, a municipal guard looked over the young girl's shoulder to make sure they were not conspiracies. One day models for design, sent by the princess's professor, Van Blaremberg, were almost refused entrance, because among the helmeted and laurel-crowned heads a statue of the allied tyrants had been seen. They were forced to give up teaching the dauphin arithmetic; this was a hieroglyphic language which might be used for correspondence in cipher.

Everything which entered the tower was rigorously examined: the bread was cut in two, the dishes were tasted, the *carafes* and coffee-pots could not be filled except in presence of the commissioners. One day a chess-board had been sent to the dauphin; a municipal guard by the name of Molinon had all the squares unglued to make sure that nothing was hidden below. The king himself was not spared these investigations; even his pockets were searched. In the night of August 24 and 25 — his fête-day — his sword was taken from him. The following night a municipal guard named Venineux came with a cudgel in his hand to search the king's apartment, under the pretext that some means of escape might be concealed there. Others persisted in remaining during the evening in the queen's chamber until the hour for retiring, and she had the greatest difficulty in making them leave it. Most of these men assumed the most insolent attitude toward the captives, and addressed them in the grossest language, singing the carmagnole and obscene songs. "If the executioner does not guillotine this family," the municipal guard, Turlot, said, "I shall guillotine them myself." "In what quarter do you live?" the queen one day asked another municipal guard, who was waiting at dinner. "In La Patrie," he replied rudely. "La Patrie," the queen replied sadly; "ah! that is France."

At this time the allied armies were advancing, almost without resistance, under the command of the Duke of Brunswick. Marie Antoinette, who had been apprised of it by Hue, was also aware of the great agitation which the success of the Prussians had caused among the Jacobins, and of the increased fury against the king and herself which had resulted from it. And yet this is what this woman, accused of having prepared the ruin and dismemberment of France, said to her faithful confidant: "All things tell me that I am soon to be separated from the king; I hope that you will remain with him. As a Frenchman and as one of his most faithful servants, imbue yourself thoroughly with the sentiments which you should express to him, and which I have often manifested to him. Remind the king, when you are able to speak to him alone, that impatience to break our irons must never wrest from him any sacrifice unworthy of his glory. *Above all, no dismemberment of France.* On this point let no consideration mislead him; do not let him be afraid either for his sister or for me. Represent to him that we both prefer to see our captivity indefinitely prolonged rather than owe its termination to the abandonment of the least important stronghold. If Divine Providence permits us to recover our liberty, the king has determined to establish his residence temporarily at Strasburg. This is also my desire. It is possible that this important city may be tempted to resume its place in the German coalition. We must prevent this and retain it in France. . . . *The interest of France before everything.*" We know what was the response of the Convention to these patriotic sentiments.

As Hue was not adequate to the service of the entire royal family, Louis XVI. asked that a man be given him for the rougher work. This request was granted, but it was by sending a former employee at the barriers, named Tison, who was sold to the Commune. This man and his wife were installed at the Temple, less as servants than as spies. Some days after, on August 26, a new auxiliary was given Hue, but this man, whatever may have been the prejudices against him at the beginning, proved himself devoted and faithful to the end. This was Cléry, the dauphin's former *valet de chambre.*

On September 2, unusual animation was manifested round the Temple. The king and his family had descended, as usual, to the garden. Their attendants made them re-enter the tower precipitately to save them from the stones that were thrown from the windows. Toward five o'clock a municipal guard, an ex-Capuchin, named Mathieu, rushed like a madman into the queen's chamber, where all the royal family were assembled, and addressing the king, said, " Monsieur, you do not know what is passing: a general call to arms has been beaten; the tocsin has sounded; the cannon of alarm has been fired; the emigrants are at Verdun. If they come, we shall all perish ; but you will perish first." " I have done everything for the happiness of my people," the king replied; " there is nothing left for me to do." The dauphin, terrified, ran away crying. Mathieu, turning to Hue, said, " I arrest you ! " and barely leaving him time to make a bundle of his clothing, he carried him off to the Hôtel de Ville.

After this violent scene, the queen could not sleep at night. The agitation increased in Paris; the general call to arms was beaten. At eight o'clock on the morning of the 3d, Manuel came to the tower, and assured the king that Madame de Lamballe and all the persons taken from the Temple were well, and peacefully settled at La Force. At one o'clock, Louis XVI. wished to go down to the garden; the municipal guard would not allow him to do so. About three o'clock, frightful cries were heard. A crowd made up of ragged men, drunken women, children in tatters, surrounded the Temple, shouting revolutionary songs and threats of death. The prisoners could distinguish the cries: " La Lamballe! The Austrian ! " It was the assassins of the ill-fated Princesse de Lamballe, who had dragged her disfigured body so far, and were washing it in the fountain of the Temple, in order to show it to her friend. Her chemise, stained with blood and mud, was stuck on the end of a pike, as a hideous trophy. At the end of another pike, the head of the unhappy victim was fixed; her long curly hair, which, as a refinement of horror, they had carefully powdered and crimped, floated around the bloody instrument.

The commissioners, uncertain as to what they ought to do, not daring to attempt an " impolitic, dangerous, and *perhaps unjust* " resistance, had done nothing but stretch a tri-coloured scarf across the gate. The band stopped for a moment and growled before this improvised barrier. They were refused entrance to the tower, but they were permitted to enter the garden. The municipal guard Dangou harangued them ; and the variable mob, convinced, perhaps, by the orator's sinister argument, gave up their intention of forcing their way into the prison. Leaving the body of the princess in the street, but taking her head, to the great delight of the gatekeeper, Rocher, they gathered under the windows, shouting and hooting; the workmen who were employed on the tower, and Rocher himself, joined with them ; and resolved to get some amusement at least out of the grief and " grimaces " of the prisoners, they called the royal family in loud shouts. Some of them added, " If the Austrian does not show herself, we must go up to her and make her kiss La Lamballe's head."

The king had just left the table; he was playing a game of trictrac with the queen. Cléry had gone down to dine with Tison and his wife, when the woman suddenly gave a scream and fainted; she had seen the head of the princess. Cléry rushed upstairs; his face was so agitated that the queen noticed it, and asked, "Why do you not go to your dinner?" "Madame, I am not well." The municipal guard on duty closed the door, and going to the window, drew the curtains. Several municipal guards and officers of the guards arrived. The king asked them if his family was safe. "The report has been circulated," they replied, "that you and your family are no longer in the tower; the mob demand that you appear at the window, but we shall not permit it. The people must show greater confidence in their magistrates." The cries redoubled outside; they could hear distinctly the insults uttered against the queen. The bandit who held the head of Madame de Lamballe had mounted upon the débris of the houses lately torn down to isolate the tower, that he might bring his hideous trophy nearer the wall; another carried the bleeding heart of the ill-fated princess upon the end of his sword.

Another municipal guard came in escorted by four men, sent by the people to find out if the captives were still at the Temple. One of these men, in the uniform of a National Guard, having two epaulettes and armed with a large sword, insisted that the prisoners appear at the windows. The municipal guards objected. "No; do not go. How terrible!" one of them, named Menessier, exclaimed. An altercation ensued; the king asked the cause of it. "Very well, Monsieur," the National Guard replied rudely; "since you wish to know, the people desire to show you the head of Madame de Lamballe. I advise you to appear if you do not wish the people to come up here."

At this horrible revelation the queen fainted. "This is the only time," Madame Royale remarks, "that her resolution forsook her." Madame Elisabeth and Cléry lifted her and placed her in an armchair. Her children burst into tears; the man stood there insensible to their grief. "Monsieur," the king could not resist saying, "we are prepared for anything; but you might have dispensed with communicating this frightful misfortune to the queen."

This was his only revenge. When Malesherbes asked him a little later for the name of this wretch, he said, "I had no need to recognize him." The man left with his comrades; "their purpose was accomplished."

When the queen recovered, she mingled her tears with those of her children, and with her family passed into Madame Elisabeth's room, where the clamours of the mob were less audible. The assassins were still there with their abominable trophy; it was only after repeated and long parleys that they were persuaded to leave. It was eight o'clock in the evening before calm was restored round the Temple. Do we need to add that after this horrible scene the unhappy Marie Antoinette did not sleep? She passed the night in tears and prayers.

But the ingenious cruelty of the persecutors was not exhausted. Every day the jailers conceived some new vexation, some new insult. When the queen returned to her room from the garden, a parody on a couplet from " Marlborough,"

> " See, there goes Madame up the tower;
> When she 'll descend, there 's none can tell,"

shouted by voices thick with wine, greeted her maliciously as she passed. They left under the eyes of the king and his family the most ignoble numbers of the " Père Duchesne," infamous caricatures, or hateful inscriptions : " Madame Veto will dance it. . . . We shall know how. . . . We must strangle the little whelps." Sometimes it was a rough sketch of a gallows, from which hung a corpse, with these words, " Louis taking a bath of air;" sometimes a guillotine, at the foot of which one read, " Louis spitting in a sack ! "

One day when some vague panic had spread through Paris, announcing the victorious march and approaching entrance of the allied armies, Rocher, with abuse on his lips and rage in his eyes, bounded up the stairs, and shaking his fists in the king's face, yelled, " If they come, I will kill thee ! "

" One evening," Madame Royale relates, " a municipal guard on arriving uttered a thousand insults and threats, and repeated what we had already been told, that we should perish if the enemies came. He added that my brother alone aroused his pity; but that being the son of a tyrant, he should die. Such were the scenes which my family had to endure every day."

On September 21, the Convention succeeded the Legislative Assembly; the same day, on the motion of a player of low rank, Collot d'Herbois, it decreed the abolition of royalty. At four o'clock in the evening, the municipal guard, Lubin, escorted by four mounted gendarmes and numerous citizens, came to proclaim this decision under the windows. Lubin had the voice of a stentor. The royal family could distinctly hear the terms of the decree, which solemnly broke with the secular traditions of France. Hébert, the famous "Père Duchesne," and Destournelles, who was afterward minister of public taxes, were at that moment on guard at the Temple; while Lubin was reading, they watched the king with malicious curiosity. The king noticed it; without manifesting any emotion, he continued to read a book which he had in his hand. The queen showed the same control; there was not a sign which could furnish these wretches with the base enjoyment which they sought.

. The same evening Cléry, having to ask for curtains and coverings for the young prince, thus formulated his request, "The king demands for his son," etc. "You are very bold to make use of a title abolished by the will of the people," Destournelles said to him. "You can say to *Monsieur*," he continued, pointing to Louis XVI., "that he must cease to assume a title which the people do not recognize." The king did not move an eyelash. On the following day Madame Elisabeth recommended Cléry to write henceforth, "It is necessary for the service of Louis XVI., Marie Antoinette, Louis Charles," etc.

On the 29th, five or six municipal guards presented themselves in the queen's chamber, where all the family were gathered. One of them, Charbonnier, read a decree of the Commune, which ordered that " all paper, ink, pens, pencils, and even written papers be taken from the person and from the rooms of the prisoners, and also from the *valet de chambre* and others in service at the tower; that no weapon whatsoever, offensive or defensive, be left them; in a word, that all necessary precautions be observed to prevent any intercourse of *Louis the Last* with other persons than the municipal officers."

The king and princesses were forced to deliver what they had; the commissioners searched the rooms and wardrobes, looking everywhere, " even rudely," and carrying off the objects named in the decree; nevertheless, the queen and Madame Royale succeeded in hiding and keeping their pencils.

On the evening of the same day, as the king had finished his supper and was preparing to go up to his own room, a municipal guard told him to wait; a quarter of an hour later, those six municipal guards who had already been there in the morning, Hébert at their head, read a new decree, ordering a separation of the prisoners, and the king's immediate transfer to the great tower. The king, although notified of this resolution, was keenly affected by it; the queen burst into tears. Hébert, however, did not allow himself to be moved. They were forced to separate. Cléry accompanied his master to his new prison.

Despite Santerre's urgent exertions, and the fact that a portion of the five hundred thousand francs set apart for the maintenance of the royal family had been appropriated for these works, the fallen monarch's apartment was not completed; there was no furniture except a bed in the chamber; the painters and paper-hangers were still working there, and the odour was unbearable. Cléry passed the first night on a chair in the king's chamber; the following day he obtained permission for his *valet de chambre* to occupy a small room near him. At the usual hour, nine o'clock, the king wished to go to his wife's apartment for breakfast; he was not permitted to do so. The queen, Madame Elisabeth, and the children were served separately. The queen would not take anything; her grief was sombre and gloomy. At ten o'clock Cléry entered with a municipal guard; he came to get some books for the king. In seeing him, the grief of the prisoners redoubled; they burst into tears, and asked the faithful servant a thousand questions, to which he could reply only with reserve, because of the presence of the municipal guards. The queen, addressing these last, renewed her request to join her husband, at least for a few moments, and at meal-hours. "These entreaties were no longer lamentations and tears, but cries of grief," remarks Cléry. "Very well," said a municipal guard, frightened or touched by this explosion; "they can dine together to-day. To-morrow we shall do what the Commune prescribes." His colleagues consented, but forbade them to speak in low tones, or in a foreign tongue; they must converse aloud, and *in good French.* Although the favour was very small, the joy was great. The queen, with her children in her arms, Madame Elisabeth with hands lifted to heaven, thanked God for this unexpected happiness; the municipal guards themselves were touched; some of them could not restrain their tears. One of the cruellest, the cobbler Simon, that hideous figure which was beginning to appear in the history of the Temple, said, loud enough to be heard, "I believe that these b—— of women would make me weak." And addressing Marie Antoinette, he added, "When you assassinated the people on August 10, you did not weep." "The people are sadly deceived," the poor woman replied gently.

The dinner was served in the king's chamber, to which all the

family repaired; as sorrowful as was the meeting, they had suffered so keenly from the separation that the reunion was almost
joyful. Nothing more was said of the decree of the Commune;
and the prisoners were able to come together every day at meal-
hours, and also during their walk toward noon. " In the morning," Madame Royale writes, " we remained long enough for Cléry
to dress our hair, because he could not come to my mother's
room, and because this gave us a few moments more with my
father."

Misfortune develops ingenuity. Thanks to clever scheming;
thanks to the devoted complicity of a former cook to the king,
named Turgy, who had found means to attach himself and two
of his comrades, Marchand and Chrétien, to the service of the
tower; thanks to the occasional good-will of certain municipal
guards, who were better disposed than the others, — Cléry succeeded in securing some news and communicating it to the captives. Was this harmless complot suspected? On October 26
Cléry was arraigned before the revolutionary tribunal. The examination happily was favourable; and at midnight of the same
evening, the *valet de chambre* resumed his duties at the Temple.

During Cléry's short absence a great change had been made in
the existence of the prisoners. The queen, her children, and Madame Elisabeth had been transferred to the great tower. For a
month the poor women had sighed for this change, which would
at least bring them under the same roof with the king; but it
would be an error to attribute this decision of the Commune to a
feeling of compassion or justice. The hatred of the executioners
for the queen was not yet sated, and they were skilful in tormenting their royal victim; the very day that they brought her
nearer to her husband, they separated her from her son. The
care which she lavished upon this child, the gratitude which he
showed her, the affectionate caresses with which he overwhelmed
her, had been her sole consolation since her arrival at the Temple;
her enemies grudged her this last and bitter enjoyment.

" On the observations made by one of the members of the
service at the Temple," according to the decree of the Council
of Service, ratified on the same day by the General Council,
" that the son of Louis Capet was day and night under the direction of women, mother and aunt, considering that this child is
at the age when he should be under the direction of men, the
Council decrees that the son of Louis Capet be at once taken

from the hands of women, and be placed and remain in those of his father day and night."

They allowed him to go up every day at the hour of dinner " to the apartment of his mother and aunt, during the time that his father was resting, but to come down again between four and five o'clock."

In obedience to the cruel words of the commissioners, the decree was executed *at once* without even notifying the unhappy mother. The child was taken to his father and did not return.

CHAPTER XXIII.

THE great tower, a last remnant of an important house of
Templars, afterward transformed into a storehouse for the
archives of the Order of Malta, formed an imposing mass one
hundred and fifty feet high, with walls of an average thickness of
nine feet. It had four arched stories, supported in the middle by
a large pillar running from the foundation to the roof. The interior, some thirty feet square, formed only one room on each
floor; but in order to lodge the royal captives there, the second
and third stories had each been divided by board partitions into
four rooms. The ground floor, under the name of council-chamber, was set apart for the municipal officers; the first was used
as guard-room. One of the four turrets, placed at the four angles of the tower, held the staircase which led up to the battlements; seven gates had been placed on it at short distances from
one another. To go from the staircase into each story one was
obliged to pass through two doors, — one of oak, studded with
nails, the other of iron.

On the second story, destined for the king, the first room was
an antechamber, which gave access to all the others. The Declaration of the Rights of Man, printed in large letters, and framed
in a tri-coloured border, had been posted on the walls, which were
hung with paper stamped with a design representing broad stones.
Opposite the entrance-door was the king's chamber; the turret

which adjoined it served as study and oratory; Cléry's bedroom was on the left, and also a fourth room which was used as dining-room, and was separated from the antechamber by a glass partition. Each apartment was lighted by one window; but on the outside had been placed heavy bars of iron and shades, which intercepted the air and the light; the embrasures had a thickness of nine feet.

The king's chamber was the only one with a fireplace; the rest of the apartment was heated by a large stove placed in the centre.

The furniture was very simple: a large bed, hung with green damask for the king, a folding-bed for the dauphin, a mahogany chest of drawers, a rosewood desk, and a few chairs; two barometers on the walls; on the mantel-shelf, a mirror and a clock, which was soon carried off, because on its face was stamped, " Lepaute, watchmaker to the king." The oratory contained a small stove, a rush-bottomed chair, a cane-seated chair, and a stool covered with horsehair. In the dining-room were a mahogany table, a serving-table, two corner buffets in rosewood, and some chairs.

The third floor, reserved for the princesses, was arranged like the second. The queen's chamber was above that of the king; Madame Royale lodged in her mother's room; the turret served as cabinet. The paper was of a pale shade, crossed with green and blue bands; the bed was hung with green damask. The furniture consisted of a chest of drawers in mahogany, a large sofa, and a few chairs. On the chimney, which smoked badly, the clock, through involuntary or intended irony, represented Fortune turning her wheel. Madame Elisabeth slept in the adjoining room, upon a wretched iron bed, provided with a spread of Jouy canvas. Tison and his wife, the two spies, occupied the third room; the antechamber was used by the municipal guards, who remained there day and night. The fourth floor was empty. Finally, between the pointed roof of the tower and the battlements, ran the gallery, where the royal family went occasionally to take the air; but their jailers had taken care to place blinds between the battlements, to keep the prisoners from seeing and being seen.

The most minute precautions had been taken to guard the captives. At the great gate of the street there was a keeper, named Darque, former beadle to the grand prior; at the gate of the

tower, the *concierge*, Mathey, and the two jailers, Rocher and
Risbey, the wretches of whom we have already spoken. Eight
commissioners, whose service lasted forty-eight hours, and who
relieved one another every day in two sections, were charged with
the surveillance. During the day one of them was constantly
with Louis XVI., the other with Marie Antoinette; the six others
sat in the council-chamber. An effective of 287 men, — reduced
after the death of the king to 240, — under the orders of a commander-general, and of a *chef de légion* with two cannons and
twenty men of the artillery, made up the guard of the Temple.
A *chef*, named Gagnié, with two special *chefs*, a pastry-cook and
a meat cook, and three culinary officers, whom we have already
named, Turgy, Chrétien, and Marchand, were charged with the
table service; the domestic service was intrusted to Cléry and to
the household of Tison.

The king rose at seven o'clock and prayed until eight. He
read the office of the chevaliers du Saint Esprit, and as the
Commune had refused to allow mass to be said at the Temple,
even on feast-days, he had bought a copy of the breviary used
in the diocese of Paris. At nine o'clock he went to breakfast in the
queen's apartment. Cléry went up at the same time, arranged
the hair of the princesses, and by order of Marie Antoinette,
taught Madame Royale to dress her own hair; the unhappy
queen, clearly foreseeing the future, wished that her daughter
should be able to dispense with all service. After breakfast the
king gave the dauphin lessons until eleven o'clock; the young
prince played afterward until noon. This was the hour for their
walk; and the whole royal family descended, no matter what the
weather, because the guard, who changed at that moment,
wished to assure themselves of the presence of the prisoners.
The walk lasted until two o'clock, when they ascended again for
dinner.

After dinner the king and queen played trictrac or piquet, or
rather pretended to play, in order that they might say a few
words to each other. During this time the dauphin and Madame
Royale played battledore and shuttlecock, or siam, or some other
game, in the antechamber; Madame Elisabeth presided at these
amusements. This was the moment she chose to question Cléry,
or to give him instructions; the young prince and his sister, by
their noisy games, facilitated these conversations between their
aunt and the faithful servant, and warned them by a sign if some

of the municipal guards, or what was worse, if Tison and his wife, whom the good behaviour of the royal family had not disarmed, were coming. At four o'clock the queen went upstairs with her children; in conformity to the decree of the commissioners, she could take her son with her during the time that the king slept. At six o'clock the child returned to his father, who made him work or play until the hour for supper. The monarch, in order to carry on the education of his son more intelligently, studied the Latin authors, says Cléry, or read books of travel and natural history, during four hours of each day. At nine o'clock, immediately after supper, the queen undressed her son and put him to bed. The princesses then went upstairs, and the king did not retire until eleven o'clock. The queen during the day embroidered a great deal, and occupied herself with the education of her daughter; she made her study and read aloud. Madame Elisabeth passed a part of her time kneeling at the side of her bed, praying; every day she recited her office and read religious books, which she had secured through Cléry. The queen often asked her to read them aloud. Vexations and insults were not spared the prisoners in the great tower any more than they had been in the small tower. On October 7, the king had in the name of equality been despoiled of his orders. Everything was arbitrary, and depended upon the humour or caprices of the keepers. One day a municipal guard forbade Cléry to go to the queen to dress her hair; the unhappy woman was forced to descend to her husband's apartments, carrying all that was necessary for her toilet. Another wished to follow her, when at noon, according to her custom, she entered Madame Elisabeth's room to take off her morning dress; owing to the unseemly importunity of this man, the queen was obliged to give up changing her dress. Certain commissioners made the most bizarre exactions : one broke all the macaroons and cracked open all the peach-stones, to make sure that no note was hidden in them; another forced Cléry to drink some essence of soap, destined for the king's beard, on the ground that it might be poison; and still another cut off the margins of a book, which Madame Elisabeth was sending to the Duchesse de Sérent, in the fear that she had written something in invisible ink on them.

Another day the queen broke her comb; she begged Turgy to buy her another. "Buy one of horn," the municipal guard, Dorat-Cubières, said; "boxwood would be too good for her." The queen feigned not to hear. Dorat-Cubières was formerly a poet who had paid homage to the royal family in his colourless little verses; no one had at that time been a more obsequious flatterer than he.

The commissioners continued to forbid the entrance of newspapers to the Temple; only those were allowed to enter which contained some infamy against the fallen sovereigns, — like that letter of a gunner who demanded the head of the tyrant Louis XVI., that he might load his cannon with it and send it to the enemy, or that odious article in which some one declared that the little whelps confined at the tower must be smothered.

One day a municipal officer approached the queen and princesses and said, " Mesdames, I have a piece of good news for you; many of the emigrant traitors have been taken. If you are patriots, you will rejoice over it." " My mother," relates Madame Royale, " said nothing, as usual, and did not appear to hear. Often her contemptuous calmness and dignified bearing overawed these men; they rarely dared address any remarks to her."

Amid all these outrages, among these base men, who made it their sport to insult misfortune, history greets with emotion a few men who esteemed it an honour to hold aloof from these wretches, and surround this fallen grandeur with their respect. These were the teacher Lepître, the grocer Cortey, Moëlle, Lebœuf, Jobert, and especially Toulan, former member of the Commune of August 10, who had become Royalist in his daily contact with these royal victims of the Revolution, — Toulan, whom the princesses designated by the beautiful name of Faithful; last among these was Michonis, at first a fierce Revolutionist like Toulan, but who, like him, touched by so much misfortune so heroically borne, became one of the most zealous servants of those whose jailer he had formerly asked to be, and who, again like Toulan, sacrificed his life for them. We shall meet them again in the course of this history, and shall tell of the ingenious plotting of these obscure but courageous and devoted men, whom fortune did not favour, but who during these sad days at least avenged the honour of humanity and, like the heroes of the sacred books, delivered the soul of France.

On November 1 a deputation from the Convention came to examine for themselves " the condition of the persons of Louis Capet and his family, and to look into the measures of safety adopted by the General Council of the Commune and the commander-general of the National Guard of Paris, for the preservation of the hostages intrusted to their charge." The deputation was composed of the ex-Capuchin Chabot, Du Prat, and Drouet, the man from Varennes; it was accompanied by Santerre and the commissioners on duty. The deputies, arriving at the Temple about ten o'clock in the morning, ascended to the second story, where they found the royal family gathered. The queen shuddered at the sight of Drouet. This man insolently seated himself near her, and Chabot, following his example, took a chair. "We are come," Drouet said, "to ask you if you are comfortable, if you are in need of anything, if you have any complaints to make?" "I have no complaints to make," the king replied; "I will not complain so long as I am with my family." Cléry called attention to the fact that the tradesmen were not paid accurately. "The nation does not bother itself about an écu," Chabot replied. The deputies inspected the departments in detail, assured themselves that neither pens nor ink nor paper had been left at the disposition of the prisoners; then they proceeded to the third floor, where they made the same examination.

After dinner they returned to the king's lodging, asked the same questions, and received the same response. Drouet went up to the queen's apartments. "He was pale and his voice was weak; he asked the queen in a melancholy tone if she had no complaint to make; the queen made no answer; he repeated the question twice. 'It is, however, important to know if you have any complaint to make of anything or any one.' The queen gave him a proud look, and without a word walked away and seated herself upon the sofa with her daughter. Drouet, opening and extending his arms like a man astonished, but who feels more spite than regret, bowed and went out. Marie Thérèse, seeing her mother's emotion, pressed her in her arms and kissed her hands, when she heard her say these words to Madame Elisabeth, 'My sister, why did the man from Varennes come up here? Is it because to-morrow is All Saints' Day?'"

Yes; the next day was All Saints', and also the anniversary of Marie Antoinette's birth. But how was this anniversary, formerly so joyously observed, celebrated to-day, and what good wishes did the people of Paris address to the sovereign with whom in times past they had been so enamoured? "We heard," Madame Royale relates, "a great noise of people demanding the heads of my father and mother; they had the cruelty to come and cry it under our windows."

On November 14 the king was taken ill with a somewhat serious cold; he asked for his dentist. The Commune deliberated for three days, and refused. On the 22d fever set in; this time the Commune grew uneasy, and permitted Louis XVI.'s first physician, Monsieur le Monnier, to visit the tower, but he never entered without being searched, and was not allowed to speak except in audible tones. The queen and the princesses passed their days at the king's bedside, sharing with Cléry the task of waiting upon him; but at night they were obliged to return to their upper story, leaving the august patient alone with his *valet de chambre*. The queen had unsuccessfully requested that her son should not remain in the fever-poisoned air, but should sleep in her room; the municipal officers would not permit it. In this unwholesome atmosphere the child was, in his turn, taken ill; whooping-cough declared itself. The unhappy mother, however, solicited in vain the favour to pass the night with her son; the municipal guards repulsed her brutally, and the poor woman was forced to return to her apartments, consumed with anxiety and a prey to sleeplessness.

Only during the day had she permission to sit by her child's bedside, and lavish attentions upon him. Under the weight of this sadness and anxiety, the entire royal family, the queen, Madame Elisabeth, and Madame Royale caught the disease. Cléry himself was in his turn confined to his bed, and it was then the young prince who, although scarcely recovered from his cough, carried remedies to the devoted servant.

In this school of misfortune, the child had developed and ripened his natural good qualities. He was most charmingly considerate of every one, but especially of his mother; he never said a word which might awaken in her painful memories. He lavished the most delicate attentions upon her. If he saw a municipal guard coming who was more civil or less odious than the others, he ran to the queen, saying, " Mamma, to-day it is such a one." If, on the contrary, it was a sinister figure which recalled sad events, he remained silent, or only pronounced the name in low tones. One day, when he was looking attentively at a commissioner, whom he seemed to recognize, the man asked where he had seen him. The young prince refused to reply; but bending toward his sister, he said in a low voice, " It was at the time of our journey from Varennes."

On December 2 a new Commune succeeded the revolutionary

Commune of August 10. The same evening at ten o'clock the members inaugurated their entrance into office by coming to the Temple to inspect the prisoners; but if these last hoped for some amelioration from this change, they were deceived. The new commissioners, not so rough, perhaps, as the former ones, showed a more calculating maliciousness and a more tyrannical watchfulness. Instead of one municipal officer with the king and with the queen, there were two, and henceforth it became much more difficult for Cléry to transmit news to them, or to obtain the slightest alleviation of their discomfort. On the 3d the queen, who was ill, had been unable to take any kind of nourishment; she asked Turgy for some bouillon for supper. Turgy brought it; but the queen, knowing the woman Tison was also indisposed, ordered the bouillon to be given to her. Turgy bade the municipal officers to wait upon her in order that he might go and get some more, but they refused to do so, and Marie Antoinette was obliged to do without her supper.

On the 7th a municipal guard, Moëlle, came and read in a broken voice a decree ordering " knives, razors, scissors, penknives, and all other sharp instruments of which the law deprives persons reputed criminal to be taken from the prisoners, and a most thorough search for them to be made, both on the prisoners and in their apartments." The king was forced to deliver all he had in his pockets, and what could be found in his room, — a knife which had come to him from his father, a penknife, a small dressing-case in red morocco, his razors, a compass for rolling up the hair, even an instrument for cleaning the teeth; the princesses their knives, scissors, and everything which they used in their needle-work. " Must we not also give up our needles, for they prick very sharply?" the queen asked ironically. The poor women were obliged after this to abandon certain pieces of work which had been a distraction for them during the long hours of captivity. One day Madame Elisabeth was mending the king's clothes; and no longer having scissors, she cut the thread with her teeth. "What a contrast!" the prince said to her; " you wanted for nothing at your pretty little house at Montreuil." " Ah, my brother," she replied, " can I feel regret when I share your misfortune?"

In the evening at dinner the question was agitated whether knives and forks should be left the prisoners. Some of the commissioners wished to take them away. At Moëlle's entreaties, however, the opinion of the more humane prevailed; and it was decided that the royal family should keep their knives and forks, but that they should be taken away at the end of every meal.

Was it as a compensation for these fresh annoyances that on the 9th the municipal officer Lepître obtained the grant of a clavichord which stood at the entrance to Madame Élisabeth's room, and permitted the queen to give music-lessons to her daughter? The first piece which came into her hands bore the title, "The Queen of France."

At five o'clock on the morning of December 11 a general call to arms was beaten in the streets of Paris. The cavalry and cannons occupied the garden of the Temple. Through Turgy and Cléry the royal family already knew the cause of this unusual display of troops. On December 3 the Convention had decided that Louis Capet should be arraigned at its bar. They had come to execute this decree.

At nine o'clock the king, according to custom, went up to breakfast in the queen's apartment; he remained there an hour, but despite their anguish of soul, under the watchful eyes of the municipal guards the prisoners could say nothing to one another. Looks took the place of words; at last they were obliged to separate. The king returned to his room; the dauphin as usual accompanied him. Unconscious of the danger, and ignorant of events, the young prince insisted upon playing a game of siam; he was not lucky at it, and twice he could not get beyond the number sixteen. "Every time that I reach this point of sixteen," he said, with a slight irritation, "I cannot win." The king said nothing, but an involuntary tremor crossed his face at this naïvely cruel comparison.

At eleven o'clock the dauphin had stopped playing, and was taking a reading-lesson, when two municipal guards came to carry him to his mother. Louis XVI. asked the cause of his sudden removal. They only replied that it was the order of the Commune; the accused was to be separated from his family. The ill-fated father embraced the child tenderly, and Cléry took the boy to his mother.

At one o'clock the king set out for the Convention, escorted by the mayor of Paris, Chambon, the procurator of the Commune, Chaumette, the secretary registrar, Coulombeau, and Santerre. At six o'clock in the evening he returned to the Temple; his first care was to ask to be taken to his family; the guards refused, on the grounds that they had no orders. " But at least," he said, " my son will pass the night with me; his bed and his effects are here." The same silence. After dinner the king again insisted; they replied simply that they must await the instructions of the Convention.

The queen and the princesses had passed the day in mortal anxiety. The queen had made every attempt to learn something from the municipal officers who guarded her; it was the first time that she had consented to question them. The municipal officers refused to say anything. On the king's return Marie Antoinette at once asked to see him; she sent her request to the mayor, Chambon; the mayor did not even deign to reply.

The unhappy woman, exhausted by grief, did not have the strength left to weep; it almost seemed as if even the sight of her son left her insensible. " My brother passed the night in her room," Madame Royale relates; " he had no bed. She gave him hers, and sat up all night, plunged in such gloom that we did not wish to leave her; but she forced my aunt and me to go to bed."

On the following day the queen renewed her solicitations; she asked again to see her husband and to read the journals which gave an account of the trial. She urged that if the favour of seeing the king was refused her, it might at least be granted to his children. The journals were forbidden. The request for a meeting of the children with their father was referred to the Convention. After a long deliberation the Assembly decided, on December 15, by a false sentiment of pity which the very terms of the decree denied, that " Louis Capet might see his children, but that the latter should not, until the final judgment was passed, communicate with their mother and their aunt."

This was granting and refusing at the same time. The unhappy prince did not wish to accept a favour which would have been anguish for his wife; he preferred to lay upon himself a new sacrifice, and to leave to the queen the comfort of her children's society. The same evening he ordered the dauphin's bed to be taken up to the apartment of the princesses. Cléry kept the linen and clothes; it was agreed that every two days he should send what was necessary.

During six long weeks the king remained isolated from his family; the queen and princesses obtained news of him only through the devotion of Turgy and Cléry, who hid notes in balls of cotton or wool, which they threw under the beds, or let down in the shutters of the windows, by means of pieces of carefully hoarded string, and also through the tender-heartedness of a few municipal guards, more humane than their colleagues. Some of them assured the queen that the king would not perish, and that his cause would be referred to the Primary Assemblies, who would certainly save him, — generous illusions, or charitable lies, which little deceived the prisoners.

The sinister trial continued its course. On December 12 Louis XVI. had chosen as his defender Tronchet, to whom on the next day he added Malesherbes, and a little later De Sèze. On the 15th a deputation from the Convention came to communicate to him the accusations against him. Every day after this the three defenders visited the Temple, where, after minute search by the municipal guards, they were admitted to confer with their client. On December 25, Christmas Day, the king, alone with himself and God, wrote in full with his own hand his testament, that admirable monument of his Christian resignation and love for his people.

On the 26th the accused was conducted for the second time to the Convention; fearing lest the noise of the drums and the numerous company which were to come for him might frighten the queen, he had her notified in the morning.

It is not in our province to give here a detailed recital of that memorable and melancholy session. This was the day on which De Sèze pronounced that eloquent speech which more than once caused a shudder of emotion to pass through the hearts of the most prejudiced judges. This was also the day on which Malesherbes, challenged by the member Treilhard, who asked him, "What makes you so bold in pronouncing here names which the Convention has proscribed?" made him this simple and heroic response, "Contempt for you, and contempt for life."

When De Sèze had finished his speech, the king rose, and in a firm voice pronounced these words, —

"Monsieurs, this gentleman has just laid before you my means of defence; I shall not repeat them. In speaking to you perhaps for the last time, I declare that my conscience reproaches me for nothing, and that my defenders have told you only the truth."

But what did the members of the Convention care for conscience, and could they not reply like Pilate, "What is truth?"

On the next day De Sèze gave several copies of his speech to the king. A municipal guard, named Vincent, undertook to carry secretly a copy of it to the queen. The unhappy woman read it with breathless attention; but she did not delude herself with any hope, and with a feverish but firm hand, she wrote on the first leaf: "Oportet unum mori pro populo."

Tuesday, the 1st of January, 1793, was a sad day at the tower. In the morning Cléry approached the king's bedside and begged permission to offer him his felicitations. "I accept your good wishes," the prince replied, extending his hand, which the faithful servant bathed with his tears. As soon as he was up, he begged a municipal guard to go and inquire after his family, and present to them his good wishes for the new year. His tone was so heart-rending that one of the commissioners, touched, said to Cléry, "Why does the king not ask to see his family? Now that the examination is over, there would be no difficulty about it." Meanwhile the municipal guard who had gone to the queen's lodging returned and announced that his family thanked him for his good wishes, and sent him theirs. The king was moved. "What a New Year's day!" he said sadly.

In the evening Cléry repeated to him his conversation with the commissioner, and assured him that the Convention would certainly authorize him to see his family. "In a few days," the prince replied, "they will not refuse me this consolation; we must wait."

Yet the unhappy sovereign's thoughts recurred constantly to his family; he returned to them continually in his conversations with his defenders, and his voice grew tender. His eyes were bathed in tears when he spoke of his sister, whose life had been naught "but affection, devotion, and courage;" of his children, "already so unhappy at their age;" of the queen, who was so insulted, so calumniated, so misunderstood.

"If they—the French people—knew her great worth," he said; "if they knew to what degree of perfection she had risen since our misfortunes,—they would revere her, they would prize her; but for a long time her enemies and mine have by disseminating slanders among the people succeeded in transforming that love of which she was so long the object into hatred."

Then rapidly passing in review the queen's conduct and the calumnies by means of which her enemies had sought to defame her, he added,—

"The malcontents show this relentlessness in decrying and traducing the queen only in order to prepare the people for her destruction. Yes, my friends, her death is resolved upon. They would fear, if they allowed her to live, that she might revenge me. Ill-fated princess! my marriage promised her a throne; to-day what prospect does it offer her?"

In pronouncing these words, he pressed Malesherbes's hands, and his eyes filled with tears.

On January 15 the Convention declared Louis Capet guilty. On the 17th, after a session of twenty-two hours, a factitious majority of *five* voices pronounced sentence of death against him; the same evening Malesherbes, trembling with emotion, came to announce it to the captive. The next day a decree of the Commune decided that all communication should be broken off between Louis XVI. and his counsellors, and that the condemned should be strictly watched day and night. The king protested in vain against this increased rigour; his protest was not heard.

On the 20th the Convention, by three hundred and eighty voices against three hundred and ten, rejected all reprieval. At two o'clock on the afternoon of the same day the executive committee repaired to the Temple, and the minister of justice, Garat, with his hat on his head, ordered the Secretary Grouvelle to read the decree of the Assembly. When it was finished, Louis XVI. quietly took the decree, placed it in his pocket-book, then drawing out a paper, said, "Monsieur le Ministre, be good enough to submit this document to the Convention." It was a letter in which the condemned asked for a delay of three days, in order to "prepare himself to appear before his God," and the permission to see a priest whom he named as freely as he wished. He added to this the address of this priest, the Abbé Edgeworth de Firmont, whom his sister had recommended to him, and urged that he should be allowed to converse with his family without witnesses.

During this cruel scene the king's manner had been so resolute, so full of lofty majesty, that Hébert himself was touched by it. "The nobility and dignity of his bearing and of his language," he declared, "wrung from me tears of rage;" and not wishing to allow his emotion to be seen, he withdrew.

The respite was refused; the Convention were in haste to have done with it; the other requests were granted. The Abbé Edgeworth was sent for, and Garat himself brought him in his carriage to the Temple. He assured the king that there was no charge whatsoever against his family, and that they would be sent out of France.

The unhappy prisoners had first heard of Louis XVI.'s condemnation on the morning of Sunday, the 20th, through the newspaper-venders who cried it under their windows. At eight o'clock on the evening of the same day they learned that a decree of the Convention permitted them to go down to the king's apartment; they hastened to it. The prince had asked the Abbé Edgeworth to pass into the turret, lest the sight of the priest might cause the princesses pain; he waited in the dining-room. The Convention had decided that he should be alone with his family; but the Commune, always ingenious in tormenting their victim, had stipulated that the municipal guards should assist at the interview behind a glass door. The room was lighted by a wretched Argand lamp; the table had been pushed to one side, the chairs placed at the end, in order to give more space; on the table, a *carafe* of water and a glass. "Bring some water which is not iced," the king, who in this cruel anguish of heart retained all his presence of mind, had said; "if the queen should drink this, it might hurt her."

At half-past eight the door opened; the queen entered first, holding her son by the hand; then Madame Royale and Madame Elisabeth. They all rushed into the king's arms. A gloomy silence reigned for several minutes, broken only by sobs. The king sat down, the queen at his left, Madame Elisabeth at his right, Madame Royale almost opposite; the young prince remained standing between the king's knees. All bent toward him, and often put their arms about him.

"We found him — the king — sadly changed," Madame Royale records. "He wept from grief for us, and not from fear of death; he described his trial to my mother, excusing the scoundrels who were putting him to death. . . . Then he gave some religious instructions to my brother, especially recommending him to pardon those who were putting him to death, and giving both him and me his benediction."

Then in order to produce a stronger impression upon the young dauphin, he took him upon his knees and said to him:

"'My son, you have heard what I have just said to you; but as an oath is something even more sacred than words, swear, in raising your

hand, that you will fulfil the last wishes of your father.' My brother obeyed him, bursting into tears, and this touching bounty made our tears also flow the more abundantly."

The queen wished to pass the night near the king with her family. The unhappy prince refused; he had need of calm, to prepare himself for death. The queen insisted at least in seeing him for a moment on the following morning; he consented to this, but "when we had gone," Madame Royale recounts, "he told the guards not to allow us to come down again, because our presence was too painful for him."

This touching interview lasted three quarters of an hour, amid sobs and tears. During this time four municipal guards, ill dressed and with their hats upon their heads, stood in the embrasure of the window, warming themselves at the stove, and watching through the glass partition. At a quarter past ten, the king rose, and all followed his example. The queen held him by the right hand, leaning against his shoulder, and scarcely able to stand; the dauphin, on the same side, was clasped in his mother's right arm, pressed against her heart, and he himself held in his little hand the king's right and the queen's left hands, kissing them and watering them with his tears; Madame Royale, on the left, embraced the king round the waist; Madame Elisabeth, a little behind her niece, had seized the top of the king's left arm between her two hands and raised to heaven her eyes, bathed in tears. Louis XVI. endeavoured to preserve his calmness; but he struggled painfully not to give way. "I assure you," he said, "that I shall see you to-morrow morning at eight o'clock." "You promise us?" they repeated altogether. "Yes, I promise you." "Why not at seven o'clock?" the queen asked. "Very well! Yes, at seven o'clock," he replied. "Adieu!" He uttered this adieu with so heart-rending an expression that the sobs grew louder. Madame Royale fainted; Cléry raised her, and Madame Elisabeth held her up. The king, wishing to put an end to this harrowing scene, clasped these dear objects of his affection to his breast a last time; and freeing himself gently from their affecting embrace, he murmured, "Adieu! Adieu!" and slowly re-entered his room. "Ah! Monsieur," he said to the Abbé Edgeworth, "what an interview! Why must I love and be so tenderly loved? But it is over; let us forget all else and think only of the one matter. In this moment all my affections and all my thoughts should centre upon that."

Meanwhile, the princesses returned to their apartment; and although the doors were closed, their sobs and groans could still be heard in the king's lodging. · "The executioners!" the queen exclaimed; and turning to the dauphin, she said to him, "My son, promise me that you will never think of avenging your father's death." Then placing a long and bitter kiss upon the child's blond hair, she undressed him and put him to bed. As for herself, she threw herself dressed upon her bed, "where," says Madame Royale, "we could hear her all night trembling with cold and grief."

At a quarter past six on the following day, a municipal guard entered. The queen was up; she thought that he had come to seek her for that last interview, which her husband had promised her the night before. Vain hope! the municipal guard came to get a book of prayers for the king's mass. The unhappy woman still hoped, continued to hope, listening with heart-breaking anxiety for a sound of steps ascending the stairs. . . . Useless waiting; no one came.

The king had retired at half-past-twelve; as soon as he was in bed he had fallen into a sound sleep. At five he rose, made his toilet as usual, heard mass kneeling, and received the sacrament. When he had accomplished his religious duty, he called Cléry and gave him various objects, saying to him in a broken voice : —

"'Give this seal to my son, . . . this ring to the queen; say to her that I leave her with sorrow' (it was his marriage ring). . . . 'This little package contains the hair of each of my family; you will give this to her also. . . . Say to the queen, to my dear children, to my sister, that I had promised to see them this morning; but I wish to spare them the pain of so cruel a parting. How much does it cost me to go away without receiving their last embraces !' He wiped away several tears, and added in the most sorrowful tone, 'I charge you to bid them farewell for me.'"

At nine o'clock Santerre appeared, escorted by municipal guards and gendarmes. The king came out of his cabinet, where he was conversing with the Abbé Edgeworth, and asked, "You are come for me?" "Yes," Santerre replied. "I am occupied," the prince replied in a tone of authority; "await me here."

He re-entered the cabinet, received the last benediction from his confessor, came out again, and addressing the municipal guard, Jacques Roux, an apostate priest, who stood nearest him,

he said, "I beg you to give this paper to the queen, to my wife."
It was his testament. "That is not my business," Jacques
Roux retorted brutally. "I am here to lead you to the scaffold."
"It is well," the king replied; and turning toward another muni-
cipal guard, he handed him the paper. Then taking his hat from
the hands of Cléry, he said to Santerre in a tone of command,
"Let us go."

One hour later, at twenty minutes past ten o'clock, the head of
Louis XVI. fell on the scaffold of the Place de la Révolution ; and
while round the guillotine a frenzied mob welcomed with wild
clamours the royal blood which was flowing for them, in the third
story of the tower two women and two children in tears, clasped
in each other's arms, were praying for the victim and for his
executioners.

CHAPTER XXIV.

THE queen was a widow; she knew by the cries of joy of an unbridled populace that the regicide was consummated. Her eyes were dry; she had no more tears. She panted for breath; a violent shock only could bring her out of her gloomy torpor. Eager to feed upon her misfortune and to gather the sad details of it, she hoped that Cléry, the last faithful servant who had remained with the ill-fated monarch, would be able to come to talk with her of him who was no more; she expressed this desire to the municipal officers. The municipal officers refused. She asked for simple mourning garments for herself and her family; they replied that the Commune would deliberate upon it.

How long this day of January 21 was, passed in the midst of a thick fog which wrapped the capital as in a shroud! In the evening the dauphin and his sister went to bed, but Madame Royale could not sleep; the queen and Madame Elisabeth watched by the bedside of the young prince, who, alone of all those in the third story of the tower, slept peacefully. "He is now," said Marie Antoinette, "at the age of his brother when he died at Meudon. Happy were those of our house who went first; they did not witness the ruin of our family."

It was half-past two in the morning, but Tison and his wife were awake. Astonished at hearing voices at that hour, they came to the door to look after their prisoners. "I beg of you," Madame Elisabeth said to them gently, "let us weep in peace." "The inquisition," Monsieur de Beauchesne remarks, "ceased, disarmed by this angelic voice; and the conspiracy of tears was not reported."

On the following day, when the dauphin awakened, the queen took him in her arms and said to him, "My child, we must think of the good God." "Mamma," he replied, "I have thought of the good God ; but when I call upon him, it is always my father who rises before me."

On January 23, after two days of waiting, the Commune generously accorded the mourning garments demanded by the widow and orphans; but they refused to allow Cléry, as the queen had requested, to continue for the son the office which he had filled for the father. This was another blow for the queen. "Nothing," says Madame Royale, "could calm her suffering; we could awaken no hope in her heart; she had grown indifferent to life and to death. She regarded us at times with a pity which made us start." This pity saved her, and maternal love drew her out of this gloomy despondency. Madame Royale had for some time been suffering from pain in her leg; anxiety and sorrow had soured her blood. "Happily," she writes, "a few days after January 21 grief augmented my illness, which gave the queen some occupation." The report of it spread even through Paris, and the princess's former nurse solicited the favour of coming to care for her; her demand was scornfully repulsed, but the attendance of the former physician of the Children of France, Brunier, was allowed. Brunier came to the Temple ; and his emotion can be imagined when he found his august patrons in such destitution that they did not even have linen with which to bind up the young patient's leg; he was forced to bring some from his house. Thanks to his good care and to that of the surgeon La Caze, the princess was restored to health in a month. On the 27th and the 30th the mourning clothes were brought. When the queen first saw her children in black, she could not keep from remarking with a sigh, " My poor children, with you it is for a long time ; with me it is forever."

The garments fitted ill ; this was a piece of good fortune. Mademoiselle Pion, a former waiting-woman to Madame Royale, was allowed to come to the Temple to alter them. The sight of this friendly face cheered the captives a little. " Their looks," Mademoiselle Pion relates, " told me more than their words could have done, and Monseigneur le Dauphin, whose age excused his playfulness, profited by it to ask me, under the show of a game, all the questions which the royal family could desire."

It seemed, moreover, as if the surveillance had been somewhat relaxed. " The guards," Madame Royale remarks, " believed that we were to be sent away." Kind-hearted municipal officers gained admittance to the tower. Toulan and Lepître found means through an ingenious ruse to be on duty together, and often on Sunday. The first time that they came after January 21, " We found the royal family," says one of them, " plunged in the deepest affliction. The queen, her sister, and the children, on perceiving us, burst into tears ; we dared not advance. The queen motioned to us to enter her chamber. ' You did not deceive me,' she said to us : ' they have allowed the best of kings to die.' " The two municipal guards managed to give the captives some newspapers, and it was thus that the unhappy women learned the details of the regicide.

Some days later, on February 7, Lepître brought a song which he had composed on the death of Louis XVI., and which Madame Cléry had set to music. When, three weeks later, on March 1, he returned to the Temple, the queen led him into Madame Elisabeth's room, where the dauphin sang the romance accompanied by his sister.

" Our tears flowed," Lepître relates ; " and we observed a gloomy silence. But who could paint the scene which I had before my eyes ? — the daughter of Louis XVI. at her harpsichord ; her mother seated near her, holding her son in her arms, and, her eyes wet with tears, directing with difficulty the playing and the voice of her children ; Madame Elisabeth standing at her sister's side, mingling her sighs with her nephew's sad tones."

It was not only, however, to offer these Platonic consolations to the royal family that Toulan and Lepître were come to the Temple ; they had conceived a more decisive and more audacious project. In Paris there were still to be found, lost in the crowd, a few devoted Royalists: former servants of the Court, former agents of the royal family, prowled round the Temple seeking means of gaining admittance, and still more of effecting the escape of the prisoners. Foremost among these was the Baron de Batz, regarded with distrust by the emigrants, suspected even by Fersen, — we know not why, — but faithful as any one, a fearless soldier, a conspirator fertile in resources, " the infamous Batz," as Barrère called him, who had, on January 21, sought to carry off Louis XVI., and who, not having succeeded in rescuing the king, risked all to rescue his family. There was also the Chevalier de Jarjayes, a major-general, the husband of one of the queen's most devoted women, a former agent of the king abroad, who, since the imprisonment of his masters, had been unwilling to leave the capital that he might study means of being useful to them. This momentary abatement in the surveillance of which Madame Royale speaks, had perhaps suggested to them the thought that an escape might be possible. At the beginning of March a plan was fixed upon by Jarjayes, Toulan, and Lepître. The first undertook to prepare the flight outside the Temple, the other two to render it possible within. Jarjayes had men's clothes made for the queen and Madame Elisabeth, and Toulan and Lepître brought them to the tower. The princesses, dressed in these costumes, girt with tri-coloured sashes, and provided with credentials similar to those of the municipal guards, were to escape in this disguise. It was more difficult to carry away the children, especially the young king, who was more carefully watched. How baffle this vigilance? However, they found a means of effecting this. Every evening the man charged to clean the lamps came to light them; for this task he was accompanied by two children, of about the same size as Madame Royale and Louis XVII., and he went out usually before seven o'clock, the hour at which the sentinels were relieved. A devoted Royalist, Monsieur Ricard, inspector of the national domains, was to take the place of this man; and coming in the evening when the guard had been changed, he should, with his tin box in his hand, penetrate to the queen's apartment. There, from the hands of Toulan, who was to reprove him harshly and loudly for not having come himself instead of allowing the children to do his work, he was to receive the royal children, dressed as little lamp-lighters, and they should thus go to rejoin their mother, who had left before them.

At the time and place agreed upon, three cabriolets were to be held in readiness. The queen and her son were to take their places in the first with Monsieur de Jarjayes; Madame Royale in the second with Lepître; Madame Élisabeth in the third with Toulan. Regulation passports left no cause of uneasiness as to the journey. The plan had been concerted in such a way that no one could set out in pursuit of the fugitives for five or six hours after their departure. This was a sufficient start to allow them to gain the coast of Normandy, where a boat was to be waiting near Havre which should transport them to England.

Everything was settled; and the queen approved the project, which was to be put into execution on March 8. Unfortunately, on the 7th, a serious agitation, caused by the scarcity of food, and the bad news which was received from the army, broke out in Paris; the French had been forced to evacuate Aix la Chapelle, and to raise the siege of Maestricht. The Austrians had entered Liège. Under the shock of this news the sections demanded the closing of the barriers, to prevent the exit of all suspected travellers. The council thought it sufficient to suspend the delivery of passports for foreign countries. It would not have been prudent, however, in the midst of this agitation and distrust, to attempt an escape which would have been difficult at all times, but which was more difficult at a moment when the attention of the public was more especially on the alert. They were forced to postpone, then abandon the project.

If, however, the flight of the royal family had become impossible; if that of the young king, among others, who was especially watched, was confronted by almost insurmountable obstacles, — would it not at least be possible to save the queen, who was most exposed to the hatred of the populace? The two intrepid allies, Toulan and Jarjayes, contrived a new plan. In this plan it was still Toulan, alone this time, who undertook to effect Marie Antoinette's escape, and to conduct her to a fixed spot, where she should rejoin Jarjayes. He, in his turn, had arranged means of conducting her to a place of safety. But would the queen accept this scheme? Would she consent to fly alone, leaving her sister-in-law, her children especially, in the hands of their executioners? The prayers of Toulan and Jarjayes, Madame Elisabeth's supplications, the certainty that this estimable aunt would be an estimable second mother to the orphans, had finally overcome Marie Antoinette's reluctance. She had, not without terri-

ble revulsions of feeling and a great desire to refuse, consented
to yield to the wishes of her rescuers. The day for the escape
was approaching; it was the evening before. The children were
in bed; but Madame Royale was not asleep. The queen and
Madame Elisabeth were talking together; one can divine with
what agony, with what suffering, at this imminent separation.
" The queen, resolved upon the sacrifice which was asked of her,"
relates Monsieur de Beauchesne, who has collected the precious
souvenirs of the Duchesse d'Angoulême concerning this moving scene, "was seated at her son's bedside. ' May it be God's
will that this child be happy!' she said. ' He will be, my sister,'
Madame Elisabeth replied, showing the queen the dauphin's naïve,
open, sweet, proud countenance. 'All youth is short-lived, like
all joy,' Marie Antoinette murmured, with unutterable anguish of
heart. 'One finishes with happiness as with everything else!'
Then rising, she walked up and down her room for some time,
saying, 'And you yourself, my good sister, how and when shall
I see you again? It is impossible! It is impossible!'"

And when on the morrow Toulan came, ready for the departure,
and happy in the thought that he was going to save the widow of
his king, the queen advanced toward him and said, " You will bear
me ill-will, but I have thought it over. There is only danger
here; death is better than remorse."

Then she intrusted him with the following note for Jarjayes,
made known for the first time by Chauveau-Lagarde: —

" We have had a beautiful dream, — that is all : *but we have gained
much from it*, in finding on this occasion a new proof of your complete
devotion to me. My confidence in you is unbounded. You will always
find in me determination and courage; but interest for my son is the
only impulse which guides me. *Despite the happiness which I should have
experienced in being away from this place*, I cannot consent to separation
from him. I could enjoy nothing without my children, and *this thought
does not leave a regret*."

" I shall die unhappy," the queen said again to Toulan, " if
I am unable to give you some evidence of my gratitude."
" And I, Madame," Toulan replied, " if I am unable to give you
a proof of my devotion." The faithful municipal guard was
soon to give a new proof of this devotion. He knew with what
ardour the queen and the princesses desired to possess the last
souvenirs of the king, — those precious objects which the ill-fated

monarch had delivered to Cléry for Marie Antoinette, and which the Commune had not allowed Cléry to carry to the royal persons for whom they were destined. Louis XVI.'s ring and seal, the little package of hair, taken from the faithful servant when he left the Temple on the 1st of March, — all these were placed under seal, and kept in the apartment of the condemned. With rare adroitness Toulan found a means of carrying them off, and bringing these dear relics of the martyr to the queen. The queen received them with tears of emotion and joy; but she feared lest some denunciation by Tison, some minute perquisition, might disclose these precious tokens of her husband's affection, and to place them in safety, she decided to send them out of the country. It was again to the two valiant accomplices, Toulan and Jarjayes, that she appealed; Toulan received the objects, and Jarjayes agreed to carry them to Monsieur and the Comte d'Artois, with letters from the royal prisoners.

"Having a faithful servant, upon whom we can count," the queen wrote to Monsieur, "I take advantage of the opportunity to send to my brother and friend what can only be intrusted to his hands. The bearer will tell you by what miracle we have been able to get possession of these precious tokens. I reserve for myself the right of telling you the name of him who is so useful to us. The impossibility under which we have laboured until now of sending you news of us, and the excess of our misfortunes, make us feel still more keenly our cruel separation; may it not be long! I embrace you meanwhile, as I love you, and you know that is with all my heart."

And she wrote to the Comte d'Artois: —

"Having at last found a means of confiding to our brother one of the sole tokens which remain to us of the being whom we all cherish and mourn, I thought that you would be heartily glad to have something which came from him; keep it as a mark of the tender friendship with which I embrace you from my heart."

The mission was performed. Jarjayes, however, did not set out at once. He continued to hope. But when Barnave was arrested, the general, who had served more than once as intermediary in the transactions between the Constitutionalists and the court, feared that he himself might be arrested; and dreading a confrontation with the eloquent deputy, which might have been compromising for both, and especially for the queen, he decided to take refuge at Turin. It was from there that, through the medium of the king of Sardinia, he succeeded in transmitting the souvenirs of Louis XVI. and Marie Antoinette's letters to Monsieur and the Comte d'Artois. But before leaving, he received from the "great and ill-fated sovereign" the following note: —

"Adieu! I believe that if you are really determined to go, it would be better to set out at once. *Mon Dieu!* how I pity your poor wife! T. will tell you the solemn promise which I make to return you to her, if it is possible for me.

"How happy I shall be if we can soon be reunited! I shall never be able to thank you enough for what you have done for us.

"Adieu! This word is cruel."

Thus the isolation became daily greater; the iron circle closed in round the prisoners; they still preserved, however, — this note proves it, — the hope of a possible and perhaps near deliverance. An illusion too soon dispelled! On March 27, Robespierre demanded the banishment of the Bourbons, with the exception of Marie Antoinette, who should be arraigned before the revolutionary tribunal, and of the son of Capet, who should continue in confinement in the tower of the Temple. The Convention for once passed on to the order of the day; but had the Commune wind of the generous designs of Toulan and Jarjayes? Their mistrust became more suspicious; their hatred more persecuting.

One day, March 25, the queen's chimney caught fire.

"In the evening," says Madame Royale, "Chaumette, procurator of the Commune, for the first time came to see my mother, and asked her if she desired anything. My mother asked only for a door of communication into my aunt's room; during the two terrible nights which we had passed with her, my aunt had slept on one of the mattresses laid on the floor. The municipal officers refused this request; but Chaumette said that in the state of prostration in which my mother was, it might be necessary for her health, and that he would speak of it to the General Council. At ten o'clock on the morning of the following day, he returned with Pache, the mayor, and that frightful Santerre, commander-general of the National Guards. Chaumette said to my mother that he had spoken to the Council General of her request for the door, and that it had been refused. She made no reply. Pache asked her if she had no complaints to make. My mother said no, and paid no attention to what he said."

Fresh precautions were taken: a wall was erected in the garden; Venetian blinds were hung round the top of the tower; all the holes were carefully stopped up. On August 1 the Commune decided "that no person on guard at the Temple should draw anything of any sort on the walls; that the commissioners on duty should have no communication whatsoever with the prisoners, or undertake any commission for them; that Tison and his wife should not be allowed to leave the tower, or communicate with any one outside." This new prohibition, however, so hard for the captives, was also hard for the Tisons; they no longer had the right to see any one, not even their relatives. One day when their daughter had been allowed to come up to their room, — it was on the 19th of April, — Tison became violently angry; and not knowing upon whom to vent his rage, he naturally fell upon the prisoners, and upon those who appeared to manifest some interest in them. He declared to Pache, who was at the tower, that certain municipal guards spoke in low tones to the queen and to Madame Elisabeth. Ordered to give their names, he denounced Toulan, Lepître, Brunot, Moëlle, Vincent, and Dr. Brunier, and added that the captives had had some correspondence with people outside. As a proof he related that one day after supper, the queen, in drawing out her handkerchief, had let fall a pencil, and that in a box in Madame Elisabeth's room there were sealing-wafers, wax, and pens. His wife, when sent for, repeated the same thing; the denunciation, signed by the two spies, was sent to the Commune, which, after having affixed seals to the houses of the suspected municipal guards, decided that a minute perquisition should be made at the Temple.

At a quarter to eleven on the evening of the 20th the princesses had just retired when Hébert arrived, escorted by several municipal guards; he had wished to add to the odium of the inquisition the terror of a surprise in the middle of the night. The prisoners got up in haste. Hébert read them a decree of the Commune which gave order to search them at discretion. They looked in all the furniture, everywhere, even under the mattresses. The young prince was asleep; they snatched him roughly from his bed to search it; his mother took him in her arms, all numb with the cold. The visit lasted five hours, until four o'clock in the morning. They found nothing except upon the queen a pocket-book of red morocco, which contained some addresses and a steel pencil-holder, without lead, and in Madame Elisabeth's room a stick of red sealing-wax which had been partially used, and a little boxwood powder. From Marie Thérèse they took a medallion of the Sacred Heart and a prayer for France. Hébert and his acolytes, furious at having seized nothing more than these trifles, forced the queen and Madame Elisabeth to sign the *procès-verbal* of perquisition, threatening them, if they refused, to take from them Louis XVII. and Marie Thérèse. Three days after, they returned, and this time they discovered under Madame Elisabeth's bed a man's hat in a band-box; it was a hat which Louis XVI. had worn at the beginning of his captivity at the Temple, and which his sister had asked of him, in order that she might keep it as a souvenir of him. Such a relic was suspicious; the commissioners carried off the hat, despite Madame Elisabeth's supplications, but they were forced to avow in the *procès-verbal* that they had found no "vestige of a correspondence with any one outside, or a connivance between them — the prisoners — and the six members of the council inculpated in Tison's report." The six municipal guards were none the less suspended from their duties, and the two who were the most compromised, Toulan and Lepître, were struck off from the list of commissioners charged with the surveillance of the Temple.

Meanwhile the friends of the royal family abroad were not inactive; Fersen redoubled his negotiations with all the courts.

But how bring about accord, when the courts, when even the faithful friends of the monarchy, were divided? Catherine II. did not love Marie Antoinette; Austria mistrusted Prussia; Russia was dissatisfied with Austria; Fersen himself was full of prejudices against La Marck and Mercy. He was not discouraged, however. In the month of September, 1792, he had tried to make England take action, because she, not being then at war with France, would perhaps have been heard at Paris; but Pitt had remained cold, and had gone no further than protestations of Platonic interest. Spain alone had made some expostulations through the medium of her ambassador. The assassination of January 21 had been the Convention's response to the declarations of England and of Spain. After the death of Louis XVI. Austria had thought of demanding the queen.

"Not having believed the murder of the king of France possible," wrote Mercy to La Marck, who had become Prince d'Aremberg, "all was perhaps not done which might have been done to prevent this horror. Let us at least try to prevent the same from happening to this ill-fated queen, who should now be the constant object of our solicitude."

But these measures were soon abandoned in the fear that they might be vain and perhaps harmful.

"Will not the interest which the emperor manifests for his aunt," writes Fersen, "be an excuse for the malcontents, and a means which they will use to ruin her, arousing hatred for the Austrian, and pointing out the queen as a foreigner and the accomplice in the crimes which they imputed to the king?"

Was it not better by means of money and promises to win over some of the influential leaders, like Laclos, Santerre, Dumouriez? — Dumouriez especially, who was then at the head of a victorious army, and who, a former servant of the monarchy, might harbour the thought of restoring it and Louis XVII. Some time after, in fact, the Constitutionalists, as if to justify the supposition of the devoted Swede, proposed to the Baron de Breteuil to obtain a decree of banishment for the queen and her children; they demanded for this six millions, payable when the prisoners should be safe on foreign soil. The baron asked the six millions of Pitt, who made objections, and the affair came to nothing. A little later, however, a confidential follower of Dumouriez came in his turn to make advances to Monsieur de Breteuil. The general was weary of the despotism of the Convention, indignant over the death of the king and the atrocities which were being committed at Paris. The baron again appealed to England, who again procrastinated. But with or without the emigrants, Dumouriez pursued his plan. On March 12 he had a lively altercation with the commissioners of the Convention. On the 25th, he received at his headquarters the Austrian Colonel Mack, who had been sent by the Prince of Coburg, and after having poured out to him all his grievances against the revolutionary government, he exclaimed, —

"It is impossible for us to remain longer tranquil spectators of such horrors. I wish to disperse this criminal Convention, reestablish the constitutional royalty, proclaim the dauphin king of France, and save the queen's life."

Some days after, harmony was established between the German prince and the French general. Coburg agreed not to molest Dumouriez; and he, at the head of his army, was to march on Paris, dissolve the Convention, and restore the monarchy.

"A despatch sent by the Vicomte de Caraman to the Baron de Breteuil," wrote Fersen joyously in his journal, "has brought news of the arrangement made by Dumouriez with the Prince of Coburg. I sent a courier to carry the news to Sweden. There was great rejoicing. I felt the more joy because I no longer feared for the queen."

New intrigues, however, were already springing up. In case the monarchy was re-established, who was to have the regency? Monsieur's followers demanded it for him; the queen's friends, laying their support upon precedence, claimed it for her; and it was possible that Dumouriez, if victor, would lay claim to a title to which the greatness of the service rendered by him would seem to give him some right. Fersen, to prevent these conflicts and settle the attitude to be taken, wished to send, on the one hand, the Marquis de Limon to Vienna and to Hamm, to persuade Monsieur to renounce his pretensions; on the other, the bishop of Pamiers, Monseigneur d'Agoût, to Paris, to "see the queen at the moment of her liberation, inform her of her position, and advise her as to what she should do," and he himself wrote a long letter to Marie Antoinette explaining to her his whole policy. They must make use of Dumouriez, without putting themselves in his power; for he was a " knave who, in truth, only yielded to necessity, and desired to act uprightly only when he saw the impossibility of longer resistance." He was, nevertheless, a useful auxiliary in the re-establishment of the monarchy in its entirety, such as the queen wished, and as circumstances permitted; for he could, on the one hand, neutralize the influence of the emigrants, and on the other resist the powers such as England and Austria, who were interested in " giving to France a government which would keep her in a state of weakness." A council of regency should be formed, and care taken to have the various influences counterbalance one another, — the princes by Dumouriez, Monsieur by the Baron de Breteuil. " We must write to the emperor, to the kings of Prussia and England. They have been most friendly toward us, especially the king of Prussia. We should also write to the empress, but the letter must be simple and dignified, for I am not satisfied with her conduct; she has never answered your letter." In any case, " until the moment when you are recognized as regent, and have formed your council, we must do the least possible, and pay all the world with polite speeches."

Thus everything was being settled, the places doled out, honours distributed, as if the enterprise, which had not yet been begun, was already accomplished. The heart is oppressed in reading, in all its details, of this plan of restoration which was not to be realized, and in thinking that she upon whose head Fersen's ardent imagination already saw the crown of France was to wear no other crown than that of a martyr. But at this moment who was doubtful of success? When the generals of the republic abandoned the republic, how was it possible not to believe in the restoration of the monarchy? The illusion was of short duration; the same day on which Fersen wrote to the queen the outline of this plan of action, he learned of the complete ruin of his dreams. Four days before, Dumouriez had fled; abandoned by his army, fired upon by the volunteers, he had been forced to take refuge at Mons, with all his staff.

One last hope remained, — the exchange of the prisoners of the Temple for the commissioners of the Convention, who had been given up by Dumouriez and imprisoned at Maestricht. Negotiations were opened; they miscarried, and this last chance vanished.

Instead of deliverance disease visited the tower. So much moral and physical suffering had undermined the health of the prisoners. Madame Royale had come to sleep in her mother's room, in the fear lest the queen or dauphin should be taken ill in the night and remain without assistance. The health of the young prince was also declining; the poor child, habituated to an active life, took almost no exercise, and at eight years old, — the age when one has need of happiness and expansion, — lived " perpetually in the midst of tears and shocks, alarms and constant terror."

After January 21 the queen refused to descend to the garden; she could not bring herself to pass before her husband's empty chamber. Fearing, however, that the lack of fresh air might prove deleterious for her children, she had at the end of February solicited permission to take them up to the platform of the tower; the Commune, by chance humane on that day, had granted it. This at least meant fresh air and a little liberty when Madame Elisabeth succeeded in enticing the guards behind the roof of the tower, that the queen might be out of sight, or when they had to do with some kind-hearted municipal guard like Moëlle. But what was this walk, limited to a space of a few square feet? — for the sharp peak which surmounted the tower occupied the middle of the platform, and they were forced to content themselves with making the round of the parapet. No more games, no more sporting, no more races, as in the garden. Without doubt the view was beautiful, the air was stimulating; but the wind was also violent at this height, and the shades of the walls often treacherous.

One day in the beginning of May, on returning from this sad promenade, the young prince complained of a pain in his side; at seven o'clock on the evening of the 9th he was taken with a violent fever, accompanied by headache. He could not remain in bed because he choked. The queen, uneasy, asked that the usual physician of her children, Brunier, should be sent for. The council only laughed at the poor mother's anxiety. The municipal guards said that she was tormenting herself over nothing; Hébert had seen the child without fever at five o'clock, and moreover Brunier was suspected; he had respectfully taken off his hat in the presence of his former rulers, and had been denounced by Tison with Toulan and Lepître. The fever augmented. Madame Royale, in order not to remain in this unwholesome atmosphere, left her mother's chamber, and Madame Elisabeth replaced her at night. The malady did not yield to maternal care; the queen again asked for a physician. This time the Commune determined to accord one, but it was not Brunier, but Thierry, the regular prison doctor, "because it would offend the principle of equality to send any other." Thierry came in the morning, and found the child with a little fever; he returned during the day and affirmed that the fever was higher. Happily he was an estimable person, both as man and practitioner. He attended the young patient with devotion, and showed the consideration and courage to go and confer about the treatment with Brunier, who, acquainted with the prince's temperament for years, could better indicate the remedy. The remedy in fact — it was a purgative — proved beneficial; but the queen did not sleep at night, because the last time that her son had been purged he had had fearful convulsions. The disease, however, yielded; but the fever and the pain in the side returned from time to time. The health of the unhappy child was beginning to break down; it never recovered entirely. During the months of May, June, and July one finds in the Memoirs of the Citizen Robert, an apothecary, numerous medicines furnished for him. On June 11 it is even recorded that the young prince had hurt himself while playing on a stick, and the truss-maker of the prison was obliged to visit him. To divert him while he was in bed, the queen read "Gil Blas" aloud to him.

The effect of the agitations in Paris continued to make itself felt at the Temple. On May 31, the prisoners were forbidden to mount to the tower to take the air. Some days after, at six in the evening, Chaumette came with Hébert; both were intoxicated. Chaumette asked the queen if she had any desires to express, or any complaints to make. The queen replied in the negative, and paid no more attention to her sinister visitors; but their prolonged presence was odious to her. Madame Elisabeth, in order to deliver her sister-in-law from this torture, asked Chaumette why he had come and why he remained. The procurator of the Commune replied, "It is because I am making the rounds of the prisons; and all prisons being equal, I came to the Temple as elsewhere." The following night Louis XVII. was taken ill; these accidents occurred frequently to the poor child, deprived of air and exercise. Thierry came to see him, and this time the indisposition had no evil consequences.

The friends of the queen, meanwhile, still watched round the Temple. Through the connivance of kind-hearted municipal guards, some of them succeeded in gaining admittance to the prison, — as that La Caze of whom Fersen speaks, who found Marie Antoinette little changed, but Madame Elisabeth so unrecognizable that he only recognized her when the queen called her *my sister*. Another time, an English lady, Madame Atkyns, found her way to the queen, and offered to change clothes with her to facilitate her escape, but she must leave alone; Marie Antoinette again refused. The intrepid and indefatigable Baron de Batz especially was always on the watch to seize a favourable opportunity, always ready to risk his head to save the remnant of the royal family. A former member of the Constituent Assembly and the possessor of a large fortune, which he had generously placed at the disposition of the king, he had found means of buying up or winning over several members of the Convention and some municipal guards; hidden in Paris, sometimes in one house, sometimes in another, he baffled the police, and alone aroused terror among those who terrorized France. His principal retreat was in the Rue Richelieu with a grocer named Cortey, a secret Royalist, who, through his relations with Chrétien, a juror of the revolutionary tribunal, and the principal agent of the Committee of the Section Lepelletier, had succeeded in having himself inscribed among the officers intrusted with the guard of the tower. Through him Batz, under the name of Forget, was included among the men on duty at the Temple, and could thus study the premises with a view to the enterprise which he was contemplating. When he had examined everything, he opened his mind to a municipal guard who had formerly been an ardent Revolutionist, but who also, converted by the sight of the virtues of the prisoners, concealed under the show of noisy civism an invincible devotion to the royal family, — a devotion for which he was to pay with his life. Michonis, a man of brains and of great self-possession, was the very accomplice fitted for Batz; he undertook to organize everything within the tower. At the same time the baron made sure in his section of the active co-operation of some thirty faithful followers whose courage and discretion he knew; but to succeed it was necessary for Michonis and Cortey to be on duty together.

The desired day finally arrived. Cortey entered the Temple with his detachment, among whom Batz figured under his assumed name; he distributed the guards in such a way as to place his thirty loyal men at the posts in the tower, on the staircase, or in the patrols between midnight and two o'clock in the morning. At the same hour Michonis was to be on guard in the apartment of the princesses, while his colleagues would remain in the council-chamber.

It was Michonis who should open the gate for the prisoners and should throw round them large military cloaks, with which some of Cortey's men had taken the precaution to provide themselves. The princesses, in this disguise, and carrying weapons, should be placed in a patrol in the midst of which the young king would be hidden. The patrol would be led by Cortey, who alone, in his quality of commander-general, had the power to have the large gates opened during the night. Outside in the Rue Charlot all was prepared for a rapid flight; the measures had been well taken. " They were," says Sénar, who was well acquainted with them, " as audacious as they were well directed."

The hour approached; it was eleven o'clock. Suddenly Simon arrived, breathless; a gendarme had delivered this note to him, " Michonis will betray you to-night; be on your guard." When Simon had read this denunciation, he had sprung up and notified his colleagues, who had charged him to watch. "If I had not seen you here," he said to Cortey, " I should not have been tranquil." From these words, pronounced in a rude voice, from Simon's attitude, Batz saw that he was betrayed. For one moment he thought

of breaking the spy's head with a pistol-shot; but he reflected that
the noise of the report would cause a general stir, which would compromise those whom he wished to save. Simon mounted to the
tower, and enjoined Michonis to cease his duties and follow him.
Michonis obeyed with imperturbable composure. In going out
he passed a word to Cortey, but he had already chosen his course
of action; under pretext of some noise heard outside, he sent
out a patrol, in which he had placed the Baron de Batz. The
enterprise had miscarried, but the conspirators were saved.
Michonis, conducted to the Commune, underwent a severe examination; but he replied with such presence of mind that he
disconcerted his judges, and Simon was treated as a visionary
calumniator.

Meanwhile remorse had also made its appearance at the tower.
For some time past the woman Tison had shown signs of mental
derangement: she no longer wished to go out; she laughed,
screamed, wept all alone; she talked of her faults, of her denunciations, of prison, of the scaffold, of the royal family, declaring
herself unworthy to approach them. At night she had frightful
dreams, uttered horrible screams, which disturbed the sleep of
the captives. One evening at ten o'clock her daughter was sent
for to calm her. The late hour frightened her still more; she
would not come down, but screamed, "They are going to put
us in prison!" She rolled back and forth on the stairs. She perceived the queen, and threw herself at her feet, saying, "Madame,
I ask pardon of your Majesty; I am an unfortunate woman. I
am the cause of your death and of that of Madame Elisabeth."
Turgy entered; she ran to him, and again threw herself on her
knees, persistently repeating, "I am an unhappy woman; I am
the cause of the queen's death and of Madame Elisabeth's."

The princesses lifted her up, tried to calm her, and cared for
her with a pity and charity which the conduct of the woman little warranted. They assured her that they pardoned her; but
nothing could quiet this madness, which was the daughter of remorse. The unhappy woman continued to writhe in cries and
convulsions. Eight men had to be called to hold her; on
June 29 she was removed to the château. Eight days later,
July 6, it became necessary to transfer her to the Hôtel Dieu,
where a woman, instructed to watch her in her turn, was given
charge of her.

And the queen, in her compassion, wrote to Toulan in one of

those notes which the faithful Turgy succeeded in hiding from the researches of the municipal guard, "Is the woman Tison well cared for?"

Tison's wickedness could not withstand this noble pardon of past wrongs. Seized with remorse, he also endeavoured to efface the memory of his past conduct by devoting himself, like Turgy, to the service of those whom he had so long spied upon.

The Convention and the Commune, however, did not feel any such repentance; they were pitiless in their hatred; they persecuted because they feared. The image of the royalty, which they had thought to destroy on January 21, pursued them like a threatening phantom. Louis XVI. was dead, but Louis XVII. lived. The name of the infant king recurred unceasingly in the hopes of his partisans, and in the thoughts of his father's executioners. On June 30, some members of the Section du Pont Neuf went to the Committee of Public Safety, and announced that a plot had been formed, under the direction of General Dillon, to overthrow the Convention, abduct Louis XVII., and proclaim him king under the regency of Marie Antoinette. On the following day, July 1, the Committee of Public Safety replied to this denunciation by decreeing that the young Louis Capet should be separated from his mother, placed in " the best-defended apartment of the Temple," and given into the hands of an instructor chosen by the Commune. The Convention hastened to sanction the resolution of this committee; on July 3 the decree was put into execution.

At half-past nine in the evening, six municipal officers proceeded to the Temple to carry off the royal child. The young prince was asleep. A shawl, hung round his bed in place of a curtain, shielded him from the air and light. The queen and Madame Elisabeth, seated near his bed, were with their own hands mending his worn-out clothes; Madame Royale was reading aloud in the " Semaine Sainte," which Turgy had found means of procuring for Madame Elisabeth in the month of March. Thus religion presided at these sad vigils. Her austere voice sanctified these labours, and fortified these tender hearts against the sacrifices already consummated, and those which yet awaited them.

Suddenly the door opened; the municipal guards entered. " We come," said one of them, " to notify you of the order of the committee that the son of Capet shall be separated from his mother and his family." The queen rose, pale and trembling. "Take my son from me?" she cried; "that is not possible! They cannot think of separating me from my son. My care is necessary to him." "The committee has passed the resolution," retorted the municipal guards; "the Convention has ratified it. We must assure its immediate execution." "No," replied the unhappy mother; "do not exact this separation of me." Then with clasped hands, moist eyes, and heaving breast, she placed herself near the bed with her sister-in-law, and her daughter, like a lioness who would defend her young. In these movements the shawl fell; the child awoke; hearing the tumult, seeing his mother in tears, these threatening men, he cried, stretching out his arms to her, "Mamma, do not leave me." And the mother snatched up her son, covered him with kisses, pressed him to her heart, and clung to the foot of the bed to keep them from taking him from her. "You will have to kill me before you tear him from me." Then relinquishing her pride, and stooping to entreaty, forgetting that she was queen, and remembering only that she was a mother, she begged the ravishers to have pity upon her and her child; she burst into tears, sobs, and supplications. Madame Elisabeth and Madame Royale wept and prayed at her side; they endeavoured, but in vain, to soften the hearts of the jailers; these men had no hearts. "What is the use of all this fuss?" one of the municipal guards exclaimed brutally; "they are not going to kill thy son. Deliver him to us with a good grace, or we shall know how to get hold of him." And another proposed to call up the guard to carry off the child by force.

"One hour," Madame Royale records, "passed thus in resistance on her part, — on the queen's part, — in insults and threats on the part of the municipal guards, in tears and protestations from us all. At last they threatened so resolutely to kill him as well as me that she was forced to yield through love of us."

Yes; in order to wrest the son from his mother, they had the contemptible courage to threaten this mother to kill her children. The pen falls in presence of such infamy.

Madame Elisabeth and Madame Royale lifted the young prince; the poor mother had no strength left to do it. They dressed him slowly; God knows with what looks, with what heart-breaks, with what calculated slowness. When the toilet was finished, the queen placed her son before her, and drawing from her Christian faith strength to address him, she laid her two hands upon the head of the child and said to him in a solemn voice, " My son, we are about to leave each other. Be mindful of your duty when I am no longer near to remind you of it. Never forget the good God, who is trying you, and your mother, who loves you. Be good, patient, and upright, and your father will bless you from the heights of heaven."

Then, placing upon the forehead of the little one a last benediction in a last kiss, she delivered him into the hands of his guardians. The child broke away from them and clung to his mother's dress. " You must obey," she said sadly; " you must." " Come," one of the municipal guards said roughly, " I hope you have no more moralizing for him; I must confess that you have mightily imposed upon our patience." " You might dispense with reading him a lecture," a second one remarked. " Do not be uneasy," replied a third; " the nation, which is always great and generous, will see to his education." Then the six municipal guards, roughly dragging the young prince after them, left the room.

For some moments the steps of the retreating jailers and the cries of the struggling child could be heard. Then there was silence, and the three women remained alone, weeping by the side of an empty bed. The Commune at least spared them the torture of having witnesses to their grief; from that day forth the municipal guards no longer remained in the prisoners' chamber; every evening they were locked in. The guards only came three times a day to bring their meals, and make sure that the bars of the windows had not been disturbed. They no longer had any one to serve them; Madame Elisabeth and Madame Royale made the beds, and waited on the queen. The poor women preferred this; they could at least pray and weep in peace.

The Convention had declared that it would provide for the education of the son of Capet. It is known how this was done. The preceptor which it gave Louis XVII. was the cobbler Simon, — one of the roughest and most malevolent among the municipal guards who were intrusted with the guard of the prisoners at the Temple. After a few months this beautiful and winsome child, with his red cheeks, curly hair, gay spirit, ardent and tender heart, was only a poor, sickly, broken-down little creature; his guardians were killing his body with lashes, and unable to kill his soul, they were destroying his intelligence by imprecations and obscene songs. "Citizens," Simon had asked the committees, when he had been given charge of the young king, — "citizens, what do you decide for the whelp? He has been taught to be insolent; I can cow him. So much the worse if he dies of it! I do not answer for that. After all, what do you wish? Transport him for life?" "No." "Kill him?" "No." "Poison him?" "No." "Well, what then?" "Get rid of him!"

Such was the programme which the Convention marked out for Simon, and which he accomplished with singular conscientiousness, if one can make use of the word "conscientiousness" in speaking of such a man!

It is not for us to repeat here the history of this long and painful martyrdom. The recital of it, drawn by the masterly hands of Messieurs de Beauchesne and Chantelauze, has made every mother weep.

Since Louis XVII. had been intrusted to this strange preceptor, he had not left his room. The guards of the Temple had not seen him. The rumour had spread about Paris that he had been stolen from his dungeon, and been carried in triumph to St. Cloud. To put an end to these rumours, which created some agitation, the Committee of Public Safety decided on July 7 that four commissioners — Dumont, Maure, Chabot, and Drouet — should visit the tower. The first act of the commissioners was to make the child descend to the garden, that he might be seen by the soldiers going on guard. Once there, the young prince began to call his mother in a loud voice, and to complain at being separated from her. "Show me," he cried, "the law which orders that I be separated from my mother." These cries annoyed the commissioners. "They made him be quiet," Madame Royale laconically remarks. How? She does not say; but one can divine. He was hastily taken back to his chamber, where Simon was instructed to put him to work, and to train him.

In leaving the son, the deputies entered the mother's apartment. At the sight of Drouet, the queen could not restrain a gesture of repulsion; when she had mastered it, "she complained in a most touching way of the cruelty which they had shown in taking her son from her;" she entreated that he be given back to her, that she at least be permitted to see him at meals. Neither prayers nor arguments could move the hard hearts of the commissioners; they merely replied that the Commune had thought it necessary to take this measure.

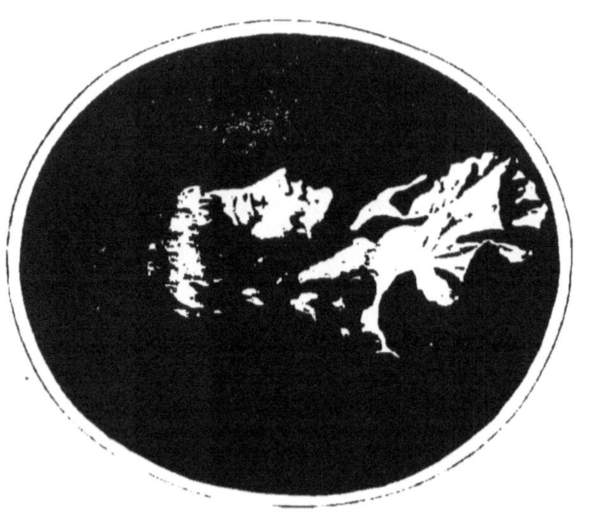

These men felt nothing. "We visited the Temple," Drouet reported coldly to the Convention. "In the first apartment we found the son of Capet tranquilly playing checkers with his mentor. We mounted to the apartment of the women; we found there Marie Antoinette, her daughter, and her sister enjoying perfect health. Certain persons are pleased to spread among foreign nations the report that they are ill-treated; but according to their own statement, made in the presence of the commissioners of the Convention, nothing is wanting to their comfort." Not a word of the dramatic scene in the garden, of the queen's touching supplications.

No; it was not upon the compassion of those in power, but upon the devotion of a few friends, and upon herself, that the poor woman could count to obtain a sight of her son, and to have news of him. From time to time the young prince went up to take the air on the platform of the tower; the queen discovered that through a little window of her apartment she could see the child as he passed on the stairs. " Say to Fidèle" (Toulan), Madame Elisabeth wrote, — " my sister desired that you should know it, — that we see the little one every day through the window of the closet opening on the stairs." The unhappy woman remained there for hours together watching for her son to pass; when he had gone by, they ascended to the platform, which had been divided into two parts by a partition, and there through a little crack they again caught a glimpse of the young king. " We mounted to the top of the tower very often," Madame Royale relates, " because my brother went up, and because my mother's only pleasure was to see him through a little crack as he passed at a distance. She stayed there for hours together, to wait for the moment when she could see the child; it was her sole hope, her sole occupation." Occasionally also, they had news of the little prisoner, either through municipal guards or Turgy or Tison, who apparently wished to efface the memory of his former unworthy conduct by redoubled zeal. This news was harrowing: Simon ill-treated his royal pupil " beyond all conception." Madame Elisabeth was forced to beg Tison, through pity, to conceal these horrors from the poor mother; she knew, or suspected, quite enough of them. One day, however, — it was the day on which the people had just heard of the victorious march of the allied armies, — the queen was on the top of the tower waiting at her post of observation; she saw the child and his jailer come up. The child was pale, suffering, and held his head bowed; he had put off mourning for his father; he wore the carmagnole and a red cap. His jailer accompanied him, with oaths and blasphemies on his lips, and insults, brutal treatment, blows, for the poor little thing. That day the queen had seen too much. She threw herself weeping into Madame Elisabeth's arms, pushed back the young Marie Thérèse, who wished in her turn to approach the crack, and returned to her room crushed. " My fears did not deceive me," she said to Madame Elisabeth, bursting into tears; " I knew that he suffered. My heart told me that he would be unhappy a hundred leagues from me. For two days I have suffered, I have been agitated, I have trembled; it is because I felt the tears which my poor child was shedding far from me fall upon my heart. I have no more interest in anything. God has abandoned me. I no longer dare to pray." Then suddenly repenting of this last remark, " Pardon, my God, and you, my sister, pardon me! I believe in you as in myself. I am so tormented that I am sure some new misfortune threatens me. My child! my poor child! I feel, from the breaking of my own heart, the faltering of his."

Marie Thérèse was at her side; Madame Elisabeth, fearing that she might have heard these despairing words, went to console her; the young girl said her prayers and fell asleep.

This new misfortune which the queen dreaded soon fell upon her. On August 1, upon a report by Barrère, the Convention decided that Marie Antoinette should be brought up before the revolutionary tribunal, and transferred at once to the Conciergerie.

" On August 2, at two o'clock in the morning," Madame Royale records, " they came to awaken us, and read to my mother the decree of the Convention, which ordered that, upon the requisition of the procurator of the Commune, she should be conducted to the Conciergerie for her trial. She heard the reading of this decree without emotion, and without saying a word. My aunt and I at once asked to follow my mother; but this favour was not granted us. While she did up her clothing in a package, the municipal guards did not leave her; she was even obliged to dress before them. They asked for her pockets, which she gave up; they searched them, and took all that was in them, although there was nothing of the least importance. They made a package of the objects, which they said they would send to the tribunal, where it would be opened before her. They left her nothing except a handkerchief and a smelling-bottle, fearing lest she might feel ill. My mother, after having tenderly embraced me, charged me to have courage, to take the best care of my aunt, and to obey her as a second mother, and repeated to me the same instructions which my father had given me; then throwing herself into my aunt's arms, she recommended her children to her. I made no reply, so frightened was I at the thought of seeing her for the last time; my aunt said some words to her in a low tone. Then my mother went away without casting her eyes upon us, doubtless fearing lest her resolution might abandon her. She stopped again at the foot of the tower, while the municipal guards drew up an official report discharging the *concierge* of her person. In going out, she struck her head against a grating, not remembering to stoop down; they asked her if she had hurt herself. 'Oh, no,' she said; 'nothing can hurt me now.' Then getting into a carriage with the municipal guard and two gendarmes, she set out for the Conciergerie."

CHAPTER XXV.

WE have arrived at the last stage: after the Conciergerie,
there is nothing but the scaffold.

It was three in the morning when the queen arrived at her new
prison; instead of entering her in the jail's book at the office, she
was conducted directly to the room destined for her. It was a
little room on the ground floor, low, damp, and cold, reached by
a long dark corridor, and closed by a massive door provided with
two enormous bolts. The floor, situated below the level of the
court, was paved with bricks, set in the ground; on the walls,
down which the water ran when the Seine was high, fragments
of old paper could still be seen stamped with the *fleur-de-lis*, and
eaten by the lime. This chamber, called the council-chamber,
because, before the Revolution, the magistrates of the Parliament
of Paris came here at certain epochs to hear the claims of the
prisoners, had been occupied by General Custine, who had been
forced to vacate it hastily to make place for the queen. One low
window, carefully grated, and opening on the inner court of the
prison, lighted this sombre cell. A cot, a table, two straw-bottomed
chairs, a cane-seated armchair, composed its wretched furnish-
ings; on the bed, straps tied together in several places with cord,
a rotting straw mattress, a second mattress, torn, a woollen
coverlet full of holes, coarse gray linen sheets; there were no
curtains, but an old screen. The gendarmes, who slept on a bed
similar to the queen's, found it too hard, and complained. There
was also a willow work-basket, a wooden box for powder, and
another of tin for pomade.

On entering, the queen involuntarily glanced round at the
bareness of these walls. The day was already breaking. She
hung her watch on a nail, and threw herself upon her bed.

The hatred of her executioners, however, could not even leave her the consolation of solitude. In the morning two gendarmes came and settled themselves in the prisoner's chamber to watch her. To them was added a woman to serve her; she was an old creature, eighty years of age, named Larivière, the former *concierge* at the Admiralty, whose son was turnkey of the prison. But soon this woman, whose attitude had inspired a certain confidence in the queen, was changed; she was replaced by a young woman thirty-six years old, the woman Harel, a "veritable fishwife," says Rougeville, whose husband was employed in the offices of the secret police, and who had no other mission than to spy upon the captive. The queen distrusted her instinctively, and almost never spoke to her.

Two new beds were brought at the same time: one was destined for the waiting-woman, the other for the gendarmes, who never lost sight of their prisoner, even, says Rougeville, "when she attended to the natural necessities of life."

A robber of the worst kind, named Barassin, a convict, and a spy, with the face of a brute and the heart of a hyena, who was charged in the prisons with the most disgusting and most disagreeable duties, occasionally visited the royal cell, to fulfil there his repulsive functions. One day Beaulieu, then confined at the Conciergerie, questioned him as to the way in which Marie Antoinette was treated. .

"Like the others," he replied.

"How? Like the others?"

"Yes, like the others; that can only surprise the aristocrats."

"And what does the queen do in her sad chamber?"

"The Capet! Oh, she is sheepish enough; she mends her stockings, that she may not wear them into holes."

"Upon what does she sleep?"

"Upon a cot like your own."

"How is she dressed?"

"She wore a black dress, which was badly torn; she looked like a magpie."

What a thrilling picture, set forth in all its brutality!

Marie Antoinette, hastily carried off from the tower, had been able to take very little clothing with her. On the morrow she had sent a request for some; and the municipal guards of the Temple transmitted to those of the Conciergerie a jacket and skirt, two pairs of lisle-thread stockings, one pair of under-stockings, and a stocking to knit, enclosed in a basket, which the poor mother had begun for her son. Madame Elisabeth and her niece put into the package all the wool and silk that they could find; they knew how much the queen had always liked to be occupied. Even at the time of her prosperity she had had the habit of constantly working; at the Conciergerie this would be her sole distraction. But even this distraction was denied her; the prisoner's hope and her sister-in-law's affectionate ingenuity were deceived. Her guardians refused to give the queen any knitting-needles, fearing, said the municipal guards, lest she might use them to take her life. The poor woman was forced to do nothing in her prison but pray, meditate, dwell on the sad past and on the sad future. Her only pastime was to watch her jailers play cards, or to read the few volumes which the compassion of some more humane guard or the devotion of a faithful servant, like Hue or Montjoye, succeeded in procuring for her, — "Cook's Travels," among others; and when she was asked what books she desired, she replied, "The most frightful adventures."

At the same time that the prisoner at the Conciergerie was denied needles, the guards at the Temple took from their prisoners the tapestries worked by the queen and those upon which they were working, on the pretext that there might be in these pieces of embroidery mysterious signs and means of correspondence.

Marie Antoinette had never drunk wine, and she could not stand the water of the Seine. The only drink which did not make her ill was the water of Ville d'Avray; during her captivity at the Temple a supply of this water had always been brought to her. Madame Elisabeth begged the municipal guards to have a little carried to the Conciergerie, and on August 5 the police administrators consented. Every day two bottles of the water of Ville d'Avray were taken from the supply at the Temple for the use of the widow of Louis XVI. By the side of the persecutors there were still some friendly hearts. The terror which weighed upon France had not crushed out the holy aspirations of devotion and pity. Michonis was always there; it was he who watched over the queen, and who, appointed administrator of the police, had obtained the inspection of her cell. It was he who served as intermediary between the Temple and the Conciergerie, and who, on August 19, for example, made the demand for the four chemises and a pair of shoes, of which the prisoner was in such pressing need. Turgy and Toulan, for their part, continued their correspondence by signs; and it was through them that to the very end Madame Elisabeth and Madame Royale received news of the " person," as they called Marie Antoinette. But the greatest precaution was necessary. The report of these communications had finally leaked out; at once the princesses, fearing a perquisition, threw away all the paper, ink, and pencils which they had kept hidden under their clothing; they no longer had anything but gall-nuts and almond-milk for their correspondence with Toulan.

Huc had done even better: he had gained admittance to the Conciergerie, and had succeeded (without great difficulty, moreover, for the way had been carefully prepared) in winning over the *concierge* Richard and his wife, — the one whom Madame Elisabeth in her notes mentions under the name of *Sensible*. It was through them that he secured news of the prisoner, which he transmitted to Toulan, which he in turn communicated to Turgy, by means of signals on the cornet, — news which poured a little balm into the hearts of the captives at the Temple. To transmit to the queen news of her children, to inform Madame Royale and Madame Elisabeth of the queen's condition, — such was the double purpose which Huc, the *Constant* of the correspondence, proposed to himself, and which this generous quartette of accomplices, Turgy and Toulan, Richard and his wife, faithfully helped him to accomplish.

The Richards were truly kind-hearted people. All that they could do to alleviate the painful captivity of Marie Antoinette they did; and they easily found aids in these pious complots. One day the prisoner desired to eat a melon; Madame Richard ran to the nearest market. " I must have an excellent melon," she said to the merchant, whom she knew. " I divine for whom," the vender replied; " choose, take the very nicest." She herself turned the melons topsy-turvy to find the best. Madame Richard wished to pay. " Keep your money," the worthy woman replied, " and say to the queen that there are among us those who lament."

Even some of the most prominent revolutionary leaders were touched by the misfortunes of their victim, or seduced by the bribe of a sum of money. Manuel had been one of the first converted; Camille Desmoulins was seized with pity. He wished at all risks to save the prisoner; he only succeeded in ruining himself after her. Hébert himself, the infamous " Père Duchesne,"

—Hébert was won over; but he was suspected, and to avert suspicion he showed himself more violent than ever. The ex-Capuchin Chabot was tempted by the bribe of a million, which the Marquise de Janson offered him; and Fersen, as ever intrepid and indefatigable, planned with La Marck and Mercy to send the ballet-master Noverre and the financier Ribbes to Paris, to win over Danton, by offering him money and the diamonds taken on Sémonville. In another direction the Prince de Coburg renewed his offers to exchange the queen for the commissioners taken by Dumouriez. The rumour of this more friendly feeling on the part of certain government leaders spread throughout Paris, and one day the wife of Richard spoke to the queen of a possibility of deliverance; but the queen, rendered more clear-sighted by misfortune, only shook her head and said, " They sacrificed the king; they will put me to death as they did him. No; I shall never again see my unhappy children or my tender and virtuous sister;" and saying these words, she burst into tears.

However that might be, this compassion on the part of her guardians brought about some abatement in the severity of the surveillance. Certain gendarmes showed pity for the prisoner. One of them broke his pipe, because he observed that the tobacco-smoke was unpleasant to the queen and kept her from sleeping at night. Others, knowing her fondness for flowers, brought her pinks, tuberoses, rockets. The woman Harel was softened. Through the complicity of police administrators and *concierges*, various persons, even priests, were admitted to the Conciergerie, and to the queen's cell. The Abbé Emery, also confined there, could, from within the prison, it is true, confess her, and converse with her for a few minutes; and Fouquier-Tinville declared that at the Conciergerie there were greater facilities than at the Temple for holding communication with the outer world.

It was these facilities, doubtless, which kept alive among a few faithful servants the thought of carrying off the prisoner, and thus saving France from another crime.

"A great many people were interested in my mother," Madame Royale relates. " I have learned since her death that they wished to rescue her from the Conciergerie, and that unhappily the project failed. I have been assured that the gendarme who guarded her, and the wife of the *concierge*, had been won over by some of our friends; that she had seen several devoted persons in her prison, among others a priest who had administered the sacrament, which she received with great devoutness. The opportunity of escape was once missed because she had been instructed to speak to the second guard, and by mistake she spoke to the first. Another time she was outside of her room, and had passed the corridor, when a gendarme opposed her departure (although he had been bribed), and obliged her to return, thus causing the enterprise to fail."

We know little of the first of these projects. It is probable, however, that it had been conceived by the Baron de Batz, — that "infamous monster," upon whose head the Convention had put a price; that the gendarmes had been bought over, and that the plan miscarried because the queen failed to speak to that one of her guardians who, having two cloaks, one on top of the other, should have given her one, in order to lead her out of the Conciergerie, whence a young man called Rousset was to conduct her to a place of safety.

The second project, better known, appears to have been the complot mentioned in history under the name of the *affaire de l'œillet.*

Among the faithful friends who prowled around the Conciergerie, ready to sacrifice their lives to save that of Marie Antoinette, was a chevalier of St. Louis, named Rougeville, one of those who had been at Louis XVI.'s side on the 20th of June and on the 10th of August. Through the intermediation of an American, the widow Dutilleul, and a wood-vender named Fontaine, Rougeville became acquainted with Michonis. They were made to understand one another; they soon came to an agreement, and one day, Wednesday, the 28th of August, Rougeville accompanied Michonis to the Conciergerie. The prisoner was dressed in a black caraco; her gray hair was cut in the back and on the forehead; she had grown so thin that Rougeville scarcely recognized her, and so weak that she had difficulty in standing; on her fingers she wore three poor rings. "Ah, it is you, Monsieur Michonis," she said; and approaching him, she asked him, as usual, for news of her children. Then perceiving Rougeville, she was seized with such emotion that she fell back into an armchair. A deep flush rose to her face; her limbs trembled, and tears flowed from her eyes. Rougeville sought to reassure her, and approaching her, motioned to her to take some pinks, among which he had hidden a piece of paper. The queen, however, was still so agitated that she did not at first understand, and Rougeville let the pinks fall back of the stove.   Then he went out with Michonis. They came back almost immediately, recalled by the gendarme; and while Michonis occupied the attention of these last, the queen, who had retired behind a screen, conversed with Rougeville, and entreated him not to expose himself thus to danger.   "I have weapons and money," Rougeville replied; "take courage."   And he promised her that she should be rescued; that he would bring her money to bribe the gendarmes, etc.   "Does your heart fail you?" he asked.   "It never fails me," the queen answered; "but it is deeply wounded."   And laying her hand upon her heart, she added, "If I am feeble and crushed, this is not."   Michonis, fearing lest this scene, if prolonged, might attract the attention of the gendarme, made a sign to Rougeville, and both went out.   "I am then bidding you an eternal adieu?" the queen said to Michonis, who told her that he had not been re-elected police administrator. "No, Madame," he answered; "if I am no longer administrator, being still a municipal officer, I shall have the right to come to visit you as much as you care to have me."

In the second interview, Rougeville had been able to apprise his royal interlocutor of the presence of the pinks.   As soon as he was gone, the queen, taking advantage of the fact that the woman Harel was playing cards with the gendarme, quickly picked up the flowers and read the notes enclosed in the bouquet. They contained an offer of money and vague phrases such as these: "What do you mean to do?   I have been in prison; I escaped by a miracle; I shall come on Friday."   The queen hastened to destroy these notes by tearing them into a thousand pieces, then she endeavoured to answer them; and having neither paper nor pen, she was forced to try to prick out a few words upon a little piece of paper with a pin: "I am constantly watched; I neither talk nor write; I trust in you; I shall come."

Was she then acquainted with the conspirators' plan?   Did she believe that the gendarme had already been bribed?   Although this seems improbable, it appears certain that it was she herself who, while the woman Harel was gone for some water, handed this little paper to the gendarme Gilbert, to have him deliver it to Rougeville.   Gilbert took the note, placed it in his waistcoat and took it to the woman Richard, who hastened to deliver it to Michonis when he returned on the following day, the 29th. Rougeville also returned on the 30th, as he had promised, in a new disguise, and if he is to be believed, took advantage of the opportunity to give the prisoner a certain sum in louis and assignats.

The execution of the project had been fixed for the night of September 2 and 3. The *concierge* and his wife had been bribed. Two administrators had received money. Michonis was to go at ten o'clock in the evening, take away the queen on the pretext of carrying her to the Temple, by order of the municipality, and once outside, he was to effect her escape; Rougeville would then receive her, and conduct her to a place of safety, to the château of Livry, says one version, and from there into the territory of the empire. In order not to compromise the *concierge*, a discharge should be put on his jail-book. The conspirators came, in fact, on the day named; for fifty louis the gendarmes had promised to say nothing; but at the last moment one of them, although he had received the sum, thought better of his promise. Despite Michonis's entreaties, who urged the orders of the municipality, he declared that if they carried the queen away, he would call the guard. The attempt had failed; and on September 3, the gendarme Gilbert denounced the complot. Rougeville succeeded in escaping; but Michonis was arrested on the 4th. Richard and his wife were incarcerated; and two deputies from the Convention, Amar and Sevestre, accompanied by a member of the municipality, visited the Conciergerie to hold an inquest. Marie Antoinette was questioned twice; with admirable presence of mind she tried to repudiate all the charges which could weigh upon Michonis and Rougeville. The examiners discovered nothing; and without the account which two months later Rougeville gave to Fersen, without the memoir which a little later he sent to the Comte de Metternich, and still later to the Cinq-Cents, we should not know to-day the details of the plan elaborated by these two faithful servants of the monarchy.

The Convention, however, shuddered at the danger which it had run of losing its prey. On September 10, police officials came to take from the queen her last jewels, regarded with suspicion, doubtless, because they might be used to bribe the guards: the little rings which Rougeville had seen on her fingers, and which only contained hair, a gold watch, a Breguet, — this last friend of prisoners, whose hours it counts, — some seals, and a medallion also enclosing hair, the dauphin's, it is said. At the same time the captive was put in close confinement, the gendarme and the woman Harel dismissed from her chamber, a sentinel placed at her door, with orders to allow her to communicate with no one except the *concierge* and his wife, and another sentinel stationed in the court, with instructions to permit no one whatsoever to go within ten steps of the window on any possible pretext.

This was not all. The cell to which the chevalier of St. Louis had been able to gain admittance, and from which the queen had almost escaped, was evidently not sure enough to hold her henceforth. On September 11, police officials came to the Conciergerie "for the purpose of choosing a place for the detention of the Widow Capet other than that in which she was then confined." They visited with care the various rooms of the prison, and ended by deciding on the one which was used as the pharmacy. It was decided that the chemist, Jacques Antoine Lacour, should clear it on the same day, to allow Citizen Godard to make "with the least possible delay" the alterations necessary to transform it into a cell. The wide casement, which opened on the court of the women, should be closed up as far as the fifth cross-bar, with a sheet of iron the thickness of a line, and the rest should be grated with bars of iron placed close together; the second window, looking on the infirmary, should be wholly blocked by means of a sheet of iron of the same thickness, and the small window, which opened on the corridor, entirely suppressed. The door already there was provided on the outside with two bolts; a second very heavy one was added, opening on the inside, and secured with a safety-lock. There was a gargoyle for draining the water; they determined to stop it up. When the alterations were finished, the queen was transferred to this cell; she never again left it except to go to the revolutionary tribunal.

The surveillance was rendered still more minute; no more women were allowed to serve the prisoner. The woman Harel had been dismissed after the affair of the pinks; it was the *concierge* who dressed the queen's hair every morning. A gendarme in her room day and night, separated by a simple screen; two sentinels under the window of the court; incessant perquisitions in the cell by police officials and members of the Committee of Public Safety; no light in the evening; no work during the day, since at her arrival at the Conciergerie even her knitting-needles had been taken away from her. The queen read and prayed. "The greater part of her time," remarks an eye-witness, "was consecrated to prayer." Misfortune had developed and strengthened her religious sentiments, which she owed to her Christian education, and which the whirl of society had not blotted from her memory. "Her imprisonment," writes Madame Royale, "had made her very religious." No more ink or pencil, — they had been taken from her long ago; the queen was constrained to write with a point on the wall the state of her linen. Her clothing was falling to pieces; she had only two dresses, — a black and a white, both equally worn out, — and only three chemises, which were given to her in succession every ten days. The daughter of the *concierge* was constantly busy mending her linen, clothes, her shoes; she put a new binding on her black dress. The captive's health, shattered by emotion, crushed by privations, bad air, and lack of exercise, had become impaired, and horrible hemorrhages came to add to her suffering and weakness.

Fortunately Hue, who still kept up his relations with the Conciergerie, had succeeded, through the medium of a police official, Dangé, in having a man appointed as Richard's successor who was in every respect as humane as he. This was Bault, *concierge* at La Force. Under a rough and severe manner, under the dress of a Jacobin, Bault hid a compassionate heart; and seconded by his wife and daughter, he sought to procure for his august prisoner such alleviation as was compatible with the surveillance of which he himself was the object. On the ground that he alone was responsible for the prisoners intrusted to him, he sent the gendarmes out of the royal chamber, put the key in his pocket, and the queen had no longer to endure their odious presence, which was rendered still more odious by the conversation of these men, their blasphemies, the noise of their glasses, and their tobacco-smoke. The gendarmes, consigned to the outer court, accompanied the *concierge*, it is true, whenever he entered the cell, but they no longer remained there. The queen's food, without being luxurious, was carefully prepared; in the morning it consisted of coffee, and at dinner of boiled meat, roasted fowl, vegetables, and dessert; but the poor woman had little appetite, and often she ate nothing. This modest bill of fare, however, offended the democratic sentiments of certain municipal officers; they notified the *concierge* that the accused should be fed like the others, — on the coarsest prison fare. " I will not do it," Bault replied. "She is my prisoner; I am responsible for her with my head. Some one might attempt to poison her; I must attend to her food myself; not a drop of water shall enter here without my permission." The municipal officers yielded. The *concierge* continued to have the charge of the queen's food; he gave her at least what was wholesome and proper, and the water was always clear and limpid.

To exercise humanity, however, he was forced to hide his feelings under the mask of rigour and persecution. Autumn was approaching; the month of October was cold and rainy; Bault thought to protect his prisoner against the dampness of this room without fire, where the water stood on the pavement and trickled down the walls, by hanging an old carpet round her bed. When the administrators saw this, they did not conceal their dissatisfaction. "Do you not see," the *concierge* said to them, "that it is to break the sound, and keep her from hearing anything from the next room?" "That's right," the commissioners replied; "you have done well." They would have blamed a measure of pity; they approved of a thought of mistrust.

Another time, however, Bault was less fortunate; he had asked for a coverlet of English cotton, to add to the meagre covering which barely sheltered the captive from the cold and dampness. Fouquier-Tinville grew angry, and replied brutally, "You deserve to be sent to the guillotine;" but the *concierge* was not crushed, and not being able to obtain a coverlet, he substituted a mattress for it. On her part, Madame Bault, who had a garden at Charenton, reserved its best products for the queen, — the most delicate fruits, — and sometimes the venders at the *halles* added peaches and melons, as in Richard's time.

The unhappy sovereign, in the midst of her painful solitude, thought constantly of her children, of her son especially. One day when Bault entered her cell, she approached him and sought to slip into his hand a pair of gloves and a ringlet of hair; but Bault was not alone: the gendarmes accompanied him, as usual. They saw the action, and darting toward the *concierge*, exclaimed, "What has she just given you?" Bault was forced to open his hand; the gloves and the hair were seized and carried to Fouquier-Tinville. The queen, more fortunate some days later, let fall at his feet a poor little garter, which she had woven, with the aid of two toothpicks, out of the threads pulled from her bedclothing. This time she was not seen. Bault picked up the melancholy and precious souvenir, and Hue afterward succeeded in delivering it to the Duchesse d'Angoulême, sole remnant of that great family, decimated at the Temple and at the Conciergerie.

A last and most unforeseen consolation was reserved for the unhappy woman: through the complicity of the jailers, a loyal priest was one night able to come to her cell, say mass there, and even administer the sacrament. That night there was greater calmness and perhaps a ray of hope in the prisoner's heart. Men seemed to abandon her; but God did not desert her.

The devotion of her friends, moreover, was persistent. In October a complot to snatch the victim from the hands of her executioners was again sketched out. Who was at the head of it? Was it Rougeville? Was it Batz? It is not known. The subaltern agents alone are known, — the wig-maker Basset, a hunchback woman named Fournier, the household Lemille. A certain number of soldiers at Paris, at Courbevoie, and at Vincennes had been bribed; they were to stir up a riot, take possession of the Convention and the Jacobins, and under cover of the tumult deliver the queen. The complot was extensive; like all the others, it failed. The conspirators, denounced by spies in whom they imprudently confided, were arrested on October 12, and paid for their generous design with their heads.

While these brave people were struggling to rescue this daughter of the Cæsars from the scaffold, and while her jailers were endeavouring to sweeten her last moments, what were her family doing to deliver her? When she was transferred to the Conciergerie, Mercy hastened to write to the Prince de Coburg, general-in-chief of the Austrian army, who had just entered Valenciennes, entreating him to direct a body of cavalry on Paris at once, that it might prevent the crime which was visibly preparing. " Can posterity believe," he exclaimed, " that so great a crime could be consummated at a few days' march from the victorious armies of Austria and England, *without these armies making some effort to prevent it?*"

Coburg, however, was not the man for a bold *coup-de-main.* Either from force of habit, calculation, or impotence, he preferred to go into winter quarters; and Mercy was driven to write, two months later, " I tremble for the queen. Can any one in reading the journals restrain a shudder of terror?"

When Mercy uttered this cry of alarm, it was too late; the last act of the great drama had begun, and, to borrow the words of La Marck, the " ineffaceable stain rested upon the Austrian government, that at forty leagues from Paris they had done nothing to save the aunt of their emperor."

CHAPTER XXVI.

TWO months had passed since the queen had been transferred
to the Conciergerie, to be arraigned before the revolutionary
tribunal; and her enemies in their hatred had been unable to
draw up an indictment against her. Hébert, eager to efface the
memory of an instant of pity by redoubled violence, and impatient to see "the life of the Austrian wolf shortened," exclaimed
in vain, "The people seek noon at fourteen o'clock in waiting to
judge the Austrian tigress, and in demanding proofs to condemn
her; whereas if justice were done her, she would be chopped up like
mince-meat." The cruel imagination of the habitual purveyors of
the guillotine set to work in vain to forge pretexts and invent crimes.
Héron's work, even revised and corrected by Marat, was so absurd that the Committee of Public Safety gave up making use
of it. On October 3, Billaud-Varennes ascended the tribune and
said, " The woman Capet has not been punished. . . . I demand
that the Convention expressly decrees that the revolutionary tribunal immediately attend to the trial and judgment of the woman
Capet." The decree was passed; but two days after, on October
5, Fouquier-Tinville complained that in communicating it to
him, the Convention had at the same time transmitted " no documents relative to Marie Antoinette." The tribunal did not know
what to do, and Fouquier had scruples. The Committee of Public Safety opened the national archives to him, and ordered the
papers on the trial of Louis XVI. to be given him, — useless

trouble; he found nothing. Pache, Chaumette, and Hébert, at the end of their resources, visited the Temple on Monday, October 7, tortured Madame Royale and Madame Elisabeth at length with infamous questions, but could not extract from their replies any denunciation whatever against the queen. More fortunate on the preceding evening with Louis XVII., however, they had extorted from the innocence of a child of eight, drunk with brandy and terrorized by Simon's brutal treatment, an odious calumny against his mother.

Fouquier-Tinville could now lay the foundations of his "work of hell;" his imagination and the hatred of the populace would do the rest.

At six o'clock on the evening of October 12, Marie Antoinette was summoned to the Palace of Justice, to the great audience-hall. Dressed in a wretched black gown, she seated herself opposite the public prosecutor, upon a bench between two gendarmes. The hall was dark; two meagre candles, placed before the clerk of the court, Fabricius, gave a dim light; and the queen could not distinguish, in the shadow in which they hid themselves, the powerful men of the day, who had come with feverish and malicious curiosity to be present at the agony of the widow of the last king of France.

The president, Herman, opened the examination; he passed in review all the edifice which had been laboriously erected by Fouquier, — all the grievances of the Revolutionists against this woman, who by herself had withstood the Revolution; the pretended millions sent to her brother, her relation with the princes, the so-called Austrian committee, the veto opposed to the decrees against the emigrants and against the priests, the complots against the people.

Question. "Was it you who taught Louis Capet that art of profound dissimulation with which he so long deceived the French people, ignorant that villany and perfidy could be carried to such a point?"

Answer. "Yes, the people have been deceived, cruelly deceived; but neither by my husband nor by myself."

They came to the flight to Varennes.

Q. "You were the principal instigator in Louis Capet's treachery; and it was because of your counsels, and perhaps of your persecutions, that he wished to fly from France, to put himself at the head of the furious, who desired to rend their fatherland?"

A. " My husband never wished to fly from France. I followed him everywhere ; but if he had desired to leave his country, I should have employed every means to dissuade him from it ; but that was not his intention."

The queen was pressed with questions upon this subject, as she had been pressed at the time of the affair of the pinks. As on September 4, she replied with a composure and an uncompromising presence of mind, which confounded Herman.

Q. " You have never for a moment wavered in your desire to destroy liberty ; you wished to reign at any price, and remount the throne over the bodies of the patriots ? "
A. " We did not need to remount the throne, since we were on it ; we have never desired aught but the welfare and happiness of France. Let France be happy, and we shall always be content."
Q. " What interest do you feel in the arms of the republic ? "
A. " I desire the happiness of France above everything."
Q. " You regret, without doubt, that your son should have lost the throne, which he might have ascended if the people, at last enlightened as to their rights, had not shattered this throne ? "
A. " I shall regret nothing for my son when my country is happy."

Herman referred again to the banquet of the body-guards, to the events of October, to the queen's relations at the Temple and at the Conciergerie with the police administrators and municipal officers, to the conspiracy of the pinks, etc., closely watching the replies of the august accused, seeking to extract from them some avowal which might prop up Fouquier's monstrous and fragile scaffolding, waiting for her, in the shadow, so to speak, as the tiger waits for his prey. The queen replied with rare ease and simple dignity, without haughtiness and without weakness ; in this entanglement of involved and purposely confused questions, she discerned the snares, foiled the artifices, and with astonishing tact knew at the same time how to defend herself and compromise no one.

Herman, conquered in the struggle, officially appointed two defenders for her, Chauveau-Lagarde and Tronçon-Ducoudray, and gave the order to take her back to the Conciergerie. The queen returned to her cell, where, after that day, she was placed under the special surveillance of an officer of the *gendarmerie*, who did not again quit her.

Chauveau-Lagarde was in the country when a messenger came

to apprise him of the great and painful mission, which had been confided to him. He set out for Paris at once, and on the evening of the 13th, repaired to the Conciergerie, with his colleague Tronçon-Ducoudray. On the preceding evening, Fouquier had placed in the record-office of the revolutionary tribunal the indictment which he had succeeded in drawing up. The queen examined it with contemptuous firmness, and coldly made various observations without troubling herself about the gendarme, who could overhear her. The lawyer, more moved than she, and frightened by the voluminous and confused mass of documents which constituted the indictment, begged her to demand a delay, which was indispensable for the examination of these papers. "To whom must I appeal?" she asked. "To the National Convention," the defender murmured in a low voice. "No," she replied quickly, turning her head; "no, never!" Her pride as queen and her dignity as widow would not allow her to recognize the authority of her husband's murderers.

Chauveau-Lagarde insisted, pleaded the interest of the memory of Louis XVI., that of her children, of Madame Elisabeth, and, he records, —

"At the words 'sister,' 'wife,' and 'mother,' nature triumphed over the sovereign ; and the queen, without offering an objection, with a sigh, took her pen, and wrote to the Assembly in our name a few lines full of nobleness and dignity, in which she complained that they had not allowed us sufficient time to examine the documents relative to the trial, and requested the necessary delay for us."

The request, transmitted to the public prosecutor, remained without reply. On the next day, Monday, October 14, at eight o'clock in the morning, the discussion began.

The judges and the jury were at their posts. The judges were Herman, president, Coffinhal, the tool of Robespierre, and his most energetic partisan, Deliège, Maire, Donzé-Verteuil. The jury consisted of the ex-Marquis Antonelle, Renaudin, one of the cruellest of this band of cruel or cowardly men, Fiévée, Besnard, Thoumain, Desboisseaux, Baron Sambat, Devèze, the surgeon Souberbielle, who wished to decline adjudicating, but the president imposed silence upon him in these terms: "If any one should challenge you, it would be the prosecuting party, for you have cared for the accused, and you may have been touched by the greatness of her misfortune ;" the innkeeper Chrétien, the musician Lumière, the printer Nicholas, the wigmaker Ganney, the carpenter Trinchard, joyous at having to pass judgment "upon this wild beast, who had devoured a part of the republic."

The queen was introduced; from a remnant of coquetry, according to Mercier, or rather from an imperishable sense of dignity, she had given greater attention to her widow's dress. Her hair, whitened by grief, was arranged more artistically; she had added to her ordinary linen cap two floating lappets, and under these lappets she had fastened some black crape. She stood there, majestic and proud, before these men who called themselves her judges. Questioned by the president, she declared her name to be Marie Antoinette of Austria, thirty-eight years of age, widow of the king of France, being, at the time of her arrest, in the place of meeting of the National Assembly.

The hall was crowded. Several members of the Committee of Public Safety — Vadier, Amar, Vouland, Moise, Bayle — were seated by the side of the public prosecutor, intently observing the jury and the audience, encouraging the hesitating, upholding the feeble, watching the agony of their victim. The *tricoteuses* were also at their post. Since the institution of the revolutionary tribunal, they had never before had such a piece of good fortune; and they were come to feed upon the sufferings of her who had been a queen, and more, an adored queen.

Herman recommended firmness and impartiality to the jury. Then, addressing the accused, he charged her to be attentive (*sic*) to what she was about to hear. The witnesses were called; and the clerk, Fabricius, read the indictment.

Antoine Quentin, Fouquier-Tinville, public prosecutor for the revolutionary tribunal, —

"*Deposed*, That on the examination made of all the documents transmitted to the public prosecutor it had resulted that, like the Messalinas, Brunehauts, Fredegondas, and Médicis who were formerly styled queens of France, and whose eternally odious names would never be effaced from the annals of history, Marie Antoinette, widow of Louis Capet, had, since her sojourn in France, been the scourge and leech of the French people; that before the fortunate Revolution which gave the sovereignty to the French people, she had held political relations with the man called king of Bohemia and Hungary; that these relations were contrary to the interests of France; that, not content with having, in concert with the brothers of Louis Capet and the infamous and execrable Calonne, at that time minister of finance, abominably squandered the finances of France (fruit of the sweat of the people) to gratify inordinate pleasure and to pay the agents of her criminal intrigues, it was well known that she had at different epochs sent millions to the emperor, which he had used and still used to wage war against the republic ; and that through her excessive prodigality she had succeeded in exhausting the national treasury."

Fouquier then enumerated all the grievances collected by Herman in the first examination. He accused the queen of having on Oct. 1, 1789, arranged between the officers of the body-guards and those of the Flemish regiment "a repast which had degenerated into a veritable orgy, as she had wished it to do," to have led on the banqueters "to sing, in the effusion of drunkenness, songs expressing the heart-felt loyalty to the throne, and deep-rooted aversion for the people, to raise the white cockade aloft, and to trample the national cockade under foot;" of having, "through her agents, occasioned in Paris and its environments a scarcity of food, which had given place to another insurrection, as a consequence of which a numerous throng of citizens had marched to Versailles on the 5th of the same month;" of having "held in her palace cabals in which the flight to Varennes had been determined upon with Lafayette and Bailly;" of having "herself arranged and prepared everything for this flight, as she herself had admitted in her examination;" of having "wished for the horrible massacre of the zealous patriots who were on the Champ de Mars on July 17, 1791;" of having "conceived the idea of exciting discussion in these nightly councils, long known with reason as the Austrian Cabinet, against [*sic*] the laws which had been passed by the Legislative Assembly." He further set forth: —

"That the Widow Capet had digested and matured with her perfidious agents the horrible conspiracy which had broken out on the day of August 10, which had only miscarried through the courageous and marvellous efforts of the patriots ; that to this end she had assembled in her residence at the Tuileries — even in the vaults — the Swiss Guards, who, according to the terms of the decrees, should no longer compose the guard of Louis Capet ; that she had kept them in a state of drunkenness from the 9th until the morning of the 10th, the day agreed upon for the execution of this horrible conspiracy ; that she had likewise, for the same purpose, assembled on the 9th a crowd of those creatures known as the *chevaliers du poignard*, who had already figured in the same place on Feb. 28, 1791, and afterward on June 20, 1792.

"That the Widow Capet, fearing, without doubt, that this conspiracy might not have the full effect which she desired, had, about half-past nine on the evening of August 9, gone into the room where the Swiss Guards and others devoted to her were making cartridges; that in order to encourage them to hasten the manufacture of these cartridges, and to excite them the more, she had taken some cartridges and sharpened the balls — words fail me to express so atrocious a deed; . . . that there was no doubt but that it had been agreed upon in the council, which took place throughout that night, that the guards should fire upon the people, and that Louis Capet and Marie Antoinette (who herself was the chief leader of this conspiracy) had given the order to fire."

At the end of his address to the court, Fouquier reviewed in a few rapid phrases, and as if he himself was ashamed of it, the infamous calumny which could only have been originated in the licentious imagination of the "Père Duchesne," and he resumed his entire brief under three principal heads. The queen was accused: —

"1. Of having maliciously and purposely, in concert with the brothers of Louis Capet and the ex-minister Calonne, squandered in a frightful manner the finances of France, and of having sent innumerable sums to the emperor, and of having thus exhausted the national treasury.

"2. Of having both directly and through her counter-revolutionary agents kept up communications and correspondence with the enemies of the republic; of having directly and indirectly informed these same enemies of the plans of attack and of the campaign agreed upon and decided in the council.

"3. Of having through her intrigues and manoeuvres and those of her agents laid conspiracies and complots against the interior and exterior security of France; and of having to this end enkindled civil war at various points in the republic, and armed the citizens one against another; and of having by this means shed the blood of incalculable numbers of citizens."

Such was the indictment; but where were the proofs? What documents had Fouquier produced to the support of his statements? Documents, — the tribune had not even given the defenders time to verify them. Proofs, — there were none; it was for the witnesses to furnish them if they could.

The queen had listened in silence to the long reading of the clerk; she had not shown the least sign of emotion. As Fouquier repeated Hébert's calumny, a scarcely perceptible curl of

disdain had crossed her lips; but her bearing had remained calm
and assured. The rest of the time she had let her fingers wan-
der carelessly over the arm of the chair on which she was seated,
as over a pianoforte.

The hearing of the witnesses began. The first called was Lecointre of Versailles, — Lecointre, who had formerly proclaimed
himself "one of the most faithful subjects" of the king and
queen, that day and for four years before one of their most implacable enemies; Lecointre, one of those upon whom had
weighed most heavily the responsibility of the events of October, 1789. It was about those events that he was called upon to
speak. He repeated all the diatribes which he had formerly published in the journal of Gorsas; he endeavoured to incriminate
Marie Antoinette. Marie Antoinette replied both to the allegations of Lecointre and the questions of the president only by
clear and precise denials.

The adjutant-general, Lapierre, and the gunner, Roussillon, testified, — the first concerning the flight to Varennes, the second
concerning the events of August 10. Roussillon claimed that
at the time of the pillage of the Tuileries he had seen bottles
under the bed of the accused, — an evident proof that she had
given the Swiss Guards something to drink in order to intoxicate
them. Here again the queen confronted the grotesque insinuations of this croaking subaltern with proud denial. It seemed,
moreover, that in the accounts of the witnesses, the judges sought
not so much proofs against her, who was already doomed, as
against certain personages whom they wished to ruin, — against
Lafayette, Bailly, Pétion, or the police administrators, such as
Michonis, Marino, Jobert, etc. The prosecution had advanced
little when Hébert was called.

Hébert related vague facts: he found a book of the accused in
which were counter-revolutionary signs, — a heart pierced by an
arrow; he suspected Toulon of having taken off his hat before
the members of the ex-royal family. Then this wretch, who was
possessed of every baseness, — this man who had lived as a knave
and who died like a coward, — repeated in detail the unclean
calumny which had furnished Fouquier with the last paragraph
of his indictment.

Strange thing, the audience remained silent! The applause upon
which Hébert had counted failed him; the *tricoteuses*, then, had
greater decency than he. The president himself, in the questions

which he put to the accused, seemed to forget the declaration of the substitute of the procurator of the Commune; he questioned her concerning Michonis, concerning the affair of the pinks, and he left in obscurity, through a remnant of shame, perhaps, the odious accounts of the "Père Duchesne."

But a man was found who had no less indecency than Hébert. A juror, — why has his name not been published? Did he blush later, or did the editor of the "Bulletin du Tribunal Révolutionnaire" blush for him? — an unknown juror addressed Herman, saying, —

"Citizen President, I beg you to have the goodness to call the accused's attention to the fact that she has made no answer to the point on which the citizen Hébert spoke, regarding what passed between herself and her son."

This man should have been content; his infamous act was crowned with success. The queen had until then met the allegations of the witnesses and the denunciations of the public prosecutor with a calm face and impassive heart. At the juror's question her face flushed and her heart bounded; she half rose from her chair, and with an indignant gesture and a vibrating voice she said, "If I have not replied, it is because nature refuses to reply to such a charge made against a mother." Then casting a glance over the audience, she continued, "I appeal to all those who are here!"

Before this sublime outcry of a mother's heart I know not what magnetic current passed through the Assembly. The *tricotcuses* were touched despite themselves; a little more and they would have applauded, as they had applauded on October 6. Heart-rending cries were heard; women, it is said, were carried out fainting, and the tribunal was forced to threaten the disturbers of order. Hébert shuddered and bowed his head; the queen's cry had struck him a mortal blow.

To cut short these expressions, which were too favourable to the accused, the judges demanded that the hearing of the witnesses be resumed; but the notary, Silly, tried in vain to re-awaken the hatred by giving testimony concerning the flight of June 20, 1791. No one paid attention; the emotion of the audience must have time to calm down; and at three o'clock the court was adjourned.

So many shocks had not crushed the queen; her conscience sustained her. "Do you see how proud she is?" a woman murmured, as she saw her leave the hall with a firm step. The queen heard the remark; she was moved by it; she feared that she might have shown too much dignity in her replies. Then, turning toward her defenders, she asked them what they thought of the declarations of the witnesses; and upon the assurance which they gave her that nothing positive had yet resulted from the discussion, she said, "I fear no one except Manuel."

At five o'clock the audience was resumed. The depositions continued, but as in the morning, no definite fact, no allegation based on proofs; only recriminations, vague insinuations, suppositions.

Terrasson had seen the accused during the return from Varennes cast vindictive glances at the National Guards. Reine Millot, a domestic, had heard the Duc de Coigny say in 1778 that Marie Antoinette had sent at least twenty millions to her brother, as if it were probable that Monsieur de Coigny, whose title she could not have known, since she called him "Count," would have made a confidence of this kind to a servant of low grade. She also knew that one day the queen had carried two pistols on her person to kill the Duc d'Orléans, and that the king had been forced to put her under arrest in her room for two weeks. How did she know it? She did not say. Labenette, the editor of the " Journal du Diable," Marat's subaltern rival, declared that the queen had sent three men to assassinate him. And beyond these ridiculous or odious statements, not a proof, — nothing, absolutely nothing.

Manuel himself, the only witness whom Marie Antoinette seemed to fear, did not accuse her. He only protested that he had never had any intercourse with the court, nor with the wife of the former king. And to tell the truth, in this trial Manuel, like Bailly, who followed him, both memorable examples of the inconstancy of popular enthusiasm, was more in the position of an accused person than a witness. In vain judges called up a whole new series of witnesses; in vain they revived the affair of the pinks; in vain Dufraisne, Gilbert, the Richards, the woman Harel, were pressed with questions concerning Rougeville's visit to the Conciergerie. Still nothing. At eleven o'clock in the evening the meeting was adjourned; judges, jury, and witnesses had need of repose.

The queen, overcome with fatigue, tortured by these long discussions of fifteen hours, exhausted by the heat, by indignation. by contempt, was thirsty; she asked for a drink. The ushers were absent; not one in this crowd, every one of whom would, ten years before, have solicited the honour of going to get her a glass of water, and would have offered it to her on their knees, had the courage to render her a service which simple humanity demanded. The officer of *gendarmerie* who accompanied her, De Busne, alone dared to show his devotion; he gave her a drink. The queen felt herself grow faint; her sight became confused; in returning to her cell, she was almost taken ill. "I can no longer see," she murmured; "I am exhausted; I cannot walk." De Busne, respectful and moved to compassion, offered her his arm, and helped her descend the three slippery steps which led to her room. On the following morning, De Busne, suspected of humanity and convicted of counter-revolutionary pity, was thrown into prison.

At nine o'clock on the morning of the 15th the audience was resumed. It was the last day of this horrible agony; the morrow was to be the day of death.

The first witness who appeared was the conqueror of the Antilles, — D'Estaing, "sailor and soldier," as he was called. D'Estaing, who had military intelligence and bravery, but who was wanting in one sense, — the sense of respect for himself and others, — began by saying that he had a complaint against the accused, because she had prevented him from becoming marshal of France; but he brought no actual charge against her, and his very testimony was an homage to the queen's noble heart. "If the Parisians come to assassinate me," he had heard her say on October 5, "I shall be at my husband's feet; but I will not fly."

D'Estaing was followed by the two La Tour du Pin, his former companions in arms, soon to be his companions on the scaffold, — all three were guillotined on April 28, 1794, — his equals in rank, his superiors in moral grandeur. Their testimony incriminated the queen as little as his had done. The former minister of war greeted her with the same respect as formerly in the gallery at Versailles. He was asked if he knew the accused. He replied, bowing, "Ah, yes, I had the honour of knowing Madame." Inculpated like her, he defended himself and her with an ease and a courage which disconcerted the judges. They were seeking accusers; they only found apologists.

Yet Herman's passion was ingenious in harassing Marie Antoinette. He referred constantly to the former grievances alleged against her; he laid bare her whole life; he gathered from the pamphlets of courtiers, and from those of demagogues, old calumnies, begot of the spites of the antechamber and the hatred of the street: the outlays for Trianon, the trial of the necklace, the nomination of ministers, the pretended millions sent to the emperor.

Question. "Where did you get the money with which you built and furnished the Petite Trianon, where you gave entertainments of which you were always the goddess?"

Answer. "It was a fund which had been set aside for that purpose."

Q. "It must have been a large one; for the Petite Trianon must have cost enormous sums."

A. "It is possible that the Petite Trianon did cost immense sums, — more, perhaps, than I could wish. We were led into the outlays little by little. Besides, I desire more than any one that the people be instructed as to what passed there."

Q. "Was it not at the Petite Trianon that you first became acquainted with the woman La Motte?"

A. "I have never seen her."

Q. "Was she not to have been your victim in the affair of the famous necklace?"

A. "She could not have been, since I did not know her."

Q. "You persist, then, in denying that you knew her?"

A. "My object is not denial; I spoke the truth, and shall continue to speak it."

Q. "Did you not force the ministers of finance to deliver funds to you; and when some among them refused to do so, did you not threaten them with your indignation?"

A. "Never!"

Q. "Did you not solicit Vergennes to send six millions to the king of Bohemia and Hungary?"

A. "No!"

They opened a package sealed with the signet of the Commune, and containing the objects found on the queen on August 2, at the moment when she was registered in the jail-book at the Conciergerie. They found therein pocket-books, portraits, and locks of hair. Could not the prosecution find here some document convicting the accused? Would there not be by chance some counter-revolutionary badges? And might not this red morocco pocket-book, or this little book in green moire, have received the confidence of some complot against liberty? No:

these portraits were those of the Princesse de Lamballe, and of two friends of her childhood, the " ladies of Mecklenburg and of Hesse."   The pocket-book contained nothing but the address of the queen's physician and of the women in charge of her linen. This hair was that of her husband and of her children.

In default of accusers among the servants of the old *régime* and of the former court, or among the men of '89, were they not to be found at least among the servants of the Revolution, among the men of '93, among the partisans of Robespierre and Hébert? These were they who defiled before the tribunal, — Simon, the governor of the boy Capet ; Mathey, the *concierge* of the tower of the Temple.   Had they anything important to allege?   Against the administrators of the police, grave accusations, insignificant insinuations, suppositions ; against the queen, nothing.

There was one, however, a police spy, Tisset, the author of an infamous collection, " The Account given to the *Sans-culottes* of the French Republic by the very high, very powerful, and very expeditious Dame Guillotine," who, luckier or more adroit than the others, came with his hands full of facts.   Tisset had discovered at the house of the treasurer of the civil list, Septeuil, numerous notes of payment made to Favras, Bouillé, and other conspirators.   He had seen, he had held in his fingers, two bonds of eighty thousand livres, signed Antoinette.   These bonds had been deposited at the commission of the Vingt-Quatre, which had since then been dissolved.

And the former secretary of the commission of the Vingt-Quatre, Garnerin, declared that he had also seen the bond of eighty thousand livres signed Antoinette, payable to the above-named Polignac.   This bond, like the other papers, had been delivered to Valazé, member of the commission.   Garnerin knew even more ; he knew that the court had authorized the formation of monopolies, in order to " secure an increase in the price of provisions, and thereby disgust the people with the Revolution and with liberty."   The queen, called upon, stated that she had no knowledge whatsoever of these monopolies ; but, in her turn, she asked some questions : she demanded what was the date of these bonds, which Garnerin had already reduced to one, and Tisset, confused, replied that one of them was of the 10th of August, 1792, as if on that day, during the attack on the Tuileries, or in the reporters' *loge*, the queen could have sent a bond of eighty thousand livres to Septeuil.   The accusation fell under ridicule, and Valazé dealt it a final blow by transforming the bond of eighty thousand livres into a receipt for fifteen or twenty thousand, the receiver of which he could not recall ; and even this receipt was not produced. It was after this defeat of the prosecution that the audience was suspended, at three o'clock in the afternoon. The queen was not taken back to her cell; some one brought her a bowl of soup, which she hastily ate ; she had need of strength for this final session, which did not adjourn until well into the night.

At five o'clock the tribunal re-entered the hall. This time the municipal officers and police administrators, Lebœuf, Jobert, Moëlle, Vincent, Bugnot, Dangé, Michonis, etc., were called upon to testify; but these men, the majority of whom acted toward the captive with a deference and devotion for which several were to pay with their heads, had nothing to allege against her. Brunier, physician to the Children of France, who had been summoned at various times to the Temple to ·attend them, had also nothing to say. He was reproached for having treated the children of the accused with all the servility of the old *régime*. "It was decorum, and not servility," Brunier courageously replied.

Didier-Jourdeuil declared that he had seen a letter addressed by the accused to the commander of the Swiss Guards, the Comte d'Affry, in which she had said to him, "Can we count upon your Swiss Guards? Will they act as they should when the time comes?" Marie Antoinette, however, denied this letter, and Jourdeuil could not produce it. What had been gained by this session, as by those which had preceded it? The ridiculous testimony of Michael Gointre, who suspected the queen of having founded a factory for counterfeit assignats at Passy, or Herman's absurd question, whether she had not conceived the project of annexing Lorraine to Austria. But not one important allegation, not one authentic document; not one support for the monstrous work of the public prosecutor. "The queen," one of her historians has eloquently remarked, "only consented to justify herself in order to justify others, and in these long debates, not one word escaped her which could imperil a devoted friend, or quiet· the conscience of the judges."

The list of witnesses was exhausted; the tortures of the examination were over. The president asked the accused if she had anything to add to her defence.

"Yesterday," she replied simply, anticipating the judgment of history, — "yesterday, I did not know the witnesses; I was ignorant of what they would testify against me. Not one uttered a positive accusation against me. I close by saying that I was only the wife of Louis XVI., and that it was my manifest duty to conform to his wishes."

Herman declared the debates ended, and Fouquier-Tinville took the floor. We shall not analyze his long address, which was only the reproduction of the indictment, and which is already known. There was one point, however, to which Fouquier did not dare to refer; that was Hébert's deposition.

The defenders rose. At midnight the president had notified them that the prosecution was about to close, and that they had a quarter of an hour in which to prepare themselves. Chauveau-Lagarde spoke first; he had assumed as his part to reply to the accusation concerning communication with the enemies outside the kingdom, whereas his colleague was to defend the queen against the accusation of intelligence with enemies within. "In this affair," he said, "I am only at a loss with regard to one thing; it is not to find replies, but to find objections." And the two lawyers "with as much zeal as eloquence," says the "Bulletin du Tribunal Révolutionnaire," "reduced to nothing the scaffolding which had been so laboriously erected by Fouquier."

"How tired you must be, Monsieur Chauveau-Lagarde!" the queen murmured in the ear of her defender, "I am deeply sensible of all your efforts." These words were overheard; and forthwith, under the very eyes of their august client, Chauveau-Lagarde and Tronçon-Ducoudray were arrested.

Herman resumed the discussion, or rather he pronounced another violent speech, designed to show the jury what was the final task expected of them. "It is the French people," he said, "who accuse Marie Antoinette;" and reviewing in a few malicious words the public life of the accused, recalling the political events which had followed one another during the five years before, evoking "the ghosts of our brothers murdered in consequence of the infernal machinations of this modern Médicis," he submitted these •four questions : —

"1. Is it certain that manœuvres and dealings with foreign powers and enemies outside of the republic have existed, the said manœuvres and dealings tending to furnish them with assistance and money, to give them entrance to French territory, and to facilitate the progress of their armies therein?

"2. Is Marie Antoinette of Austria, widow of Louis Capet, convicted of having co-operated in these manœuvres and of having had these dealings?

"3. Is it certain that there has been a complot and conspiracy tending to enkindle civil war in the interior of the republic, arming the citizens against one another?

"4. Is Marie Antoinette of Austria, widow of Louis Capet, convicted of having participated in this complot and conspiracy?"

The jury withdrew to the deliberating chamber, and the accused was led out. At the end of about an hour, the jury returned and unanimously replied in the affirmative to all the questions.

Herman, with a last show of hypocrisy, exhorted the audience to restrain every sign of approbation; and ordering Marie Antoinette to be brought back, he read her the declaration of the jury.

Fouquier arose, and pursuant to Article 1, of the first section of Act 1, of the second part of the Penal Code, he demanded sentence of death against the accused. The president asked the queen if she had any objection to make to the application of the sentence. The queen shook her head without saying a word.

The president consulted his colleagues; the tribunal rendered their judgment aloud; and Herman declared that Marie Antoinette of Lorraine of Austria, widow of Louis Capet, was condemned to death.

The queen remained impassive; there was not a contraction of her face, not a tear in her eyes; prostrated with fatigue, exhausted by loss of blood, weakened by want of food, — she had taken almost nothing for eleven hours, — her incomparable energy sustained her. She did not say a word; she did not make a gesture; serene and proud, she left the audience-hall with her head erect, and returned to the Conciergerie, where the gendarmes conducted her to the cell of those condemned to death.

CHAPTER XXVII.

IT was half-past four in the morning; in a few hours the executioner would come to claim his victim. The queen asked
for some ink; before dying she needed to free her soul and send
to her children and her sister-in-law her last thoughts with her
last tears. It was to Madame Elisabeth that she wrote: —

"October 16, 4.30 in the morning.

"It is to you, my sister, that I send my last words. I have just been
condemned, not to a shameful death, — it is only that for criminals, —
but to go to rejoin your brother. Innocent, like him, I hope to show the
same firmness as he in his last moments. I am calm, as one always is
when his conscience is untroubled. I feel profound regret in abandoning
my children. You know that I only lived for them and for you, my
good and tender sister, — you who have through your affection sacrificed
everything to be with us. In what a position do I leave you!

"I have learned, through the speeches during the trial, that my
daughter has been separated from you. Alas, the poor child! I do not
dare to write to her; she would not receive my letter. I do not even
know whether this will reach you; receive for both of my children my
benediction. I hope that one day, when they are older, they will be
able to return to you, and enjoy to the full your tender care. May they
both remember what I have constantly instilled in their minds, — that
their principles and the uncompromising fulfilment of their duties form the
chief basis of life; that their mutual affection and confidence will make
its happiness! May my daughter feel that because of her age she should
always aid her brother by the counsels which her greater experience and

her affection will suggest to her! May my son, on his side, show his sister every attention and render her every service which affection may prompt! Finally, may they both feel that whatever their situation, they will never be truly happy except through their union! May they take pattern from us! How much consolation our affection brought us in our misfortune, and in happiness one enjoys doubly what one can share with a friend! and where is a tenderer or more sympathetic one to be found than in one's own family? May my son never forget his father's last words, which I repeat to him with emphasis: 'Let him never try to avenge our death!'

"I have to speak to you of a thing very painful to my heart: I know how much trouble this child has caused you. Pardon him, my dear sister; think at his age how easy it is to make a child say what one wishes, and even what he does not understand. There will come a day, I hope, when he will the more fully appreciate the worth of your kindness and your tenderness for both of them.

"It remains for me yet to confide to you my last thoughts. I would have liked to write to you at the beginning of the trial; but, besides the fact that I was not permitted to write, it proceeded so rapidly that I should really not have had time.

"I die in the apostolic and Roman Catholic faith, — in that of my fathers, that in which I was brought up, and which I have always professed. Having no spiritual consolation to expect, not knowing whether priests of this religion still exist here, — and the place in which I am would expose them to too great danger if they once entered it, — I sincerely ask pardon of God for all the faults which I may have committed throughout my life; I hope that in his goodness he will receive my last prayers, as well as those which I have long made, that he may receive my soul in his pity and bounty. I demand pardon of all those whom I know, and of you, my sister, in particular, for all the sorrows which I have, without wishing it, caused them and you. I pardon all my enemies for the evil which they have done me. I say adieu to my aunts and to all my brothers and sisters. I had some friends; the idea of being separated from them forever, and the thought of their sufferings, are among the greatest regrets which I carry with me in dying. May they at least know that I thought of them to the last!

"Adieu, my good and tender sister; may this letter reach you! Think ever of me; I embrace you with all my heart, and also those poor dear children. *Mon Dieu!* how heart-breaking it is to leave them forever! Adieu! adieu! I shall now turn all my thoughts to my spiritual duties. As I am not free in my actions, a priest will perhaps be brought to me; but I protest here that I shall not say a word to him, and that I shall treat him as an absolutely strange being."

The queen had wept in writing this letter, — not for herself, but for her children. She wept in thinking of the unworthy hands in which she was leaving her son, of what he had already been made to say and do, of what he perhaps might still be made to say and do. But she could not allow herself to be softened by these thoughts; she had need of all her courage and all her strength to die. She forced back her tears, gave the letter to the *concierge*, Bault, and kneeling down, poured out her whole soul to God. She rose hastily, ate the wing of a chicken and a roll, removed her ragged chemise, stained by the hemorrhages which had exhausted her for the last month, put on another which the wife of the *concierge* had procured for her; and exhausted by so many emotions, she threw herself all dressed upon her bed, wrapped her feet in a coverlet, and fell asleep.

At six o'clock the guard awakened her, saying, "Here is a curé of Paris, who asks if you wish to confess." "A curé of Paris," she murmured; "there are few left." The priest advanced; he was dressed as a layman; it was an Abbé Girard, curé of St. Landry, in the Cité. The queen thanked him; but faithful to the pledge which she had given in her letter, she refused to accept the ministration of a schismatic priest; moreover, she had no need of his offices. God had granted her the grace of sending a faithful priest to her a few days before; and if Madame Royale is to be believed, that very morning, kneeling before her window, she had received the absolution and benediction of the curé of Ste. Marguerite, in confinement opposite to her.

The queen was cold: the cool atmosphere of the first nights of autumn, the mists from the river, the dampness of the prison, froze the blood in her veins. On the advice of the Abbé Girard, she placed a pillow upon her feet, and gave herself up to meditation and silent prayer.

At seven o'clock another person entered the cell; it was the last actor in this lugubrious drama, — the executioner. "You come early, Monsieur," Marie Antoinette said to him; "could you not delay?" "No, Madame; I was ordered to come." The queen cut her hair herself, and Sampson proceeded rapidly to the fatal toilet. Then they waited. The priest attempted some exhortations; the queen listened to them with inattentive ears. Her thoughts were no longer there. But when the Abbé Girard ventured to say, "Your death will expiate —" she interrupted him, exclaiming, "Ah, faults! but no crime."

At five in the morning the call to arms was beaten in the forty-eight sections of Paris. At seven o'clock all the military force was out. Cannons had been placed at the extremity of the bridges, squares, and carrefours from the palace to the Place de la Révolution. At ten o'clock numerous patrols circulated in the streets. The mob crowded around the doors of the Conciergerie, impatient and taunting; thousands of *sans-culottes* were there, insulting their victim and awaiting their prey.

At eleven o'clock there was a movement. The gate of the prison opened; the queen appeared, majestic and proud as at Versailles, — dressed in a loose gown of white piqué, as for a day of triumph, remarks an eye-witness; on her feet, slippers of black prunella, with very high heels, of the fashion of Saint-Huberty; a fichu of white muslin round her neck; upon her head a linen cap without lappets, — she had been unable to obtain permission to go to the scaffold bareheaded; the elbows drawn back by a heavy cord, the end of which was held by the executioner; her complexion was pale, except a slight flush on her cheeks; her eyes were blood-shot, the eyelids immovable and rigid; her lips curled with ineffable disdain; about her, gendarmes; near her, the curé of St. Landry. "Do you wish me to accompany you?" the priest asked her. "As you wish," the queen replied indifferently.

Thirty thousand men formed the line from the Conciergerie to the Place de la Révolution. This military preparation, this fear of a possible escape, of a complot to rescue the condemned on the way, this immense crowd which surged like waves, was a last and involuntary homage rendered to the greatness of Marie Antoinette; for the new rulers had not the same consideration for this fallen sovereign as for her husband. The wagon which awaited her, drawn up a few steps from the door, was not a coach, as for Louis XVI., but the ignoble cart for common convicts, with its wheels covered with mud, a plank for a seat, without straw or hay in the bottom, a heavy white horse to drag it, a man in a blouse, with a severe and sinister face, to drive it. The queen could not restrain a start of surprise at sight of this strange vehicle; but she at once mastered this passing emotion.

A short but rather broad ladder was placed against the step at the back of the cart. Sampson offered his hand to the condemned to aid her in ascending it; the queen refused by a gesture, and walked up alone without support. She placed herself upon the seat, with her back turned to the horse; the priest seated himself next her. "This is the moment, Madame, to arm yourself with courage." "Courage?" she replied energetically. "I have so long served an apprenticeship in it that it is not likely to fail me to-day." The priest persisted; she silenced him by repeating to him with firmness "that she was not of his religion, that she died professing that of her husband, and that she should never forget the principles so oft instilled in her."

The executioner and his assistant stood behind the queen, their hats in their hands, leaning against the side of the wagon, and carelessly allowing the cords which bound the hands of the victim to hang as they pleased.

A pale autumn sun shone on this scene. The cart started; the gendarmes had difficulty in opening a passage for it in the midst of this compact mass of *sans-culottes* and *tricoteuses*, who were to earn a good day's living. A strange silence reigned in the crowd, but at the entrance to the Rue St. Honoré the clamours began. Gross jests, sinister jokes, infamous insults, cries of death arose, like unhealthy vapours, from the depths of this mad populace, and mingled with the cries of "Vive la république!" "Down with tyrants!" A few wretches clapped their hands; the comedian Gramont, mounted on a horse, caracoled round the cart, giving the signal for the outrages. The queen, impassive and serene, "neither downcast nor haughty," towered above this rabble; her glance rested upon this hideous mob almost without seeing it, and her ears were struck with these sounds without hearing them. Only occasionally some insult more odious than the others succeeded in reaching her, and brought back to earth for an instant her thoughts, which were obstinately rising toward heaven.

Nobody at the windows; there must be nothing above the brutal level of the street. All sympathy must be silent. Hatred alone had the right to show itself; yet it is said that some of the spectators fainted from grief.

The cart advanced slowly. The queen, a journalist wrote, should "drink death with lingering slowness." Before St. Roch the *cortège* halted: this was one of the stations which the ingenious rage of the executioners had arranged for the victim along the road to her Calvary. On the porch of the church the fine flower of the revolutionary furies — the battalion of the Citizeness Lacombe — was packed. Gramont stood up in his stirrups, brandishing his sword and crying, "There she is, the infamous Antoinette; she is mad, my friends!" This was the signal. A long murmur rose from the crowd. Shouts, imprecations, insults, blended together in one immense yell of hatred and insult. What delight for these women, for these *lickers of the guillotine*, as the Commune pithily called them, if they could catch a tremor on the face of the queen, or a tear in her eyes! But this pleasure was not granted them; under the blow of outrage the queen remained unmoved; she saw nothing, she heard nothing.

A hundred steps farther on, opposite the Jacobins, it seemed as if she wished to decipher the inscription over the arcade of the passage. She leaned toward the constitutional priest and appeared to question him. As sole response the priest raised a little Christ in ivory; and the queen resumed her silence and serenity.

At noon the funeral *cortège* came out on the Place de la Révolution; through a last and cruel irony the scaffold had been erected near the Pont Tournant, at the foot of the statue of Liberty. The queen gazed long on the Tuileries, where she had entered for the first time on June 8, 1773, a radiant dauphiness, greeted by the enthusiastic acclamations of the people of Paris; whence she had come out, on Aug. 10, 1792, amid the furious cries of this same people, who were so cruelly variable; on these high trees in the shade of which her son had so often played, and whose leaves, yellowed by the autumn sun, were falling to the ground; on this palace, where she had lived three mortal years after the events of October, 1789, and opposite to which she was to die. Under the weight of these memories and of these thoughts, her head fell forward and her face paled. For a moment she staggered, oppressed with unfathomable grief; but at once she drew herself up, stepped down from the cart "lightly and quickly," and "although her hands were still bound," climbed the steps of the scaffold without assistance, and "with more calmness and tranquillity in her bearing than when she had left the prison."

In ascending the steps, she inadvertently placed her foot upon that of the executioner. Sampson uttered a cry of pain. The queen turned and said, with a freedom and dignity incomprehensible at such a moment, "Monsieur, I beg your pardon!" Then she lifted her eyes to heaven and murmured a last prayer.

Four minutes after the national knife had accomplished its

work.   The executioner held up for some time before the people
this bleeding head, whose eyelids still quivered with a convulsive
movement, and whose cheeks were still tinted a deep crimson.
" Vive la république!" the people replied.   It was a quarter
past twelve.

All was over; the daughter of the Cæsars had gone to rejoin
the son of Saint Louis in heaven.   The crowd dispersed, silent
and as if appalled, a prey to that involuntary terror which op-
presses even the most hardened consciences after the accomplishment of a great crime.

Meanwhile a man issued from this malevolent and glutted
populace, glided up under the scaffold, and dipped his handkerchief in the blood which was running from the scaffold, as in the
blood of a martyr.

History has preserved the blood of this victim, as it has the
name of the gendarme Maingot; it has preserved it that it might
with it mark Marie Antoinette's murderers on the forehead.
" The first crime of the Revolution," says Chateaubriand, " was
the death of the king ; but the most frightful was the death of the
queen."   " Paris has only one more crime to commit," wrote
the Cardinal de Bernis, in learning of the murder of October 16 ;
" the last adds to all the others a degree of horror and infamy
unknown up to the present day."   And Napoleon said, " The
queen's death was a crime worse than regicide," — a crime absolutely unjustifiable, since it had no pretext whatsoever to offer
as excuse ; a crime eminently impolitic, since it struck down
" a foreign princess, the most sacred of hostages; " a crime
cowardly beyond measure, since the victim was a woman " who
possessed only honours without power."

Two weeks later the grave-digger, Joly, buried in an obscure
corner of the cemetery of the Madeleine the mutilated remains
of the great victim, and submitted for the approbation of the
president of the revolutionary tribunal, Herman, a bill worded
in this fashion : —

<blockquote>
The Widow Capet, for the bier . . . . 6 livres.
For the grave and grave-diggers 25   "
</blockquote>

This was the last *memorandum of supplies furnished for the use
of the Queen of France !*

INDEX.